THE GOOD, THE BAD,
AND THE UNDEAD

By Kim Harrison

DEAD WITCH WALKING
EVERY WHICH WAY BUT DEAD
A FISTFUL OF CHARMS

THE GOOD, THE BAD AND THE UNDEAD

KIM HARRISON

HARPER
Voyager

Harper*Voyager*
An Imprint of HarperCollins*Publishers*
77–85 Fulham Palace Road,
Hammersmith, London W6 8JB

www.harpercollins.co.uk

Published by Voyager 2006
5

A catalogue record for this book
is available from the British Library

ISBN-13 978 0 00 723611 4
ISBN-10 0 00 723611 5

Printed and bound in Great Britain by
Clays Limited, St Ives plc

*To the man who knows caffeine comes first,
chocolate comes second, romance comes third—
and when they ought to be reversed*

Acknowledgements

I'd like to thank Will for his help and inspiration with the jewelry of the Hollows, and Dr. Caroline White for her invaluable assistance with much of the Latin. But I'd especially like to thank my editor, Diana Gill, for giving me the freedom to push my writing into areas I'd never though to go, and my agent, Richard Curtis.

THE GOOD, THE BAD,
AND THE UNDEAD

One

I hitched the canvas strap holding the watering canister higher up on my shoulder and stretched to get the nozzle into the hanging plant. Sunlight streamed in, warm through my blue institutional jumpsuit. Past the narrow plate-glass windows was a small courtyard surrounded by VIP offices. Squinting from the sun, I squeezed the handle of the watering hose, and the barest hint of water hissed through.

There was a burst of clattering computer keys, and I moved to the next plant down. Phone conversation filtered in from the office past the reception desk, accompanied by a belly laugh that sounded like the bark of a dog. Weres. The higher up in the pack they were, the more human looking they managed, but you could always tell when they laughed.

I glanced down the row of hanging plants before the windows to the freestanding fish tank behind the receptionist's desk. Yup. Cream-colored fins. Black spot on right side. This was the one. Mr. Ray raised koi, showing them in Cincinnati's annual fish show. Last year's winner was always displayed in his outer office, but now there were two fish, and the Howlers' mascot was missing. Mr. Ray was a Den boy, a rival of Cincinnati's all Inderland baseball team. It didn't take much to put two and two together and get stolen fish.

"So," the cheerful woman behind the desk said as she

stood to drop a ream of paper into the printer's hopper. "Mark is on vacation? He didn't tell me."

I nodded, not looking at the secretary dressed in her snappy cream-colored business suit as I dragged my watering equipment down another three feet. Mark was taking a short vacation in the stairwell of the building he had been servicing before this one. Knocked out with a short-term sleepy-time potion. "Yes, ma'am," I added, raising my voice and adding a slight lisp. "He told me what plants to water, though." I curled my red manicured nails under my palms before she spotted them. They didn't go with the working plant-girl image. I should have thought of that earlier. "All the ones on this floor, and then the arboretum on the roof."

The woman smiled to show me her slightly larger teeth. She was a Were, and fairly high up in the office pack by her amount of polish. And Mr. Ray wouldn't have a dog for a secretary when he could pay a high enough salary for a bitch. A faint scent of musk came from her, not unpleasant. "Did Mark tell you about the service elevator at the back of the building?" she said helpfully. "It's easier than lugging that cart up all those stairs."

"No, ma'am," I said, pulling the ugly cap with the plant-man logo on it tighter to my head. "I think he's making everything just hard enough that I don't try to take his territory." Pulse quickening, I pushed Mark's cart with its pruning shears, fertilizer pellets, and watering system farther down the line. I had known of the elevator, along with the placement of the six emergency exits, the pulls for the fire alarm, and where they kept the doughnuts.

"Men," she said, rolling her eyes as she sat before her screen again. "Don't they realize that if we wanted to rule the world, we could?"

I gave her a noncommittal nod and squirted a tiny amount of water into the next plant. I kinda thought we already did.

A tight hum rose over the whirl of the printer and the faint office chatter. It was Jenks, my partner, and he was clearly in a bad mood as he flew out of the boss's back office and to me. His dragonfly wings were bright red in agitation, and pixy dust sifted from him to make temporary sunbeams. "I'm done with the plants in there," he said loudly as he landed on the rim of the hanging pot in front of me. He put his hands on his hips to look like a middle-age Peter Pan grown up to be a trashman in his little blue jumpsuit. His wife had even sewn him a matching cap. "All they need is water. Can I help you out here with anything, or can I go back and sleep in the truck?" he added acerbically.

I took the watering canister off me, setting it down to unscrew the top. "I could use a fertilizer pellet," I prompted, wondering what his problem was.

Grumbling, he flew to the cart and started rummaging. Green twist ties, stakes, and used pH test strips flew everywhere. "Got one," he said, coming up with a white pellet as large as his head. He dropped it in the canister and it fizzed. It wasn't a fertilizer pellet but an oxygenator and slime-coat promoter. What's the point of stealing a fish if it dies in transport?

"Oh my God, Rachel," Jenks whispered as he landed on my shoulder "It's polyester. I'm wearing polyester!"

My tension eased as I realized where his bad mood came from. "It'll be okay."

"I'm breaking out!" he said, scratching vigorously under his collar. "I can't wear polyester. Pixies are allergic to polyester. Look. See?" He tilted his head so his blond hair shifted from his neck, but he was too close to focus on. "Welts. And it stinks. I can smell the oil. I'm wearing dead dinosaur. I can't wear a dead animal. It's barbaric, Rache," he pleaded.

"Jenks?" I screwed the cap lightly back onto the canister and hung it over my shoulder, pushing Jenks from me in the process. "I'm wearing the same thing. Suck it up."

"But it stinks!"

I eyed him hovering before me. "Prune something," I said through gritted teeth.

He flipped me off with both hands, hovering backward as he went. Whatever. Patting my back pocket of the vile blue jumpsuit, I found my snippers. While Miss Office Professional typed a letter, I snapped open a step stool and began to clip leaves off the hanging plant beside her desk. Jenks started to help, and after a few moments I breathed, "Are we set in there?"

He nodded, his eyes on the open door to Mr. Ray's office. "The next time he checks his mail, the entire Internet security system is gonna trip. It will take five minutes to fix if she knows what she's doing, four hours if she doesn't."

"I only need five minutes," I said, starting to sweat in the sun coming in the window. It smelled like a garden in there, a garden with a wet dog panting on the cool tile.

My pulse increased, and I moved down another plant. I was behind the desk, and the woman stiffened. I had invaded her territory, but she had to put up with it. I was the water girl. Hoping she attributed my rising tension to being so close to her, I kept working. My one hand rested on the lid of the watering canister. One twist and it would be off.

"Vanessa!" came an irate shout from the back office.

"Here we go," Jenks said, flying up to the ceiling and the security cameras.

I turned to see an irate man, clearly a Were by his slight size and build, hanging halfway out of the back office. "It did it again," he said, his face red and his thick hands gripping the archway. "I hate these things. What was wrong with paper? I like paper."

A professional smile wreathed the secretary's face. "Mr. Ray, you yelled at it again, didn't you? I told you, computers are like women. If you shout at them or ask them to do too many things at once, they shut down and you won't even get a sniff."

He growled an answer and disappeared into his office, un-aware or ignoring that she had just threatened him. My pulse leapt, and I moved the stool right beside the tank.

Vanessa sighed. "God save him," she muttered as she got up. "That man could break his balls with his tongue." Giving me an exasperated look, she went into the back office, her heels thumping. "Don't touch anything," she said loudly. "I'm coming."

I took a quick breath. "Cameras?" I breathed.

Jenks dropped down to me. "Ten minute loop. You're clear."

He flew to the main door, perching himself on the molding above the lintel, to hang over and watch the exterior hallway. His wings blurred to nothing and he gave me a tiny thumbs-up.

My skin tightened in anticipation. I took off the fish tank lid, then pulled the green fishnet from an inner pocket of the jumpsuit. Standing atop the step stool, I pushed my sleeve to my elbow and plunged the net into the water. Immediately both fish darted to the back.

"Rachel!" Jenks hissed, suddenly at my ear. "She's good. She's halfway there."

"Just watch the door, Jenks," I said, lip between my teeth. *How long could it take to catch a fish?* I pushed a rock over to get to the fish hiding behind it. They darted to the front.

The phone started ringing, a soft hum. "Jenks, will you get that?" I said calmly as I angled the net, trapping them in the corner. "Got you now . . ."

Jenks zipped back from the door, landing feet first on the glowing button. "Mr. Ray's office. Hold please," he said in a high falsetto.

"Crap," I swore as the fish wiggled, slipping past the green net. "Come on, I'm just trying to get you home, you slimy finned thing," I coaxed through gritted teeth. "Almost . . . almost . . ." It was between the net and the glass. If it would just hold still . . .

"Hey!" a heavy voice said from the hall.

Adrenaline jerked my head up. A small man with a trim beard and a folder of papers was standing in the hallway leading to the other offices. "What are you doing?" he asked belligerently.

I glanced at the tank with my arm in it. My net was empty. The fish had slipped past it. "Um, I dropped my scissors?" I said.

From Mr. Ray's office on my other side came a thump of heels and Vanessa's gasp. "Mr. Ray!"

Damn. So much for the easy way. "Plan B, Jenks," I said, grunting as I grabbed the top of the tank and pulled.

In the other room, Vanessa screamed as the tank tipped and twenty-five gallons of icky fish water cascaded over her desk. Mr. Ray appeared beside her. I lurched off the stool, soaked from the waist down. No one moved, shocked, and I scanned the floor. "Gotcha!" I cried, scrabbling for the right fish.

"She's after the fish!" the small man shouted as more people came in from the hallway. "Get her!"

"Go!" Jenks shrilled. "I'll keep them off you."

Panting, I followed the fish in a hunched, scrabbling walk, trying to grab it without hurting it. It wiggled and squirmed, and my breath exploded from me as I finally got my fingers around it. I looked up as I dropped it into the canister and screwed the lid on tight.

Jenks was a firefly from hell as he darted from Were to Were, brandishing pencils and throwing them at sensitive parts. A four-inch pixy was holding three Weres at bay. I wasn't surprised. Mr. Ray was content to watch until he realized I had one of his fish. "What the hell are you doing with my fish?" he demanded, his face red with anger.

"Leaving," I said. He came at me, his thick hands reaching. I obligingly took one of them, jerking him forward and into my foot. He staggered back, clutching his stomach.

"Quit playing with those dogs!" I cried at Jenks, looking for a way out. "We have to go."

Picking up Vanessa's monitor, I threw it at the plate-glass window. I'd wanted to do that with Ivy's for a long time. It shattered in a satisfying crash, the screen looking odd on the grass. Weres poured into the room, angry and giving off musk. Snatching the canister, I dove through the window.

"After her!" someone shouted.

My shoulders hit manicured grass and I rolled to my feet.

"Up!" Jenks said by my ear. "Over there."

He darted across the small enclosed courtyard. I followed, looping the heavy canister to hang across my back. Hands free, I climbed the trellis. Thorns pierced my skin, ignored.

My breath came in a quick pant as I reached the top. The snapping of branches said they were following. Hauling myself over the lip of the flat-topped, tar-and-pebble roof, I took off running. The wind was hot up here, and the skyline of Cincinnati spread out before me.

"Jump!" Jenks shouted as I reached the edge.

I trusted Jenks. Arms flailing and feet still going, I ran right off the roof.

Adrenaline surged as my stomach dropped. It was a parking lot! He sent me off the roof to land in a parking lot!

"I don't have wings, Jenks!" I screamed. Teeth gritted, I flexed my knees.

Pain exploded as I hit the pavement. I fell forward, scraping my palms. The canister of fish clanged and fell off as the strap broke. I rolled to absorb the impact.

The metal canister spun away, and still gasping from the hurt, I staggered after it, fingers brushing it as it rolled under a car. Swearing, I dropped flat on the pavement, stretching for it.

"There she is!" came a shout.

There was a ping from the car above me, then another.

The pavement beside my arm suddenly had a hole in it, and sharp tingles of shrapnel peppered me. They were shooting at me?

Grunting, I wiggled under the car and pulled the canister out. Hunched over the fish, I backed up. "Hey!" I shouted, tossing the hair from my eyes. "What the hell are you doing? It's just a fish! And it isn't even yours!"

The trio of Weres on the roof stared at me. One hefted a weapon to his eye.

I turned and started running. This was not worth five hundred dollars anymore. Five thousand, maybe. *Next time,* I vowed as I pounded after Jenks, *I'd find out the particulars before I charge my standard fee.*

"This way!" Jenks shrilled. Bits of pavement were ricocheting up to hit me, echoing the pings. The lot wasn't gated, and as my muscles trembled from adrenaline, I ran across the street and into the pedestrian traffic. Heart pounding, I slowed to look behind me to see them silhouetted against the skyline. They hadn't jumped. They didn't need to. I had left blood all over that trellis. Still, I didn't think they would track me. It wasn't their fish; it was the Howlers'. And Cincinnati's all Inderland baseball team was going to pay my rent.

My lungs heaved as I tried to match the pace of the people around me. The sun was hot, and I was sweating inside my polyester sack. Jenks was probably checking my back, so I dropped into an alley to change. Setting the fish down, I let my head thump back into the cool wall of the building. I'd done it. Rent was made for yet another month.

Reaching up, I yanked the disguise amulet from around my neck. Immediately I felt better, as the illusion of a dark-completed, brown-haired, big-nosed woman vanished, revealing my frizzy, shoulder-length red hair and pale skin. I glanced at my scraped palms, rubbing them together gingerly. I could have brought a pain amulet, but I had wanted as few charms as possible on me in case I was caught and my "intent to steal" turned into "intent to steal and do bodily harm." One I could dodge, the other I'd have to answer to. I was a runner; I knew the law.

While people passed at the head of the alley, I stripped off the damp coveralls and stuffed it into the Dumpster. It was a vast improvement, and I bent to unroll the hem of my leather pants down over my black boots. Straightening, I eyed the new scrape mark in my pants, twisting to see all the damage. Ivy's leather conditioner would help, but pavement and leather didn't mesh well. Better the pants scraped than me, though, which was why I wore them.

The September air felt good in the shade as I tucked in my black halter top and picked up the canister. Feeling more myself, I stepped into the sun, dropping my cap on a passing kid's head. He looked at it, then smiled, giving me a shy wave as his mother bent to ask him where he had gotten it. At peace with the world, I walked down the sidewalk, boot heels clunking as I fluffed my hair and headed for Fountain Square and my ride. I had left my shades there this morning, and if I was lucky, they'd still be there. God help me, but I liked being independent.

It had been nearly three months since I had snapped under the crap assignments my old boss at Inderland Security had been giving me. Feeling used and grossly unappreciated, I had broken the unwritten rule and quit the I.S. to start my own agency. It had seemed like a good idea at the time, and surviving the subsequent death threat when I couldn't pay the bribe to break my contract had been an eye opener. I wouldn't have made it if not for Ivy and Jenks.

Oddly enough, now that I was finally starting to make a name for myself, it was getting harder, not easier. True, I was putting my degree to work, stirring spells I used to buy and some I had never been able to afford. But money was a real problem. It wasn't that I couldn't get the jobs; it was that the money didn't seem to stay in the cookie jar atop the fridge very long.

What I made from proving a Werefox had been slipped some bane by a rival den had gone to renewing my witch license; the I.S. used to pay for that. I recovered a stolen familiar for a warlock and spent it on the monthly rider on my health insurance. I hadn't known that runners were all but uninsurable; the I.S. had given me a card, and I'd used it. Then I had to pay some guy to take the lethal spells off my stuff still in storage, buy Ivy a silk robe to replace the one I ruined, and pick up a few outfits for myself since I now had a reputation to uphold.

But the steady drain on my finances had to be from the cab fares. Most of Cincinnati's bus drivers knew me by sight and wouldn't pick me up, which was why Ivy had to come cart me home. It just wasn't fair. It had been almost a year since I accidentally removed the hair from an entire busload of people while trying to tag a Were.

I was tired of being almost broke, but the money for recovering the Howlers' mascot would put me in the clear for another month. And the Weres wouldn't follow me. It wasn't their fish. If they filed a complaint at the I.S., they'd have to explain where they had gotten it.

"Hey, Rache," Jenks said, dropping down from who knew where. "Your back is clear. And what is Plan B?"

My eyebrows rose and I looked askance at him as he flew alongside, matching my pace exactly. "Grab the fish and run like hell."

Jenks laughed and landed on my shoulder. He had ditched his tiny uniform, and he looked like his usual self in a long-sleeve hunter-green silk shirt and pants. A red bandana was about his forehead to tell any pixy or fairies whose territory we might walk through that he wasn't poaching. Sparkles glittered in his wings where the last of the pixy dust stirred up by the excitement remained.

My pace slowed as we reached Fountain Square. I scanned for Ivy, not seeing her. Not worried, I went to sit on the dry side of the fountain, running my fingers under the rim of the retaining wall for my shades. She'd be here. The woman lived and died by schedules.

While Jenks flew through the spray to get rid of the last of the "dead dinosaur stink," I snapped open my shades and put them on. My brow eased as the glare of the September afternoon was muted. Stretching my long legs out, I casually took off the scent amulet that was around my neck and dropped it into the fountain. Weres tracked by smell, and if they did follow me, the trail would end here as soon as I got in Ivy's car and drove away.

Hoping no one had noticed, I glanced over the surrounding people: a nervous, anemic-looking vampire lackey out doing his lover's daytime work; two whispering humans, giggling as they eyed his badly scarred neck; a tired witch—no, warlock, I decided, by the lack of a strong redwood smell—sitting at a nearby bench eating a muffin; and me. I took a slow breath as I settled in. Having to wait for a ride was kind of an anticlimax.

"I wish I had a car," I said to Jenks as I edged the canister of fish to sit between my feet. Thirty feet away traffic was stop-and-go. It had picked up, and I guessed it was probably after two o'clock, just beginning the span of time when humans and Inderlanders started their daily struggle to coexist in the same limited space. Things got a hell of a lot easier when the sun went down and most humans retired to their homes.

"What do you want with a car?" Jenks asked as he perched himself on my knee and started to clean his dragonfly-like wings with long serious strokes. "I don't have a car. I've never had a car. I get around okay. Cars are trouble," he said, but I wasn't listening anymore. "You have to put gas in them, and keep them in repair, and spend time cleaning them, and you have to have a place to put them, and then there's the money you lavish on them. It's worse than a girlfriend."

"Still," I said, jiggling my foot to irritate him. "I wish I had a car." I glanced at the people around me. "James Bond never had to wait for a bus. I've seen every one of his movies, and he never waited for a bus." I squinted at Jenks. "It kinda loses its pizzazz."

"Um, yeah," he said, his attention behind me. "I can see where it might be safer, too. Eleven o'clock. Weres."

My breath came fast as I looked, and my tension slammed back into me. "Crap," I whispered, picking up the canister. It was the same three. I could tell by their hunched stature and the way they were breathing deeply. Jaw clenched, I stood up and put the fountain between us. *Where was Ivy?*

"Rache?" Jenks questioned. "Why are they following you?"

"I don't know." My thoughts went to the blood I had left on the roses. If I couldn't break the scent trail, they could follow me all the way home. But why? Mouth dry, I sat with my back to them, knowing Jenks was watching. "Have they winded me?" I asked.

He left in a clatter of wings. "No," he said when he returned a bare second later. "You've got about half a block between you, but you gotta get moving."

Jiggling, I weighed the risk of staying still and waiting for Ivy with moving and being spotted. "Damn it, I wish I had a car," I muttered. I leaned to look into the street, searching for the tall blue top of a bus, a cab, anything. *Where the hell was Ivy?*

Heart pounding, I stood. Clutching the fish to me, I headed for the street, wanting to get into the adjacent office building and the maze I could lose myself in while waiting for Ivy. But a big black Crown Victoria slowed to a stop, getting in my way.

I glared at the driver, my tight face going slack when the

window whined down and he leaned over the front seat. "Ms. Morgan?" the dark man said, his deep voice belligerent.

I glanced at the Weres behind me, then at the car, then him. A black Crown Victoria driven by a man in a black suit could only mean one thing. He was from the Federal Inderland Bureau, the human-run equivalent of the I.S. *What did the FIB want?* "Yeah. Who are you?"

Bother crossed him. "I talked to Ms. Tamwood earlier. She said I could find you here."

Ivy. I put a hand on the open window. "Is she all right?"

He pressed his lips together. Traffic was backing up behind him. "She was when I talked with her on the phone."

Jenks hovered before me, his tiny face frightened. "They winded you, Rache."

My breath hissed in through my nose. I glanced behind me. My gaze fell on one of the Weres. Seeing me watching him, he barked out a hail. The other two started to converge, loping forward with an unhurried grace. I swallowed hard. I was dog chow. That's it. Dog chow. Game over. Hit the reset button.

Spinning, I grabbed the door handle and jerked it up. I dove in, slamming the door behind me. "Drive!" I shouted, turning to look out the back window.

The man's long face took on a tinge of disgust as he glanced behind him in his rearview mirror. "Are they with you?"

"No! Does this thing move, or do you just sit in it and play with yourself?"

Making a low noise of irritation, he accelerated smoothly. I spun in my seat, watching the Weres come to a halt in the middle of the street. Horns blew from the cars forced to stop for them. Turning back around, I clutched my fish canister and closed my eyes in relief. I was going to get Ivy for this. I swear, I was going to use her precious maps as weed block in the garden. She was supposed to pick me up, not send some FIB flunky.

Pulse slowing, I turned to look at him. He was a good head taller than me, which was saying something—with nice shoulders, curly black hair cut close to his skull, square jaw, and a stiff attitude just begging for me to smack him. Comfortably muscled without going overboard, there wasn't even the hint of a gut on him. In his perfectly fitting black suit, white shirt, and black tie, he could be the FIB poster boy. His mustache and beard were cut in the latest style—so minimal that they almost weren't there—and I thought he might do better to lighten up on his aftershave. I eyed the handcuff pouch on his belt, wishing I still had mine. They had belonged to the I.S., and I missed them dearly.

Jenks settled himself at his usual spot on the rearview mirror where the wind wouldn't tear his wings, and the stiff-necked man watched him with an intentness that told me he had little contact with pixies. Lucky him.

A call came over the radio about a shoplifter at the mall, and he snapped it off. "Thanks for the ride," I said. "Ivy sent you?"

He tore his eyes from Jenks. "No. She said you'd be here. Captain Edden wants to talk you. Something concerning Councilman Trent Kalamack," the FIB officer added indifferently.

"Kalamack!" I yelped, then cursed myself for having said anything. The wealthy bastard wanted me to work for him or see me dead. It depended on his mood and how well his stock portfolio was doing. "Kalamack, huh?" I amended, shifting uneasily in the leather seat. "Why is Edden sending you to fetch me? You on his hit list this week?"

He said nothing, his blocky hands gripping the wheel so tight that his fingernails went white. The silence grew. We went through a yellow light shifting to red. "Ah, who are you?" I finally asked.

He made a scoffing noise deep in his throat. I was used to

wary distrust from most humans. This guy wasn't afraid, and it was ticking me off. "Detective Glenn, ma'am," he said.

"Ma'am," Jenks said, laughing. "He called you ma'am."

I scowled at Jenks. He looked young to have made detective. The FIB must have been getting desperate. "Well, thank you, Detective Glade," I said, mangling his name. "You can drop me off anywhere. I can take the bus from here. I'll come out to see Captain Edden tomorrow. I'm working an important case right now."

Jenks snickered, and the man flushed, the red almost hidden behind his dark skin. "It's Glenn, *ma'am*. And I saw your important case. Want me to take you back to the fountain?"

"No," I said, slumping in my seat, thoughts of angry young Weres going through my head. "I appreciate the lift to my office, though. It's in the Hollows, take the next left."

"I'm not your driver," he said grimly, clearly unhappy. "I'm your delivery boy."

I shifted my arm inside as he rolled the window up from his control panel. Immediately it grew stuffy. Jenks flitted to the ceiling, trapped. "What the hell are you doing?" he shrilled.

"Yeah!" I exclaimed, more irate than worried. "What's up?"

"Captain Edden wants to see you now, Ms. Morgan, not tomorrow." His gaze darted from the street to me. His jaw was tight, and I didn't like his nasty smile. "And if you so much as reach for a spell, I'll yank your witch butt out of my car, cuff you, and throw you in the trunk. Captain Edden sent me to get you, but he didn't say what kind of shape you had to be in."

Jenks alighted on my earring, swearing up a blue streak. I repeatedly flicked the switch for the window, but Glenn had locked it. I settled back with a huff. I could jam my finger in Glenn's eye and force us off the road, but why? I knew where I was going. And Edden would see that I had a ride home. It ticked me off, though, running into a human who had more gall than I did. What was the city coming to?

A sullen silence descended. I took my sunglasses off and leaned over, noticing the man was going fifteen over the posted limit. Figures.

"Watch this," Jenks whispered. My eyebrows rose as the pixy flitted from my earring. The autumn sun coming in was suddenly full of sparkles as he surreptitiously sifted a glowing dust over the detective. I'd bet my best pair of lace panties it wasn't the usual pixy dust. Glenn had been pixed.

I hid a smile. In about twenty minutes Glenn would be itching so bad he wouldn't be able to sit still. "So, how come you aren't scared of me?" I asked brazenly, feeling vastly better.

"A witch family lived next door when I was a kid," he said warily. "They had a girl my age. She hit me with just about everything a witch can do to a person." A faint smile crossed his square face to make him look very un-FIBlike. "The saddest day of my life was when she moved away."

I made a pouty face. "Poor baby," I said, and his scowl returned. I wasn't pleased, though. Edden sent him to pick me up because he had known I couldn't bully him.

I hated Mondays.

Two

The gray stone of the FIB tower caught the late afternoon sun as we parked in one of the reserved slots right in front of the building. The street was busy, and Glenn stiffly escorted me and my fish in through the front door. Tiny blisters between his neck and collar were already starting to show a sore-looking pink against his dark skin.

Jenks noticed my eyes on them and snorted. "Looks like Mr. FIB Detective is sensitive to pixy dust," he whispered. "It's going to run through his lymphatic system. He's going to be itching in places he didn't know he had."

"Really?" I asked, appalled. Usually you only itched where the dust hit. Glenn was in for twenty-four hours of pure torture.

"Yeah, he won't be trapping a pixy in a car again."

But I thought I heard a tinge of guilt in his voice, and he wasn't humming his victory song about daisies and steel glinting red in the moonlight, either. My steps faltered before crossing the FIB emblem inlaid in the lobby floor. I wasn't superstitious—apart from when it might save my life—but I was entering what was generally humans-only territory. I didn't like being a minority.

The sporadic conversation and clatter of keyboards remind me of my old job with the I.S., and my shoulders eased. Justice's wheels were greased with paper and fueled by quick feet on the streets. Whether the feet were human or Inderlander was irrelevant. At least to me.

The FIB had been created to take the place of both local and federal authorities after the Turn. On paper, the FIB had been enacted to help protect the remaining humans from the—ah—more aggressive Inderlanders, generally the vamps and Weres. The reality was, dissolving the old law structure had been a paranoiac attempt to keep us Inderlanders out of law enforcement.

Yeah. Right. The out-of-the-closet, out-of-work Inderland police and Federal agents had simply started their own bureau, the I.S. After forty years the FIB was hopelessly outclassed, taking steady abuse from the I.S. as they both tried to keep tabs on Cincinnati's varied citizens, the I.S. taking the supernatural stuff the FIB couldn't.

As I followed Glenn to the back, I shifted the canister to hide my left wrist. Not many people would recognize the small circular scar on the underside of my wrist as a demon mark, but I preferred to err on the side of caution. Neither the FIB nor the I.S. knew I had been involved in the demon-induced incident that trashed the university's ancient-book locker last spring, and I'd just as soon keep it that way. It had been sent to kill me, but it ultimately saved my life. I'd wear the mark until I found a way to pay the demon back.

Glenn wove between the desks past the lobby, and my eyebrows rose in that not a single officer made one ribald comment about a redhead in leather. But next to the screaming prostitute with purple hair and a glow-in-the-dark chain running from her nose to somewhere under her shirt, we were probably invisible.

I glanced at the shuttered windows of Edden's office as we passed, waving at Rose, his assistant. Her face flashed red as she pretended to ignore me, and I sniffed. I was used to such slights, but it was still irritating. The rivalry between the FIB and the I.S. was long-standing. That I didn't work for the I.S. anymore didn't seem to matter. Then again, it could be she simply didn't like witches.

I breathed easier when we left the front behind and entered a sterile fluorescent-lit hallway. Glenn, too, relaxed into a slower pace. I could feel the office politics flowing behind us like unseen currents but was too dispirited to care. We passed an empty meeting room, my eyes going to the huge dry-marker board where the week's most pressing crimes were plastered. Pushing out the usual human-stalked-by-vamp crimes was a list of names. I felt ill as my eyes dropped. We were walking too fast to read them, but I knew what they had to be. I'd been following the papers just like everyone else.

"Morgan!" shouted a familiar voice, and I spun, my boots squeaking on the gray tile.

It was Edden, his squat silhouette hastening down the hallway toward us, arms swinging. Immediately I felt better.

"Slugs take it," Jenks muttered. "Rache, I'm outta here. I'll see you at home."

"Stay put," I said, amused at the pixy's grudge. "And if you say one foul word to Edden, I'll Amdro your stump."

Glenn snickered, and it was probably just as well I couldn't hear what Jenks muttered.

Edden was an ex–Navy SEAL and looked it, keeping his hair regulation short, his khaki pants creased, and his body under his starched white shirt honed. Though his thick shock of straight hair was black, his mustache was entirely gray. A welcoming smile covered his round face as he strode forward, tucking a pair of plastic-rimmed reading glasses into his shirt pocket. The captain of Cincinnati's FIB division came to an abrupt halt, wafting the smell of coffee over me. He was my height almost exactly—making him somewhat short for a man—but he made up for it in presence.

Edden arched his eyebrows at my leather pants and less-than-professional halter top. "It's good to see you, Morgan," he said. "I hope I didn't catch you at a bad time."

I shifted my canister and extended my hand. His stubby thick fingers engulfed mine, familiar and welcoming. "No, not at all," I said dryly, and Edden put a heavy hand on my shoulder, directing me down a short hallway.

Normally I would have reacted to such a show of familiarity with a delicate elbow in a gut. Edden, though, was a kindred spirit, hating injustice as much as I did. Though he looked nothing like him, he reminded me of my dad, having gained my respect by accepting me as a witch and treating me with equality instead of mistrust. I was a sucker for flattery.

We headed down the hallway shoulder-to-shoulder, Glenn lagging behind. "Good to see you flying again, Mr. Jenks," Edden said, giving the pixy a nod.

Jenks left my earring, his wings clattering harshly. Edden had once snapped Jenks's wing off while stuffing him into a water cooler, and pixy grudges went deep. "It's Jenks," he said coldly. "Just Jenks."

"Jenks, then. Can we get you anything? Sugar water, peanut butter . . ." He turned, smiling from behind his mustache. "Coffee, Ms. Morgan?" he drawled. "You look tired."

His grin banished the last of my bad mood. "That'd be great," I said, and Edden gave Glenn a directive look. The detective's jaw was clenched, and several new welts ran down his jawline. Edden grasped his forearm as the frustrated man turned away. Pulling Glenn down, Edden whispered, "It's too late to wash the pixy dust off. Try cortisone."

Glenn gave me a closed stare as he straightened and walked back the way we had come.

"I appreciate you dropping in," Edden continued. "I got a break this morning, and you're the only one I could call to capitalize on it."

Jenks made a scoffing laugh. "Whatsa matter, got a Were with a thorn in his paw?"

"Shut up, Jenks," I said, more from habit than anything else. Glenn had mentioned Trent Kalamack, and that had me itchy. The captain of the FIB drew to a stop before a plain door. Another equally plain door was a foot away. Interrogation rooms. He opened his mouth to explain, then shrugged and pushed the door open to show a bare room at half-light. He ushered me in, waiting until the door shut before turning to the two-way mirror and silently shifting the blinds.

I stared into the other room. "Sara Jane!" I whispered, my face going slack.

"You know her?" Edden crossed his short, thick arms on his chest. "That's lucky."

"There's no such thing as luck," Jenks snapped, the breeze from his wings brushing my cheek as he hovered at eye level. His hands were on his hips and his wings had gone from their usual translucence to a faint pink. "It's a setup."

I drew closer to the glass. "She's Trent Kalamack's secretary. What is she doing here?"

Edden stood beside me, his feet spread wide. "Looking for her boyfriend."

I turned, surprised at the tight expression on his round face. "Warlock named Dan Smather," Edden said. "Went missing Sunday. The I.S. won't act until he's gone for thirty days. She's convinced his disappearance is tied to the witch hunter murders. I think she's right."

My stomach tightened. Cincinnati was not known for its serial killers, but we had endured more unexplained murders in the last six weeks than the last three years combined. The recent violence had everyone upset, Inderlander and human alike. The one-way glass fogged under my breath and I backed up. "Does he fit the profile?" I asked, already knowing the I.S. wouldn't have brushed her off if he had.

"If he were dead he would. So far he's only missing."

The dry rasp of Jenks's wings broke the silence. "So why bring Rache into it?"

"Two reasons. The first being Ms. Gradenko is a witch." He nodded to the pretty woman past the glass, frustration thick in his voice. "My officers can't question her properly."

I watched Sara Jane look at the clock and wipe her eye. "She doesn't know how to stir a spell," I said softly. "She can only invoke them. Technically, she's a warlock. I wish you people would get it straight that it's your level of skill, not your sex, that makes you a witch or warlock."

"Either way, my officers don't know how to interpret her answers."

A flicker of anger stirred. I turned to him, my lips pressed. "You can't tell if she's lying."

The captain shrugged, his thick shoulders bunching. "If you like."

Jenks hovered between us, his hands on his hips in his best Peter Pan pose. "Okay, so you want Rache to question her. What's the second reason?"

Edden leaned a shoulder against the wall. "I need someone to go back to school, and as I don't have a witch on my payroll, that's you, Rachel."

For a moment I could only stare. "Beg pardon?"

The man's smile made him look even more like a contriving troll. "You've been following the papers?" he needlessly asked, and I nodded.

"The victims were all witches," I said. "All single except for the first two, and all experienced in ley line magic." I stifled a grimace. I didn't like ley lines, and I avoided using them whenever I could. They were gateways to the ever-after and demons. One of the more popular theories was that the victims had been dabbling in the black arts and simply lost control. I didn't buy that. No one was stupid enough to bind a demon—except Nick, my boyfriend. And that had been only to save my life.

Edden nodded, showing me the top of his head of thick black hair. "What has been kept quiet is that all of them, at one point or another, have been taught by a Dr. Anders."

I rubbed my scraped palms. "Anders," I murmured, searching my memory and coming up with a thin-faced, sour-looking woman with her hair too short and her voice too shrill. "I had a class with her." I glanced at Edden and turned to the one-way glass, embarrassed. "She was a visiting professor from the university while one of our instructors was on sabbatical. Taught Ley Lines for the Earth Witch. She's a condescending toad. Flunked me out on the third class because I wouldn't get a familiar."

He grunted. "Try to get a B this time so I can get reimbursed for tuition."

"Whoa!" Jenks shouted, his tiny voice pitched high. "Edden, you can just plant your sunflower seeds in someone else's garden. Rachel isn't going anywhere near Sara Jane. This is Kalamack trying to get his manicured fingers on her."

Edden pushed himself away from the wall, frowning. "Mr. Kalamack is not implicated in this whatsoever. And if you take this run gunning for him, Rachel, I'll sling your lily-white witch butt back across the river and into the Hollows. Dr. Anders is our suspect. If you want the run, you leave Mr. Kalamack out of this."

Jenks's wings buzzed an angry whine. "Did you all slip antifreeze in your coffee this morning?" he shrilled. "It's a setup! This has nothing to do with the witch hunter murders. Rachel, tell him this has nothing to do with the murders."

"This has nothing to do with the murders," I said blandly. "I'll take the run."

"Rachel!" Jenks protested.

I took a slow breath, knowing I would never be able to explain. Sara Jane was more honest than half the I.S. agents I had once worked with: a farm girl struggling to find her way in the city and help her indentured-servant family. Though she wouldn't know me from Jack, I owed her. She was the sole person who had shown me any kindness during my three days of purgatory trapped as a mink in Trent Kalamack's office last spring.

Physically, we were as unalike as two people could possibly be. Where Sara Jane sat stiffly upright at the table in her crisp business dress with every blond hair in place and makeup applied so well it was almost invisible, I stood in scraped-up leather pants with my frizzy red hair wild and untamed. Where she was petite, having a china-doll look with her clear skin and delicate features, I was tall with an athletic build that had saved my life more times than I have freckles on my nose. Where she was amply curved and padded in all the right places, I stopped at the curves, my chest not much more than a suggestion. But I felt a kinship with her. We were both trapped by Trent Kalamack. And by now she probably knew it.

Jenks hovered beside me. "No," he said. "Trent is using her to reach you."

Irritated, I waved him away. "Trent can't touch me. Edden, do you still have that pink folder I gave you last spring?"

"The one with the disc and datebook containing evidence that Trent Kalamack is a manufacturer and distributor of illegal genetic products?" The squat man grinned. "Yeah. I keep it by my bed for when I can't sleep at night."

My jaw dropped. "You weren't supposed to open it unless I went missing!"

"I peek at my Christmas presents, too," he said. "Relax. I won't do anything unless Kalamack kills you. I still say blackmailing Kalamack is risky—"

"It's the only thing keeping me alive!" I said hotly, then

winced as I wondered if Sara Jane might have heard me through the glass.

"—but probably safer than trying to bring him to justice—at the present time. This, though?" He gestured to Sara Jane. "He's too smart for this."

If it had been anyone but Trent, I'd have to agree. Trent Kalamack was pristine on paper, as charming and attractive in public as he was ruthless and cold behind closed doors. I had watched him kill a man in his office, making it look like an accident with a swiftly implemented set of preparations. But as long as Edden didn't act on my blackmail, the untouchable man would leave me alone.

Jenks darted between me and the mirror. He came to a hovering standstill, worry creasing his tiny features. "This stinks worse than that fish. Walk away. You gotta walk away."

My gaze focused past Jenks, upon Sara Jane. She had been crying. "I owe her, Jenks," I whispered. "Whether she knows it or not."

Edden shifted to stand beside me, and together we watched Sara Jane. "Morgan?"

Jenks was right. There was no such thing as luck—unless you bought it—and nothing happened around Trent without reason. My eyes were fixed upon Sara Jane. "Yeah. Yeah, I'll do it."

Three

My gaze was drawn to Sara Jane's nails as she fidgeted across from me. Last time I had seen her, they were clean but worn down to the quick. Now they were long and shapely, polished a tasteful shade of red. "So," I said, looking from the fitfully flashing enamel to her eyes. They were blue. I hadn't known for sure. "You last heard from Dan on Saturday?"

From across the table, Sara Jane nodded. There hadn't been a flicker of recognition when Edden introduced us. Part of me was relieved, part disappointed. Her lilac scent pulled the unwelcome memory of helplessness I had felt while a mink caged in Trent's office.

The tissue in Sara Jane's hand was about the size of a walnut, clenched into a ball with her trembling fingers. "Dan called me as he was coming off of work," she said, the tremor reflected in her voice. She glanced at Edden, standing beside the closed door with his arms crossed and his white sleeves rolled up to his elbows. "Well, he left a message on my machine—it was four in the morning. He said he wanted to have dinner together, that he wanted to talk to me. He never showed up. That's why I know something's wrong, Officer Morgan." Her eyes went wide and her jaw clenched as she struggled not to cry.

"It's Ms. Morgan," I said uncomfortably. "I don't work for the FIB on a regular basis."

Jenks's wings shifted into motion as he remained perched on my foam cup. "She doesn't really work regularly at all," he said snidely.

"Ms. Morgan is our Inderland consultant," Edden said, frowning at Jenks.

Sara Jane dabbed at her eyes. The tissue still in her grip, she nudged her hair back. She had cut it, and it made her look even more professional as it bumped about her shoulders in a straight yellow sheet. "I brought a picture of him," she said, digging in her purse to pull out a snapshot and push it at me. I looked down to see her and a young man on the deck of one of the steamers that take tourists out on the Ohio River. They were both smiling. His arm was around her, and she was leaning into him. She looked happy and relaxed in blue jeans and a blouse.

I took a moment to study Dan's picture. He was clean-cut, sturdy looking, and wearing a plaid shirt. Just the kind of man one would expect a farm girl to bring home to Mom and Dad.

"Can I keep this?" I asked, and she nodded. "Thanks." I tucked it in my bag, not comfortable with how her eyes were fixed upon the picture as if she could bring him back by her will alone. "Do you know how we can get in touch with his relatives? He may have had a family emergency and needed to leave without notice."

"Dan is an only child," she said, dabbing at her nose with the crumpled tissue. "Both his parents are gone. They were serfed on a farm up north. Life expectancy isn't high for a farmer."

"Oh." I didn't know what else to say. "Technically, we can't enter his apartment until he's declared missing. You don't happen to have a key, do you?"

"Yes. I—" She blushed through her makeup. "I let his cat in when he works late."

I glanced down at the lie-detecting amulet in my lap as it briefly shifted from green to red. She was lying, but I didn't need an amulet to figure that out. I said nothing, not wanting to embarrass her further by making her admit she had the key for other, more romantic reasons.

"I was there today about seven," she said, eyes downcast. "Everything looked fine."

"Seven in the morning?" Edden uncrossed his arms and levered himself upright. "Isn't that when you—you witches, I mean—are tucked in bed?"

She gazed up at him and nodded. "I'm Mr. Kalamack's personal secretary. He works in the mornings and evenings, so my schedule is split. Eight to noon in the morning and four to eight in the afternoon. It took a while to become accustomed to it, but with four hours for myself in the afternoon, I was able to spend more time with . . . Dan," she finished.

"Please," the young woman pleaded suddenly, her gaze shifting between Edden and me. "I know something's wrong. Why won't anyone help me?"

I shifted uncomfortably as she struggled for control. She felt helpless. I understood her better than she knew. Sara Jane was the latest in Trent's long string of secretaries. As a mink I had listened in on her interview, unable to warn her as she was lured into believing Trent's half-truths. For all her intelligence, she hadn't a chance to escape his charm and extravagant offers. With his offer of employment, Trent had given her family a golden ticket out of their indentured servitude.

And Trent Kalamack was truly a benevolent employer, offering high wages and outstanding benefits. He gave people what they desperately wanted, asking in return nothing but their loyalty. By the time they realized how deep he demanded that loyalty go, they knew too much to extricate themselves.

Sara Jane had escaped the farm, but Trent had then bought it, probably to ensure that she would keep her mouth shut when she found out about his dealings in the illegal drug Brimstone, as well as the desperately sought-after genetic medicines outlawed during the Turn. I'd almost tagged him with the truth, but the sole other witness had died in a car explosion.

Publicly, Trent served on the city's council, untouchable because of his vast wealth and generous donations to charities and underprivileged children. Privately, no one even knew if he was a human or Inderlander. Even Jenks couldn't tell, which was unusual for a pixy. Trent quietly ran a good slice of Cincinnati's underworld, and both the FIB and the I.S. would sell their bosses to have a court date with him. And now Sara Jane's boyfriend was missing.

I cleared my throat, recalling the temptation of Trent's offer myself. Seeing Sara Jane under control again, I asked, "You said he works at Pizza Piscary's?"

She nodded. "He's a driver. That's how we met." She bit her lip and dropped her eyes.

The lie-detecting amulet was a steady green. Piscary's was an Inderland eatery serving everything from tomato soup to gourmet cheesecake. Piscary himself was said to be one of Cincinnati's master vampires. Nice enough, from what I'd heard: not greedy with his vamp takes, even-tempered, on record as being dead for the last three hundred years. 'Course, he was probably older than that, and the nicer and more civilized an undead vampire seemed, the more depraved he or she generally was. My roommate thought of him as sort of a friendly uncle, which made me feel oh-so-warm and fuzzy inside.

I handed Sara Jane another tissue, and she smiled weakly. "I can go out to his apartment today," I said. "Do you think you could meet me there with the key? Sometimes a professional can spot things others miss." Jenks snorted, and I shifted my legs, bumping the underside of the table to make him dart into the air.

Sara Jane showed relief. "Oh, thank you, Ms. Morgan," she gushed. "I can go right now. I just have to call my employer and let him know I'll be a little late." She gripped her purse, looking like she was ready to fly out of the room. "Mr. Kalamack told me to take all the time I need this afternoon."

I glanced at Jenks's attention-getting buzz. He had a worried I-told-you-so look. How nice of Trent to let his secretary take all the time she needs to find her boyfriend when he's probably stuffed in a closet so she'll keep her mouth shut. "Ah, let's make it tonight," I said, thinking of my fish. "I need to look up a few things." *And whip up a few antigoon spells, check my splat gun, and collect my fee . . .*

"Of course," she said, settling back as her expression clouded.

"And if nothing turns up there, we'll go on to the next step." I tried to make my smile reassuring. "I'll meet you at Dan's apartment a little after eight?"

Hearing the dismissal in my voice, she nodded and stood. Jenks flitted into the air, and I rose as well. "All right," she said. "It's out at Redwood—"

Edden shuffled his feet. "I'll tell Ms. Morgan where it is, Ms. Gradenko."

"Yes. Thank you." Her smile was starting to look stilted. "I'm just so worried. . . ."

I disguised putting my lie-detecting amulet away by digging through my bag and pulling out one of my cards. "Please let me or the FIB know if you hear from him in the meantime," I said as I handed it to her. Ivy had the cards professionally printed, and they looked slick.

"Yes. I will," she murmured, her lips moving as she read VAMPIRIC CHARMS, the name Nick had given my and Ivy's agency. She met my eyes as she tucked the card in her purse.

I shook her hand, deciding her grip was firmer this time. Her fingers, though, were still cold.

"I'll show you out, Ms. Gradenko," Edden said as he opened the door. At his subtle gesture, I sank back into my chair to wait.

Jenks buzzed his wings for my attention. "I don't like it," he said as our eyes met.

A flash of ire took me. "She wasn't lying," I said defensively. He put his hands on his hips, and I waved him off my cup to take a sip of my lukewarm coffee. "You don't know her, Jenks. She hates vermin, but she tried to keep Jonathan from tormenting me though it might have meant her job."

"She felt sorry for you," Jenks said. "Pitiful little mink with a concussion."

"She gave me part of her lunch when I wouldn't eat those disgusting pellets."

"The carrots were drugged, Rache."

"She didn't know that. Sara Jane suffered as much as I did."

The pixy hovered six inches before me, demanding I look at him. "That's what I'm saying. Trent could be using her to get to you again, and she wouldn't even know it."

My sigh pushed him back. "She's trapped. I have to help her if I can." I looked up as Edden opened the door and poked his head in. He had an FIB hat on, and it looked odd with his white shirt and khakis as he gestured for me.

Jenks flitted to my shoulder. "You and your 'rescue impulses' are going to get you killed," he whispered as I found the hallway.

"Thanks, Morgan," Edden said as he grabbed my canister of fish and led me up front.

"No problem," I said as we entered the FIB's back offices. The hustle of people enfolded me, and my tension eased in the blessed autonomy it offered. "She wasn't lying about anything other than having a key to let his cat out. But I could have told you that without the spell. I'll let you know what I find out at Dan's apartment. How late can I call you?"

"Oh," Edden said loudly as we slipped past the front desk and headed for the sunlit sidewalk. "No need, Ms. Morgan. Thank you for your help. We'll be in touch."

I stopped short in surprise. A curl of escaped hair brushed my shoulder as Jenks's wings clattered against themselves in a harsh noise. "What the hell?" he muttered.

My face warmed as I realized he was brushing me off. "I did not come down here just to invoke a lousy lie-detecting amulet," I said as I jerked into motion. "I told you I'd leave Kalamack alone. Get out of my way and let me do what I'm good at."

Behind me, conversations were going quiet. Edden never hesitated in his slow stride to the door. "It's an FIB matter, Ms. Morgan. Let me help you out."

I followed, tight to his heels, not caring about the dark looks I was getting. "This run is mine, Edden," I almost yelled. "Your people will mess it up. These are Inderlanders, not humans. You can have the glory. All I want is to be paid." *And see Trent in jail,* I added silently.

He pushed open one of the glass double doors. The sun-warmed concrete threw up a wave of heat as I stomped out after him, almost pinning the short man against the building as he gestured for a cab. "You gave me this run and I'm taking it," I exclaimed, yanking a curl out of my mouth as the wind blew it up into my face. "Not some stuck-up, arrogant cookie in an FIB hat who thinks he's the greatest thing since the Turn!"

"Good," he said lightly, shocking me into taking a step back. Putting my canister on the sidewalk, he stuffed his FIB hat into his back pocket. "But from here on out, you are *officially* off the run."

My mouth opened in understanding. I was *officially* not here. Taking a breath, I willed the adrenaline out of my system. Edden nodded as he saw my anger fizzle out. "I'd appreciate your discretion on this," he said. "Sending Glenn out to Pizza Piscary's alone isn't prudent."

"Glenn!" Jenks shrilled, his voice scraping the inside of my skull, making my eyes water.

"No," I said. "I already have my team. We don't need Detective Glenn."

Jenks left me. "Yeah," he said as he flew between the FIB captain and me. His wings were red. "We don't play well with others."

Edden frowned. "This is an FIB matter. You will have an FIB presence with you when at all possible, and Glenn is the only one qualified."

"Qualified?" Jenks scoffed. "Why not admit he's the only one of your officers who can talk to a witch without pissing his pants?"

"No," I said firmly. "We work alone."

Edden stood beside my canister, his arms crossed to make his squat form look as immovable as a stone wall. "He's our new Inderland specialist. I know he's inexperienced—"

"He's an ass!" Jenks snapped.

A grin flashed over Edden. "I prefer rough around the edges, myself."

My lips pursed. "Glenn is a cocky, self-assured . . ." I fumbled, looking for something suitably derogatory. ". . . FIB flunky who is going to get himself killed the first time he runs into an Inderlander who isn't as nice as I am."

Jenks bobbed his head. "He needs to be taught a lesson."

Edden smiled. "He's my son, and I couldn't agree more," he said.

"He's what?" I exclaimed as an unmarked FIB car pulled up to the curb beside us. Edden reached for the handle of the back door and opened it. Edden was clearly from European decent, and Glenn . . . Glenn wasn't. My mouth worked as I tried to find something that couldn't be remotely construed as being racist. As a witch, I was sensitive to that kind of thing. "How come he doesn't have your last name?" I managed.

"He's used his mother's maiden name since joining the FIB," Edden said softly. "He's not supposed to be under my direction, but no one else would take the job."

My brow furrowed. Now I understood the cold reception in the FIB. It hadn't been all me. Glenn was new, taking a position everyone but his dad thought was a waste of time. "I'm not doing this," I said. "Find someone else to baby-sit your kid."

Edden put my canister into the back. "Break him in gently."

"You aren't listening," I said loudly, frustrated. "You gave me this run. My associates and I appreciate your offer to help, but you asked me here. Back off and let us work."

"Great," Edden said as he slammed the car's back door shut. "Thanks for taking Detective Glenn with you out to Piscary's."

A cry of disgust slipped from me. "Edden!" I exclaimed, earning looks from the passing people. "I said no. There is one sound coming past my lips. One sound. Two letters. One meaning. No!"

Edden opened the front passenger door and gestured for me to get in. "Thanks bunches, Morgan." He glanced into the backseat. "Why were you running from those Weres, anyway?"

My breath came in a slow, controlled sound. *Damn.*

Edden chuckled, and I put myself in the car and slammed the door, trying to get his stubby fingers in it. Scowling, I looked at the driver. It was Glenn. He looked as happy as I felt. I had to say something. "You don't look anything like your dad," I said snidely.

His gaze was fixed with a ramrod stiffness out the front window. "He adopted me when he married my mother," he said through clenched teeth.

Jenks zipped in trailing a sunbeam of pixy dust. "You're Edden's son?"

"You got a problem with that?" he said belligerently.

The pixy landed on the dash with his hands on his hips. "Nah. All you humans look alike to me."

Edden bent to put his beaming round face in the window. "Here's your class schedule," he said, handing me a yellow half page of paper with printer holes along the sides. "Monday, Wednesday, Friday. Glenn will buy any books you need."

"Hold it!" I exclaimed, alarm washing through me as the yellow paper crackled in my fingers. "I thought I was just going to poke around the university. I don't want to take a class!"

"It's the one Mr. Smather was taking. Be there, or you won't get paid."

He was smiling, enjoying this. "Edden!" I shouted as he backed up onto the sidewalk.

"Glenn, take Ms. Morgan and Jenks to their office. Let me know what you find at Dan Smather's apartment."

"Yes *sir!*" he barked. His knuckles gripping the wheel showed a fierce pressure. Pink patches of Ivy-Aid decorated his wrists and neck. I didn't that care that he had heard most of the conversation. He wasn't welcome, and the sooner he understood that, the better.

Four

"**R**ight at the next corner," I said, resting my arm on the open window of the unmarked FIB car. Glenn ran his fingertips through his close-cropped hair as he scratched his scalp. He hadn't said a word the entire way, his jaw slowly unclenching as he realized I wasn't going to make him talk to me. There was no one behind us, but he signaled before turning onto my street.

He had sunglasses on, taking in the residential neighborhood with its shady sidewalks and patchy lawns. We were well within the Hollows, the unofficial haven for most of Cincinnati's resident Inderlanders since the Turn, when every surviving human fled into the city and its false sense of security. There has always been some mingling, but for the most part humans work and live in Cincinnati since the Turn, and Inderlanders work and—uh—play in the Hollows.

I think Glenn was surprised the suburb looked like everywhere else—until you noticed the runes scratched in the hopscotch grid, and that the basketball hoop was a third again taller than NBA regulation. It was quiet, too. Peaceful. Some of that could be attributed to Inderland's schools not letting out until almost midnight, but most was self-preservation.

Every Inderlander over the age of forty had spent their earliest years trying to hide that they weren't human, a tradition that is unraveling with the cautious fear of the hunted, vampires included. So the grass is mown by sullen teenagers on Friday, the cars are dutifully washed on Saturday, and the trash makes tidy piles at the curb on Wednesday. But the streetlights are shot out by gun or charm as soon as the city replaces them, and no one calls the Humane Society at the sight of a loose dog, as it might be the neighbor's kid skipping school.

The dangerous reality of the Hollows remains carefully hidden. We know if we color too far out of humanity's self-imposed lines, old fears will resurface and they will strike out at us. They would lose—badly—and as a whole, Inderlanders like things balanced just as they are. Fewer humans would mean that witches and Weres would start taking the brunt of vampires' needs. And while the occasional witch "enjoyed" a vampiric lifestyle at his or her own discretion, we'd bind together to take them out if they tried to turn us into fodder. The older vampires know it, and so they make sure everyone plays by humanity's rules.

Fortunately, the more savage side of Inderlanders naturally gravitates to the outskirts of the Hollows and away from our homes. The strip of nightclubs along both sides of the river is especially hazardous since swarming, high-spirited humans draw the more predatorial of us like fires on a cold night, promising warmth and reassurance of survival. Our homes are kept as human looking as possible. Those who strayed too far from the Mr. and Mrs. Cleaver veneer were encouraged in a rather unique neighborhood intervention party to blend in a little more . . . or move out to the country where they couldn't do as much damage. My gaze drifted over the tongue-in-cheek sign peeping out from a bed of foxgloves. DAY SLEEPER. SOLICITORS WILL BE EATEN. *For the most part, anyway.*

"You can park up there on the right," I said, pointing.

Glenn's brow furrowed. "I thought we were going to your office."

Jenks flitted from my earring to the rearview mirror. "We are," he said snidely.

Glenn scratched his jawline, his short beard making a rasping sound under his nail. "You run your agency out of a house?"

I sighed at his patronizing lilt. "Sort of. Anywhere here is fine."

He pulled to the curb at Keasley's house, the neighborhood's "wise old man" who had both the medical equipment and know-how of a small emergency room for those who could keep their mouths shut about it. Across the street was a small stone church, its steeple rising high above two gigantic oaks. It sat on an unreal four city lots and had come with its own graveyard.

Renting out a defunct church hadn't been my idea but Ivy's. Seeing tombstones out the small stained-glass window of my bedroom had taken a while to get used to, but the kitchen it came with made up for having dead humans buried in the backyard.

Glenn cut the engine, and the new silence soaked in. I scanned the surrounding yards before I got out, a habit begun during my not-so-distant death threats, which I thought prudent to continue. Old man Keasley was on his porch as usual, rocking and keeping a sharp eye on the street. I gave him a wave and got a raised hand in answer. Satisfied he would have warned me if I had needed it, I got out and opened the back door for my canister of fish.

"I'll get it, ma'am," Glenn said as his door thumped shut.

I gave him a tired look over the car's roof. "Drop the ma'am, will you? I'm Rachel."

His attention went over my shoulder and he visibly stiffened. I whipped around expecting the worst, relaxing as a cloud of pixy children descended in a high-pitched chorus of conversation too fast for me to follow. Papa Jenks had been missed—as usual. My sour mood evaporated as the darting swooping figures in pale green and gold swirled about their dad in a Disney nightmare. Glenn took his sunglasses off, his brown eyes wide and his lips parted.

Jenks made a piercing whistle with his wings, and the horde broke enough for him to hover before me. "Hey, Rache," he said. "I'll be out back if you want me."

"Sure." I glanced at Glenn and muttered, "Is Ivy here?"

The pixy followed my gaze to the human and grinned, undoubtedly imagining what Ivy would do when meeting Captain Edden's son. Jax, Jenks's eldest child, joined his father. "No, Ms. Morgan," he said, pitching his preadolescent voice deeper than it normally fell. "She's doing errands. The grocery store, the post office, the bank. She said she'd be back before five."

The bank, I thought, wincing. She was supposed to wait until I had the rest of my rent. Jax flew three circles about my head, making me dizzy. " 'Bye, Ms. Morgan," he called out, zipping off to join his siblings, who were escorting their dad to the back of the church and the oak stump Jenks had moved his very large family into.

My breath puffed out as Glenn came around the back of the car, offering to carry my canister. I shook my head and hefted it; it wasn't that heavy. I was starting to feel guilty for having let Jenks pix him. But then I hadn't known I was going to have to baby-sit him at the time. "Come on in," I said as I started across the street to the wide stone steps.

The sound of his hard-soled shoes on the street faltered. "You live in a church?"

My eyes narrowed. "Yeah. But I don't sleep with voodoo dolls."

"Huh?"

"Never mind."

Glenn muttered something, and my guilt deepened. "Thanks for driving me home," I said as I climbed the stone steps and pulled open the right side of the twin wooden doors for him. He said nothing, and I added, "Really. Thanks."

Hesitating on the stoop, he stared at me. I couldn't tell what he was thinking. "You're welcome," he finally said, his voice giving me no clue, either.

I led the way through the empty foyer into the even more empty sanctuary. Before we rented out the church, it had been used as a daycare. The pews and altar had been removed to make a large play area. Now all that remained were the stained-glass windows and a slightly raised stage. The shadow of a huge, long-gone cross spread across the wall in a poignant reminder. I glanced at the tall ceiling, seeing the familiar room in a new way as Glenn looked it over. It was quiet. I'd forgotten how peaceful it was.

Ivy had spread tumbling mats over half of it, leaving a narrow walkway running from the foyer to the back rooms. At least once a week we'd spar to keep fresh, now that we were both independents and not on the streets every night. It invariably ended with me a sweating mass of bruises and her not even breathing hard. Ivy was a living vamp—as alive as I was and in possession of a soul, infected by the vamp virus by way of her, at the time, still-living mother.

Not having to wait until she was dead before the virus began molding her, Ivy had been born possessing a little of both worlds, the living and dead, caught in the middle ground until she died and became a true undead. From the living she retained a soul, allowing her to walk under the sun, worship without pain, and live on holy ground if she wanted, which she did to tick her mother off. From the dead came her small but sharp canines, her ability to pull an aura and scare the crap out of me, and her power to hold spellbound those who allowed it. Her unearthly strength and speed were decidedly less than a true undead, but still far beyond mine. And though she didn't need blood to remain sane, as undead vampires did, she had an unsettling hunger for it, which she was continually fighting to suppress, since she was one of the few living vamps who had sworn off blood. I imagine Ivy must have had an interesting childhood, but I was afraid to ask.

"Come on in to the kitchen," I said as I went through the archway at the back of the sanctuary. I took off my shades as I passed my bathroom. It had once been the men's bathroom, the traditional fixtures replaced with a washer and dryer, a small sink, and a shower. This one was mine. The women's bathroom across the hall had been converted into a more conventional bathroom with a tub. That one was Ivy's. Separate bathrooms made things a heck of a lot easier.

Not liking the way Glenn was making silent judgments, I closed the doors to both Ivy's and my bedrooms as I passed them. They had once been clergy offices. He shuffled into the kitchen behind me, spending a moment or two taking it all in. Most people did.

The kitchen was huge, and part of the reason I had agreed to live in a church with a vampire. It had two stoves, an institutional-size fridge, and a large center island overhung with a rack of gleaming utensils and pots. The stainless steel shone, and the counter space was expansive. With the exception of my Beta in the brandy snifter on the windowsill, and the massive antique wooden table Ivy used for a computer desk, it looked like the set of a cooking show. It was the last thing one would expect attached to the back of church—and I loved it.

I set the canister of fish on the table. "Why don't you sit down," I said, wanting to call the Howlers. "I'll be right back." I hesitated as my manners clawed their way up to the forefront of my mind. "Do you want a drink . . . or something?" I asked.

Glenn's brown eyes were unreadable. "No, ma'am." His voice was stiff, with more than a hint of sarcasm, making me want to smack him a good one and tell him to lighten up. I'd deal with his attitude later. Right now I had to call the Howlers.

"Have a seat, then," I said, letting some of my own bother show. "I'll be right back."

The living room was just off the kitchen on the other side of the hallway. As I searched for the coach's number in my bag, I hit the message button on the answering machine.

"Hey, Ray-ray. It's me," came Nick's voice, sounding tinny through the recording. Shooting a glance at the hallway, I turned it down so Glenn couldn't hear. "I've got 'em. Third row back on the far right. Now you'll have to make good on your claim and get us backstage passes." There was a pause, then, "I still don't believe you've met him. Talk to you later."

My breath came in anticipation as it clicked off. I had met Takata four years ago when he spotted me in the balcony at a solstice concert. I had thought I was going to be kicked out when a thick Were in a staff shirt escorted me backstage while the warm-up band played.

Turned out Takata had seen my frizzy hair and wanted to know if it was spelled or natural, and if natural, did I have a charm to get something that wild to lie flat? Starstuck and repeatedly embarrassing myself, I admitted it was natural, though I had encouraged it that night, then gave him one of the charms my mother and I spent my entire high school career perfecting to tame it. He laughed then, unwinding one of his blond dreadlocks to show me his hair was worse than mine, static making it float and stick to everything. I hadn't straightened my hair since.

My friends and I had watched the show from backstage, and afterward, Takata and I led his bodyguards on a merry chase through Cincinnati the whole night. I was sure he would remember me, but I hadn't a clue as to how to get in touch with him. It wasn't as if I could call him up and say,

"Remember me? We had coffee on the solstice four years ago and discussed how to straighten curls."

A smile twitched the corner of my mouth as I fingered the answering machine. He was all right for an old guy. 'Course, anyone over the age of thirty had seemed old to me at the time.

Nick's was the only message, and I found myself pacing as I picked up the phone and punched in the Howlers' number. I plucked at my shirt as the number rang. After running from those Weres, I had to take a shower.

There was a click, and a low voice nearly growled, "'Ello. Ya got the Howlers."

"Coach!" I exclaimed, recognizing the Were's voice. "Good news."

There was a slight pause. "Who is this?" he asked. "How did you get this number?"

I started. "This is Rachel Morgan," I said slowly. "Of Vampiric Charms?"

There was a half-heard shout directed off the phone, "Which one of you dogs called the escort service? You're athletes, for God's sake. Can't you pin your own bitches without having to buy them?"

"Wait!" I said before he could hang up. "You hired me to find your mascot."

"Oh!" There was a pause, and I heard several war whoops in the background. "Right."

I briefly weighed the trouble of changing our name against the fuss Ivy would raise: a thousand glossy black business cards, the page ad in the phone book, the matched oversized mugs she had imprinted our name on in gold foil. It wasn't going to happen.

"I recovered your fish," I said, bringing myself back. "When can someone pick it up?"

"Uh," the coach muttered. "Didn't anyone call you?"

My face went slack. "No."

"One of the guys moved her while they cleaned her tank and didn't tell anyone," he said. "She was never gone."

Her? I thought. *The fish was a her? How could they tell?* Then I got angry. I had broken into a Were's office for nothing? "No," I said coldly. "No one called me."

"Mmmm. Sorry about that. Thanks for your help, though."

"Whoa! Wait a moment," I cried, hearing the brush-off in his voice. "I spent three days planning this. I risked my life!"

"And we appreciate that—" the coach started.

I spun in an angry circle and stared out at the garden through the shoulder-high windows. The sun glinted on the tombstones beyond. "I don't think you do, *Coach*. We're talking bullets!"

"But she was never lost," the coach insisted. "You don't have our fish. I'm sorry."

"Sorry won't keep those Weres off my tail." Furious, I paced around the coffee table.

"Look," he said. "I'll send you some tickets to the exhibition game coming up."

"Tickets!" I exclaimed, astounded. "For breaking into Mr. Ray's office?"

"Simon Ray?" the coach said. "You broke into Simon's office? Damn, that's rough. 'Bye now."

"No, wait!" I shouted, but the phone clicked off. I stared at the humming receiver. Didn't they know who I was? Didn't they know I could curse their bats to crack and their pop flies to land foul? Did they think I would sit back and do nothing when they owed me my rent!

I flopped into Ivy's gray suede chair with a feeling of helplessness. "Yeah, right," I said softly. A noncontact spell required a wand. Tuition at the community college hadn't covered wand making, just potions and amulets. I didn't have the expertise, much less the recipe, for anything that complicated. I guess they knew who I was right enough.

The sound of a foot scraping linoleum came from the kitchen, and I glanced at the hall. Swell. Glenn had heard the entire thing. Embarrassed, I pulled myself up from the chair. I'd get the money from somewhere. I had almost a week.

Glenn turned as I entered the kitchen. He was standing next to that canister of useless fish. Maybe I could sell it. I put the phone beside Ivy's computer and went to the sink. "You can sit down, Detective Edden. We're going to be here a while."

"It's Glenn," he said stiffly. "It's against FIB policy to report to a member of your family, so keep it to yourself. And we're going to Mr. Smather's apartment now."

I made a scoffing bark of laughter. "Your dad just loves to bend the rules, doesn't he?"

He frowned. "Yes ma'am."

"We aren't going to Dan's apartment until Sara Jane gets off work." Then I slumped. Glenn wasn't the one I was angry with. "Look," I said, not wanting Ivy to find him while I was in the shower. "Why don't you go home and meet me back here about seven-thirty?"

"I'd prefer to stay." He scratched at the welt showing a light pink under his watchband.

"Sure," I said sourly. "Whatever. I gotta shower, though." Clearly he was concerned I'd go without him. The worry was well-founded. Leaning to the window over the sink, I shouted out into the lavish, pixy-tended garden, "Jenks!"

The pixy buzzed in through the hole in the screen so fast, I was willing to bet he'd been eavesdropping. "You bellowed, princess of stink?" he said, landing beside Mr. Fish on the sill.

I gave him a weary look. "Would you show Glenn the garden while I shower?"

Jenks's wings blurred into motion. "Yeah," he said, going to make wide wary circles around Glenn's head. "I'll baby-sit. Come on, cookie. You're going to get the five-dollar tour. Let's start in the graveyard."

"Jenks," I warned, and he gave me a grin, tossing his blond hair artfully over his eyes.

"This way, Glenn," he said, darting out into the hall. Glenn followed, clearly not happy.

I heard the back door shut, and I leaned to the window. "Jenks?"

"What!" The pixy darted back in the window, his face creased with irritation.

I crossed my arms in thought. "Would you bring in some mullein leaves and jewelweed flowers when you get the chance? And do we have any dandelions that haven't gone to seed?"

"Dandelions?" He dropped an inch in surprise, his wings clattering. "You going soft on me? You're going to make him an anti-itch spell, aren't you?"

I leaned to see Glenn standing stiffly under the oak tree, scratching his neck. He looked pitiful, and as Jenks kept telling me, I was a sucker for the underdog. "Just get them, all right?"

"Sure," he said. "He's not much good like that, is he?"

I choked back a laugh, and Jenks flew out the window to join Glenn. The pixy landed on his shoulder, and Glenn jumped in surprise. "Hey, Glenn," Jenks said loudly. "Head off toward those yellow flowers over there behind that stone angel. I want to show you to the rest of my kids. They've never met an FIB officer before."

A faint smile crossed me. Glenn would be safe with Jenks if Ivy came home early. She jealously guarded her privacy and hated surprises, especially ones in FIB uniforms. That Glenn was Edden's son wouldn't help. She was willing to let sleeping grudges lie, but if she felt her territory was being threatened, she wouldn't hesitate to act, her odd, political status of dead-vamp-in-waiting letting her get away with things that would put me in the I.S. lockup.

Turning, my eyes fell upon the fish. "What am I going to do with you—Bob?" I said around a sigh. I wasn't going to take him back to Mr. Ray's office, but I couldn't keep him in the canister. I cracked the top, finding that his gills were pumping and he was laying almost on his side. I thought perhaps I ought to put him in the tub.

Canister in hand, I went into Ivy's bathroom. "Welcome home, Bob," I murmured, dumping the canister into Ivy's black garden tub. The fish flopped in the inch of water, and I hurriedly ran the taps, jiggling the flow to try to keep it room temp. Soon Bob the fish was swimming in graceful sedate circles. I turned off the water and waited until it finished tinkling in and the surface grew smooth. He really was a pretty fish, striking against the black porcelain: all silver, with long, cream fins and that black circle decorating one side to look like a reverse full moon. I dabbled my fingertips in the water, and he darted to the other end of the tub.

Leaving him, I crossed the hall to my bathroom, got a change of clothes out of the dryer, and started the shower. As I picked the snarls out of my hair while waiting for the water to warm, my eyes fell upon the three tomatoes ripening upon the sill. I winced, glad they hadn't been anywhere for Glenn to see. A pixy had given them to me as payment for smuggling her across the city as she fled an unwanted marriage. And while tomatoes weren't illegal anymore, it was in bad taste to have them on display when one had a human guest.

It had been just over forty years since a quarter of the world's human population had been killed by a military-generated virus that had escaped and spontaneously fastened to a weak spot in a biogenetically engineered tomato. It was shipped out before anyone knew—the virus crossing oceans with the ease of an international traveler—and the Turn began.

The engineered virus had a varied effect upon the hidden Inderlanders. Witches, undead vampires, and the smaller species such as pixies and fairies, weren't affected at all. Weres, living vamps, leprechauns, and the like got the flu. Humans died by the droves, taking the elves with them as their practice of bolstering their numbers by hybridizing with humanity backfired.

The U.S. would have followed the Third World countries into chaos if the hidden Inderlanders hadn't stepped in to halt the spread of the virus, burn the dead, and keep civilization running until what was left of humanity finished mourning. Our secret was on the verge of coming out by way of the what-makes-these-people-immune question when a charismatic living vamp named Rynn Cormel pointed out that our combined numbers equaled humanity's. The decision to make our presence known, to live openly among the humans we had been mimicking to keep ourselves safe, was almost unanimous.

The Turn, as it came to be called, ushered in a nightmarish three years. Humanity took their fear of us out on the world's surviving bioengineers, murdering them in trials designed to legalize murder. Then they went further, to outlaw all genetically engineered products, along with the science that created them. A second, slower wave of death followed the first once old diseases found new life when the medicines humanity had created to battle everything from Alzheimer's to cancer no longer existed. Tomatoes are still treated like poison by humans, even though the virus is long gone. If you don't grow them yourself, you have to go to a specialty store to find them.

A frown pinched my forehead as I looked at the red fruit beading up with shower fog. If I was smart, I'd put it in the kitchen to see how Glenn would react at Piscary's. Bringing a human into an Inderland eatery wasn't a crackerjack idea.

If he made a scene, we might not only get no information, we might get banned, or worse.

Judging that the water was hot enough, I eased into it with little "ow, ow, ows." Twenty minutes later I was wrapped in a big pink towel, standing before my ugly pressboard dresser with its dozen or so bottles of perfume carefully arranged on top. The blurry picture of the Howlers' fish was tucked between the glass and the frame. Sure looked like the same fish to me.

The delighted shrieks of pixy children filtered in through my open window to soften my mood. Very few pixies could manage to raise a family in the city. Jenks was stronger in spirit than most would ever know. He had killed before to keep his garden so his children wouldn't starve. It was good to hear their voices raised in delight: the sound of family and security.

"Which scent was it, now?" I murmured, fingers hovering over my perfumes as I tried to remember which one Ivy and I were currently experimenting with. Every so often a new bottle would show up without comment as she found something new for me to try.

I reached for one, dropping it when Jenks said from right beside my ear, "Not that one."

"Jenks!" I clutched my towel closer and spun. "Get the hell out of my room!"

He darted backward as I made a grab for him. His grin widened as he looked down at the leg I accidentally showed. Laughing, he swooped past me and landed on a bottle. "This one works good," he said. "And you're going to need all the help you can get when you tell Ivy you're going to make a run for Trent again."

Scowling, I reached for the bottle. Wings clattering, he rose, pixy dust making temporary sunbeams shimmer through the glittering bottles. "Thanks," I said sullenly, knowing his nose was better than mine. "Now get out. No, wait." He hesitated by my small stained-glass window, and I vowed to sew up the pixy hole in the screen. "Who's watching Glenn?"

Jenks literally glowed with parental pride. "Jax. They're in garden. Glenn is shooting wild cherry pits straight up with a rubber band for my kids to catch before they hit the ground."

I was so surprised, I almost could ignore that my hair was dripping wet and I was wearing nothing but a towel. "He's playing with your kids?"

"Yeah. He's not so bad—once you get to know him." Jenks vaulted through the pixy hole. "I'll send him inside in about five minutes, okay?" he said through the screen.

"Make it ten," I said softly, but he was gone. Frowning, I shut the window, locked it, and checked twice that the curtains hung right. Taking the bottle Jenks had suggested, I gave myself a splash. Cinnamon blossomed. Ivy and I had been working for the last three months to find a perfume that covered her natural scent mixing with mine. This was one of the nicer ones.

Whether undead or alive, vampires moved by instinct triggered by pheromones and scent, more at the mercy of their hormones than an adolescent. They gave off a largely undetectable smell that lingered where they did, an odoriferous signpost telling other vamps that this was taken territory and to back off. A far cry better than the way dogs did it, but living together the way we were, Ivy's smell lingered on me. She had once told me it was a survival trait that helped increase a shadow's life expectancy by preventing poaching. I wasn't her shadow, but there it was anyway. What it boiled down to was, the smell of our natural scents mingling tended to act like a blood aphrodisiac, making it harder for Ivy to best her instincts, nonpracticing or not.

One of Nick's and my few arguments had been over why I put up with her and the constant threat she posed to my free will if she forgot her vow of abstinence one night and I couldn't fend her off. The truth was, she considered herself my friend, but even more telling was that she had loosened the death grip she kept on her emotions and let me be her friend as well. The honor of that was heady. She was the best runner I'd ever seen, and I was continually flattered that she left a brilliant career at the I.S. to work with me/save my ass.

Ivy was possessive, domineering, and unpredictable. She also had the strongest will of anyone I had met, fighting a battle in herself that if she won would rob her of her life after death. And she was willing to kill to protect me because I called her my friend. God, how could you walk away from something like that?

Apart from when we were alone and she felt safe from recrimination, she either held herself with a cool stiffness or fell into a classic vampire mode of sexy domination that I had discovered was her way of divorcing herself from her feelings, afraid that if she showed a softening she would lose control. I think she had pinned her sanity on living vicariously through me as I stumbled through life, enjoying the enthusiasm with which I embraced everything, from finding a pair of red heels on sale to learning a spell to laying a big-bad-ugly out flat. And as my fingers drifted over the perfumes she had bought for me, I wondered again if perhaps Nick was right and our odd relationship might be slipping into an area I didn't want it to go.

Dressing quickly, I made my way back to the empty kitchen. The clock above the sink said it was edging toward four. I had loads of time to make a spell for Glenn before we left.

Pulling out one of my spelling books from the shelf under the center island counter, I sat at my usual spot at Ivy's antique wooden table. Contentment filled me as I opened the yellowed tome. The breeze coming in the window had a chill that promised a cold night. I loved it here, working in my beautiful kitchen surrounded by holy ground, safe from everything nasty.

The anti-itch spell was easy to find, dog-eared and spotted with old splatters. Leaving the book open, I rose to pull out my smallest copper vat and ceramic spoons. It was rare that a human would accept an amulet, but perhaps if he saw me making it, Glenn might. His dad had taken a pain amulet from me once.

I was measuring the springwater with my graduated cylinder when there was a scuffing on the back steps. "Hello? Ms. Morgan?" Glenn called as he knocked and opened the door. "Jenks said I could come right in."

I didn't look up from my careful measuring. "In the kitchen," I said loudly.

Glenn edged into the room. He took in my new clothes, running his eyes from my fuzzy pink slippers, up my black nylons to my matching short skirt, past my red blouse, to the black bow holding my damp hair back. If I was going to see Sara Jane again, I wanted to look nice.

In Glenn's hands was a wad of mullein leaves, dandelion blossoms, and jewelweed flowers. He looked stiffly embarrassed. "Jenks—the pixy—said you wanted these, ma'am."

I nodded to the island counter. "You can put them over there. Thanks. Have a seat."

With a stilted haste, he crossed the room and set the cuttings down. Hesitating briefly, he pulled out what was traditionally Ivy's chair and eased into it. His jacket was gone, and his shoulder holster with his weapon looked obvious and aggressive. In contrast, his tie was loose and the top button of his starched shirt was unfastened to show a wisp of dark chest hair.

"Where's your jacket?" I asked lightly, trying to figure out his mood.

"The kids . . ." He hesitated. "The pixy children are using it as a fort."

"Oh." Hiding my smile, I rummaged in my spice rack to find my vial of celandine syrup. Jenks's capacity to be a pain in the butt was inversely proportional to his size. His ability to be a stanch friend was the same. Apparently Glenn had won Jenks's confidence. How about that?

Satisfied the show of his gun wasn't intended to cow me, I added a dollop of celandine, swishing the ceramic measuring spoon to get the last of the sticky stuff off. An uncomfortable silence grew, accented by the whoosh of igniting gas. I could feel his gaze heavy upon my charm bracelet as the tiny wooden amulets gently clattered. The crucifix was self-explanatory, but he'd have to ask if he wanted to know what the rest were for. I had only a paltry three—my old ones were burnt to uselessness when Trent killed the witness wearing them in a car explosion.

The mix on the stove started to steam, and Glenn still hadn't said a word. "So-o-o-o," I drawled. "Have you been in the FIB long?"

"Yes ma'am." It was short, both aloof and patronizing.

"Can you stop with the ma'am? Just call me Rachel."

"Yes ma'am."

Ooooh, I thought, *it was going to be a fun evening.* Peeved, I snatched up the mullein leaves. Tossing them into my green-stained mortar, I ground them using more force then necessary. I set the mush to soak in the cream for a moment. *Why was I bothering to make him an amulet? He wasn't going to use it.*

The brew was at a full boil, and I turned the flame down, setting the timer for three minutes. It was in the shape of a cow, and I loved it. Glenn was silent, watching me with a wary distrust as I leaned my back against the edge of the counter. "I'm making you something to stop the itching," I said. "God help me, but I feel sorry for you."

His face hardened. "Captain Edden is making me take you. I don't need your help."

Angry, I took a breath to tell him he could take a flying leap off a broomstick, but then shut my mouth. "I don't need your help" had once been my mantra. But friends made things a lot easier. My brow furrowed in thought. What was it that Jenks did to persuade me? Oh, yeah. Swear and tell me I was being stupid.

"You can go Turn yourself for all I care," I said pleasantly. "But Jenks pixed you, and he says you're sensitive to pixy dust. It's spreading through your lymph system. You want to itch for a week just because you're too stiff-necked to use a paltry itch spell? This is kindergarten stuff." I flicked the copper vat with a fingernail and it rang. "An aspirin. A dime a dozen." It wasn't, but Glenn probably wouldn't accept it if he knew how much one of these cost at a charm shop. It was a class-two medicinal spell. I probably should have put myself inside a circle to make it, but I'd have to tap into the ever-after to close one. And seeing me under the influence of a ley line would probably freak Glenn out.

The detective wouldn't meet my eyes. His foot twitched as if he was struggling to not scratch his leg through his pants. The timer dinged—or mooed, rather—and leaving him to make up his mind, I added the blossoms of jewelweed and dandelion, crushing them against the side of the pot with a clockwise—never withershins—motion. I was a white witch, after all.

Glenn gave up all pretense at trying not to scratch and slowly rubbed his arm through his shirtsleeve. "No one will know I've been spelled?"

"Not unless they did a spell check on you." I was mildly disappointed. He was afraid to openly show he was using magic. The prejudice wasn't unusual. But then, after having taken an aspirin once, I'd rather be in pain than swallow another. I guess I wasn't one to talk.

"All right." It was a very reluctant admission.

"Okey-dokey." I added the grated goldenseal root and turned it to a high boil. When the froth took on a yellow tint that smelled like camphor, I turned off the heat. Nearly done.

This spell made the usual seven portions, and I wondered if he'd demand I waste one on myself before trusting I wasn't going to turn him into a toad. That was an idea. I could put him in the garden to police the slugs from the hostas. Edden wouldn't miss him for at least a week.

Glenn's eyes were on me as I pulled out seven clean redwood disks about the size of a wooden nickle and arranged them on the counter where he could see. "Just about done," I said with a forced cheerfulness.

"That's it?" he questioned, his brown eyes wide.

"That's it."

"No lighting candles, or making circles, or saying magic words?"

I shook my head. "You're thinking of ley line magic. And it's Latin, not magic words. Ley line witches draw their power right from the line and need the trappings of cere-mony to control it. I'm an earth witch." *Thank God.* "My magic is from ley lines, too, but it's naturally filtered through plants. If I was a black witch, much of it would come through animals."

Feeling as if I was back doing my graduate lab-work exam, I dug in the silverware drawer for a finger stick. The sharp prick of the blade on my fingertip was hardly notice-able, and I massaged the required three drops into the po-tion. The scent of redwood rose thick and musty, overpowering the camphor smell. I had done it right. I had known I had.

"You put blood in it!" he said, and my head came up at his disgusted tone.

"Well, duh. How else was I supposed to quicken it? Put it

in the oven and bake it?" My brow furrowed, and I tucked a strand of my hair that had escaped my bow back behind my ear. "All magic requires a price paid by death, Detective. White earth magic pays for it by my blood and killing plants. If I wanted to make a black charm to knock you out, or turn your blood to tar, or even give you the hiccups, I'd have to use some nasty ingredients involving animal parts. The really black magic requires not just my blood but animal sacrifice." *Or human or Inderlander.*

My voice was harsher than I had intended, and I kept my eyes down as I measured out the doses and let them soak into the redwood disks. Much of my stunted career at the I.S. involved bringing in gray spell crafters—witches that took a white charm such as a sleep spell and turned it to a bad use—but I'd brought in black charm makers as well. Most had been ley line witches, since just the ingredients needed to stir a black charm were enough to keep most earth witches white. Eye of newt and toe of frog? Hardly. Try blood drawn from the spleen of a still-living animal and its tongue removed as it screamed its last breath into the ether. Nasty.

"I won't make a black charm," I said when Glenn remained silent. "Not only is it demented and gross, but black magic always comes back to get you." *And when I had my way, it involved my foot in his gut or my cuffs on his wrists.*

Choosing an amulet, I massaged three more drops of my blood onto it to invoke the spell. It soaked in quickly, as if the spell pulled the blood from my finger. I extended the charm to him, thinking of the time I had been tempted to stir a black spell. I survived, but came away with my demon mark. And all I'd done was look at the book. Black magic always swings back. Always.

"It's got your blood in it," he said in revulsion. "Make another, and I'll put mine in it."

"Yours? Yours won't do squat. It has to be witch blood.

Yours doesn't have the right enzymes to quicken a spell." I held it out again, and he shook his head. Frustrated, I gritted my teeth. "Your dad used one, you whiny little human. Take it so we can all move on with our lives!" I thrust the amulet belligerently at him, and he gingerly took it.

"Better?" I said as his fingers encircled the wooden disk.

"Um, yeah," he said, his square-jawed face suddenly slack. "It is."

"Of course it is," I muttered. Slightly mollified, I hung the rest of my amulets in my charm cupboard. Glenn silently took in my stash, each hook carefully labeled thanks to Ivy's anal-retentive need to organize. Whatever. It made her happy and was no skin off my nose. I closed the door with a loud thump and turned.

"Thank you, Ms. Morgan," he said, surprising me.

"You're welcome," I said, glad he had finally dropped the ma'am. "Don't get any salt on it, and it should last for a year. You can take it off and store it if you want when the blisters go away. It works on poison ivy, too." I started to clean up my mess. "I'm sorry for letting Jenks pix you like that," I said slowly. "He wouldn't have if he had known you were sensitive to pixy dust. Usually the blisters don't spread."

"Don't worry about it." He stretched for one of Ivy's catalogs at the end of the table, pulling his hand back at the picture of the curved stainless-steel knives on special.

I slid my spelling book away under the center island counter, glad he was loosening up. "When it comes to Inderlanders, sometimes the smallest things can pack the hardest punch."

There was a loud boom of the front door closing. Stiffening, I crossed my arms before me, only now recognizing that it had been Ivy's motorcycle tooling up the road a moment before. Glenn met my eyes, sitting straighter as he recognized my alarm. Ivy was home.

"But not always," I finished.

Five

Eyes on the empty hallway, I motioned for Glenn to stay seated. I didn't have time to explain. I wondered how much Edden had told him, or if this was going to be one of his nasty but effective ways to smooth Glenn's edges.

"Rachel?" came Ivy's melodious voice, and Glenn stood, checking the creases in his gray slacks. *Yeah, that would help.* "Did you know there's an FIB car parked in front of Keasley's?"

"Sit down, Glenn," I warned, and when he didn't, I moved to stand between him and the open archway to the hall.

"Yuck!" Ivy exclaimed, her voice muffled. "There's a fish in my bathtub. Is it the Howlers'? When are they coming to get it?" There was a hesitation, and I managed a sick smile at Glenn. "Rachel?" she called out, closer. "Are you in here? Hey, we should go out to the mall tonight. Bath and Body-works is re-releasing an old scent with a citrus base. We need to hit the sample bottles. See how it works. You know, celebrate you making rent. What is that you have on now? The cinnamon? That's a nice one, but it only lasts three hours."

Would have been nice to have known that earlier. "I'm in the kitchen," I said loudly.

Ivy's tall, black-clad form strode past the opening. A canvas sack of groceries hung from her shoulder. Her black silk duster fluttered after her boot heels, and I could hear her looking for something in the living room. "I didn't think you would be able to pull the fish thing off," she said. There was a hesitation, then, "Where in hell is the phone?"

"In here," I said, crossing my arms uneasily.

Ivy pulled up short in the archway as she saw Glenn. Her somewhat Oriental features went blank in surprise. I could almost see the wall come down as she realized we weren't alone. The skin around her eyes tightened. Her small nose flared, taking in his scent, cataloging his fear and my concern in an instant. Lips tight, she put her canvas bag of groceries on the counter and brushed her hair out of her eyes. It fell to her mid-back in a smooth black wave, and I knew it was bother, not nerves, that had prompted her to tuck it behind an ear.

Ivy had once had money, and still dressed like it, but her entire early inheritance had gone to the I.S. to pay off her contract when she quit with me. Put simply, she looked like a scary model: lithe and pale, but incredibly strong. Unlike me, she wore no nail polish, no jewelry apart from her crucifix twin black chain anklets about one foot, and very little makeup; she didn't need it. But like me, she was basically broke, at least until her mother finished dying and the rest of the Tamwood estate came to her. I was guessing that wouldn't be for about two hundred years—bare minimum.

Ivy's thin eyebrows rose as she looked Glenn over. "Bringing your work home again, Rachel?"

I took a breath. "Hi, Ivy. This is Detective Glenn. You talked to him this afternoon? Sent him to *pick me up?*" My look went pointed. We were going to talk about that later.

Ivy turned her back on him to unpack the groceries. "Nice to meet you," she said, her tone flat. Then to me, she muttered, "Sorry. Something came up."

Glenn swallowed hard. He looked shaky but was holding

up. I guess Edden hadn't told him about Ivy. I really liked Edden. "You're a vampire," he said.

"Ooooh," Ivy said. "We've got a bright one here."

Fingers fumbling around the string of his new amulet, he pulled a cross from behind his shirt. "But the sun is up," he said, sounding as if he had been betrayed.

"My my my," Ivy said. "And a weatherman, too?" She turned with a snide look. "I'm not dead yet, Detective Glenn. Only the true undead have light restrictions. Come back in sixty years and I might be worried about a sunburn." Seeing his cross, she smiled patronizingly and pulled out from behind her black spandex shirt her own, extravagant crucifix. "That only works on undead vamps," she said as she turned back to the counter. "Where did you get your schooling? B-movies?"

Glenn backed up a step. "Captain Edden never said you worked with a vampire," the FIB officer stammered.

At Edden's name, Ivy spun. It was a blindingly fast motion, and I started. This wasn't going well. She was starting to pull an aura. *Damn.* I glanced out the window. The sun would be down soon. *Double damn.*

"I heard about you," the officer said, and I cringed at the arrogance in his voice, which he was using to cover his fear. Even Glenn couldn't be stupid enough to antagonize a vamp in her own house. That gun at his side wasn't going to do him any good. Sure, he could shoot her, and kill her, but then she'd be dead and she'd rip his freaking head off. And no jury in the world would convict her of murder, seeing as he killed her first.

"You're Tamwood," Glenn said, his bravado clearly scraped from a misplaced feeling of security. "Captain Edden gave you three hundred hours of community service for taking out everyone on his floor, didn't he? What was it he made you do? A candy striper, right?"

Ivy stiffened, and my mouth dropped open. He was that stupid.

"It was worth it," Ivy said softly. Her fingers were shaking as she set the bag of marshmallows gently on the counter.

My breath caught. *Shit.* Ivy's brown eyes had gone black as her pupils dilated. I stood, shocked at how quickly it had happened. It had been weeks since she vamped out on me, and never without warning. The angry shock of finding someone in an FIB uniform in her kitchen might have accounted for some of it, but in hindsight I had a sick feeling that letting her walk in on Glenn hadn't been the best thing. His fear had hit her hard and fast, giving her no time to prepare herself against temptation.

His sudden fright had filled the air with pheromones. They acted as a potent aphrodisiac only she could taste, jerking into play thousand-year-old instincts fixed deep in her virus-changed DNA. In a breath, they had turned her from my slightly disturbing roommate to a predator that could kill both of us in three seconds flat if the desire to sate her long-suppressed hunger outweighed the consequences of draining an FIB detective. It was that balance that frightened me. I knew where I was on her personal scale of hunger and reason. Where Glenn stood, I hadn't a clue.

Like flowing dust, her posture melted and she leaned back against the counter on one bent elbow, hip cocked. Deathly still, she ran her gaze up Glenn until it locked upon his eyes. Her head tilted with a sultry slowness until she was eyeing him from under her straight bangs. Only now did she take a slow, deliberate breath. Her long pale fingers flicked about the deep V-neck of her spandex shirt tucked into her leather pants.

"You're tall," she said, her gray voice pulling remembered fear from me. "I like that." It wasn't sex she was after, it was dominance. She would have bespelled him if she could have, but she'd have to wait until she was dead before she had power over the unwilling.

Swell, I thought as she pushed herself from the counter and headed for him. She'd lost it. It was worse than the time she found Nick and I snuggled up together on her couch not watching pro wrestling. I still didn't know what had set her off then—she and I had a concrete understanding that I wasn't her girlfriend, plaything, lover, shadow, or whatever the newest term for vampire flunky was these days.

My thoughts scrambled for a way to bring her back without making things worse. Ivy drifted to a stop before Glenn, the hem of her duster seeming to move in slow motion as it edged forward to touch his shoes. Her tongue slipped across her very white teeth, hiding them even as they flashed. With a recognizable restrained power, she put a hand to either side of him at head height, pinning him to the wall. "Mmmm," she said, breathing in through parted lips. "Very tall. Lots of leg. Beautiful, beautiful dark skin. Did Rachel bring you home for me?"

She leaned into him, almost touching. He was only a few inches taller than she was. She tilted her head as if to give him a kiss. A drop of sweat slid down his face and neck. He didn't move, tension pulling every muscle tight.

"You work for Edden," she whispered, her eyes fixed on the line of moisture as it pooled at his collarbone. "He'd probably be upset if you died." Her eyes darted to his at the sound of his quick breath.

Don't move, I thought, knowing if he did, instincts would take over. He was in trouble with his back to the wall like that. "Ivy?" I said, trying to distract her and avoid having to tell Edden why his son was in intensive care. "Edden gave me a run. Glenn is along for the ride."

I willed myself not to shudder as she turned the black pits her eyes had become to me. They tracked me as I put the island counter between us. She stood unmoving but for a hand tracing Glenn's shoulder and neck, her finger running a perfect half inch above him. "Uh, Ivy?" I said hesitantly. "Glenn might want to leave now. Let him go."

My request seemed to break through, and she took a quick, clean breath. Bending her elbow, she pushed herself away from the wall.

Glenn darted out from under her. Weapon drawn, he stood in the archway to the hall, his feet spread and his gun trained upon Ivy. The safety clicked off, and his eyes were wide.

Ivy turned her back on him and went to the bag of forgotten groceries. It might look as if she was ignoring him, but I knew she was aware of everything down to the wasp bumping about at the ceiling. Back hunched, she set a bag of shredded cheese on the counter. "Tell that bloodsack of a captain I said hi the next time you see him," she said, her soft voice carrying a shocking amount of anger. But the hunger—the need to dominate—was gone.

Knees weak, I let my breath out in a long puff of air. "Glenn?" I suggested. "Put the gun away before she takes it from you. And the next time you insult my roommate, I'm going to let her tear your throat out. Understand?"

His eyes flicked to Ivy before he holstered the weapon. He stayed in the archway, breathing hard.

Thinking the worst had to be over, I opened the fridge. "Hey, Ivy," I said lightly, to try and get everyone back to normal, "toss me the pepperoni?"

Ivy met my gaze from across the kitchen and blinked the last of her runaway instincts from her. "Pepperoni," she said, her voice huskier than usual. "Yeah." She felt a cheek with the back of her hand. Frowning at herself, she crossed the kitchen with what I recognized as a deliberately slow pace. "Thanks for bringing me down," she said softly as she handed me the pouch of cut meat.

"I should have warned you. I'm sorry." I put the pepperoni away and straightened, giving Glenn a black look. His face was grayed and drawn as he wiped the perspiration away. I think he just figured out we were in the same room with a predator held back by pride and courtesy. Maybe he learned something today. Edden would be pleased.

I shuffled through the groceries and pulled out the perishables. Ivy leaned close as she put a can of peaches away. "What's he doing here?" she asked, loud enough for Glenn to hear.

"I'm baby-sitting."

She nodded, clearly waiting for more. When it wasn't forthcoming, she added, "It's a paying job, right?"

I glanced at Glenn. "Uh, yeah. A missing person." I snuck a glance at her, relieved to see her pupils were almost back to normal.

"Can I help?" she asked.

Ivy had done almost nothing but run for missing persons since she quit the I.S., but I knew she would side with Jenks that it was a ploy of Trent Kalamack's once she learned it was Sara Jane's boyfriend. Putting off telling her would only make it worse, though. And I wanted her to come out to Piscary's with me. I'd get more information that way.

Glenn stood with an affected casualness as Ivy and I put the groceries away, not seeming to care that we were ignoring him. "Oh, come on, Rachel," the vamp cajoled. "Who is it? I'll put my feelers out." She looked as far from a predator now as a duck. I was used to the shifts in temperament, but Glenn looked bewildered.

"Uh, a witch named Dan." I tuned away, hiding my head in the fridge as I put the cottage cheese away. "He's Sara Jane's boyfriend, and before you get all huffy, Glenn is coming with me to look at his apartment. I figure we can wait until tomorrow to check out Piscary's; he works there as a driver. But no way is Glenn coming with me to the university." There was a heartbeat of silence, and I cringed, waiting for her shout of protest. It never came.

I looked past the door of the fridge, going slack in surprise. Ivy had put herself at the sink and was hunched over it, a hand to either side. It was her "count to ten" spot. It had never failed her yet. She pulled her eyes up and put them on me. My mouth went dry. It had failed.

"You are not taking this run," she said, the smooth monotone of her voice pulling the chill of black ice through me.

Panic flashed before settling into a churning burn in the pit of my stomach. All that existed was her pupil-black eyes. She inhaled, taking my warmth. Her presence seemed to swirl behind me until I fought to keep from turning around. My shoulders tensed and my breath came fast. She had pulled a full-blown, soul-stealing aura. Something was different, though. This wasn't anger or hunger I was seeing. This was fear. *Ivy was afraid?*

"I'm taking the run," I said, hearing a thin thread of fear in my voice. "Trent can't touch me, and I already told Edden I would."

"No you aren't."

Silk duster furling, she jerked into motion. I started, finding her right before me almost as soon as I noticed she had moved. Face whiter than usual, she pushed the fridge door shut. I jumped to get out of the way. I met her eyes, knowing if I showed the fright that was making my stomach knot, she would feed on it, making her fervor stronger. I'd learned a lot in the last three months, some of it the hard way, some of it I wished I hadn't needed to know.

"The last time you took on Trent, you almost died," she said, sweat trickling down her neck to disappear behind the deep V of her shirt. *She was sweating?*

"The key word there is 'almost,'" I said boldly.

"No. The key word is 'died.'"

I could feel the heat coming from her and stepped back. Glenn was in the archway, watching me with wide eyes as I argued with a vamp. There was a knack to it. "Ivy," I said calmly, though I was shaking inside. "I'm taking this run. If you want to come with Glenn and me when we talk to Piscary—"

My breath cut off. Ivy's fingers were around my throat. Gasping, my air exploded from me as she slammed me up against the kitchen wall. "Ivy!" I managed before she picked me up with one hand and pinned me there.

Air coming in short, insufficient pants, I hung off the floor.

Ivy put her face next to mine. Her eyes were black, but they were wide with fear. "You aren't going to talk to Piscary," she said, panic a silver ribbon through the gray silk of her voice. "You aren't taking this run."

I braced my feet against the wall and pushed. A breath of air made it past her fingers, and my back smacked back into the wall. I kicked out at her, and she shifted to the side. Her hold on me never altered. "What the hell are you doing?" I rasped. "Let me go!"

"Ms. Tamwood!" Glenn shouted. "Drop the woman and step to the center of the room!"

Digging my fingers into her one-handed grip, I looked past Ivy. Glenn was behind her, his feet braced, ready to shoot. "No!" my voice grated. "Get out. Get out of here!"

Ivy wouldn't listen to me if he was here. She was afraid. What the hell was she afraid of? Trent couldn't touch me.

There was a sharp whistle of surprise as Jenks darted in. "Howdy, campers," he said sarcastically. "I see Rachel told you about her run, huh, Ivy?"

"Get out!" I demanded, my head pounding as Ivy's grip tightened.

"Holy crap!" the pixy exclaimed from the ceiling, his wings flashing into a frightened red. "She's not kidding."

"I know . . ." Lungs hurting, I pried at the fingers around my neck, managing a ragged breath. Ivy's pale face was drawn. The black of her eyes was total and absolute. And laced with fear. Seeing the emotion on her was terrifying.

"Ivy, let her go!" Jenks demanded as he hovered at eye level. "It's not that bad, really. We'll just go with her."

"Get out!" I said, taking a clean breath as Ivy's eyes went confused and her grip faltered. Panic took me as her fingers shook. Sweat trickled down her forehead, pinched in confusion. The whites of her eyes showed strong against the black.

Jenks darted to Glenn. "You heard her," the pixy said. "Get out."

My heart raced as Glenn hissed, "Are you crazy? We leave, and that bitch will kill her!"

Ivy's breath came in a whimper. It was as soft as the first snowflake, but I heard it. The smell of cinnamon filled my senses.

"We gotta get out of here," Jenks said. "Either Rachel will get Ivy to let go, or Ivy will kill her. You might be able to separate them by shooting Ivy, but Ivy will track her down and kill her the first chance she gets if she overthrows Rachel's dominance."

"Rachel is dominant?"

I could hear the disbelief in Glenn's voice, and I frantically prayed they'd get out before Ivy finished throttling me.

The buzz of Jenks's wings was as loud as my blood humming in my ears. "How else do you think Rachel got Ivy to back off of you? You think a witch could do that if she wasn't in charge? Get out like she said."

I didn't know if dominant was the right word. But if they didn't leave, the point would be moot. The honest to God's truth was, in some twisted fashion Ivy needed me more than I needed her. But the "dating guide" Ivy had given me last spring so I would stop pressing her vamp-instinct buttons hadn't had a chapter on "What to Do If You Find Yourself the Dominant." I was in uncharted territory.

"Get—out," I choked as the edges of my sight shifted to black.

I heard the safety click back on. Glenn reluctantly holstered his weapon. As Jenks flitted from him to the rear door and back again, the FIB officer retreated, looking angry and frustrated. I stared at the ceiling and watched the stars edging my sight as the screen door squeaked shut.

"Ivy," I rasped, meeting her eyes. I stiffened at their black terror. I could see myself in their depths, my hair wild and my face swollen. My neck suddenly throbbed under her fingers where they pressed against my old demon bite. God help me, but it was starting to feel good, the remembrance of the euphoria that had surged through me last spring as the demon sent to kill me had ripped my neck open and filled it with vamp saliva.

"Ivy, open your fingers a little so I can breathe," I managed, spittle dripping down my chin. The heat from her hand made the smell of cinnamon stronger.

"You told me to let him go," she snarled, baring her teeth as her grip tightened until my eyes bulged. "I wanted him, and you made me let him go!"

My lungs tried to work, moving in short splurges as I struggled for air. Her hold slackened. I took a grateful gulp of air. Then another. Her face was grim, waiting. Dying with a vampire was easy. Living with one took more finesse.

My jaw ached where it rested upon her fingers. "If you want him," I whispered, "go get him. But don't break your fast in anger." I took another breath, praying it wouldn't be my last. "Unless it's for passion, it won't be worth it, Ivy."

She gasped as if I had hit her. Face thunderstruck, her grip loosened without warning. I fell into a heap against the wall.

Hunching into myself, I gagged on the air. I felt my throat, my stomach knotting as the demon bite on my neck continued to tingle in bliss. My legs were askew, and I slowly straightened them. Sitting with my knees to my chest, I shook my charm bracelet back to my wrist, wiped the spit from me, and looked up.

I was surprised to find Ivy still there. Usually when she broke down like this, she went running to Piscary. But then, she had never broken down quite like this before. She had been afraid. She had pinned me to the wall because she had been afraid. Afraid of what? Of me telling her she couldn't tear out Glenn's throat? Friend or not, I'd leave if I saw her take someone in my kitchen. The blood would give me nightmares forever.

"Are you okay?" I rasped, hunching into myself when it triggered a spate of coughing.

She didn't move, sitting at the table with her back to me. She had her head in her hands.

I had figured out shortly after we had moved in together that Ivy didn't like who she was. Hated the violence even as she instigated it. Struggled to abstain from blood even as she craved it. But she was a vampire. She didn't have a choice. The virus had fixed itself deep into her DNA and was there to stay. You are what you are. That she had lost control and let her instincts have sway meant failure to her.

"Ivy?" I got to my feet, listing slightly as I stumbled to her. I could still feel the impressions of her fingers around my neck. It had been bad, but nothing like the time she had pinned me to a chair in a cloud of lust and hunger. I pushed my black bow back where it belonged. "You all right?" I reached out, then drew back before touching her.

"No," she said as my hand dropped. Her voice was muffled. "Rachel, I'm sorry. I—I can't . . ." She hesitated, taking a ragged breath. "Don't take this run. If it's the money—"

"It's not the money," I said before she could finish. She turned to me, and my anger that she might try to buy me off died. A shiny ribbon of moisture showed where she had tried to wipe it away. I'd never seen her cry before, and I eased myself down in the chair beside her. "I have to help Sara Jane."

She looked away. "Then I'm going out to Piscary's with you," she said, her voice holding a thin memory of its usual strength.

I clutched my arms about myself, one hand rubbing the faint scar on my neck until I realized I was unconsciously doing it to feel it tingle. "I was hoping you would," I said as I forced my hand down.

She gave me a frightened, worried smile and turned away.

Six

Pixy children swarmed around Glenn as he sat at the kitchen table as far from Ivy as he could without looking obvious about it. Jenks's kids seemed to have taken an unusual liking to the FIB detective, and Ivy, sitting before her computer, was trying to ignore the noise and darting shapes. She gave me the impression of a cat sleeping before a bird feeder, seemingly ignoring everything but very aware if a bird should make a mistake and get too close. Everyone was overlooking that we had nearly had an incident, and my feelings for being saddled with Glenn had waned from dislike to a mild annoyance at his new, and unexpected, tact.

Using a diabetic syringe, I injected a sleepy-time potion into the last of the thin-walled, blue paint balls. It was after seven. I didn't like leaving the kitchen a mess, but I had to make these little gems up special, and there was no way I would go out to meet Sara Jane at a strange apartment unarmed. *No need to make it that easy for Trent,* I thought as I took off my protective gloves and tossed them aside.

From the nested bowls under the counter I pulled out my gun. I had originally kept it in a vat hanging over the island counter, until Ivy pointed out I'd have to put myself in plain sight to reach it. Keeping it at crawling height was better. Glenn perked up at the sound of iron hitting the counter, waving the chattering, green-clad adolescent pixy girls off his hand.

"You shouldn't keep a weapon out like that," he said scornfully. "Do you have any idea how many children are killed a year because of stupid stunts like that?"

"Relax, Mr. FIB Officer," I said as I wiped the reservoir out. "No one has died from a paint ball yet."

"Paint ball?" he questioned. Then he turned condescending. "Playing dress-up, are we?"

My brow furrowed. I liked my mini splat gun. It felt nice in my hand, heavy and reassuring despite its palm size. Even with its cherry red color, people generally didn't recognize it for what it was and assumed I was packing. Best of all, I didn't need a license for it.

Peeved, I shook a pinky-nail-sized red ball out from the box resting on the shelf above my charms. I dropped it in the chamber. "Ivy," I said, and she looked up from her monitor, no expression on her perfect, oval face. "Tag."

She went back to her screen, her head shifting slightly. The pixy children squealed and scattered, flowing out of the window and into the dark garden to leave shimmering trails of pixy dust and the memory of their voices. Slowly the sound of crickets came in to replace them.

Ivy wasn't the type of roommate who liked to play Parcheesi, and the one time I sat with her on the couch and watched *Rush Hour*, I had unwittingly triggered her vamp instincts and nearly got bitten during the last fight scene as my body temp rose and the smell of our scents mingling hit her hard. So now, with the exception of our carefully orchestrated sparing sessions, we generally did things with lots of space between us. Her dodging my splat balls gave her a good workout and improved my aim.

It was even better at midnight in the graveyard.

Glenn ran a hand over his close-cut beard, waiting. It was clear something was going to happen, he just didn't know what. Ignoring him, I set the splat gun on the counter and started to clean up the mess I'd made in the sink. My pulse increased and tension made my fingers ache. Ivy continued to shop on the net, the clicks of her mouse sounding loud. She reached for a pencil as something got her attention.

Snatching the gun, I spun and pulled the trigger. The puff of sound sent a thrill through me. Ivy leaned to the right. Her free hand came up to intercept the ball of water. It hit her hand with a sharp splat, breaking to soak her palm. She never looked up from her monitor as she shook the water from her hand and read the caption under the casket pillows. Christmas was three months away, and I knew she was stumped as to what to get her mother.

Glenn had stood at the sound of the gun, his hand atop his holster. His face slack, he alternated his gaze between Ivy and me. I tossed him the splat gun, and he caught it. Anything to get his hand away from his pistol. "If that had been a sleepy-time potion," I said smugly, "she'd be out cold."

I handed Ivy the roll of paper towels we kept on the island counter for just this reason, and she nonchalantly wiped her hand off and continued to shop.

Head bowed, Glenn eyed the paint-ball gun. I knew he was feeling the weight of it, realizing it wasn't a toy. He walked to me and handed it back. "They ought to make you license these things," he said as it filled my grip.

"Yeah," I agreed lightly. "They should."

I felt him watching as I loaded it with my seven potions. Not many witches used potions, not because they were outrageously expensive and lasted only about a week uninvoked, but because you needed to get a good soaking in saltwater to break them. It was messy and took a heck of a lot of salt. Satisfied that I'd made my point, I tucked the loaded splat gun into the small of my back and put on my leather jacket to cover it. I kicked off my pink slippers and padded into the living room for my vamp-made boots by the back door. "Ready to go?" I asked as I leaned against the wall in the hallway and put them on. "You're driving."

Glenn's tall shape appeared in the archway, dark fingers expertly tying his tie. "You're going like that?"

Brow furrowing, I looked down at my red blouse, black skirt, nylons, and ankle-high boots. "Something wrong with what I've got on?"

Ivy made a rude snort from her computer. Glenn glanced at her, then me. "Never mind," he said flatly. He snuggled his tie tight to make him look polished and professional. "Let's go."

"No," I said, getting in his face. "I want to know what you think I should put on. One of those polyester sacks you make your female FIB officers wear? There's a reason Rose is so uptight, and it has nothing to do with her having no walls or her chair having a broken caster!"

Face hard, Glenn sidestepped me and headed up the hallway. Grabbing my bag, I acknowledged Ivy's preoccupied wave good-bye and strode after him. He took up almost the entire width of the hall as he walked and put his arms into his suit's jacket at the same time. The sound of the lining rubbing against his shirt was a soft hush over the noise of his hard-soled shoes on the floorboards.

I kept to my cold silence as Glenn drove us out of the Hollows and back across the bridge. It would have been nice had Jenks come with us, but Sara Jane said something about a cat, and he prudently decided to stay home.

The sun was long down and traffic had thickened. The lights from Cincinnati looked nice from the bridge, and I felt a flash of amusement as I realized Glenn was driving at the head of a pack of cars too wary to pass him. Even the FIB's unmarked vehicles were obvious. Slowly my mood eased. I cracked the window to dilute the smell of cinnamon, and Glenn flipped the heater on. The perfume didn't smell as nice anymore, now that it had failed me.

Dan's apartment was a town house: tidy, clean, and gated.

Not too far from the university. Good access to the freeway. It looked expensive, but if he was taking classes at the university, he could probably swing it just fine. Glenn pulled into the reserved spot with Dan's house number on it and cut the engine. The porch light was off and the drapes were pulled. A cat was sitting on the second-story balcony railing, its eyes glowing as it watched us.

Saying nothing, Glenn reached under the seat and moved it back. Closing his eyes, he settled in as if to nap. The silence grew, and I listened to the car's engine tick as it cooled off in the dark. I reached for the radio knob, and Glenn muttered, "Don't touch that."

Peeved, I sank back. "Don't you want to question some of his neighbors?" I asked.

"I'll do it tomorrow when the sun is up and you're at class."

My eyebrows rose. According to the receipt Edden had given me, class ran from four to six. It was an excellent time to be knocking on doors, when humans would be coming home, diurnal Inderlanders well up, and nightwalkers stirring. And the area felt like a mixed neighborhood.

A couple came out of a nearby apartment, arguing as they got into a shiny car and drove away. She was late for work. It was his fault, if I was following the conversation properly.

Bored, and a little nervous, I dug in my bag until I found a finger stick and one of my detection amulets. I loved these things—the detection amulet, not the finger stick—and after pricking my finger for three drops of blood to invoke it, I found that there was no one but Glenn and me within a thirty-foot radius. I draped it about my neck like my old I.S. badge as a little red car pulled into the lot. The cat on the railing stretched before dropping out of sight onto the balcony.

It was Sara Jane, and she whipped her car into the spot directly behind us. Glenn took notice, saying nothing as we got out and angled our paths to meet her.

"Hi," she said, her heart-shaped face showing her worry in the light from the street lamp. "I hope you weren't waiting long," she added, her voice carrying the professional air of the office.

"Not at all, ma'am," Glenn said.

I tugged my leather coat closer against the cold as she jingled her keys, fumbling for one that still carried a shiny, new-cut veneer and opened the door. My pulse increased, and I glanced at my amulet with thoughts of Trent going through me. I had my splat gun, but I wasn't a brave person. I ran away from big-bad-uglies. It increased my life span dramatically.

Glenn followed Sara Jane in as she flipped on the lights, illuminating the porch and apartment both. Nervous, I crossed the threshold, wavering between closing the door to keep anyone from following me in and leaving it open to keep my escape route available. I opted to leave it cracked.

"You got a problem?" Glenn whispered as Sara Jane made her confident way to the kitchen, and I shook my head. The town house had an open floor plan with almost the entire downstairs visible from the doorway. Stairs ran a straight, unimaginative pathway to the second floor. Knowing my amulet would warn me if anyone new showed up, I relaxed. There was no one here but us three and the cat yowling on the second-floor balcony.

"I'll go up and let Sarcophagus in," Sara Jane said as she headed for the stairs.

My eyebrows rose. "That's the cat, right?"

"I'll come with you, ma'am," Glenn offered, and he thumped upstairs after her.

I did a quick reconnaissance of the downstairs while they were gone, knowing we'd find nothing. Trent was too good to leave anything behind; I just wanted to see what kind of a guy Sara Jane liked. The kitchen sink was dry, the garbage can was stinky, the computer monitor was dusty, and the cat box was full. Clearly Dan hadn't been home in a while.

The floorboards above me creaked as Glenn walked through the upstairs. Perched on the TV was the same picture of Dan and Sara Jane aboard the steamer. I picked it up and studied their faces, setting the framed photo back on the TV as Glenn clumped downstairs. The man's shoulders took up almost the entirety of the narrow stairway. Sara Jane was silent behind him, looking small and walking sideways in her heels.

"Upstairs looks fine," Glenn said as he rifled through the stack of mail on the kitchen counter. Sara Jane opened the pantry. Like everything else, it was well-organized. After a moment of hesitation, she pulled out a pouch of moist cat food.

"Mind if I check his e-mails?" I asked, and Sara Jane nodded, her eyes sad. I jiggled the mouse to find that Dan had a dedicated, always-on line just like Ivy. Strictly speaking, I shouldn't have been doing this, but as long as no one said anything . . . From the corner of my eye I watched Glenn run his eyes over Sara Jane's smartly cut business dress as she tore the bag of cat food open, and then down my outfit as I bent over the keyboard. I could tell by his look that he thought my clothes were unprofessional, and I fought back a grimace.

Dan had a slew of unopened messages, two from Sara Jane and one with a university address. The rest were from a hard-rock chat room of some sort. Even I knew better than to open any of them, tampering with evidence should he turn up dead.

Glenn ran a hand across his short hair, seemingly disappointed that he had found nothing unusual. I was guessing it wasn't because Dan was missing but that he was a witch, and as such should have dead monkey heads hanging from the ceiling. Dan appeared to be an average, on his own young man. He was perhaps tidier than most, but Sara Jane wouldn't date a slob.

Sara Jane set a bowl of food on the placement next to a water bowl. A black cat slunk downstairs at the clink of porcelain. It hissed at Sara Jane, not coming to eat until she left the kitchen. "Sarcophagus doesn't like me," she said needlessly. "He's a one-person familiar."

A good familiar was like that. The best chose their owners, not the other way around. The cat finished the food in a surprisingly short amount of time, then jumped onto the back of the couch. I scratched the upholstery and he came close to investigate. He stretched out his neck and touched my finger with his nose. It was how cats greeted each other, and I smiled. I'd love to have a cat, but Jenks would pix me every night for a year if I brought one home.

Remembering my stint as a mink, I shuffled through my purse. Trying to be discreet, I invoked an amulet to do a spell check on the cat. Nothing. Not satisfied, I dug deeper for a pair of wire-rimmed glasses. Ignoring Glenn's questioning look, I popped open the hard case and carefully put the so-ugly-they-could-work-as-birth-control glasses on. I had bought them last month, spending three times my rent with the excuse that they were tax deductible. The ones that didn't make me look like a nerd reject would've cost me twice that.

Ley line magic could be bound in silver just as earth magic could be kept in wood, and the wire frames were spelled to let me see through disguises invoked by ley line magic. I felt kind of cheesy using them, thinking that it dumped me back into the realm of warlocks in that I was using a charm that I couldn't make. But as I scratched Sarcophagus's chin, sure now by the lack of any change that he wasn't Dan trapped in a cat's form, I decided I didn't care.

Glenn turned to the phone. "Would you mind if I listened to his messages?" he asked.

Sara Jane's laugh was bitter. "Go ahead. They're from me."

The snap of the hard case was loud as I put my glasses away. Glenn punched the button, and I winced as Sara Jane's recorded voice came into the silent apartment. "Hey, Dan. I waited an hour. It was Carew Tower, right?" There was a hesitation, then a distant, "Well, give me a call. And you'd better get some chocolate." Her voice turned playful. "You've got some serious groveling to do, farm boy."

The second was even more uncomfortable. "Hi, Dan. If you're there, pick up." Again a pause. "Um, I was just kidding about the chocolate. I'll see you tomorrow. Love you. 'Bye."

Sara Jane stood in the living room, her face frozen. "He wasn't here when I came over, and I haven't seen him since," she said softly.

"Well," Glenn said as the machine clicked off, "we haven't found his car yet, and his toothbrush and razor are still here. Wherever he is, he hadn't planned on staying. It looks like something has happened."

She bit her lip and turned away. Amazed at his lack of tact, I gave Glenn a murderous look. "You have the sensitivity of a dog in heat, you know that?" I whispered.

Glenn glanced at Sara Jane's hunched shoulders. "Sorry, ma'am."

She turned, a miserable smile on her. "Maybe I should take Sarcophagus home. . . ."

"No," I quickly assured her. "Not yet." I touched her shoulder in sympathy, and the smell of her lilac perfume pulled from me the chalky taste-memory of drugged carrots. I glanced at Glenn, knowing he wouldn't leave so I could talk to her alone. "Sara Jane," I asked hesitantly. "I have to ask you this, and I apologize. Do you know if anyone has threatened Dan?"

"No," she said, her hand rising to her collar and her face going still. "No one."

"How about you?" I asked. "Have you been threatened any way? Any way at all?"

"No. No of course not," she said quickly, her eyes dropping and her pale features going even whiter. I didn't need an amulet to know she was lying, and the silence grew uncomfortable as I gave her a moment to change her mind and tell me. But she didn't.

"A-Are we done?" she stammered, and nodding, I adjusted my bag on my shoulder. Sara Jane headed to the door, her steps quick and stilted. Glenn and I followed her out onto the cement landing. It was too cold for bugs, but a broken spiderweb stretched by the porch light.

"Thank you for letting us look at his apartment," I said as she checked the door with trembling fingers. "I'll be talking with his classmates tomorrow. Perhaps one of them will know something. Whatever it is, I can help," I said, trying to put more meaning into my voice.

"Yes. Thank you." Her eyes went everywhere but to mine, and she had fallen into her professional office tone again. "I appreciate you coming over. I wish I could be more help."

"Ma'am," Glenn said in parting. Sara Jane's heels clicked smartly on the pavement as she walked away. I followed Glenn to his car, glancing back to see Sarcophagus sitting in an upstairs window watching us.

Sara Jane's car gave a happy chirp before she set her purse inside, got in, and drove away. I stood in the dark beside my open door and watched her taillights vanish around a corner. Glenn was facing me, standing at the driver side with his arms resting on the roof of the car. His brown eyes were featureless in the buzz of the street lamp.

"Kalamack must pay his secretaries very well for the car she has," he said softly.

I stiffened. "I know for a fact he does," I said hotly, not liking what he was implying. "She's very good at her job. And she still has enough money to send home for her family to live like veritable kings compared to the rest of the farm's employees."

He grunted and opened his door. I got in, sighing as I fastened my belt and settled into the leather seats. I stared out the window at the dark lot, growing more depressed. Sara Jane didn't trust me. But from her point of view, why should she?

"Taking this kind of personal, aren't you?" Glenn asked as he started the car.

"You think because she's a warlock she doesn't deserve help?" I said sharply.

"Slow down. That's not what I meant." Glenn shot me a quick look as he backed the car into motion. He flipped the heater on full before he shifted into drive, and a strand of hair tickled my face. "I'm just saying you're acting like you have a stake in the outcome."

I ran a hand over my eyes. "Sorry."

"It's okay," he said, sounding as if he understood. "So . . ." He hesitated. "What gives?"

He pulled into traffic, and in the light of a street lamp I glanced at him, wondering if I wanted to be that open with him. "I know Sara Jane," I said slowly.

"You mean you know her type," Glenn said.

"No. I know her."

The FIB detective frowned. "She doesn't know you."

"Yeah." I rolled the window all the way down to get rid of the smell of my perfume. I couldn't stand it anymore. My thoughts kept returning to Ivy's eyes, black and frightened. "That's what makes it hard."

The brakes made a slow squeak as we stopped at a light. Glenn's brow was furrowed, and his beard and mustache made deep shadows on him. "Would you talk human, please?"

I gave him a quick mirthless smile. "Did your dad tell you about how we nearly brought Trent Kalamack in as a dealer and manufacture of genetic drugs?"

"Yeah. That was before I transferred to his department. He said the only witness was an I.S. runner who died in a car bombing." The light changed, and we moved forward.

I nodded. Edden had told him the basics. "Let me tell you about Trent Kalamack," I said as the wind pushed against my hand. "When he caught me rifling through his office looking for a way to bring him into the courts, he didn't turn me in to the I.S., he offered me a job. Anything I wanted." Cold, I angled the vent toward me. "He'd pay off my I.S. death threat, set me up as an independent runner, give me a small staff, everything—if I worked for him. He wanted me to run the same system I had spent my entire professional life fighting. He offered me what looked like freedom. I wanted it so badly, I might have said yes."

Glenn was silent, wisely not saying anything. There wasn't a cop alive who hadn't been tempted, and I was proud that I had passed that test. "When I turned him down, his offer became a threat. I was spelled into a mink at the time, and he was going to torture me mentally and physically until I would do anything to get it to stop. If he couldn't have me willingly, he'd be satisfied with a warped shadow eager to please him. I was helpless. Just like Sara Jane is."

I hesitated to gather my resolve. I had never admitted that aloud before—that I had been helpless. "She thought I was a mink, but she gave me more dignity as an animal than Trent gave me as a person. I have to get her away from him. Before it's too late. Unless we can find Dan and get him safe, she doesn't have a chance."

"Mr. Kalamack is just a man," Glenn said.

"Really!" I said with a bark of sarcastic laughter. "Tell me, Mr. FIB Detective, is he human or Inderlander? His family has been quietly running a good slice of Cincinnati for two generations, and no one knows what he is. Jenks can't tell what he smells like, and neither can the fairies. He destroys people by giving them exactly what they want—

and he enjoys it." I watched the passing buildings without seeing them.

Glenn's continued silence pulled my eyes up. "You really think Dan's disappearance has nothing to do with the witch hunter murders?" he asked.

"Yeah." I resettled myself, not comfortable with having told him so much. "I only took this run to help Sara Jane and pull Trent down. You going to run tattling to your dad now?"

The lights from oncoming traffic illuminated him. He took a breath and let it out. "You do anything in your little vendetta to jeopardize me proving Dr. Anders is the murderer, and I'll tie you to a bonfire in Fountain Square," he said softly in threat. "You will go to the university tomorrow, and you will tell me everything you learn." His shoulders eased. "Just be careful."

I eyed him, the passing lights illuminating him in flashes that seemed to mirror my uncertainty. It sounded as if he understood. Imagine that. "Fair enough," I said, settling back. My head turned as we turned left instead of right. I glanced at him with a feeling of déjà vu. "Where are we going? My office is the other way."

"Pizza Piscary's," he said. "There's no reason to wait until tomorrow."

I eyed him, not wanting to admit I'd promised Ivy I wouldn't go out there without her. "Piscary's doesn't open until midnight," I lied. "They cater to Inderlanders. I mean, how often does a human order a pizza?" Glenn's face went still in understanding, and I picked at my nail polish. "It will be at least two before they slow down enough to be able to talk to us."

"That's two in the morning, right?" he asked.

Well, duh, I thought. That was when most Inderlanders were hitting their stride, especially the dead ones. "Why don't you go home, sleep in, and we'll all go out tomorrow?"

He shook his head. "You'll go tonight without me."

A puff of affront escaped me. "I don't work like that, Glenn. Besides, if I do, you'll go out there alone, and I promised your dad I'd try to keep you alive. I'll wait. Witches' honor."

Lie, yes. Betray the trust of a partner—even unwelcome ones—no.

He gave me a quick, suspicious glance. "All right. Witches' honor."

Seven

"**R**ache," Jenks said from my earring. "Take a squint at that guy. Is he trolling or what?"

I tugged my bag up higher onto my shoulder and peered through the unseasonably warm September afternoon at the kid in question as I walked through the informal lounge. Music tickled my subconscious, the volume of his radio set too low to hear well. My first thought was that he must be hot. His hair was black, his clothes were black, his sunglasses were black, and his black duster was made of leather. He was leaning against a vending machine trying to look suave as he talked to a woman in a gothic black lace dress. But he was blowing it. No one looks sophisticated with a foam cup in his hand, no matter how sexy his two-day stubble is. And no one wore goth but out-of-control teen living vamps and pathetically sad vamp wannabes.

I snickered, feeling vastly better. The big campus and the conglomeration of youth had me on edge. I had gone to school at a small community college, taking the standard two-year program followed by a four-year internship with the I.S. My mother would have never been able to afford tuition at the University of Cincinnati on my dad's pension, extra death benefit aside.

I glanced at the faded yellow receipt Edden had given me.

It had the time and days my class met, and right down at the lower right-hand corner was the cost of it all—tax, lab fees, and tuition all totaled up into one appalling sum. Just this one class was nearly as much as a semester at my alma mater. Nervous, I shoved the paper in my bag as I noticed a Were in the corner watching me. I looked out of place enough without wandering around with a class schedule in my grip. I might as well have hung a card around my neck saying, "Continuing Adult Education Student." God help me, but I felt old. They weren't much younger than I was, but their every move screamed innocence.

"This is stupid," I muttered to Jenks as I left the informal commissary. I didn't even know why the pixy was with me. Must be Edden had sicked him on me to make sure I went to class. My vamp-made boots clicked smartly as I strode through the windowed, elevated walkway connecting the Business Arts building with Kantack Hall. A jolt went through me as I realized my feet were hitting the rhythm of Takata's "Shattered Sight," and though I still couldn't really hear the music, the lyrics settled themselves deep into my head to drive me nuts. *Sift the clues from the dust, from my lives, of my will./ I loved you then. I love you still.*

"I should be with Glenn, interviewing Dan's neighbors," I complained. "I don't need to take the freaking class, just talk to Dan's classmates."

My earring swung like a tire swing, and Jenks's wings tickled my neck. "Edden doesn't want to give Dr. Anders any warning that she's a suspect. I think it's a good idea."

I frowned, my steps growing muffled as I found the carpeted hallway and began watching the numbers on the doors count up. "You think it's a good idea, do you?"

"Yeah. But there's one thing he forgot." He snickered. "Or maybe he didn't."

I slowed as I saw a group standing outside a door. It was probably mine. "What's that?"

"Well," he drawled, "now that you're taking the class, you fit the profile."

Adrenaline zinged through me and vanished. "How about that?" I murmured. *Damn Edden anyway.*

Jenks's laughter was like wind chimes. I shifted my heavy book to my other hip, scanning the small gathering for the person most likely to spill the best gossip. A young woman looked up at me, or Jenks rather, smiling briefly before turning away. She was dressed in jeans like me, with an expensive-looking suede coat over her T-shirt. Casual yet sophisticated. Nice combination. Dropping my bag to the carpet tile, I leaned back against the wall like everyone else, a noncommittal four feet away.

I surreptitiously looked at the book by the woman's feet. *Noncontact Extensions Using Ley Lines*. A tiny wash of relief went through me. I had the right book, at least. Maybe this wouldn't be so bad. I glanced at the frosted glass of the closed door, hearing a muted conversation from inside. Must be the previous class hadn't let out yet.

Jenks rocked my earring, pulling on it. I could ignore that, but when he started singing about inchworms and marigolds, I batted him off.

The woman beside me cleared her throat. "Just transfer in?" she asked.

"Beg pardon?" I asked as Jenks flitted back.

She popped her gum, her heavily made-up eyes going from me to the pixy. "There aren't many of us ley line students. I don't remember seeing you. Do you usually take night classes?"

"Oh." I pushed myself away from the wall and faced her. "No. I'm taking a class to, ah, move ahead at work."

She laughed as she tucked her long hair back. "Hey, I'm

right there with you. But by the time I get out of here, there's probably not going to be any jobs left for a film production manager with ley line experience. Everyone seems to be minoring in art these days."

"I'm Rachel." I extended my hand. "And this is Jenks."

"Nice to meet you," she said, taking it for an instant. "Janine."

Jenks buzzed to her, alighting on her hastily raised hand. "Pleasure is all mine, Janine," he said, actually making a bow.

She beamed, utterly delighted. Obviously she hadn't had much contact with pixies. Most stayed outside the city unless employed in the few areas pixies and fairies excelled in: camera maintenance, security, or good old-fashioned sneaking around. Even so, fairies were far more commonly employed, since they ate insects instead of nectar and their food supply was more readily available.

"Uh, does Dr. Anders actually teach the class, or does she have an aide do it?" I asked.

Janine chuckled, and Jenks flitted back to my earring. "You've heard about her?" she asked. "Yes, she teaches, seeing as there's not that many of us." Janine's eyes pinched. "Especially now. We started with more than a dozen, but we lost four when Dr. Anders told us the murderer was taking only ley line witches and to be careful. And then Dan went and quit." She slumped back against the wall, sighing.

"The witch hunter?" I asked, stifling my smile. I had chosen the right person to stand beside. I made my eyes wide. "You're kidding. . . ."

Her face went worried. "I think that's some of the reason why Dan left. And it was a shame, too. The man was so hot, he could make a sprinkler spark in a rainstorm. He had a big interview. Wouldn't tell me anything. I think he was afraid I'd apply for it, too. Looks like he got the job."

My head bobbed as I wondered if this was the news he was going to tell Sara Jane on Saturday. But then a slow burn started in me that perhaps supper at Carew Tower had been a dump dinner, and he chickened out and left without telling her anything.

"Are you sure he quit?" I asked. "Maybe the witch hunter . . ." I left my sentence open, and Janine smiled reassuringly.

"Yes, he quit. He asked if I wanted to buy his magnetic chalk if he got the job. The bookstore won't take them back once you break the seal."

My face went slack in sudden, real alarm. "I didn't know I needed chalk."

"Oh, I've got one you can borrow," she said as she rummaged in her purse. "Dr. Anders usually has us sketching something or other: pentagrams, north/south apogees . . . you name it, we've traced it. She lumps the lab in with the lecture. That's why we meet here instead of a lecture hall."

"Thanks," I said as I accepted the metallic stick and gripped it along with my book. *Pentagrams?* I hated pentagrams. My lines were always crooked. I'd have to ask Edden if he would pay for a second trip to the bookstore. But then remembering the cost of the class he would probably never be reimbursed for, I decided to go pick up my old school supplies from my mom. Swell. Better give her a call.

Janine saw my sick look, and misunderstanding it, she rushed to say, "Oh, don't worry, Rachel. The murderer isn't after us. Really. Dr. Anders said to be careful, but he's only going for experienced witches."

"Yeah," I said, wondering if I would be considered experienced or not. "I guess."

The conversations around us ceased as Dr. Anders's voice shrilled from behind the door, "I don't know who's killing my students. I've been to too many funerals this month to listen to your foul accusations. And I'll sue you from here back to the Turn if you slander my name!"

Janine looked alarmed as she picked up her book and held

it to her chest. The students in the hallway shifted from foot to foot and exchanged uneasy looks. From my earring Jenks whispered, "So much for keeping Dr. Anders in the dark about her possible suspect status." I nodded, wondering if Edden would let me drop the class now. "It's Denon in there with her," Jenks added, and I took a quick breath.

"What?"

"I can smell Denon," he reiterated. "He's in there with Dr. Anders."

Denon? I thought, wondering what my old boss was doing out from behind his desk.

There was a soft murmur, followed by a loud pop. Everyone in the hall but Jenks and me jumped. Janine reached up and touched her ear as if she had just been knocked a good one. "Didn't you feel that?" she asked me, and I shook my head. "She just set a circle without drawing a real one first."

I eyed the door along with everyone else. I didn't know you could set a circle without drawing it. I also didn't like that everybody but Jenks and I had been able to tell she had done it. Feeling as if I was in over my head, I picked my bag up.

The low rumble of my old boss's voice pulled a chill from me. Denon was a living vamp, like Ivy. But he was low-blood, rather than high, having been born a human and infected with the vamp virus later by one of the true undead. And where Ivy had political power because she'd been born a vamp and thus was guaranteed to join the undead even if she should die alone with every drop of blood in her, Denon would always be second-class, having to trust that someone would bother to finish turning him after he died.

"Get out of my room," Dr. Anders demanded. "Before I file harassment charges."

The students all shifted nervously. I wasn't surprised when the frosted glass darkened with a shape behind it. I stiffened with the rest when the door opened and Denon walked out. The man almost had to turn sideways to clear the door frame.

I still maintained my belief that Denon had been a boulder in a previous life—a smooth, river-worn boulder massing about a ton maybe? Being low-blood and having only human strength, he had to work hard to keep up with his dead brethren. The results were a trim waist and oodles of bunching muscles. They pulled at his white dress shirt as he sauntered into the hallway. The stark cotton stood in sharp contrast with his complexion, drawing my eye and holding it—just as he wanted.

The class fell back as he eased past. A cold presence seemed to flow out of the room and pool about him, the remnants of the aura he had probably pulled on Dr. Anders. A confident, dominating smile curved over him as his eyes fastened on me.

"Uh, Rachel?" Jenks muttered as he flitted to Janine. "I'll see you inside, okay?"

I said nothing, suddenly feeling too thin and vulnerable.

"I'll save you a seat," Janine said, but I didn't look from my old boss. There was a soft rustle as the hallway emptied.

I had been scared of the man, and I was ready and willing to be scared of him now, but something had changed. Though still moving with the grace of a predator, the ageless look he once carried was gone. The hungry cast in his eye, which he didn't bother to hide, told me he was still a practicing vamp, but I was guessing he had lost favor and was no longer tasting the undead, though they were probably still feeding upon him.

"Morgan," he said, his words seeming to backwash against the brick wall behind me and give me a shove forward. His voice was just like him, practiced, powerful, and full of a heavy promise. "I heard you were whoring for the FIB. Or are we just bettering ourselves?"

"Hello, Mr. Denon," I said, not dropping his pupil-black eyes. "You get bumped down to runner?" The hungry lust in his eyes faltered into anger, and I added, "Looks like you're doing the runs you gave me. Rescuing familiars out of trees? Checking for valid licenses? How are those homeless bridge trolls doing, anyway?"

Denon shifted forward, his eyes intent and his muscles tense. My face went cold, and I found my back against the wall. The sun streaming in from the distant walkway seemed to dim. Like a kaleidoscope, it swirled to look twice as far away as it was. My heart leapt, then settled back into its usual pace. He was trying to pull an aura, but I knew he couldn't do it without me giving him the fear to feed it. I wouldn't be afraid.

"Cut the crap, Denon," I said boldly, my stomach knotting. "I live with a vamp who could eat you for breakfast. Save the aura for someone who cares."

Still, he pressed close until he was the only thing I could see. I had to look up, and it ticked me off. His breath was warm, and I could smell the tang of blood on it. My pulse pounded, and I hated that he knew I was afraid of him still.

"Anyone here but you and me?" he said, his voice as smooth as chocolate milk.

Hand moving in a slow, controlled motion, I reached for the grip of my splat gun. The brick scraped my knuckles, but as my fingers touched the handle, my confidence raced back. "Just you, me, and my splat gun. Touch me, and I'll drop you." I smiled right back at him. "What do you suppose I put in my splat balls? Might be kind of hard to explain why someone from the I.S. had to come out here and hose you off with saltwater, huh? I'd say that would be good for a laugh for at least a year." I watched his eyes shift to hate.

"Back up," I said clearly. "If I pull it, I use it."

He backed up. "Walk away from this, Morgan," he threatened. "This is my run."

"That explains why the I.S. is spinning its wheels. Maybe

you should go back to ticketing parked cars and let a professional take care of it."

His breath hissed out, and I found strength in his anger. Ivy was right. There was fear in the back of his soul. Fear that someday the undead vampires that fed on him would lose control and kill him. Fear that they wouldn't bring him back as one of their brothers.

He should be afraid.

"This is an I.S. matter," he said. "Interfere, and I'll have you down in lockup." He smiled, flashing me his human teeth. "If you thought being in Kalamack's cage was bad, wait until you see mine."

My confidence cracked. The I.S. knew about that? "Don't get your falsies in a twist," I said snidely. "I'm here on a missing person, not your murders."

"Missing person," he mocked. "That's a good story. I'd stick with it. Try to keep your tag alive this time." He gave me a final glance before he started down the hallway to the sun and the distant sound of the commissary. "You won't be Tamwood's pet forever," he said, not turning around. "Then, I'm coming for you."

"Yeah, whatever," I said even as a sliver of my old fear tried to surface. I quashed it as I pulled my hand away from the small of my back. I wasn't Ivy's pet, though living with her gave me a heap of protection from Cincinnati's vamp population. She wasn't in a position of power, but as the last living member of the Tamwood family, she had a leader-in-waiting status honored by wise vamps both living and dead.

I took a deep breath to try to dispel the weakness in my knees. Great. Now I had to go into class after they had probably started.

Thinking my day couldn't possibly get any worse, I gathered myself and walked into the room lit brightly from the bank of windows overlooking the campus. As Janine had said, it was set up like a lab, with two people sitting on stools at each of the high slate tables. Janine was by herself talking to Jenks, clearly having saved me the spot next to her.

Ozone from Dr. Anders's hastily constructed circle caught at me. The circle was gone, but my sinuses tingled at the remnants of power. I glanced at its source at the front of the room.

Dr. Anders sat at an ugly metal desk before a traditional blackboard. She had her elbows on the table, her head in her hands. I could see her thin fingers trembling, and I wondered if it was from Denon's accusations or that she had pulled upon the ever-after strong enough to make a circle without the aid of a physical manifestation. The class seemed unusually quiet.

Her hair was back in a severe bun, gray streaks making unflattering lines through the black. She looked older than my mother, dressed in a conservative pair of tan slacks and a tasteful blouse. Trying not to draw attention to myself, I slipped past the first two rows of tables and sat beside Janine. "Thanks," I whispered.

Her eyes were wide as I tucked my bag under the table. "You work for the I.S.?"

I glanced at Dr. Anders. "I used to. I quit last spring."

"I didn't think you could quit the I.S.," she said, her face going even more full of wonder.

Shrugging, I pushed my hair out of the way so Jenks could land on his usual spot. "It wasn't easy." I followed her attention to the front of the room as Dr. Anders stood.

The tall woman was as scary as I remembered, with a long thin face, and a nose that wouldn't be out of place on a pre-Turn depiction of a witch. No wart, though, and her complexion wasn't green. She reeked of tenure, gathering the class's attention by simply standing. The tremor was gone from her hands as she took up a sheaf of papers.

Dropping a pair of wire-rimmed glasses down to perch on her nose, she made a show of studying her notes. I'd have been willing to bet they had a spell on them to see through ley line charms as well as correct her sight, and I wished I had the gall to put my own glasses on and see if she used ley line magic to make her look that unattractive or if it was all her. A sigh shifted her narrow shoulders as she looked up, her gaze going right to mine through her spelled glasses. "I see," she said, her voice making my spine crawl, "that we have a new face today."

I gave her a false smile. It was obvious she recognized me; her face had scrunched up like a prune.

"Rachel Morgan," she said.

"Here," I said, my voice flat.

A wisp of annoyance flashed over her. "I know who you are." Low heels clicking, she came to stand before me. Leaning forward, she peered at Jenks. "Who might you be, pixy sir?"

"Uh, Jenks, ma'am," he stammered, his wings moving fitfully to tangle in my hair.

"Jenks," she said, her tone bordering on the respectful. "I'm glad to make your acquaintance. You're not on my class list. Please leave."

"Yes ma'am," he said, and much to my surprise, the usually arrogant pixy swung himself off my earring. "Sorry, Rache," he said, hovering before me. "I'll be in the faculty lounge or the library. Nick might still be working."

"Sure. I'll find you later."

He gave Dr. Anders a head bob and zipped out the still open door.

"I'm sorry," Dr. Anders said. "Is my class interfering with your social life?"

"No, Dr. Anders. It's a pleasure seeing you again."

She pulled back at the faint sarcasm. "Is it?"

From the corner of my sight I saw Janine's mouth hanging open. What I could see of the rest of the class looked about the same. My face burned. I don't know why the woman had it in for me, but she did. She was as nice as a hungry crow to everyone else, but I got the ravenous badger.

Dr. Anders let her papers fall to my table with a slap. My name was circled in a thick red marker. Her thin lips tightened almost imperceptibly. "Why are you here?" she asked. "We are two classes into the semester."

"It's still add/drop week," I countered, feeling my pulse increase. Unlike Jenks, I had no problem fighting authority. But as the song went, authority always won.

"I don't even know how you managed to get the approval for taking this class," she said caustically. "You have none of the prerequisites."

"All my credits transferred in. And I got a year for life-experiences." True enough, but Edden was the real reason I had been able to skip right to a five-hundred-level class.

"You are wasting my time, Ms. Morgan," she said. "You are an earth witch. I thought I had made that very clear to you. You don't possess the control to work ley lines beyond what you need to close a modest circle." She leaned over me, and I felt my blood pressure rise. "I'm going to flunk you out of my class faster than before."

I took a steadying breath, glancing at the shocked faces. Clearly they had never seen this side of their beloved instructor. "I need this class, Dr. Anders," I said, not knowing why I was trying to appeal to her stunted compassion. Except that if I got kicked out, Edden might make me pay the tuition. "I'm here to learn."

At that, the prickly woman picked up her papers and retreated to the empty table behind her. Her gaze roved over the class before settling on me. "Having trouble with your demon?"

Several in the class gasped. Janine actually shrank away from me. *Damn that woman,* I thought, my hand going to cover my wrist. *Not even here for five minutes, and she alienates me from the entire class.* I should have worn a bracelet.

My jaw clenched and my breathing increased as I fought to not respond.

Dr. Anders seemed satisfied. "You can't reliably hide a demon mark with earth magic," she said, her voice raised in the sound of instruction. "You need ley line magic for that. Is that why you're here, Ms. Morgan?" she mocked.

Shaking, I refused to drop her eyes. I hadn't known that. No wonder my charms to disguise it never worked past sundown.

Her wrinkles went deeper as she frowned. "Professor Peltzer's Demonology for Modern Practitioners is in the next building over. Perhaps you should excuse yourself and see if it's not too late to change classes. We do not deal in the black arts here."

"I am not a black witch," I said softly, afraid if I raised my voice, I would start shouting. I pushed up my sleeve to show my demon mark, refusing to be ashamed of it. "I did not call the demon who gave me this. I fought it off."

I took a slow breath, unable to look at anyone, most of all Janine, who had pushed as far from me as she could get. "I'm here to learn how to keep it off of me, Dr. Anders. I will not take any demonology classes. I'm afraid of them."

The last was a whisper, but I knew everyone heard. Dr. Anders seemed taken aback. I was embarrassed, but if it kept her off my case, then it was embarrassment well spent.

The woman's footsteps were loud as she clacked to the front of the room. "Go home, Ms. Morgan," she said to the blackboard. "I know why you're here. I did not kill my past students, and I take offense in your unsaid accusation."

And with that pleasant thought, she turned, flashing the class a tight-lipped smile. "If the rest of you will please re-tain your copies of eighteenth century pentagrams? We will be having a quiz on them Friday. For next week, I want you to go over chapters six, seven, and eight in your texts and to do the even practices at the end of each. Janine?"

At the sound of her name, the woman jumped. She had

been trying to get a good look at my wrist. I was still shaking, my fingers trembling as I wrote down the assignment.

"Janine, you would do well to do the odds on chapter six, as well. Your control in releasing stored ley line energy leaves something to be desired."

"Yes, Dr. Anders," she said, white-faced.

"And go sit by Brian," she added. "You can learn more from him than Ms. Morgan."

Janine didn't hesitate. Before Dr. Anders had even finished, Janine picked up her purse and book, moving to the next table. I was left alone, feeling sick. Janine's borrowed chalk sat next to my book like a stolen cookie.

"I would also like to evaluate your linkages with your familiars on Friday, as we will be starting a section on long-term protection over the next few weeks," Dr. Anders was saying. "So please bring them in. It will take some time to get through all of you. Those at the end of the alphabet can expect to be held beyond the usual class time."

There was a weary groan from some of the students, but it lacked a certain joviality that I sensed was usually there. My stomach dropped. I didn't have a familiar. If I didn't get one by Friday, she'd flunk me. Same as last time.

Dr. Anders smiled at me with the warmth of a doll. "Is that a problem, Ms. Morgan?"

"No," I said flatly, starting to want to pin the murders on her whether she had committed them or not. "No problem at all."

Eight

Thankfully, there was no line when we pulled up to Pizza Piscary's in Glenn's unmarked FIB car. Ivy and I slid out almost as soon as the car stopped. It hadn't been a very comfortable ride for either of us, the memory of her pinning me to the kitchen wall still new-penny bright. Her manner had been odd this evening, subdued but excited. I felt like I was going to meet her parents. In a way, I suppose I was. Piscary was the way-back originator of her living-vamp family line.

Glenn yawned as he slowly got out and put his jacket on, but he woke up enough to wave off Jenks, flitting around his head. He didn't seem at all uneasy about going into what was strictly an Inderland eatery. I could almost see the chip on his shoulder. Maybe he was a slow learner.

The FIB detective had agreed to exchange his stiff FIB suit for the jeans and faded flannel shirt Ivy had tucked in the back of her closet in a box labeled LEFTOVERS in a faded black marker. They fit Glenn exactly, and I didn't want to know where she had gotten them or why they had several neatly mended tears in some rather unusual places. A nylon jacket hid the weapon he refused to leave behind, but I had left my splat gun at home. It would be useless against a room full of vamps.

A van eased into the lot to take an empty space at the far end. My attention drifted from it to the brightly lit delivery/takeout window. As I watched, another pizza went out, the car lurching into the street and speeding away with the quickness that told of a large engine. Pizza drivers have made good money since they successfully lobbied for hazard pay.

Past the parking lot was the soft lapping of water on wood. Long strips of light glinted on the Ohio River, and the taller buildings of Cincinnati reflected in wide streaks on the flat water. Piscary's was waterfront property, situated in the middle of the more affluent strip of clubs, restaurants, and nightspots. It even had a landing where yacht-traveling patrons could tie up to—but getting a table overlooking the dock would be impossible this late.

"Ready?" Ivy said brightly as she finished adjusting her jacket. She was dressed in her usual black leather pants and silk shirt, looking lanky and predatory. The only color to her face was her bright red lipstick. A chain of black gold hung about her neck in place of her usual crucifix—which was now tucked in her jewelry box at home. It matched her ankle bracelets perfectly. She had gone further to paint her nails with a clear coat, giving them a subtle shine.

The jewelry and nail polish were unusual for her, and after seeing it, I had opted to wear a wide silver band instead of my usual charm bracelet to cover my demon mark. It felt nice to get dressed up, and I'd even tried to do something with my hair. The red frizz I ended up with almost looked intentional.

I kept a step behind Glenn as we moved to the front door. Inderlanders mixed freely, but our group was more odd than usual, and I was hoping to get in and out quickly with the information we came for before we attracted attention. The van that pulled in after us was a pack of Weres, and they were noisy as they closed the gap between us.

"Glenn," Ivy said as we reached the door. "Keep your mouth shut."

"Whatever," the officer said antagonistically.

My eyebrows rose and I took a wary step back. Jenks landed upon my big hoop earrings. "This ought to be good," he snickered.

Ivy grabbed Glenn's collar, picking him up and slamming him against the wooden pillar supporting the canopy. The startled man froze for an instant, then kicked out, aiming for Ivy's gut. Ivy dropped him to evade the strike. With a vamp quickness, she picked him back up and slammed him into the post again. Glenn grunted in pain, struggling to catch his breath.

"Ooooh," Jenks cheered. "That's going to ache in the morning."

I jiggled my foot and glanced at the pack of Weres. "Couldn't you have taken care of this before we left?" I complained.

"Look, you little snack," Ivy said calmly, putting herself in Glenn's face. "You will keep your mouth shut. You do not exist unless I ask you a question."

"Go to hell," Glenn managed, his face reddening under his dark skin.

Ivy shifted him a smidgen higher, and he grunted. "You stink like a human," she continued, her eyes shifting toward black. "Piscary's is all Inderlanders or bound humans. The only way you're going to get out of here with all your parts intact and unpunctured is if everyone thinks you're my shadow."

Shadow, I thought. It was a derogatory term. Thrall was another. Toy would be more accurate. It referred to a human recently bit, now little more than a walking source of sex and food, and mentally bound to a vamp. They were kept submissive as long as possible. Decades sometimes. My old boss, Denon, had been counted among them until he curried the favor of the one who had granted him a more free existence.

Face ugly, Glenn broke her hold and fell to the ground. "Go Turn yourself, Tamwood," he rasped, rubbing his neck. "I can take care of myself. This won't be any worse than walking into a good-old-boy's bar in deep Georgia."

"Yeah?" she questioned, pale hand on her cocked hip. "Anyone there want to eat you?"

The Were pack flowed past us and inside. One jerked, doing a double take as he saw me, and I wondered if my stealing that fish was going to be a problem. Music and chatter drifted out, cutting off as the thick door shut. I sighed. It sounded busy. Now we'd probably have to wait for a table.

I offered Glenn a hand up as Ivy opened the door. Glenn refused my help, tucking his anti-itch spell back behind his shirt as he struggled to find his pride, squished under Ivy's boots somewhere. Jenks flitted from me to his shoulder, and Glenn started. "Go sit somewhere else, pixy," he said around a cough.

"Oh, no," Jenks said merrily. "Don't you know a vamp won't touch you if there's a pixy on your shoulder? It's a well-known fact."

Glenn hesitated, and my eyes rolled. *What a crock.*

We filed in behind Ivy as the Were pack was being led to their table. The place was crowded, not unusual for a workday. Piscary's had the best pizza in Cincinnati, and they didn't take reservations. The warmth and noise relaxed me, and I took off my coat. The rough-cut, thick support beams seemed to prop up the low ceiling, and a rhythmic stomping to the beat of Sting's "Rehumanize Yourself" filtered down the wide stairs. Past them were wide windows looking out over the black river and the city beyond. A three-story, obscenely expensive motorboat was tied up, the docking lights shining on the name across the bow, SOLAR. Pretty college-age kids moved efficiently about in their skimpy uniforms, some more suggestive than others. Most were bound humans, since the vamp staff traditionally took the less supervised upstairs.

The host's eyebrows rose as he took Glenn in. I could tell he was the host because his shirt was only half undone and his name tag said so. "Table for three? Lighted or non?"

"Lighted," I interjected before Ivy could say different. I didn't want to be upstairs. It sounded rowdy.

"It will be about fifteen minutes, then. You can wait at the bar if you like."

I sighed. Fifteen minutes. It was always fifteen minutes. Fifteen little minutes that dragged to thirty, then forty, and then you were willing to wait ten more so you didn't have to go to the next restaurant and start all over again.

Ivy smiled to show her teeth. Her canines were no bigger than mine were, but sharp like a cat's. "We'll wait here, thanks."

Looking almost enraptured by her smile, the host nodded. His chest, showing beneath his open shirt, was scattered with pale scars. It wasn't what the hosts were wearing at Denny's, but who was I to complain? There was a soft look about him that I didn't like in my men but some women did. "It won't be long," he said, his eyes fixing to mine as he noticed my attention on him. His lips parted suggestively. "Do you want to order now?"

A pizza went by on a tray, and as I jerked my gaze from him, I glanced at Ivy and shrugged. We weren't there for dinner, but why not? It smelled great.

"Yeah," Ivy said. "An extra large. Everything but peppers and onions."

Glenn jerked his attention from what looked like a coven of witches applauding the arrival of their dinner. Eating at Piscary's was an event. "You said we weren't going to stay."

Ivy turned, black swelling within her eyes. "I'm hungry. Is that okay with you?"

"Sure," he muttered.

Immediately Ivy regained her composure. I knew she wouldn't vamp out here. It might start a cascading reaction from the surrounding vampires, and Piscary would lose his A rating on his MPL. "Maybe we can share a table with someone. I'm starved," she said, jiggling her foot.

MPL was short for Mixed Public License. What it meant was a strict enforcement of no blood drawn on the premises. Standard stuff for most places serving alcohol since the Turn. It created a safe zone that we frail "dead means dead" folk needed. If you had too many vamps together and one drew blood, the rest had a tendency to lose control. No problem if everyone's a vampire, but people didn't like it when their loved one's night on the town turned into an eternity in the graveyard. Or worse.

The clubs and nightspots without a MPL existed, but they weren't as popular and didn't make as much money. Humans liked MPL places, since they could safely flirt without someone else's bad decision turning their date into an out of control, bloodthirsty fiend. At least until the privacy of their own bedroom, where they might survive it. And vamps liked it too—it was easier to break the ice when your date wasn't uptight about you breaking his or her skin.

I looked around the semiopen room, seeing only Inderlanders among the patrons. MPL or not, it was obvious Glenn was attracting attention. The music had died, and no one had put in another quarter. Apart from the witches in the corner and the pack of Weres in the back, the downstairs was full of vamps in various levels of sensuality ranging from casual to satin and lace. A good part of the floor was taken up in what looked like a death-day party.

The sudden warm breath on my neck jerked me straight, and it was only Ivy's bothered look that kept me from smacking whoever it was. Spinning, my tart retort died. *Swell. Kisten.*

The living vamp was Ivy's friend, and I didn't like him. Some of that was because Kist was Piscary's scion, a loose extension of the master vampire who did his daylight work for him. It didn't help that Piscary had once bespelled me against my will through Kist, something I hadn't known was possible at the time. It also didn't help that he was very, very pretty, making him very, very dangerous by my reckoning.

If Ivy was a diva of the dark, then Kist was her consort, and God help me, he looked the part. Short blond hair, blue eyes, and chin holding enough stubble to give his delicate features a more rugged cast made him a sexy bundle of promised fun. He was dressed more conservatively than usual, his biker leather and chains replaced with a tasteful shirt and slacks. His I-should-care-what-you-think-because? attitude remained, though. The lack of biker boots put him a shade taller than me with the heels I had on, and the ageless look of an undead vampire shimmered in him like a promise to be fulfilled. He moved with a catlike confidence, having enough muscle to enjoy running your fingertips over but not so much that it got in the way.

Ivy and he had a past I didn't want to know about, since she had been a very practicing vamp at the time. I was always struck with the impression that if he couldn't have her, he'd be happy with her roommate. Or the girl next door. Or the woman he met on the bus this morning . . .

"Evening, love," he breathed in a fake English accent, his eyes amused because he had surprised me.

I pushed him back with a finger. "Your accent stinks. Go away until you get it right." But my pulse had increased, and a faint, pleasant tickle from the scar on my neck brought all my proximity alarms into play. *Damn it. I'd forgotten about that.*

He glanced at Ivy as if for permission, then playfully licked his lips as she frowned her answer. I scowled, thinking I didn't need her help fending him off. Seeing it, she made a puff of exasperated air and pulled Glenn to the bar, enticing Jenks to join them with the promise of a honeyed toddy. The FIB detective glanced at me over his shoulder as he went, knowing something had passed between the three of us but not what.

"Alone at last." Kist shifted to stand shoulder-to-shoulder with me and look across the open floor. I could smell leather, though he wasn't wearing any. That I could see, at least.

"Can't you find a better opening line than that?" I said, wishing I hadn't driven Ivy away.

"It wasn't a line."

His shoulder was too close to mine, but I wouldn't shift away and let him know it bothered me. I snuck a glance at him as he breathed with a heavy slowness, his eyes scanning the patrons even as he took in my scent to gauge my state of unease. Twin diamond earrings glittered from one ear, and I remembered the other had only one stud and a healed tear. A chain made out of the same stuff as Ivy's was the only hint of his usual bad-boy attire. I wondered what he was doing here. There were better places for a living vamp to pick up a date/snack.

His fingers moved with a restless motion, always pulling my eyes back to him. I knew he was throwing off vamp pheromones to soothe and relax me—all the better to eat you with, my dear—but the prettier they are, the more defensive I get. My face went slack as I realized I had matched my breathing to his.

Subtle bespelling at its finest, I thought, purposely holding my breath to get us out of sync, and I saw him smile as he ducked his head and ran a hand over his chin. Normally only an undead vampire could bespell the unwilling, but being Piscary's scion gave Kist a portion of his master's abilities. He wouldn't dare try it here, though. Not with Ivy watching from the bar around her bottled water.

I suddenly realized he was rocking, moving his hips with

a steady, suggestive motion. "Stop it," I said as I turned to face him, disgusted. "There's an entire string of women watching you at the bar. Go bother them."

"It's much more fun to bother you." Taking my scent deep into him, he leaned close. "You still smell like Ivy, but she hasn't bitten you. My God, you are a tease."

"We're friends," I said, affronted. "She's not hunting me."

"Then she won't mind if I do."

Annoyed, I pulled away. He followed me until my back found a support post. "Stop moving," he said as he put his hand against the thick post beside my head, pinning me though air still showed between us. "I want to tell you something, and I don't want anyone else to hear it."

"Like anyone could hear you over the noise," I scoffed, the fingers behind my back bending into a fist that wouldn't make my nails cut my palm if I had to slug him.

"You might be surprised," he murmured, his eyes intent. I fixed on them, looking for and recognizing the barest hint of swelling black, even as his nearness sent a promise of heat from my scar. I'd lived long enough with Ivy to know what a vamp looked like when they were close to losing it. He was fine, his instincts curbed and his hunger sated.

I was reasonably safe, so I relaxed, easing my shoulders down. His lust-reddened lips parted in surprise at my acceptance at how close he was. Eyes bright, he breathed languorously slow, tilting his head and leaning in so his lips brushed the curve of my ear. The light shimmered on the black chain around his neck, drawing my hand up. It was warm, and that surprise kept my fingers playing with it when I should have stopped.

The clatter of dishes and conversation retreated as I exhaled into his soft, unrecognizable whisper. A delicious feeling ran through me, sending the sensation of molten metal through my veins. I didn't care that it was from him triggering my scar into play; it felt so good. And he hadn't even said a word I recognized yet.

"Sir?" came a hesitant voice from behind him.

Kist's breath caught. For three heartbeats he held himself still, unmoving as his shoulders tensed in annoyance. My hand dropped from his neck.

"Someone wants you," I said, looking beyond him to the host, shifting nervously. A smile edged over me. Kist was tempting a break in the MPL, and someone had been sent to rein him in. Laws were good things. They kept me alive when I did something stupid.

"What," Kist said flatly. I'd never heard his voice carry anything but sultry petulance before, and the power in it sent a jolt through me, its unexpectedness making it all the more demanding.

"Sir, the party of Weres upstairs? They're starting to pack."

Oh? I thought. That was not what I had expected.

Kist straightened his elbow and pushed away from the post, irritation flickering across him. I took a clean breath, my unhealthy disappointment mixing with a distressingly small waft of self-preserving relief.

"I told you to tell them we were out of bane," Kist said. "They came in reeking of it."

"We did, sir," the waiter protested, taking a step back as Kist pulled entirely away from me. "But they coerced Tarra into admitting there was some in the back, and she gave it to them."

Kist's annoyance turned into anger. "Who gave Tarra the upstairs? I told her to work the lower floor until that Were bite healed over."

Kist worked at Piscary's? Surprise, surprise. I hadn't thought the vamp had the presence of mind to do anything useful.

"She convinced Samuel to let her up there, saying she'd get better tips," the waiter said.

"Sam . . ." Kist said from between closed teeth. Emotion crossed him, the first hints of coherent thoughts that didn't revolve around sex and blood surprising me. Full lips pressed together, he scanned the floor. "All right. Pull everyone as if for a birthday and get her out of there before she sets them off. Cut off the bane. Complimentary desert for any who want it."

Blond stubble catching the light, he glanced up as if able to see through the ceiling to the noise upstairs. The music was high again, and Jeff Beck filtered down. "Loser." Somehow, it seemed to fit as they all slurred the lyrics together. The wealthier patrons in the lower floor didn't seem to mind.

"Piscary will have my hide if we lose our A rating over a Were bite," Kist said. "And as exciting as that might be, I want to be able to walk tomorrow."

Kist's easy admission of his relationship with Piscary took me aback, but it shouldn't have. Though I always equated the giving and taking of blood with sex, it wasn't, especially if the exchange was between a living and an undead vampire. The two held vastly different views, probably because one had a soul and the other didn't.

The "bottle the blood came in" mattered to most living vamps. They picked their partners with care, usually—but not always—following their sexual gender preferences on the happy chance that sex might be included in the mix. Even when driven by hunger, the giving and taking of blood often fulfilled an emotional need, a physical affirmation of an emotional bond in much the same way that sex could—but didn't always have to.

Undead vampires were even more meticulous, choosing their companions with the care of a serial killer. Seeking domination and emotional manipulation rather than commitment, gender didn't enter into the equation—though the undead wouldn't turn down the addition of sex, since it imparted an even more intense feeling of domination, akin to rape even with a willing partner. Any relationship that grew from such an arrangement was utterly one-sided, though the bitee usually didn't accept it, thinking their master was the exception to the rule. It gave me pause that Kist seemed eager for another encounter with Piscary, and I wondered, as I glanced at the young vampire beside me, if it was because Kist received a large measure of strength and status by being his scion.

Unaware of my thoughts, Kist furrowed his brow in anger. "Where's Sam?" he asked.

"The kitchen, sir."

His eye twitched. Kist looked at the waiter as if to say, "What are you waiting for?" and the man hurried away.

Bottled water in hand, Ivy snuck up behind Kist, pulling him farther from me. "And you thought I was stupid for majoring in security instead of business management?" she said. "You sound almost responsible, Kisten. Be careful, or you'll ruin your reputation."

Kist smiled to show his sharp canines, the air of harried restaurant manager falling from him. "The perks are great, Ivy, love," he said, curving a hand around her backside with a familiarity she tolerated for an instant before hitting him. "You ever need a job, come see me."

"Shove it up your ass, Kist."

He laughed, dropping his head for an instant before bringing his sly gaze back to mine. A group of waiters and waitresses were headed up the wide stairway, clapping in time and singing some asinine song. It looked annoying and innocuous, nothing like the rescue mission it really was. My eyebrows rose. Kist was good at this.

Almost as if reading my mind, he leaned close. "I'm even better in bed, love," he whispered, his breath sending a delicious dart of sensation down to the pit of my being.

He shifted out of my reach before I could push him away, and still smiling, walked off. Halfway to the kitchen he turned to see if I was watching. Which I was. Hell, everything female in the place—alive, dead, or in between—was watching.

I pulled my attention from him to find a curiously closed look on Ivy. "You aren't afraid of him anymore," she said flatly.

"No," I said, surprised to find I wasn't. "I think it's because he can do something other than flirt."

She looked away. "Kist can do a lot of things. He gets off on being dominated, but when it comes to business, he'll slam you to the ground soon as look at you. Piscary wouldn't have a fool for a scion, no matter how good he is to bleed." Her lips pressed together until they went white. "Table's ready."

I followed her gaze to the single empty table against the far wall away from the windows. Glenn and Jenks had joined us when Kist left, and as a group we wove through the tables, settling on the half-circle bench with all our backs to the wall—Inderlander, human, Inderlander—and waited for the waiter to find us.

Jenks had perched himself on the low chandelier, and the light coming through his wings made green and gold spots on the table. Glenn silently took everything in, clearly trying not to look nonplussed at the sight of the scarred, well-put-together waiters and waitresses. Whether male or female, they were all young with smiling, eager faces that had me on edge.

Ivy didn't say anything more about Kist, for which I was grateful. It was embarrassing how quickly vamp pheromones acted on me, turning "get lost" to "get over here." Thanks to the excessive amount of vamp saliva the demon pumped into me while trying to kill me, my resistance to vamp pheromones was almost nil.

Glenn carefully put his elbows on the table. "You haven't told me how class went."

Jenks laughed. "It was hell on earth. Two hours of nonstop nitpicking and putdowns."

My mouth dropped open. "How do you know that?"

"I snuck back in. What did you do to that woman, Rachel? Kill her cat?"

My face burned. Knowing Jenks had witnessed it made it worse. "The woman is a hag," I said. "Glenn, if you want to string her up for killing those people, you go right ahead. She already knows she's a suspect. The I.S. was there stirring her into a tizzy. I didn't find anything that remotely resembled possible motive or guilt."

Glenn pulled his arms from the table and sat back. "Nothing?"

I shook my head. "Just that Dan had an interview after Friday's class. I'm thinking that was the big news he was going to spring on Sara Jane."

"He dropped all his classes Friday night," Jenks said. "Just made the add/drop with a full refund. Must have done it by e-mail."

I squinted up at the pixy sitting by the lightbulbs to stay warm. "How do you know?"

His wings blurred to nothing and he grinned. "I checked out the registrar's office during class break. You think the only reason I went was to look pretty on your shoulder?"

Ivy drummed her fingernails. "You three aren't going to talk shop all night, are you?"

"Ivy girl!" came a strong voice, and we all looked up. A short, spare man in a cook's apron was making a beeline for us from across the restaurant, weaving gracefully through the tables. "My Ivy girl!" he called over the noise. "Back already. And with friends!"

I glanced at Ivy, surprised to see a faint blush coloring her pale cheeks. *Ivy girl?*

"Ivy girl?" Jenks said from on high. "What the hell is that?"

Ivy rose to give him an embarrassed-looking hug as he halted before us, making an odd picture since he was nearly six inches smaller than she was. He returned it with a fatherly pat on the back. My eyebrows rose. She *hugged* him?

The cook's black eyes glittered in what looked like pleasure. The scent of tomato paste and blood drifted to me. He was clearly a practicing vamp. I couldn't tell yet if he was dead.

"Hi, Piscary," Ivy said as she sat, and Jenks and I exchanged looks. This was Piscary? One of Cincinnati's most powerful vamps? I'd never seen such an innocuous looking vampire.

Piscary was actually an inch or two shorter than I was, and he carried his slight, well-proportioned build with a comfortable ease. His nose was narrow, and his wide-spaced, almond-shaped eyes and thin lips added to his exotic appearance. His eyes were very dark, and they shone as he took his chef's hat off and tucked it behind his apron ties. He kept his skull clean-shaven, and his honey-amber skin glinted in the light from over our table. The lightweight, pale shirt and pants he wore might have been off-the-rack, but I doubted it. They gave him the air of comfortable middle class, his eager smile enforcing the picture in my mind. Piscary ran much of the darker side of Cincinnati, but looking at him, I wondered how.

My usual healthy distrust of undead vamps sank to a wary caution. "Piscary?" I asked. "As in Pizza Piscary's?"

The vampire smiled, showing his teeth. They were longer than Ivy's—he was a true undead—and looked very white next to his dusky completion. "Yes, Pizza Piscary's is mine." His voice was deep for such a small frame, and it seemed to carry the strength of sand and wind. The faint remnants of an accent made me wonder how long he had been speaking English.

Ivy cleared her throat, jerking my attention away from his quick, dark eyes. Somehow the sight of his teeth hadn't instilled my usual knee-jerk alarm. "Piscary," Ivy said, "this is Rachel Morgan and Jenks, my business associates."

Jenks had flitted down to the hot-pepper shakers, and Piscary gave him a nod before turning to me. "Rachel Morgan," he said slowly and with care. "I've been waiting for my Ivy girl to bring you to see me. I think she's afraid I'll tell her she can't play with you anymore." His lips curved into a smile. "I'm charmed."

I held my breath as he took my hand with a high gentility that stood in sharp contrast to his looks. He lifted my fingers, bringing them close to his lips. His dark eyes were fixed on mine. My pulse quickened, but I felt as if my heart were somewhere else. He inhaled over my hand, as if scenting the blood humming within them. I stifled a shiver by clenching my jaw.

Piscary's eyes were the color of black ice. I boldly returned his gaze, intrigued at the hints beyond their depths. It was Piscary who looked away first, and I quickly pulled my hand from him. He was good. Really good. He had used his aura to charm rather than frighten. Only the old ones could do that. And there hadn't been even a twinge from my demon scar. I didn't know whether to take that as a good sign or bad.

Laughing good-naturedly at my sudden, obvious suspicion, Piscary sat down on the bench beside Ivy as three waiters struggled to get by with round platters. Glenn didn't seem at all upset Ivy hadn't introduced him, and Jenks kept his mouth shut. My shoulder pressed into Glenn as he shoved me down until I was nearly hanging off the edge to make room for Piscary.

"You should have told me you were coming," Piscary said. "I'd have saved you a table."

Ivy shrugged. "We got one okay."

Half turning, Piscary looked to the bar and shouted, "Bring up a bottle of red from the Tamwood cellar!" A sly grin came over him. "Your mother won't miss one."

Glenn and I exchanged a worried look. *A bottle of red?* "Uh, Ivy?" I questioned.

"Oh, good God," she said. "It's wine. Relax."

Relax, I thought. Easier said than done with my rear hanging half off the seat and surrounded by vampires.

"Have you ordered?" Piscary asked Ivy, but his gaze was on me, suffocating. "I have a new cheese that uses a just-discovered species of mold to age. All the way from the Alps."

"Yes," Ivy said. "An extra large—"

"With everything but onions and peppers," he finished, showing his teeth in a wide smile as he turned from me to her.

My shoulders slumped as his gaze left me. He looked like nothing more than a friendly pizza chef, and it was setting off more alarm bells than if he had been tall, thin, and slunk about seductively in lace and silk.

"Ha!" he barked, and I stifled my jump. "I'm going to make you dinner, Ivy girl."

Ivy smiled to look like a ten-year-old. "Thank you, Piscary. I'd like that."

"'Course you would. Something special. Something new. On the house. It will be my finest creation!" he said boldly. "I will name it after you and your shadow."

"I'm not her shadow," Glenn said tightly, shoulders hunched and his eyes on the table.

"I wasn't talking about you," Piscary said, and my eyes widened.

Ivy stirred uneasily. "Rachel . . . isn't my shadow . . . either."

She sounded guilty, and an instant of confusion crossed the old vamp's face. "Really?" he said, and Ivy visibly tensed. "Then what are you doing with her, Ivy girl?"

She wouldn't look up from the table. Piscary caught my

eye again. My heart pounded as a faint tingle rippled across my neck at my demon bite. Suddenly the table was too crowded. I felt pressed upon at all sides, and the claustrophobic feeling beat at me. Shocked at the change, my breath left me and I held the next one. *Damn.*

"That's an interesting scar on your neck," Piscary said, his voice seeming to scour my soul. It hurt and felt good all at the same time. "Is it vamp?"

My hand rose unbidden to hide it. Jenks's wife had sewn me up, and the tiny stitches were almost invisible. I didn't like that he had noticed them. "It's demon," I said, not caring if Glenn told his dad. I didn't want Piscary thinking I'd been bitten by a vamp, Ivy or otherwise.

Piscary arched his eyebrows in a mild surprise. "It looks vampiric."

"So did the demon at the time," I said, my stomach tightening in the memory.

The old vamp nodded. "Ah, that would explain it." He smiled, chilling me. "A ravaged virgin whose blood has been left unclaimed. What a delectable combination you are, Ms. Morgan. No wonder my Ivy girl has been hiding you from me."

My mouth opened, but I could think of nothing to say.

He stood with no warning. "I'll have your dinner out in a moment." Leaning to Ivy, he murmured, "Talk to your mother. She misses you."

Ivy dropped her eyes. With a casual grace, Piscary snagged a stack of plates and breadsticks from a passing tray. "Enjoy your evening," he said as he set them on our table. He made his way back to the kitchen, stopping several times to greet the more well-dressed patrons.

I stared at Ivy, waiting for an explanation. "Well?" I said bitingly. "You want to explain why Piscary thinks I'm your shadow?"

Jenks snickered, taking his hands-on-hips Peter Pan pose

atop the pepper shaker. Ivy shrugged in obvious guilt. "He knows we live under the same roof. He just assumed—"

"Yeah, I got it." Annoyed, I chose a breadstick and slumped against the wall. Ivy's and my arrangement was odd no matter what angle you looked at it. She was trying to abstain from blood, the lure to break her fast almost irresistible. As a witch, I could fend her off with my magic when her instincts got the better of her. I had dropped her once with a charm, and it was that memory that helped her master her cravings and keep her on her side of the hallway.

But what bothered me was that it was shame that made her let Piscary believe what he wanted—shame for turning her back on her heritage. She didn't want it. With a roommate, she could lie to the world, pretending she had a normal vamp life with a live-in source of blood yet remain true to her guilty secret. I told myself I didn't care, that it protected me against other vamps. But sometimes . . . Sometimes it rankled me that everyone assumed I was Ivy's toy.

My sulk was interrupted by the arrival of the wine, slightly warm, as most vamps liked it. It had been opened already, and Ivy took control of the bottle, avoiding my look as she poured three glasses. Jenks made do with the drop on the mouth of the bottle. Still peeved, I settled back with my glass and watched the other guests. I wouldn't drink it because the sulfur it broke down into tended to wreak havoc with me. I'd have told Ivy, but it was none of her business. It wasn't a witch thing, just my own personal quirk that gave me headaches and made me so light sensitive that I had to hide in my room with a washcloth over my eyes. It was an oddly related lingering remnant of a childhood affliction that had me in and out of the hospital until puberty kicked in. I'd take the developed sulfur sensitivity any day in exchange for my misery as a child, weak and sickly as my body tried to kill itself.

The music had started again, and my unease at Piscary

slowly filtered away, driven out by the music and background conversations. Everyone could ignore Glenn now that Piscary had talked to us. The rattled human downed his wine as if it were water. Ivy and I exchanged glances as he refilled his glass with shaking hands. I wondered if he was going to drink until he passed out or try to tough it out sober. He took a sip of his next glass, and I smiled. He was going to split the difference.

Glenn gave Ivy a wary glance and leaned close to me. "How could you meet his eyes?" he whispered, hard to hear above the surrounding noise. "Weren't you afraid he'd bespell you?"

"The man is over three hundred years old," I said, realizing Piscary's accent was Old English. "If he wanted to bespell me, he wouldn't have to look into my eyes."

Face going sallow behind his short beard, Glenn pulled away. Leaving him to mull that around for a bit, I jerked my head to get Jenks's attention. "Jenks," I said softly. "Why don't you take a quick peek in back? Check out the employees' break room? See what's up?"

Ivy topped her glass off. "Piscary knows we're here for a reason," she said. "He'll tell us what we want to know. Jenks will only get himself caught."

The small pixy bristled. "Get Turned, Tamwood," he snarled. "Why am I here if not to sneak around? The day I can't evade a baker is the day I—" He cut his thought short. "Uh," he reiterated, "yeah. I'll be right back." Pulling a red bandanna from a back pocket, he put it around his waist like a belt. It was a pixy's version of a white flag of truce, a declaration to other pixies and fairies that he wasn't poaching should he stumble into anyone's jealously guarded territory. He buzzed off just below the ceiling, headed for the kitchen.

Ivy shook her head. "He's going to get caught."

I shrugged and edged the breadsticks closer. "They won't hurt him." Settling back, I watched the contented people enjoy themselves, thinking of Nick and how long it had been since we'd been out. I'd started on my second breadstick when a waiter appeared. Already silent, the table went expectant as he cleared away the crumbs and used plates. The man's neck from behind the blue satin shirt was a mass of scars, the newest still red-rimmed and sore looking. His smile at Ivy was a little too eager, a little too much like a puppy. I hated it, wondering what his dreams had been before he became someone's plaything.

My demon bite tingled, and my gaze roved across the crowded room to find Piscary himself bringing our food. Heads turned as he passed, drawn by the fabulous smell that had to be emanating from the elevated platter. The level of conversation notably dropped. Piscary settled the platter before us, an eager smile hovering about him, his need for his cooking skills to be recognized looking odd on someone with so much hidden power. "I call it Temere's need," he said.

"Oh my God!" Glenn said in disgust, clear over the hush. "It's got tomatoes on it!"

Ivy elbowed him in the gut hard enough to knock the wind out of him. The room went silent except for the noise filtering down from upstairs, and I stared at Glenn. "Uh, how wonderful," he wheezed.

Sparing Glenn a glance, Piscary cut it into wedges with a professional flourish. My mouth watered at the smell of melted cheese and sauce. "That smells great," I said admiringly, my earlier distrust lulled by the prospect of food. "My pizzas never come out like this."

The short man raised his thin, almost nonexistent eyebrows. "You use sauce from a jar."

I nodded, then wondered how he knew.

Ivy looked to the kitchen. "Where is Jenks? He should be here for this."

"My staff is playing with him," Piscary said lightly. "I

imagine he'll be out soon." The undead vamp slid the first piece onto Ivy's plate, then mine, then Glenn's. The FIB detective pushed his plate away with one finger in disgust. The other patrons whispered, waiting to see our reaction to Piscary's latest creation.

Ivy and I immediately picked our slices up. The smell of cheese was strong, but not enough to hide the odor of spice and tomatoes. I took a bite. My eyes closed in bliss. There was just enough tomato sauce to carry the cheese. Just enough cheese to carry the toppings. I didn't care if it had Brimstone on it, it was so good. "Oh, burn me at the stake now," I moaned, chewing. "This is absolutely wonderful."

Piscary nodded, the light shining on his shaven head. "And you, Ivy girl?"

Ivy wiped her chin free of sauce. "It's enough to come back from the dead for."

The man sighed. "I'll rest easy this sunrise."

I slowed my chewing, turning with everyone else to Glenn. He was sitting frozen between Ivy and me, his jaw clenched with a mix of determination and nausea. "Uh," he said, glancing down at the pizza. He swallowed, looking as if the nausea was winning out.

Piscary's smile vanished, and Ivy glared at him. "Eat it," she said loud enough for the entire restaurant to hear.

"And start at the point, not the crust," I warned him.

Glenn licked his lips. "It has tomatoes on it," he said, and my lips pursed. This was exactly what I had been hoping to avoid. One would think we had asked him to eat live grubs.

"Don't be an ass," Ivy said caustically. "If you really think the T4 Angel virus skipped forty tomato generations and appeared in an entirely new species for your benefit, I'll ask Piscary to bite you before we leave. That way you won't die but just turn vamp."

Glenn scanned the waiting faces, realizing he was going to have to eat some pizza if he wanted to walk out under his own power. Visibly swallowing, he awkwardly picked the slice up. His eyes screwed up and he opened his mouth. The noise from upstairs seemed loud as everyone downstairs watched, their breath held.

He took a bite, his face distorting wildly. The cheese made twin bridges from him to the pizza. He chewed twice before his eyes cracked open. His jaw slowed. He was tasting it now. His eye caught mine, and I nodded. Slowly he pulled the pizza away until the cheese separated.

"Yes?" Piscary leaned to put his expressive hands atop the table, genuinely interested in what a human thought of his cooking. Glenn was probably the first in four decades to sample it.

The man's face was slack. He swallowed. "Uh," he grunted from around a partially full mouth. "It's uh . . . good." He looked shocked. "It's really good."

The restaurant seemed to heave a sigh. Piscary straightened to all of his short height, clearly delighted as the conversations started up with a new, excited edge to them. "You're welcome here anytime, FIB officer," he said, and Glenn froze, clearly worried that he had been made.

Piscary grabbed a chair behind him and swung it around. Hunched over the table across from us, he watched us eat. "Now," he said as Glenn lifted the cheese to look at the tomato sauce under it. "You didn't come here for dinner. What can I do for you?"

Ivy set her pizza down and reached for her wine. "I'm helping Rachel find a missing person," she said, flicking her long hair needlessly back. "One of your employees."

"Trouble, Ivy girl?" Piscary asked, his resonate voice surprisingly gentle with regret.

I took a sip of wine. "That's what we want to find out, Mr. Piscary. It's Dan Smather."

Piscary's few wrinkles folded into a soft frown as he gazed at Ivy. With telltale motions so slight they were almost undetectable, she fidgeted, her eyes both worried and defiant.

My attention jerked to Glenn. He was pulling the cheese off his pizza. Appalled, I watched him gingerly pile it into a mound. "Can you tell us the last time you saw him, Mr. Piscary?" the man asked, clearly more interested in denuding his pizza than our questioning.

"Certainly." Piscary eyed Glenn, his brow furrowed as if not sure whether to be insulted or pleased as the man ate the pizza, now nothing more than bread and tomato sauce. "It was early Saturday morning after work. But Dan isn't missing. He quit."

My face went slack in surprise. It lasted for three heartbeats, then my eyes narrowed in anger. It was starting to fall together, and the puzzle was a lot smaller than I had thought. A big interview, dropping his classes, quitting his job, standing his girlfriend up at a "we have to talk" dinner. My eyes flicked to Glenn, and he gave me a brief, disgusted look as he came to the same conclusion. Dan hadn't disappeared; he had gotten a good job and ditched his small-town girlfriend.

Pushing my glass away, I fought off a feeling of depression. "He quit?" I said.

The innocuous-looking vamp looked over his shoulder to the front door as a rowdy group of young vamps swirled in and what looked like the entire wait staff flocked to them with loud calls and hugs. "Dan was one of my best drivers," he said. "I'm going to miss him. But I wish him luck. He said it was what he was going to school for." The slight man brushed the flour from the front of his apron. "Security maintenance, I think he said."

I exchanged weary looks with Glenn. Ivy straightened on the bench, her usual aloof mien looking strained. A sick feeling went through me. I didn't want to be the one to tell Sara Jane she had been dumped. Dan had gotten a career job and cut all his old ties, the cowardly sack of crap. I would have bet he had a second girlfriend on the side. He was probably hiding out at her place, letting Sara Jane think he was dead in an alley and laughing as she fed his cat.

Piscary shrugged, his entire body moving with the slight motion. "If I had known he was good at security, I might have made him a better offer, though it would be hard to give more than Mr. Kalamack. I'm just a simple restaurant owner."

At Trent's name, I started. "Kalamack?" I said. "He got a job with Trent Kalamack?"

Piscary nodded as Ivy sat stiffly on the bench, her pizza sitting untouched but for the first bite. "Yes," he said. "Apparently his girlfriend works for Mr. Kalamack, too. I believe her name is Sara? You might want to check with her if you are looking for him." His long-toothed smile went devious. "She's probably the one that got him the job, if you know what I mean."

I knew what he meant, but from the sound of it, Sara Jane hadn't. My heart pounded and I started to sweat. I knew it. Trent was the witch hunter. He lured Dan with a promise of employment and probably nacked him when Dan tried to back out, realizing what side of the law Trent worked. It was him. Damn him back to the Turn, I had known it!

"Thanks, Mr. Piscary," I said, wanting to leave so I could start cooking up some spells that night. My stomach tightened, the pleasant slurry of pizza and my gulp of wine going sour in my excitement. *Trent Kalamack*, I thought bitterly, *you are mine*.

Ivy set her empty wineglass onto the table. I met her eyes triumphantly, my pleased emotion faltering as she watched herself refill it. She never, *ever*, drank more than one glass, rightly concerned about lowered inhibitions. My thoughts went back to how she had flaked out in the kitchen after I told her I was going after Trent again.

"Rachel," Ivy said, her gaze fixed on the wine. "I know

what you're thinking. Let the FIB handle it. Or give it to the I.S."

Glenn stiffened but remained silent. The memory of her fingers around my neck made it easy for me to find a flat tone. "I'll be fine," I said.

Piscary rose, his bare head coming below the hanging light. "Come see me tomorrow, Ivy girl. We need to talk."

That same wash of fear that I saw in her yesterday swept her. Something was going on that I wasn't aware of, and it wasn't something good. Ivy and I were going to have to have a talk, too.

Piscary's shadow fell over me, and I looked up. My expression froze. He was too close, and the smell of blood overwhelmed the sharp tang of tomato sauce. His black eyes fixed to mine, something shifted, as sudden and unexpected as ice cracking.

The old vamp never touched me, but a delicious tingle raced through me as he exhaled. My eyes widened in surprise. His whisper of breath followed his thoughts through my being, backwashing into a warm wave that soaked into me like water through sand. His thoughts touched the pit of my soul and rebounded as he whispered something unheard.

My breath caught as the scar on my neck suddenly throbbed in time with my pulse. Shocked, I sat unmoving as trails of promised ecstasy raced from it. A sudden need pulled my eyes wide, and my breath came fast.

Piscary's intent gaze was knowing as I took another breath, holding it against the hunger swelling in me. I didn't want blood. I wanted him. I wanted him to pull upon my neck, to savagely pin me to the wall, to force my head back and draw the blood from me, to leave behind a swelling sensation of ecstasy that was better than sex. It beat upon my resolve, demanding I respond. I sat stiffly, unable to move, my pulse pounding.

His potent gaze flowed down my neck. I shuddered at the

sensation as my stance shifted, inviting him. The pull grew worse, tantalizingly insistent. His eyes caressed my demon bite. My eyes slipped shut at the tendrils of aching promise. If he would just touch me . . . I ached for even that. My hand crept unbidden to my neck. Abhorrence and blissful intoxication warred within me, drowned out by a hurting need.

Show me, Rachel, I felt his voice chime through me. Wrapped in the thought was compulsion. Beautiful, beautiful thoughtless compulsion. My need shifted to anticipation. I would have it all and more . . . soon. Warm and content, I traced a fingernail from my ear to my collarbone, poised on the brink of a shudder as my fingernail bumped over each and every scar. The hum of conversation was gone. We were alone, wrapped in a muzzy swirl of expectation. He had bespelled me. I didn't care. God help me; it felt so good.

"Rachel?" Ivy whispered, and I blinked.

My hand was resting against my neck. I could feel my pulse lifting rhythmically against it. The room and the loud noise snapped back into existence with a painful rush of adrenaline. Piscary was kneeling before me, one hand upon mine as he looked up. His pupil-black gaze was sharp and clear as he inhaled, tasting my breath as it flowed back through him.

"Yes," he said as I pulled my hand from his, my stomach in knots. "My Ivy girl has been most careless."

Almost panting, I stared at my knees, pushing my sudden fear down to mix with my fading craving for his touch. The demon scar on my neck gave a final pulse and faded. My held breath escaped me in soft sound. It carried a hint of longing, and I hated myself for it.

In a motion of smooth grace, he stood. I stared at him, seeing and loathing his understanding of what he had done to me. Piscary's power was so intimate and certain that the thought I could stand against it rightly never occurred to him. Beside him, Kist looked like a child, even when borrowing his master's abilities. How could I ever be afraid of Kisten again?

Glenn's eyes were wide and uncertain. I wondered if everyone knew what had happened.

Ivy's fingers gripped the stem of her empty wineglass, her knuckles white with pressure. The old vamp leaned close to her. "This isn't working, Ivy girl. You either get control of your pet or I will."

Ivy didn't answer, sitting with that same frightened, desperate expression.

Still shaking, I was in no position to remind them that I wasn't a possession.

Piscary sighed, looking like a tired father.

Jenks flitted erratically to our table with a faint whine. "What the hell am I here for?" he snarled as he landed on the salt shaker and started brushing himself off. What smelled like cheese dust sifted down to the table, and there was sauce on his wings. "I could be home in bed. Pixies sleep at night, you know. But no-o-o-o," he drawled. "I had to volunteer for baby-sitting. Rachel, give me some of your wine. Do you know how hard it is to get tomato sauce out of silk? My wife is gonna kill me."

He stopped his harangue, realizing no one was listening. He took in Ivy's distressed expression and my frightened eyes. "What the Turn is going on?" he said belligerently, and Piscary drew back from the table.

"Tomorrow," the old vamp said to Ivy. He turned to me and nodded his good-bye.

Jenks looked from me to Ivy and back again. "Did I miss something?"

Nine

"**W**here's my money, Bob?" I whispered as I dropped the stinky pellets into Ivy's bathtub. Jenks had sent his brood out to the nearest park yesterday to bring back a handful of fish food for me. The pretty fish gulped at the surface, and I washed the smell of fish oil off my hands. Fingers dripping, I looked at Ivy's perfectly arranged pink towels. After a moment of hesitation, I dried my hands, then smoothed them out so she couldn't tell I'd used one.

I spent a moment trying to arrange my hair under my leather cap, then strode out into the kitchen, boots thumping. My eyes went to the clock above the sink. Fidgeting, I went to the fridge, opening it to stare at nothing. Where the devil was Glenn?

"Rachel," Ivy muttered from her computer. "Stop. You're giving me a headache."

I shut the fridge and leaned against the counter. "He said he'd be here at one o'clock."

"So he's late," she said, one finger on the computer screen as she jotted down an address.

"An hour?" I exclaimed. "Cripes. I could have been out to the FIB and back by now."

Ivy clicked to a new page. "If he doesn't show, I'll loan you bus fare."

I turned back to the window and the garden. "That's not why I'm waiting for him," I said, even though it was.

"Yeah. Right." She clicked her pen open and shut so fast it almost hummed. "Why don't you make us some breakfast while you wait? I bought toaster waffles."

"Sure," I said, feeling a tug of guilt. I wasn't in charge of breakfast—just dinner—but seeing as we ate out last night, I felt I owed her something. The deal was, Ivy did the grocery shopping if I made supper. Originally the arrangement had been to keep me from running into assassins at the store and creating a new meaning to the phrase "cleanup in aisle three." But now, Ivy didn't want to cook and refused to rene-gotiate. Just as well. The way things were going, I wouldn't have enough for a can of Spam by week's end. And rent was due Sunday.

I opened the door to the freezer and pushed aside the half-empty cartons of ice cream to find the frozen waffles. The box hit the counter with a hard clunk. Yum, yum. Ivy gave me a raised eyebrow look when I struggled to open the damp cardboard. "So-o-o-o," she drawled as I dug my red nails into the top and tore it completely off when the handy-dandy pull-tab broke. "When are they coming to get the fish?"

My eyes darted to Mr. Fish swimming in his brandy snifter on the kitchen windowsill.

"The one in my bathtub?" she added.

"Oh!" I exclaimed, flushing. "Well . . ."

Her chair creaked as she leaned back. "Rachel, Rachel, Rachel," she lectured. "I've told you before. You have to get the money up front. *Before* the run."

Angry that she was right, I jammed two waffles into the toaster and shoved them down. They popped back up, and I smacked them down again. "It wasn't my fault," I said. "The stupid fish was never missing and no one bothered to tell me. But I'll have the rent by Monday. Promise."

"It's due Sunday."

There was a distant pounding at the front door. "There's Glenn," I said, striding out of the kitchen before she could say anything more. Boots clattering, I went down the hall and into the empty sanctuary. "Come on in, Glenn!" I shouted, voice echoing against the distant ceiling. The door remained shut, so I pushed it open, stopping short in surprise. "Nick!"

"Hey. Hi," he said, his lanky height looking awkward on the wide stoop. His long face was slack in question, and his thin eyebrows were high. Tossing his black, enviably straight bangs from his eyes, he asked, "Who's Glenn?"

A smile quirked the corners of my mouth at his hint of jealousy. "Edden's son."

Nick's face went empty, and I grinned, grabbing his arm and pulling him inside. "He's an FIB detective. We're working together."

"Oh."

The volume of emotion behind that one word was better than a year's worth of dates. Nick edged past me, his sneakers hushed on the wooden floor. His blue plaid shirt was tucked into his jeans, and I caught him before he made it to the sanctuary, pulling him back into the dark foyer. The skin about his neck almost seemed to glow in the dusk, nicely tanned and so smooth it begged for my fingers to trace the outline of his shoulders. "Where's my kiss?" I complained.

The worried look pinching his eyes vanished. Giving me a lopsided smile, he put his long hands about my waist. "Sorry," he said. "You kind of threw me there."

"Aw," I gently kidded him. "What're you worried about?"

"Mmmm." He ran his gaze down me and back up. "Plenty." Eyes almost black in the dim light, he pulled me closer, sending the smell of musty books and new electronics to fill my senses. I tilted my head up to find his lips, a warm feeling starting in my middle. *Oh yeah. This was how I liked to start my day.*

Being narrow of shoulders and somewhat spare, Nick didn't exactly fit the white-knight-on-a-horse mold. But he had saved my life by binding an attacking demon, leading me to think a brainy man could be as sexy as a muscular one. It was a thought that solidified to fact the first time Nick had gallantly asked if he could kiss me, then left me breathless and pleasantly shocked after I'd said yes.

But by saying he wasn't muscle-bound, I didn't mean Nick was a weakling. His lanky build was surprisingly strong, as I learned the time we wrestled over the last spoon of Chunky Monkey and broke Ivy's lamp. And he was athletic in a lean sort of way, his long legs able to keep up with me whenever I coerced him into driving me out to the zoo for their early open hours for runners only; those hills were killers on the calves.

Nick's strongest appeal, though, was that his relaxed, flow-with-the-punches exterior hid a wickedly quick, almost frightening mind. His thoughts jumped faster than mine, taking them places I'd never think to go. Threat brought quick, decisive action with little regard to future consequences. And he wasn't afraid of anything. It was the last that I both admired and worried about. He was a magic-using human. He should be afraid. Of a lot. And he wasn't.

But best of all, I thought as I eased myself against him, *he didn't care one whit that I wasn't human.*

His lips were soft against mine, with a comfortable familiarity. Not a hint of a beard ruined our kiss. My hands linked behind his waist and I tugged him suggestively into me. Off balance, we shifted until my back hit the wall. Our kiss broke as I felt his lips curl against mine in a smile at my forwardness.

"You are a wicked, wicked witch," he whispered. "You know that, don't you? I came over here to give you the tickets, and here you are, getting me all bothered."

His bangs were a soft whisper against my fingertips. "Yeah? You probably ought to do something about that."

"I will." His grip on me loosened. "But you're just going to have to wait." His hand ran a deliciously light path across my backside as he stepped away. "Is that a new perfume?"

Playful mood faltering, I turned away. "Yes." I had thrown my cinnamon scent out that morning. Ivy hadn't said a word upon finding the thirty-dollar-an-ounce bottle making our trash smell like Christmas. It had failed me; I hadn't the stomach to wear it again.

"Rachel . . ."

It was the beginning of a familiar argument, and I stiffened. Being in the unusual circumstances of having been raised in the Hollows, Nick knew more about vamps and their scent-triggered hungers than I did. "I'm not moving out," I said flatly.

"Could you just . . ." He hesitated, his long pianist hands moving in short, jerky motions to show his frustration as he saw my jaw clench.

"We're doing okay. I'm very careful." Guilt for having not told him she had pinned me against the kitchen wall pulled my eyes down.

He sighed, his narrow body shifting. "Here." He twisted to reach into his back pocket. "You hold the tickets. I lose everything that lays around longer than a week."

"Remind me to keep moving, then," I quipped to lighten the mood as I took them. I glanced down at the seat numbers. "Third row. Fantastic! I don't know how you do it, Nick."

He flashed his teeth in a pleased smile, the hint of cunning swelling in his eyes. He'd never tell me where he'd gotten them. Nick could find anything, and if he couldn't, he knew someone who could. I had a feeling the guarded wariness he showed to authority stemmed from here. In spite of myself, I found this as yet unexplored part of Nick deliciously daring. And as long as I didn't know for sure . . .

"Do you want some coffee?" I asked, shoving the tickets into my pocket.

Nick glanced past me into the empty sanctuary. "Ivy still here?"

I said nothing, and he read my answer in the silence. "She really does like you," I lied.

"No thanks." He shifted to the door. Ivy and Nick didn't get along. I hadn't a clue why. "I've got to get back to work. I'm on lunch break."

Disappointment slumped my shoulders. "Okay." Nick worked full-time at the museum at Eden Park, cleaning artifacts when he wasn't moonlighting at the university library, helping them catalog and move their more sensitive volumes to a more secure location. I thought it amusing that our break-in to the university's ancient-book locker was probably what prompted the move. I was sure Nick had taken the job so he could "borrow" the very tomes they were trying to safeguard. He was working both jobs until the end of the month, and I knew it left him tired.

He turned to leave, and I reached after him with a sudden thought. "Hey, you still have my largest spell pot, don't you?" We'd used it for making chili three weeks ago for a Dirty Harry marathon at his place, and I'd never brought it back.

He hesitated, his hand on the door latch. "You need it?"

"Edden is making me take a ley line class," I said, not wanting to tell him that I was working on the witch hunter murders. Not yet. I wasn't going to ruin that kiss with an argument. "I need a familiar or the witch will flunk me. That means the big spell pot."

"Oh." He was silent, and I wondered if he was going to figure it out anyway. "Sure," he said slowly. "Tonight soon enough?" When I nodded, he added, "Okay. See you then."

"Thanks, Nick. 'Bye." Pleased I had wrangled a promise to see him tonight, I pushed the door open, stopping halfway when a masculine voice called out in protest. I looked to find Glenn on the stoop, juggling three sacks of fast food and a tray of drinks.

"Glenn!" I exclaimed, reaching for the drinks. "There you are. Come on in. This is Nick, my boyfriend. Nick, this is Detective Glenn." *Nick my boyfriend. Yeah, I liked that.*

Shifting the sacks to one hand, Glenn extended his hand. "How do you do," he said formally, still outside. He was dressed in a sharp-looking gray suit, making Nick's casual clothes seem untidy. My eyebrows rose at Nick's hesitation before shaking Glenn's hand. I was positive it was because of Glenn's FIB badge. *Don't want to know. Don't want to know.*

"Nice to meet you," Nick said, then turned to me. "I'll, uh, see you tonight, Rachel."

"'Kay. 'Bye." It sounded a bit forlorn even to me, and Nick shifted from foot to foot before leaning forward to give me a kiss on the corner of my mouth. I thought it was more to prove his boyfriend status than any attempt to show affection. Whatever.

Sneakers silent, Nick hastened down the steps to his salt-rusted blue pickup at the curb. I felt a wash of worry at his hunched shoulders and stilted pace. Glenn, too, was watching, but his expression was more curious than anything else.

"Come on in," I repeated as I eyed the sacks of food and shifted the door wider.

Glenn took his sunglasses off, one hand tucking them into the inner breast pocket of his suit. With his athletic build and tidy beard, he looked like a pre-Turn Secret Service guy. "That's Nick Sparagmos?" he asked as Nick drove away. "The one who was a rat?"

My hackles rose at how he had said it, as if turning into a rat or mink was morally wrong. I put a hand on my hip, the tray of drinks tilting dangerously close to spilling ice and soda pop. Obviously his dad had told him more of the story than Glenn had let on. "You're late."

"I stopped to get us all lunch," he said stiffly. "Mind if I come in?"

I fell back, and he crossed the threshold. He hooked the door with his foot, closing it with a tug behind him. The smell of fries became overpowering in the sudden dusk in the foyer. "That's a nice little outfit," he said. "How long did it take you to paint it on?"

Affronted, I looked down at my leather pants and the red silk blouse tucked into them. Wearing leather before sunset had worried me until Ivy convinced me that the high quality of the leather I bought elevated the look from "white witch trash" to "wealthy witch class." She ought to know, but I was still sensitive to it. "This is what I wear to work," I snapped. "It saves on skin grafts if I have to run and end up sliding on pavement. Got a problem with it?"

Keeping his comments to a noncommittal grunt, he followed me to the kitchen. Ivy looked up from her map, silently taking in the burger bags and drinks. "Well," she drawled. "I see you survived the pizza. I could still have Piscary bite you if you want."

My mood lifted at Glenn's suddenly closed expression. He made an ugly noise deep in his throat, and I went to put the frozen waffles away, seeing that the toaster hadn't been plugged in. "You scarfed down that pizza fast enough last night," I said. "Admit it. You li-i-i-i-iked it."

"I ate it to stay alive." Motions sharp, he stood at the table and pulled the bags to him. Seeing a tall black man in an expensive suit and shoulder holster unpacking paper-wrapped food made an odd picture. "I went home and prayed to the porcelain god for two hours straight," he added, and Ivy and I exchanged amused looks.

Pushing her work aside, Ivy took the burger that was the

most unsquished and the fullest envelope of fries. I slouched into a chair beside Glenn. He moved to the end of the table, not even trying to make it look casual. "Thanks for breakfast," I said, eating a fry before unwrapping my burger with a rustle of paper.

He hesitated, his death grip on his FIB officer persona loosening as he undid the lowest button to his jacket and sat. "The FIB is paying for it. Actually, this is my breakfast, too. I didn't get home until the sun was almost up. You put in a long day."

His faint tone of acceptance eased my shoulders another notch. "Not really. It just starts about six hours later than yours."

Wanting ketchup for my fries, I levered myself up and went to the fridge. I hesitated in my reach for the red bottle. Ivy caught my eye, shrugging after I pointed to it. *Yeah,* I thought. He was invading our lives. He ate the pizza last night. Why should Ivy and I suffer because of him? That decided, I pulled it out and set the bottle on the table with a bold thump. Much to my disappointment, Glenn didn't notice.

"So," Ivy said, reaching across the table and taking the ketchup. "You're going to baby-sit Rachel today? Don't take her on the bus. They won't stop for her."

He glanced up, starting as Ivy laced her burger with the red sauce. "Uh." He blinked, clearly having lost his thought. His eyes were fixed upon the ketchup. "Yes. I'm going to show her what we have so far on the murders."

A smile quirked the corner of my mouth at a sudden thought. "Hey, Ivy," I said lightly. "Pass me the clotted blood."

Not missing a beat, she pushed the bottle across the table. Glenn froze. "Oh my God!" he whispered harshly, his face going sallow.

Ivy snickered, and I laughed. "Relax, Glenn," I said as I squirted ketchup over my fries. I lounged in my chair, giving him a sly look as I ate one. "It's ketchup."

"Ketchup!" He pulled his paper place mat with his food closer. "Are you insane?"

"Nearly the same stuff you were slurping last night," Ivy said.

I pushed the bottle toward him. "It won't kill you. Try some."

His eyes riveted to the red plastic, Glenn shook his head. His neck was stiff, and he pulled his food closer. "No."

"Aw, come on, Glenn," I coaxed. "Don't be a squish. I was kidding about the blood." *What's the point of having a human over if you can't jerk him around a little?*

He stayed sullen, eating his burger as if it were a chore, not an enjoyable experience. But without ketchup, it might be a job. "Look," I said persuasively as I edged closer and turned the bottle around. "Here's what's in it. Tomatoes, corn syrup, vinegar, salt . . ." I hesitated, frowning. "Hey, Ivy. Did you know they put onion and garlic powder in ketchup?"

She nodded, wiping a stray bit of ketchup off the corner of her mouth. Glenn looked interested, leaning closer to read the fine print above my freshly painted nail. "Why?" he asked. "What's wrong with onions and garlic?" He got a knowing look in his brown eyes and settled back. "Ah," he said wisely. "Garlic."

"Don't be stupid." I set the bottle down. "Garlic and onions have a lot of sulfur. So do eggs. They give me migraines."

"Mmmm," Glenn said smugly as he picked the ketchup bottle up between two fingers to read the label for himself. "What's natural flavors?"

"You don't want to know," Ivy said, her voice pitched dramatically.

Glenn set the bottle down. I couldn't help my snort of amusement.

The sound of an approaching motorcycle pulled Ivy to her feet. "That's my ride," she said, crumpling her wrapper and pushing her half-eaten carton of fries to the middle of the table. She stretched, her lanky body reaching for the ceiling. Glenn ran his attention over her, then looked away.

My gaze met Ivy's. It sounded like Kist's cycle. I wondered if this had anything to do with last night. Seeing my apprehension, Ivy grabbed her purse. "Thanks for breakfast, Glenn." She turned to me. "See you later, Rachel," she added as she breezed out.

Shoulders easing, Glenn looked at the clock above the sink, then went back to eating. I was scraping the last of the ketchup up with a fry as Ivy's demand filtered in from the street, "Go Turn yourself, Kist. I'm driving." I smiled as the bike accelerated and the street grew quiet.

Finished, I crumpled my paper into a ball and stood. Glenn wasn't done, and as I cleared the table, I left the ketchup. From the corner of my sight, I watched him eye it. "It's good on burgers, too," I said, dropping to crouch beside the island counter and pick out a spell book. There was the sound of sliding plastic. Book in hand, I turned to find he had pushed the bottle away. He wouldn't meet my eyes as I sat down at the table. "Mind if I check on something before we leave?" I asked, opening to the index.

"Go ahead."

His voice had turned cold again, and deciding it was the spell book, I sighed and leaned over the faded print. "I want to stir a spell for the Howlers to change their mind about not paying me," I said, hoping he would relax if he knew what I was doing. "I thought I might pick up what I don't have in the garden while I'm out. You don't mind an extra stop, do you?"

"No." It was marginally less cold, and I took that as a good sign. He was noisily stirring the ice with his straw, and I purposely edged closer so he could see.

"Look," I said, pointing at the blurring print. "I was right. If I want to send their pop flies foul, I need a noncontact spell." For an earth witch such as myself, noncontact meant wands. I'd never made one before, but my eyebrows rose at the ingredients. I had everything but the fern seed and the wand. *How much could a dowel of redwood cost?*

"Why do you do it?"

His voice had a touch of belligerence, and blinking, I closed the book. Disappointed, I went to put it away, turning to face him with my back against the island counter. "Make spells? It's what I do. I'm not going to hurt anyone. Not with a spell, anyway."

Glenn set his super-sized cup down. His dark fingers loosened their grip and slid away. Leaning back in his chair, he hesitated. "No," he said. "How can you live with someone like that? Ready to explode with no warning?"

"Oh." I reached for my drink. "You just caught her on a bad day. She doesn't like your dad, and she took it out on you." *And you did ask for it, dickhead.* I slurped the last of my drink and threw the cup away. "Ready?" I said as I got my bag and coat from a chair.

Glenn stood and adjusted his suit coat before crossing in front of me to throw his stuff away under the sink. "She wants something," he said. "And every time she looks at you, I see guilt. Whether she means to or not, she's going to hurt you, and she knows it."

Affronted, I gave him an up-and-down look. "She's not hunting me." Trying to keep a lid on my anger, I headed down the hallway at a fast pace.

Glenn was close his hard-soled shoes a heartbeat behind mine. "Are you telling me yesterday was the first time she attacked you?"

My lips pursed, and the thumps of my boots went all the way up my spine. There had been lots of almosts before I figured out what pushed her buttons and quit doing it.

Glenn said nothing, clearly hearing the answer in my silence. "Listen," he said as we emerged into the sanctuary, "I may have looked like the dumb human last night, but I was watching. Piscary bespelled you easier than blowing out a candle. She pulled you from him by simply saying your name. That can't be normal. And he called you her pet. Is that what you are? It sure looks like it to me."

"I'm not her pet," I said. "She knows it. I know it. Piscary can think what he wants." Shoving my arms into my coat, I pushed my way out of the church and stormed down the steps. His car was locked, and I yanked at the handle. Angry, I waited for him to unlock it. "And it's none of your business," I added.

The FIB detective was silent as he opened his door, then paused to look at me over the roof of the car. He put on his shades, hiding his eyes. "You're right. It's not my business."

The door unlocked, and I got in, slamming it to make the car shake. Glenn slid softly in behind the wheel and shut his door.

"Damn right it isn't your business," I muttered in the closeness of his car. "You heard her last night. I'm not her shadow. She wasn't lying when she said that."

"I also heard Piscary say if she didn't get control of you, he would."

A flash of real fear tightened me, unwanted and unsettling. "I'm her friend," I asserted. "All she wants is a friend that isn't after her blood. Ever think of that?"

"A pet, Rachel?" he said softly as he started the car.

I said nothing, tapping my fingers on the armrest. I wasn't Ivy's pet. And not even Piscary could make her turn me into one.

Ten

The late September afternoon sun was warm through my leather jacket as I rested my arm on the car's window. The tiny vial of salt on my charm bracelet shifted in the wind to clink against my wooden cross, and reaching out, I adjusted the side mirror to watch the traffic hanging a car length behind. It was nice to have a vehicle at my beck and call. We'd be at the FIB in fifteen minutes, not the forty it would take by bus, afternoon traffic and all. "Take a right at the next light," I said, pointing.

I watched in disbelief as Glenn drove straight through the intersection. "What the Turn is wrong with you!" I exclaimed. "I have yet to get in this car and you go where I want you to."

Glenn's expression was smug behind his sunglasses. "Shortcut." He grinned, his teeth startlingly white. It was the first real smile I had seen on him, and it took me aback.

"Sure," I said, waving a hand in the air. "Show me your shortcut." I doubted it would be faster, but I wasn't going to say anything. Not after that smile.

My head turned to follow a familiar sign on one of the passing buildings. "Hey! Stop!" I shouted, spinning halfway around in my seat. "It's a charm shop."

Glenn checked behind him and made an illegal U-turn. I

gripped the top of the window as he made another, pulling up right before the shop and parking at the curb. I opened the door and grabbed my bag. "I'll just be a minute," I said, and he nodded, moving his seat backward and leaning his head against the headrest.

Leaving him to nap, I strode into the shop. The bells above the door jingled, and I took a slow breath, feeling myself relax. I liked charm shops. This one smelled like lavender, dandelion, and the bite of chlorophyll. Bypassing the ready-made spells, I went straight to the back where the raw materials were.

"May I help you?"

I looked up from a posy of bloodroot to find a tidy, eager salesman leaning over the counter. He was a witch by the smell of him—though it was hard to tell with all the scents in there. "Yes," I said. "I'm looking for fern seed and a dowel of redwood suitable for a wand."

"Ah!" he said triumphantly. "We keep our seeds right over here."

I paralleled his path from my side of the counter to a display of amber bottles. He ran his fingers over them, bringing down one the size of my pinky and extending it. I wouldn't take it, indicating he should put it on the counter. He looked affronted as I dug about in my bag, then held an amulet over the bottle. "I assure you, ma'am," he said stiffly, "it's the highest quality."

I gave him a weak smile as the amulet glowed a faint green. "I was under a death threat this spring," I explained. "You can't blame me for being cautious."

The doorbells jingled, and I glanced back to see Glenn come in.

The salesman brightened, snapping his fingers and taking a step back. "You're Rachel. Rachel Morgan, right? I know you!" He pressed the bottle into my hands. "On the house. So glad to see you survived. What were the odds on you? Three hundred to one?"

"It was two hundred," I said, slightly offended. I watched his gaze dart over my shoulder to Glenn, his smile freezing as he realized he was human. "He's with me," I said, and the man gasped, trying to disguise it with a cough. His eyes lingered on Glenn's half-hidden weapon. *The Turn take it, I missed my cuffs.*

"The wands are over here," he said, his tone giving me clear indication he didn't approve of my choice of companions. "We store them in a desiccation box to keep them fresh."

Glenn and I followed him to a clear spot beside the cash register. The man pulled a wooden box the size of a violin case out, opened it, and turned it with a flourish so I could see.

I sighed as the sent of redwood came rolling out. My hand rose to touch them, dropping as the salesman cleared his throat. "What spell are you stirring, Ms. Morgan?" he asked, his tone going professional as he eyed me over his glasses. The rims were wood, and I'd bet my panties they were spelled to see through earth magic disguise charms.

"I want to try a noncontact spell. For . . . oh . . . breaking wood already under stress?" I said, stifling a tinge of embarrassment.

"Any of the smaller ones will do," he said, his gaze shifting between Glenn and me.

I nodded, my eyes fixed upon the pencil-size wands. "How much?"

"Nine hundred seventy-five," he said. "But to you, I'd sell it for nine."

Dollars? "You know," I said slowly, "I should make sure I have everything before I actually get the wand. No sense having it lay around and pick up moisture before I need it."

The salesman's smile turned stiff. "Of course." In one smooth motion he snapped the case closed and tucked it away.

I winced, withering inside. "How much for the fern

seed?" I asked, knowing his earlier offer had been made only because I was buying a wand.

"Five-fifty."

I had that—I thought. Head bowed, I dug about in my bag. I had known wands were expensive, but not that expensive. Money in hand, I glanced up to find Glenn eyeing a rack of stuffed rats. As the salesman rang up my purchase, Glenn leaned close and, still staring at the rats, whispered, "What are those used for?"

"I have no idea." I got my receipt and jammed everything in my bag. Trying to find a shred of dignity, I headed for the door, Glenn trailing behind. The bells jingled as we reached the pavement. Again in the sun, I took a cleansing breath. I wasn't going to spend nine hundred bucks to possibly get my five-hundred-dollar fee.

Glenn surprised me by opening the car door for me, and as I settled in the seat, he leaned against the frame of the open window. "I'll be right back," he said, and strode inside. He was out in a moment with a small white bag. I watched him cross in front of the car—wondering. Timing himself between the traffic, he opened the door and slid in behind the wheel.

"Well?" I asked as he set the package between us. "What did you get?"

Glenn started the car and pulled out into traffic. "A stuffed rat."

"Oh," I said, surprised. What the devil was he going to do with it? Even I didn't know what it was for. I was dying to ask all the way to the FIB building but managed to keep my mouth shut even as we slipped into the cold shade of their underground parking.

Glenn had a reserved spot, and my heels echoed as I found the pavement. With the pained slowness I remembered from my dad, Glenn slowly unkinked himself as he got out and tugged the sleeves of his jacket down. He reached back in for his rat and gestured to the stairs.

Still silent, I followed him into the concrete stairway. We only had to go up one flight, and he held the door for me as we went in the back door. He took his shades off as we entered, and I pushed my hair out of my eyes and under my cap. The air conditioner was on, and I looked over the small entryway thinking it was worlds away from the busy front lobby.

Glenn plucked a visitor pass from behind a cluttered desk, signing me in and giving the man on the phone a nod. I clipped it on my lapel as I followed him to the open-aired offices.

"Hi, Rose," Glenn said as he came to Edden's secretary. "Is Captain Edden available?"

Ignoring me, the older woman put a finger on the paper she was typing from and nodded. "He's in a meeting. Want me to tell him you're here?"

Glenn took my elbow and started hustling me past her. "When he gets out. No rush. Ms. Morgan and I will be here for the next few hours."

"Yes sir," she said, going back to her typing.

Hours? I thought, not liking the way he hadn't let me talk to Rose; I wanted to find out what their dress code was. The FIB couldn't have that much information. The I.S. had primary jurisdiction of the crimes.

"My office is over there," Glenn said, pointing to the bank of offices with walls and a door that lined the cubicle-divided space. The few officers at their desks looked up from their paperwork as Glenn almost pushed me forward. I was getting the distinct impression that he didn't want anyone to know I was there.

"Nice," I said sarcastically as he ushered me into his office. The off-white room was almost barren, the dirt obvious in the corners. A new computer screen sat on a nearly empty desk. It had old speakers. A nasty chair sat behind it, and I wondered if there was a decent chair in the entire building.

The desk was laminated white, but the grime embedded into it from past use made it almost gray. There was nothing in the wire trash can beside it.

"Watch the phone lines," Glenn said as he swept past me and dropped his bag-o-rat on the file cabinet. His jacket came off and he meticulously hung it on a wooden hanger which then went on a hat tree. Looking over the ugly room, I wondered what his apartment was like.

The twin phone lines from the jack behind the long table ran across the open floor to his desk. It had to be an OSHA violation having them strung like that, but if he didn't care if someone pulled his phone off the desk by tripping on it, then why should I?

"Why don't you put your desk over there?" I asked, looking at the paper-cluttered table in the logical spot for a desk.

Standing hunched over his keyboard, he looked up. "My back would be to the door, and I wouldn't be able to see the main floor."

"Oh."

There were no knickknacks of any kind—nothing of a personal nature at all—the single shelf holding only folders leaking papers. It didn't look as if he had been here long. Light rectangular shadows showed where pictures had once hung. The only thing on the walls besides his detective certificate was a dusty bulletin board with hundreds of sticky notes thumbtacked to it, hanging right over that long table. They were faded and curling, with cryptic messages only Glenn could probably decipher.

"What are these?" I asked as he checked to see that the blinds on his window overlooking the open floor were closed.

"Notes from an old case I'm working on." He had a pre-occupied tone in his voice as he edged back to his keyboard and typed in a string of letters. "Why don't you sit down?"

I stood in the middle of his office, staring at him. "Where?" I finally asked.

He looked up, reddening as he realized he was standing over the only chair. "I'll be right back." He moved around his desk, coming to an awkward halt before me until I got out of his way. His gait was stilted as he edged past me and strode out.

Thinking his office was the most inhospitable slice of FIB bureaucracy I had seen yet, I took off my hat and coat, hanging them on the nail sticking out from the back of his door. Bored, I wandered to his desk. A welcome screen with a blinking prompt waited.

A rattle preceded Glenn as he pushed a rolling swivel chair into his office. Giving me an apologetic look, he set it next to his. I dropped my bag on his barren desk and sat beside him, leaning forward to see. I watched him type in three passwords: dolphin, tulip, and Monica. Old girlfriend? I wondered. They showed up on the screen as asterisks, but he was a two-fingered typist and it wasn't hard to follow.

"Okay," he said, pulling to him a notepad with a list of names and ID numbers. I glanced at the first and looked back at the screen. With a painful slowness, he furrowed his brow and started to type them in. Tap. Pause. Tap, tap.

"Oh, just give me that," I said, pulling the keyboard close. Keys chattering happily, I typed in the first, then grabbed the mouse and clicked the All button, making the only limit to the retrieval being those entries made in the last twelve months.

A query came on the screen, and I hesitated. "Which printer?" I asked.

Glenn said nothing, and I turned to see him leaning back in his chair with his arms crossed before him. "I bet you take the remote away from your boyfriend, too," he said, pulling the keyboard back in front of him and reclaiming the mouse.

"Well it's my TV," I said hotly, then added, "Sorry." Actually, it was Ivy's. Mine was lost in the big salt dip. Which was just as well since it would have looked like a toy next to Ivy's.

Glenn made a small noise at the back of his throat. He slowly typed the next name in, checking it against the list before moving to the next. I impatiently waited. My eyes went to the crumpled bag on the file cabinet. An inane desire to take the rat out filled me. This must be why he had said we'd be here for hours. It'd be faster to cut the letters out and paste them in a note.

"That's not the same printer," I said, seeing he had switched them.

"I didn't know you wanted to look at everything," he said, his voice preoccupied as he picked letters off the keyboard. "I'm sending the rest to the basement's printer." Slowly he typed in the last string of numbers and hit Enter. "I don't want to hear about tying this floor's printer up," he added.

I fought to hide a smirk. *Didn't want to hear about it? How much could there be?*

Glenn stood, and I stared up at him. "I'll get them. Stay put till I get back."

I nodded as he left. Swiveling my chair from side to side, I waited, listening to the background chatter coming in. A smile eased over me. I hadn't realized how much I missed the camaraderie of my fellow I.S. runners. I knew if I went out of Glenn's office, the conversations would stop and the looks would go cold, but if I stayed here and listened, I could pretend someone might stop by to say hi, or ask my opinion on a tough case, or tell me a dirty joke to see me laugh.

Sighing, I rose to take Glenn's rat out of the bag. I set the ugly, beady-eyed thing on the cabinet where it could watch him. A scuffing at the door pulled me around. "Oh. Hi," I said, seeing that it wasn't Glenn.

"Ma'am." The heavy FIB officer eyed first my leather

pants, then my visitor's badge. I shifted so he could see better. The badge, not my pants.

"I'm Rachel," I said. "I'm helping Detective Glenn. He's getting some printouts."

"Rachel Morgan?" he said. "I thought you were an old hag."

My mouth opened in anger, then shut in understanding. The last time he saw me, I probably did look like an old hag. "That was a disguise," I said as I crumpled the bag and threw it away. "This is the real me."

He ran his eyes over my outfit again. "Okay." He turned to leave, and I breathed easier.

He was gone when Glenn strode in, a decidedly preoccupied air about him. There was a nice-size packet of paper in his grip, and I thought the FIB's information gathering must be on par with the I.S. after all. He stood for a moment in the center of his office, then pushed the papers on his long table against the wall to one end. "Here's the first one," he said, dropping the reports on the cleared spot. "I'll be right back with the ones from the basement."

I froze in my reach for them. *The first one?* I had thought that was all of them. I took a breath to ask him, but he was gone. The thickness of the report was impressive. I wheeled my chair to the table and positioned it sideways so I wouldn't have my back to the door. Sitting, I crossed my legs and pulled the wad of pages into my lap.

I recognized the front picture of the first victim because the I.S. had released it to the papers. She had been a nice-looking older woman with a motherly smile. By the makeup and jewelry, it looked like they lifted her photo from a professional picture, like those poses you get for anniversaries and such. She had been three months from retiring from a security firm that designed magic-resistant safes. Died from "complications from rape." This was all old news. I shuffled to the coroner's report, my gaze dropping to the picture.

My gut clenched, and I flipped the report closed. Suddenly cold, I stared out of Glenn's door to the open offices. A phone rang, and someone picked it up. I took another breath, and held it. I forced myself to breathe, holding it again so I wouldn't hyperventilate.

I suppose, in a loose fashion, it could be considered rape. The woman's insides had been pulled out from between her legs and were dangling to her knees. I wondered how long she had stayed alive through the ordeal, then wished I hadn't. Stomach turning, I vowed to not look at any more pictures.

Fingers shaking, I tried to concentrate on the report. The FIB had been surprisingly through, leaving me with only one question. Stretching, I snagged the cordless phone from the desk. My jaw hurt from having clenched it too long as I dialed the number listed for next of kin.

An older man answered. "No," I assured him when he tried to hang up on me. "I'm not a dating service. Vampiric Charms is an independent runner firm. I'm currently working with the FIB to identify the person who attacked your wife."

The picture of her lying twisted and broken on the gurney flashed before me. I shoved it down to where it would probably stay until I tried to sleep. I hoped he hadn't seen the picture. I prayed he hadn't found her body.

"I apologize for calling, Mr. Graylin," I said in my best professional voice. "I have only one question. Did your wife happen to talk to a Mr. Trent Kalamack anytime before her death?"

"The councilman?" he said, his voice thick with astonishment. "Is he a suspect?"

"Perish the thought," I lied. "I'm following up one of the faint leads that we have concerning a stalker working his way up to him."

"Oh." There was a moment of silence, then, "Yes. As a matter of fact, we did."

The zing of adrenaline pulled me upright.

"We met him at a play this spring," the man was saying. "I remember because it was the *Pirates of Penzance*, and I thought the lead pirate looked like Mr. Kalamack. We had dinner afterwards at Carew Tower and laughed about it. He's not in any danger, is he?"

"No," I said, my heart pounding. "I'd ask you to keep our line of investigation quiet until we've proven it false. I'm very sorry about your wife, Mr. Graylin. She was a lovely woman."

"Thank you. I miss her." He hung up the phone in the uncomfortable silence.

I set the phone down, waiting three heartbeats before whispering an exuberant, "Yes!" Spinning my swivel chair around, I found Glenn standing in the doorway.

"What are you doing?" he asked, dropping another stack of papers before me.

I grinned, continuing to shift back and forth in my chair. "Nothing."

He went to his desk and punched a button on the phone's cradle, frowning as the last number called appeared on the tiny screen. "I never said you could call these people." His face went angry and his posture became stiff. "That man is trying to put this behind him. He doesn't need you dredging it up for him again."

"I only asked one question." Legs crossed, I swiveled, smiling.

Glenn glanced behind him into the open offices. "You are a guest here," he said roughly. "If you can't play by my rules—" He stopped. "Why are you still smiling?"

"Mr. and Mrs. Graylin had dinner with Trent a month before she was attacked."

The man straightened to his full height and drew back a step. His eyes narrowed.

"Mind if I call the next?" I asked.

He looked at the phone beside my hand, then back to the open floor. With a forced casualness, he shut his door halfway. "Keep it down."

Pleased with myself, I pulled the stack of papers closer. Glenn went back behind his computer, typing with an annoying slowness.

My mood quickly sobered as I scanned the coroner's report, skipping the picture portion this time. Apparently the man had been eaten alive from the extremities inward. They knew he had been alive at the time by the tearing pattern of the wounds. And they were fairly confident he had been eaten by the lack of body parts.

Trying to ignore the mental picture my imagination provided, I called the contact number. There was no answer, not even a machine. I called his former place of work next, my intuition settling into a nice groove at the name of the place: Seary Security.

The woman there was very nice, but she didn't know anything, telling me that Mr. Seary's wife was away at a "health resort" trying to relearn how to sleep. She did look in her files, though, telling me that they had been contracted to install a safe on the Kalamack estate.

"Security . . ." I murmured, pinning Mr. Seary's packet to the bulletin board atop Glenn's sticky notes to get it out of my way. "Hey, Glenn. You have any more of those sticky notes?"

He rummaged in his desk drawer, tossing me a pack, shortly followed by a pen. I scrawled the name of Mr. Seary's workplace and stuck it to his report. After a moment's thought, I did the same to the woman's, writing "safe designer" on it. I added a second sticky note with "Talked to T" circled in black ink.

A scuffing in the hallway brought my eyes up from the third report. I made a noncommittal smile recognizing the overweight cop, minibag of chips in hand. He acknowledged me and Glenn's nod, coming to a rest in the doorway. "Glenn's got you doing his secretary work?" he asked, his good-old-boy tone almost thick enough to cut.

"No," I said, smiling sweetly. "Trent Kalamack is the witch hunter, and I'm just taking a moment to tie the links together."

He grunted, eyeing Glenn. Glenn wearily returned his look, adding a shrug. "Rachel," he said, "this is Officer Dunlop. Dunlop, this is Ms. Morgan."

"Charmed," I said, not offering my hand lest I get it back covered in potato-chip grease.

Not getting the hint, the man walked in, crumbs falling to the tile floor. "Whatcha got?" he said, coming to peer at my thick reports stuck to the board atop Glenn's faded sticky notes.

"Too soon to say." I pushed him out of my space with a finger in his gut. "Excuse me."

He backed up but didn't leave, going instead to see what Glenn was doing. Heaven save me from cops on break. The two talked over Glenn's suspicions concerning Dr. Anders, their rising and falling voices soothing.

I blew chip crumbs off my papers, my pulse quickening as I saw that the third victim had worked at the city racetrack in weather control. It was a very difficult field of work, heavy in ley line magic. The man had been pressed to death while working late, stirring up a fall shower to dampen down the track for the next day's race. The actual implement of death was unknown. There had been nothing in the stables heavy enough. I didn't look at that picture, either.

It had been at this point that the media realized the three deaths were connected despite the varying methods of death and named the sadistic freak the "witch hunter."

A quick phone call got me his sister, who said of course he knew Trent Kalamack. That the councilman often called her brother to ask about the state of the track, but that she hadn't heard if he had talked to Mr. Kalamack before his death or not, and that she was just sick about her brother's death, and did I know how long it took for insurance checks to come in?

I finally got my condolences wedged in between her chattering and hung up on her. Everyone handled death differently, but that was offensive.

"Did he know Mr. Kalamack?" Glenn asked.

"Yup." I pinned the packet to the board and stuck a note to it with the words "weather maintenance" on it.

"And his job is important because . . ."

"It takes a heckuva lot of ley line skill to manipulate the weather. Trent raises racehorses. He could have easily been out there and talked to him and no one would have given it a second thought." I added another note with "Knew T" on it.

Old Dunlop-the-cop made an interested noise and ambled over. He hung a respectful three feet behind me this time. "Done with this one?" he asked, fingering the first.

"For now," I said, and he pulled it from the board. Some of Glenn's notes fluttered down to fall behind the table. Glenn's jaw tightened.

Feeling like someone was starting to take me seriously, I sat straighter. The overweight man ambled back to Glenn, making noises as he found the pictures. He dropped the report onto Glenn's desk, and I heard the patter of chip crumbs. Another officer came in, and an impromptu meeting seemed to be taking shape as they clustered around Glenn's computer screen. I turned my back on them and looked at the next report.

The fourth victim had been found in early August. The papers had said the cause of death was severe blood loss. What they hadn't said was that the man had been disemboweled, torn apart as if ravaged by animals. His boss had found him in the basement of his workplace, still alive and trying to push his insides back into him where they belonged. It was more difficult than usual since he only had one arm, the other hanging by his underarm skin.

"Here you go, ma'am," a voice said at my elbow, and I jerked. Heart pounding, I stared at a young FIB officer. "Sorry," he said as he extended a sheaf of papers. "Detective Glenn asked me to bring these up when they finished. Didn't mean to startle you." His eyes dropped to the report in my hand. "Nasty, isn't it?"

"Thank you," I said, accepting the reports. My fingers were trembling as I dialed the number for the victim's boss when there was no next of kin.

"Jim's," a tired voice said after the third ring.

My greeting froze in my throat. I recognized his voice. It was the announcer at Cincinnati's illegal rat fights. Heart pounding, I hung up, missing the button the first time. I stared at the wall. The room had gone silent.

"Glenn?" I said, my throat tight. I turned to see him surrounded by three officers, all looking at me.

"Yeah?"

My hands shook as I extended the report across the small space. "Will you look at the crime scene photos for me?"

His face blank, he took it. I turned to his wall of sticky notes, listening to the pages turn. Feet shuffled. "What am I looking for?" he asked.

I swallowed hard. "Rat cages?" I asked.

"Oh my God," someone whispered. "How did she know?"

I swallowed again. I couldn't seem to stop. "Thanks."

With motions slow and deliberate, I took the report and stuck it to the bulletin board. My handwriting was shaky as I wrote "T availability" and stuck it on the pages. The report said he had been a bouncer at a dance club, but if he was one of Dr. Anders's students, he had been skilled with ley lines and was more likely the head of security at Jim's rat fights.

I reached for the fifth packet with a grim feeling. It was

Trent—I knew it was Trent—but the horror of what he had done was killing any joy I might find in it.

I felt the men behind me watching as I leafed through the report, recalling that the fifth victim, found three weeks ago, had died the same way as the first. A call to her tearful mother told me she had met Trent in a specialty bookstore last month. She remembered because her daughter had been surprised that such a young, important man was interested in collectable, pre-Turn fairy-tale anthologies. After confirming that her daughter had been employed in a security subscription firm, I gave her my condolences and hung up.

The background murmurs of the excited men added to my numb state. I carefully wrote my big T, making sure the lines were clear and straight. I stuck it beside the copy of the woman's work ID picture. She had been young, with straight blond hair to her shoulders and a pretty, oval face. Just out of college. The memory of the picture I had seen of the first woman on the gurney flashed into my mind. I felt the blood drain from me. Cold and light-headed, I stood.

The men's conversations stopped as if I had rung a bell. "Where's the ladies' room?" I whispered, my mouth dry.

"Turn left. Go to the back of the room."

I didn't have time to say thanks. Low heels clacking, I strode out of the room. I looked neither left nor right, moving faster as I saw the door at the end of the room. I hit the door at a run, reaching the toilet just in time.

Retching violently, I lost my breakfast. Tears streamed down my face, the salt mixing with the bitter taste of vomit. How could anyone do that to another person? I wasn't prepared for this. I was a witch, damn it. Not a coroner. The I.S. didn't teach its runners how to deal with this. Runners were runners, not murder investigators. They brought their tags in alive, even the dead ones.

My stomach was empty, and when the dry heaves finally stopped, I stayed where I was, sitting on the floor of the FIB bathroom with my forehead against the cold porcelain, trying not to cry. I suddenly realized someone was holding my hair out of the way, and had been for a while.

"It will go away," Rose whispered, almost to herself. "Promise. Tomorrow or the next day, you'll close your eyes and it will be gone."

I looked up. Rose dropped her hand and took a step back. Beyond the propped-open door was the row of sinks and mirrors. "Really?" I said miserably.

She smiled weakly. "That's what they say. I'm still waiting. I think they all are."

Feeling foolish, I awkwardly got to my feet and flushed the toilet. I brushed myself off, glad the FIB kept their bathroom cleaner than I kept mine. Rose had gone to a sink, giving me a moment to gather myself. I left the stall feeling embarrassed and stupid. Glenn would never let me live this down.

"Better?" Rose asked as she dried her hands, and I gave her a loose-necked nod, ready to burst into tears again because she wasn't calling me a newbie or making me feel inadequate or that I wasn't strong. "Here," she said, taking my purse from a sink and handing it to me. "I thought you might want your makeup."

I nodded again. "Thanks, Rose."

She smiled, the age lines in her face making her look even more comforting. "Don't worry about it. This is a bad one."

She turned to go, and I blurted, "How do you deal with it? How do you keep from falling apart? That— What happened to them is horrible. How can a person do that to another?"

Rose took a slow breath. "You cry, you get angry, then you do something about it."

I watched her leave, the clack of her quick heels sounding sharp before the door closed.

Yeah. I can do that.

Eleven

It took more courage than I wanted to admit to walk out of the ladies' bathroom. I wondered if everybody knew I had lost it. Rose had been unexpectedly kind and understanding, but I was sure the FIB officers would use it against me. *Pretty little witch too soft to play with the big boys?* Glenn would never look past it.

I darted a nervous glance over the open-air offices, my steps faltering as I didn't find mocking, knowing faces but empty desks. No, everyone was standing outside of Glenn's office, peering in. Loud voices were coming from inside.

"Excuse me," I murmured, holding my bag close to myself as I pushed past the uniformed FIB officers. I halted just over the threshold, finding the room full of arguing people with weapons and handcuffs.

"Morgan." The cop who had been eating chips grabbed my arm and pulled me farther in. "You all right now?"

I caught myself, stumbling at my abrupt entrance. "Yes," I said hesitantly.

"Good. I called the last one for you." Dunlop met my eyes. They were brown—and it seemed I could see right to his soul, they were so frank. "Hope you don't mind. I was dying of curiosity." He ran a hand across his mustache, wiping the grease from it as his gaze went to the six reports tacked over Glenn's notes.

My gaze swept the room. Every man and woman glanced at me as the weight of my eyes fell on them, recognizing me before going back to his or her conversation. They all knew I had spewed my guts, but by their lack of comment, it seemed I had broken the ice in some twisted fashion. Perhaps falling apart proved to them that I was just as human as they were—sort of.

Glenn was sitting at his desk with his arms crossed, saying nothing as he watched the separate arguments. He gave me a wry, eyebrow-raised look. By the sound of it, most of the room wanted to arrest Trent, but a few were too cowed by his political muscle and wanted more. There was less tension in the room than I would have expected, seeing as they were all shouting at each other. Humans appeared to enjoy doing things by loud committee.

I put my purse on the floor beside the table and sat down to look at the last report. The paper had said the latest victim had been a former Olympic swimmer. He'd died in his bathtub. Drowning. He worked for a local TV station as the celebrity weatherman but had gone to school for ley line manipulation. The note stuck to it said in a stilted print that his brother didn't know if he talked to Trent or not. I pulled the report from the board and made myself look it over, paying more attention to the conversations around me than the print.

"He's laughing at us," a street-hardened, swarthy woman said as she argued with a thin, nervous-looking officer. Everyone but Glenn and I were standing, and I felt like I was at the bottom of a well.

"Mr. Kalamack isn't the witch hunter," the man protested in a nasally voice. "He gives more to Cincinnati than Santa Claus."

"That fits the profile," Dunlop butted in. "You've seen the

reports. Whoever is doing this is certifiable. Twin lives, probably a schizophrenic."

There was a soft murmur from the surrounding officers as the arguments swirled down to just this one. For what it was worth, I agreed with Dunlop. Whoever was doing this was an itsy-bitsy-skitzy. Trent filled that description nicely.

The nervous man straightened, gaze darting about the room for support. "Okay, the murderer is mental, yes," he admitted in an irritating whine. "But I've met Mr. Kalamack. The man is no more a murderer than my mother is."

I flipped to the coroner's report, learning that our Olympic swimmer had indeed died in his bathtub, but that it had been full of witch blood. A bad feeling started to push out the horror. It takes a lot of blood to fill a bathtub. A lot more than one person has; more like two dozen. Where had it all come from? A vampire wouldn't have wasted it like that.

The discussion concerning the thin cop's mother became loud, and I wondered if I should tell them about benevolent Mr. Kalamack killing his lead geneticist and blaming it on a bee sting. Nice, neat, and tidy. Murder without hardly lifting a hand. Trent had given the widowed wife and orphaned fifteen-year-old-girl the upgraded benefits package and an anonymous, full university scholarship.

"Stop thinking with your wallet, Lewis," Dunlop said, swinging his ample middle around aggressively. "Just because the man gives to the FIB charity auction, that doesn't make him a saint. I say that makes him more suspicious. We don't even know if he's human."

Glenn flicked a glance at me. "What does that have to do with anything?"

Dunlop started, clearly remembering I was here. "Absolutely nothing!" he said loudly, as if the volume of his voice could erase the hidden, underlying racial slur. "But the man has something to hide."

I silently agreed, starting to like the overweight cop despite his lack of tact.

The officers clustered at the door looked over their shoulders into the open offices. They exchanged looks and backed up. One of them said, "Afternoon, Captain," as he ducked out of the way, and I wasn't surprised when Edden's squat bulk replaced theirs in the doorframe.

"What is going on?" he said, pushing his round-framed glasses back up his nose.

Another FIB officer made a silent farewell to me and slipped out.

"Hi, Edden," I said, not getting up from my swivel chair.

"Ms. Morgan," the short man said, a hint of anger on him as he shook my offered hand and raised his eyebrows at my leather pants. "Rose said you were here. I'm not surprised to find you in the middle of an argument." He looked at Glenn, and the tall FIB officer shrugged, not a bit apologetic as he got to his feet.

"Captain," Glenn said, taking a deep breath. "We were conducting a free-flow exercise concerning the possible alternate suspects for the witch hunter murders."

"No you weren't," Edden said, and my eyes went to his at the anger in his voice. "You were gossiping about Councilman Kalamack. He's not a suspect."

"Yes sir," Glenn agreed as Dunlop gave me an unreadable look and edged quietly out of the room, surprisingly agile for his size. "But I believe Ms. Morgan is entertaining a valid thought path."

Surprised at the support, I blinked at Glenn.

Edden didn't even look at me. "Stop the college psychobabble, Glenn. Dr. Anders is our prime suspect. You'd better have a good reason for pulling your energies from there."

"Yes sir," Glenn said, not at all upset. "Ms. Morgan has found a direct link from four of the six victims to Mr. Kalamack, and a probable window of opportunity for contact with Mr. Kalamack in the other two."

Instead of being excited as I would have expected, Edden slumped. I stood up as he came close to look at the records tacked to the wall. His tired eyes went from one to the next. The last of the FIB officers left, and I went to stand beside Glenn. With a united front, maybe he might stop wasting our time and let us go after Trent.

Feet spread wide, Edden put his hands on his hips and stared at the sticky notes tacked to the reports. I found I was holding my breath, and let it out. Unable to resist, I said, "All but the last victim used ley lines heavily in their daily work. And there's a slow progression from those highly skilled down to those just out of school and not yet using their degrees."

"I know." Edden's voice was flat. "Which is why Dr. Anders is a suspect. She is the last ley line witch of any repute left in Cincinnati actively practicing. I think she's getting rid of the competition. Especially as most of the victims were working in security related fields."

"Or Trent just hasn't gotten to her yet," I said softly. "The woman is a cacti."

Edden turned, putting his back to the reports. "Morgan, why would Trent Kalamack be killing ley line witches? He has no motive."

"He has the same motive you've given Dr. Anders," I said. "Getting rid of the competition. Maybe he offered them a job, and when they refused, he killed them? It would fit in with Sara Jane's missing boyfriend." *Not to mention what he did to me.*

Creases appeared in Edden's forehead. "Which brings up the question as to why he would let his secretary come to the FIB."

"I don't know," I said, my voice rising as I became frustrated. "Maybe the two are unrelated. Maybe she lied about him knowing she came to us. Maybe the man is crazy and wants to get caught. Maybe he's so sure we can't find our asses in the dark that he's thumbing his nose at us. He had them killed, Edden. I know it. He talked to them before they died. What more do you need!"

I was almost shouting. I knew it wouldn't get me anywhere with Edden, but this bureaucracy was part of the reason I had quit the I.S. And it rankled to find myself trying to "convince the boss" again. Head bowed and hand on his chin, Glenn took a step back, leaving me alone. I didn't care.

"It's not against the law to talk to Trent Kalamack," Edden said, his eyes level with mine. "Half the city knows him."

"You're going to ignore that he talked to every one of these people?" I protested.

His face went red behind his eyeglasses. They looked too small for his round face. "I can't accuse a councilman of phone calls and casual conversations," he said. "That's his job."

My pulse quickened. "Trent killed those people," I said softly. "And you know it."

"What you know isn't worth goose shit, Rachel. It's what I can prove. And I can't prove anything with this." He flicked a hand at the nearest report, making it flutter.

"Then search his compound," I demanded.

"Morgan!" Edden shouted, shocking me. "I won't authorize a search on the evidence that he talked to the victims. I need more."

"Then let me talk to him. I'll get it."

"God bless it!" he swore. "You want me fired, Rachel? Is that it? Do you know what will happen if I let you go through his compound and find nothing?"

"Nothing," I said.

"Wrong! I will have accused a well-respected man of

murder. He is a councilman. A benefactor of most of the charities and hospitals on both sides of the state line. The FIB will become a foul word in human and Inderland households alike. My reputation will be shot!"

Frustrated, I stood toe-to-toe with him, able to look the man right in the eye. "I didn't know you became an FIB officer to better your reputation."

Glenn shifted, making a soft sound of warning. Edden stiffened, his jaw clenching until white spots appeared on his forehead. "Rachel," he said with a soft threat, "this is an official FIB investigation, and we are going to do it *my* way. You've allowed yourself to become emotionally involved, and your judgment is compromised."

"My judgment?" I shouted. "He stuck me in a freaking cage and put me in the rat fights!"

Edden took a step closer. "I'm not," he said, pointing at me, "going to let you waltz into his office and telegraph your vendetta-based suspicions while we're gathering evidence. Even if we do question him, you will—not—be—there!"

"Edden!" I protested.

"No!" he barked, rocking me back a step. "This conversation is over."

I took a breath to tell him it wasn't over until I said so, but he had walked out. Angry, I struck out after him. "Edden," I called after his swiftly vanishing shadow. For a squat man, he moved fast. A door slammed. "Edden!"

Ignoring the watching FIB officers, I stormed through the open offices, past Rose, and to his closed door. I reached for the handle, then hesitated. It was his office; angry or not, I couldn't barge in. Frustrated, I stood outside his door and shouted, "Edden!" I tucked a strand of hair behind my ear. "You and I both know Trent Kalamack is able and willing to commit murder. If you won't let me talk to him through the FIB, then I quit!"

I took off my visitor's badge as if it meant something and threw it on Rose's desk. "You hear me? I'll go talk to him by myself."

Edden's door jerked open, and I took a step back. He stood before me, his khaki slacks creased and his plaid shirt starting to come untucked. He loomed out into the hallway, pushing me almost into Rose's desk with a stubby finger. "I told you if you came into this gunning for Mr. Kalamack, I'd sling your witch ass back across the river and into the Hollows. You made a commitment to work with Detective Glenn on this, and I'm holding you to it. But if you talk to Mr. Kalamack, I'll toss you in my own lockup for harassment."

I took a breath to protest, but my resolve faltered.

"Now get out of here," Edden almost growled. "You have a class tomorrow, and I'll deduct the tuition from your compensation if you don't go."

Thoughts of rent money intruded. Despising that money, not what was right, would be what stopped me. I glared at him. "You know he killed those people," I said tightly.

Shaking in unspent adrenaline, I walked away. I passed through the silent FIB officers at their desks on my way to the front. I'd take the bus home.

Twelve

I fell hard as Ivy cut my legs from under me. I rolled away, already aching where my hip had hit the floor. My heart pounded in time with the twin pains on the back of my calves. I tossed a strand of hair that had escaped my exercise band from my eyes. Putting a hand against the wall of the sanctuary, I used it for balance as I got to my feet. Lungs heaving, I ran the back of my hand across my forehead to wipe the sweat from me.

"Rachel," Ivy said from eight feet away. "Pay attention. I almost hurt you that time."

Almost? I shook my head to clear my vision. I had never seen her move away, she was so quick. Of course, I might not have seen her move since I was falling on my can at the time.

Ivy took three loping steps toward me. Eyes wide, I twisted my body in a tight circle to the left, sending my right foot into her midsection.

Grunting, she clutched her stomach and stumbled backward. "Ow," she complained, retreating. I hunched over, putting my hands on my knees to signal I wanted a breather. Ivy obediently moved farther away and waited, trying not to show that I had hurt her.

From my position, I glanced at her standing in a band of

green and gold afternoon sun streaming in through the sanctuary's windows. The black body stocking and soft slippers she wore when we sparred with each other made her look more predatory than usual. Her straight black hair was tied back, accentuating her tall, lean appearance. Face blank and pale, she waited for me to catch my breath so we could continue.

The practice was more for me than her. She insisted it would extend my life expectancy should I run up against a big-bad-ugly without my spells or a direction to run. I always came away from of our sparring bruised and headed for my charm cupboard. How that extended my life was beyond me. More practice making pain amulets, maybe?

Ivy had arrived home early from her afternoon with Kist, surprising me with the offer to work out. I was still seething over Edden's refusal to let me question Trent and needed to burn off some anger and so said yes. As usual, within fifteen minutes I was hurting and breathing hard while she had yet to break a sweat.

Ivy danced impatiently from foot to foot. Her eyes were a nice steady brown. I kept a close watch on her when we worked out together, not wanting to push her too close to her limits. She was fine.

"What's up?" she asked as I straightened. "You're more aggressive than usual."

I bent my leg back to stretch my leg muscle and pull the cuff of my sweatpants back down about my ankle. "Every one of the victims talked to Trent before they died," I said, stretching the truth. "Edden won't let me question him." I pulled the other leg, then nodded.

Ivy's breath quickened. I dropped to a crouch as she darted forward. Too quick for thought, I ducked her blow, sweeping my leg at her feet. Calling out, she flung herself in a backflip to avoid it, landing on her hands and then feet. I jerked back to keep her foot from hitting my jaw on the way by.

"So?" Ivy questioned softly, waiting as I stood up.

"So Trent is the murderer."

"Can you prove it?"

"Not yet." I lunged for her. She danced out of the way, jumping onto the thin windowsill. As soon as her feet landed, she pushed off, somersaulting right over me. I spun to keep her in view. Red spots of exertion were starting to show on her. She was dipping into her vamp repertoire to evade me. Encouraged, I followed up, striking with my fists and elbows.

"So quit and finish the run yourself," Ivy said between blocks and counterstrikes.

My wrists smacking into her blocks hurt, but I kept at it. "I told him . . . that's what I was going to do . . ." Strike, block, block, strike. ". . . and he threatened to lock me up for harassment. Told me I should concentrate on Dr. Anders." Pull six feet back. Pant. Sweat. *Why was I doing this again?*

A smile, real and unusual flashed across her face and was gone. "Sneaky bastard," she said. "I knew God had put him on earth to be more than a happy meal."

"Edden?" I wiped at the sweat dripping from my nose. "He's more of a big kid's meal, isn't he?" I gestured for her to come get me. Eyes glinting in amusement, she obliged, attacking with a barrage of blows ending with a strike to my solar plexus that sent me reeling.

"Your concentration is slipping," she said, breathing hard as she watched me kneel, gasping, on the floor. "You should have seen that coming."

I had, but my arm was going numb and slow from having been hit too many times. "I'm all right," I wheezed. This was the first time I'd seen her break a sweat, and I wasn't going to stop now. I shakily got to my feet and held up two fingers, then one. My hand went down, and she lunged with a supernatural quickness.

Alarmed, I blocked her vamp-quick blows, retreating off

the mats and almost into the foyer. She grabbed my arm as I reached the threshold, flinging me over her and back onto the mats. My back hit with a thump, knocking the wind from me. I felt her feet padding after me. Adrenaline surged. Still not breathing, I rolled until I hit the wall. She was hot after me, landing to pin me there.

Eyes alight, she leaned over me. "Edden is a wise man," she said between breaths, a strand of hair that had escaped her tie tickling my face. Sweat dampened her brow. "You should listen to him and leave Trent alone."

"Et tu, brute?" I wheezed. Grunting, I jerked my knee up to her groin.

She sensed it coming and fell back. I had known she was too fast to let it land, but it got her off me—which was what I'd wanted.

Ivy stood her usual eight feet back and waited for me to rise. It was slower this time. I rubbed my shoulder as I took her in, avoiding eye contact to let her know I wasn't ready.

"Not bad," she admitted. "But you didn't follow it up. Mr. Big Bad Ugly isn't going to stand aside and wait for you to regain your balance, and neither should you."

I gave her a weary look from around my red frizz of hair. Trying to keep up with her, much less best her, was hard. I'd never had to think about overcoming a vampire before since the I.S. didn't send witches to tag them. And whatever else, the I.S. took care of its own, on or off the job. Unless they wanted you dead.

"What are you going to do?" she asked as I felt my ribs through my sweatshirt.

"About Trent?" I said, breathless. "Talk to him without Edden or Glenn knowing."

Ivy's rocking motion faltered. With a warning shout, she leapt forward.

Instinct and practice saved me as I ducked. She spun in a tight circle, and I jerked out of the way. Ivy followed with a series of blows that backed me to the wall. Her voice echoed against the empty walls of the sanctuary, filling it with sound.

Shocked at her sudden ferocity, I pushed myself from the wall and fought back using every trick that she had taught me. I became angry that she wasn't even trying. With her vamp speed and strength, I was a moving target dummy.

My eyes widened as Ivy's face went savage. She was going to show me something new. Swell.

She shouted and spun. I foolishly did nothing as her foot slammed into my chest, sending me into the wall of the church.

My breath whooshed out and pain crushed my lungs. She darted away, leaving me to hang gasping. Staring at the floor, I saw the green and gold sunbeams shake as the stained-glass windows to either side of me shivered. Still not breathing, I looked up to see Ivy sauntering away. Her slow, mocking pace ticked me off.

Anger burned, giving me strength. Still having not caught my breath, I jumped her.

Ivy cried out in surprise as I landed on her back. Grinning savagely, my legs went around her waist. I grabbed a fistful of her hair and jerked her head back, sliding an arm around her throat to choke her.

Gasping, she backpedaled. I let go, knowing she was going to slam me against the wall again. I dropped to the floor, and she tripped over me. She went down. I grappled for her, catching her around the neck again. She bucked against the floor, twisting her body at an impossible angle, breaking my hold.

Heart pounding, I flipped myself to my feet, finding Ivy standing eight feet away—waiting. My exhilaration at having surprised her vanished as I realized something had shifted. She was moving from foot to foot with an unnerving, fluid grace, the first sign of her vamp background getting the better of her.

Immediately I straightened and waved my arms in surrender. "That's it," I panted. "I have to get cleaned up. I'm done. I've got to do my homework."

But instead of backing off as she always did, she started to circle. Her movements were languorously slow and her eyes were fixed to mine. My heart pounded and I spun to keep her in view. Tension laced through me, tightening my muscles one by one. She came to a halt in a sunbeam, the light glinting on her black body stocking like it was oil. Her hair was free, the black band lying between us where I had accidentally ripped it off her.

"That's the trouble with you, Rachel," she said, her soft voice echoing. "You always quit when it starts to get good. You're a tease. Nothing but a goddamned tease."

"Excuse me?" I asked, the pit of my stomach clenching. I knew exactly what she meant, and it scared the crap out of me.

Her face tightened. Forewarned, I braced myself as she lunged. I blocked her fists, driving her away with a foot aimed at her knees. "Knock it off, Ivy!" I shouted as she jerked out of my reach. "I said I'm done!"

"No you aren't." Her gray voice settled over me like silk. "I'm trying to save your life, little witch. A big bad vamp isn't going to stop because you tell him to. He's going to keep coming until he gets what he wants or you drive him away. I'm going to save your life—one way or another. You'll thank me when it's over."

She darted forward. Catching my arm, she twisted it, trying to force me to the floor. I gasped and kicked her legs from under her. We went down, my breath exploding out of me. Panicking, I pushed away and rolled to my feet.

I found her waiting her usual eight feet back—circling. A subtle heat had soaked into her movements. Her head was lowered and she was eyeing me from around her hair. Her lips were parted, and I could almost see her breath passing through them.

I backed away. Fear grew as the ring of brown around her pupils flashed to black. *Damn.*

Swallowing, I ran a hand over myself, foolishly trying to wipe her sweat off. I had known better than to jump her. I had to get her smell off me, and now. My fingers touched the demon scar on my neck, and my breath caught. It was tingling from the pheromones she was pumping into the air. *Double damn.*

"Stop, Ivy," I said, cursing the quaver that had crept into my voice. "We're done." Knowing my life hung on what happened in the next few seconds, I turned my back on her in a false show of confidence. Either I would make it to my room and its two locks or I wouldn't.

The hair on the back of my neck prickled as I paced past her. My heart pounded, and I held my breath. She did nothing as I neared the hallway, and my breath slipped out.

"No, we aren't," she whispered.

The sound of moving air pulled me around.

She attacked silently, her eyes lost in black. I fended off her blows by instinct. She wasn't even trying. Ivy caught my arm, and I cried out in pain as she spun me around, crushing my back against her. I leaned forward as if trying to break her grip. As her arms tightened and her body leaned to find our balance, I slammed my head backward into her chin.

Grunting, she dropped her grip and stumbled back. Adrenaline sang through me. She was between me and my spells. If I went for the front door, I'd never make it. This was my fault. Damn it back to the Turn, I shouldn't have jumped her. I shouldn't have become aggressive. She was driven by instinct, and I had pushed her too far.

I stood, watching her come to a swaying halt in a sunbeam. Standing sideways, she tilted her head and touched the corner of her mouth.

My stomach clenched as her fingertip came away colored

in blood. Her eyes met mine as she rubbed the blood between her fingers and smiled. I shuddered at the sight of her sharp canines. "First blood, Rachel?"

"Ivy, no!" I shouted as she lunged.

She caught me before I had moved a step. Gripping my shoulder, she flung me to the front of the church. I hit the wall where the altar had once stood, slipping down to the floor. I struggled for air as she paced to me. Everything hurt. Her eyes were black pits. Her movements were smooth with power. I tried to roll away. She caught me, yanking me up.

"Come on, witch," Ivy said gently, her black, owl-feather voice in stark contrast to her painful grip on my shoulder. "I taught you better. You're not even trying."

"I don't want to hurt you," I panted, one arm clutched around my middle.

She held me to the wall under the shadow of a long gone cross. The blood from her lip made a red jewel caught at the corner of her mouth. "You can't," she whispered.

Heart pounding, I jerked to get away, failing. "Let me go, Ivy," I panted. "You don't want to do this." A cloying scent of incense pulled the memory of her pinning me to her chair last spring. "If you do this," I said frantically, "I'll leave. You'll be alone."

She leaned close, putting the flat of her free forearm against the wall by my head. "If I do this, you won't leave." A heated smile curved over her—showing a hint of teeth— and she pressed closer. "But you could get away if you really wanted to. What do you think I've been teaching you the last three months? Do you want to get away—Rachel?"

Panic lanced deep into me. My heart beat wildly, and Ivy sucked her breath in as if I had slapped her. Fear was an aphrodisiac, and I'd just given her a jolt. Lost in the blackness of instinct and need, her muscles went tension-wire tight. "Do you want to get away, little witch?" she murmured, her breath against my demon scar sending a surge of tingling through me.

My intake of breath went to my core, seeming to turn my blood to liquid metal as it conducted a pulse through me. "Get off," I panted, the delicious feeling coursing from my neck to fill me. It was my scar. She was playing on my demon scar as Piscary had done.

She licked her lips. "Make me." She hesitated, the hard hunger shifting to something more playful and insidious. "Tell me it doesn't feel good when I do this." Breath easing from her in a sigh, she watched my eyes as her finger ran a trail from my ear, across my neck, and down my collarbone.

I almost buckled at the sensation of her nail finding the faint bumps of scar tissue, stimulating the scar back into full play. My eyes closed as I remembered that the demon had taken Ivy's face when it ripped out my throat, filling the wound with a dangerous cocktail of neurotransmitters to make pain into pleasure. "Yes," I breathed, almost moaning. "God help me. It does. Please . . . stop."

Her body shifted against mine. "I know how it feels," she said. "The hunger racing from it to fill your body, the need it stirs, until the only thought burning in you is to touch the craving to fulfill it."

"Ivy?" I whimpered. "Stop. I can't. I don't want to."

My eyes flashed open at her silence. The drop of blood at the corner of her mouth was gone. I could feel the blood pounding through me. I knew my reactions were tied to the demon scar, that she was sending out pheromones to restimulate the pseudovamp saliva that remained in me to make pain into pleasure. I knew it was one of the survival adaptations vamps relied upon to bind people to them, ensuring that they had a willing supply of blood. I knew all of this, but it was getting harder to remember. Harder to care. It wasn't sexual. It was need. Hunger. Heat.

Ivy put her forehead against the wall beside mine as if to gather her resolve. Her hair made a silk curtain between us. I felt the warmth from her through her body stocking. I couldn't move, wire-tight with fear and want, wondering if she would sate it or if I would be strong enough of will to push her away.

"You don't know what it's been like living beside you, Rachel," she said, her whisper coming from behind her hair as if from a confessional grate. "I knew you'd be frightened if you knew how vulnerable your scar makes you. You've been marked for pleasure, and unless you have a vampire to claim and protect you, they all will take advantage of it, taking what they want and passing you to the next until you're nothing but a puppet begging to be bled. I was hoping you might be able to say no. That if I taught you enough, you would be able to drive a hungry vampire away. But you can't, dear heart. The neurotoxins have soaked in too far. It's not your fault. I'm sorry. . . ."

My breath came in small pants, each one sending the promise of coming pleasure through me, flowing back to renew that which ebbed, building on those that came before. I held my breath, trying to find the will to tell her to get off me. *Oh God, I was failing.*

Ivy's voice went soft, persuasive. "Piscary said this is the only way to keep you. To keep you alive. I would be kind, Rachel. I wouldn't ask anything you didn't want to give. You wouldn't be like those pathetic shadows at Piscary's, but strong, an equal. He showed me when he bespelled you that it wouldn't hurt." Her voice went little girl soft. "The demon already broke you. The pain is over. It will never hurt again. He said you would respond, and my God, Rachel, you did. It's as if a master broke you. And you're mine."

Fear flashed through me at her hard, possessive tone. She turned her head, her hair falling back to show her face. Her black eyes were an ancient hunger, faultless in their innocence. "I saw what happened under Piscary, what you felt with no more than a finger touching your skin."

I was too frightened and enraptured by the waves of feeling coming off my neck in time with my pulse to move. "Imagine," she whispered, "what it's like when it's not your finger but my teeth—slicing clean and pure through you."

The thought sent a pulse of heat through me. I went slack in her grip, my body rebelling against my railing thoughts. Tears slipped down my face, warm on my cheeks to fall on my collarbone. I couldn't tell if they were tears of fear or need.

"Don't cry, Rachel," she said, tilting her head to brush her lips upon my neck in time with her words. I almost passed out from the ache of desire. "I didn't want it to be like this, either. But for you," she whispered, "I'd break my fast."

Her teeth grazed my neck, taunting. I heard a soft moan, shocked to realize it came from me. My body cried out for it, but my soul screamed no. The eager, pliant faces at Piscary's intruded. Lost dreams. Wasted lives. Existence turned to serve someone else's need. I tried to push her away, but failed. My will was a ribbon of cotton, falling apart with the slightest tug. "Ivy," I protested, hearing my whisper. "Wait." *I couldn't say no. But I could say wait.*

She heard, pulling away to look at me. She was lost in a haze of anticipation and rapture. Numb terror struck through me. "No," I said, panting as I fought the pheromone-induced high. *I had said it. Somehow I had said it.*

Wonder and hurt crossed her face, a breath of awareness returning to her black eyes. "No?" She sounded like a hurt child.

My eyes closed in the ripples of ecstasy that flowed from my neck as her fingernails continued to trace the scars where her lips had let off. "No . . ." I managed, feeling unreal and disconnected as I weakly tried to push her away. "No."

My eyes flashed open as her grip on my shoulder tightened. "I don't think you mean that," she snarled.

"Ivy!" I shrieked as she pulled me against her. Adrenaline scoured my veins. Pain followed it, punishing me for my defiance. Terrified, I found the strength to keep her from my neck. She pulled me with an increasing power. Her lips drew back from her teeth. My muscles began to shake. Slowly she pulled me closer. Her soul was lost from her eyes. Her hunger shone like a god. My arms trembled, ready to give out.

God save me, I thought desperately, my eyes finding the cross incorporated into the ceiling.

Ivy jerked as a metallic *bong* reverberated through the air.

She stiffened. The need in her flickered. Her eyebrows rose in bewilderment and her focus wavered. Breath held, I felt her grip slacken. Fingers slipping from me, she collapsed at my feet with a sigh.

Behind her stood Nick with my largest copper spell pot.

"Nick," I whispered, tears blurring my vision. I took a breath and reached out for him, passing out as he touched my hand.

Thirteen

It was warm and stuffy. I could smell cold coffee. Starbucks: two sugars, no cream. I opened my eyes to find a red stringy mass of my hair blocking my sight. My arm aching, I pushed it out of the way. It was quiet, with only the hushed sound of traffic and the familiar hum of Nick's alarm clock to break the stillness. I wasn't surprised to find I was in his bedroom, safe on my occasional side of the bed, facing both the window and the door. Nick's dilapidated dresser with the missing knob never looked so good.

The light slanting in past the drawn curtains was faint. I was guessing it was getting close to sunset. A glance at his clock showed 5:35. I knew it was accurate. Nick was a gadget guy, and the clock received a signal from Colorado every midnight to reset it from the atomic clock there. His watch was the same way. Why someone had to be that accurate was beyond me. I didn't even wear my wristwatch.

The gold and blue afghan Nick's mother had crocheted him was snuggled under my chin, smelling faintly of ivory soap. What I recognized as a pain amulet lay on the nightstand—right beside the finger stick. Nick thought of everything. If he could have invoked it, he would have.

I sat up looking for him, knowing by the scent of coffee that he was probably nearby. The afghan pooled about me as

I swung my feet to the floor, Muscles protesting, I reached for the amulet. My ribs hurt and my back was sore. Head bowed, I pricked my finger for the three drops of blood to invoke the charm. Even before I slipped the cord over my head, I felt myself relax in immediate relief. It was all muscle aches and bruises, nothing that wouldn't heal.

I squinted in the artificial dusk. An abandoned coffee cup pulled my eyes to a slump of clothes on the chair. It moved in a gentle rhythm, becoming Nick asleep with his long legs sprawled out before him. He was sock-footed, since he wouldn't let shoes on his carpet, and his big feet pulled a smile from me.

I sat, content to do nothing for the moment. Nick's day started six hours earlier than mine, and a faint stubble made early shadows on his long face slack in slumber. His chin rested on his chest, his short black hair falling to hide his eyes. They opened as a primitive part of him felt my gaze on him. My smile grew as he stretched in the chair, a sigh slipping from him.

"Hi, Ray-ray," he said, his voice pooling like brown puddle-warm water about my ankles. "How are you doing?"

"I'm okay." I was embarrassed that he had witnessed what happened, embarrassed he'd saved me, and heartily glad he had been there to do both.

He came to sit beside me, his weight making me slide into him. My breath made a relieved, contented sound as I fell against him. He put his arm around me and gave me a sideways squeeze. I rested my head against his shoulder, taking the scent of old books and sulfur deep into me. Slowly my heartbeat became obvious as I sat and did nothing, taking strength simply from his presence.

"Are you sure you're all right?" he asked, his hand buried deep in my hair as he held me.

I pulled away to look at him. "Yes. Thanks. Where's Ivy?"

He didn't say anything, and my face went slack in alarm. "She didn't hurt you, did she?"

His hand dropped from my hair. "She's on the floor where I left her."

"Nick!" I protested, pushing myself away from him so I could sit straight. "How could you just leave her there?" I stood, looking for my bag and realizing he hadn't brought it. I was still barefoot, too. "Take me home," I said, knowing the bus wouldn't pick me up.

Nick had risen when I did. His face flashed into alarm and his eyes dropped. "Shit," he said under his breath. "I'm sorry. I thought you said no to her." His gaze flicked to mine and away, his long face looking pained, disappointed, and red with embarrassment. "Aw, shit, shit, shit," he muttered. "I'm really sorry. Yeah. Yeah, come on. I'll get you home. Maybe she hasn't woken up yet. I'm really, really sorry. I thought you said no. Oh God. I shouldn't have interfered. I thought you said no!"

He was hunched with discomfort, and bewildered, I reached out and pulled him back before he could walk out the bedroom door. "Nick?" I said as he jerked to a halt. "I did say no."

Nick's eyes widened even farther. His lips parted and he stood there, seeming unable to even blink. "But . . . you want to go back?"

I sat on the bed and looked up at him. "Well, yeah. She's my friend." I gestured in disbelief. "I can't believe you just left her lying there!"

Nick hesitated, confusion thick in his pinched eyes. "But I saw what she tried to do," he said. "She almost bit you, and you want to go back?"

My shoulders slumped and I dropped my gaze to the stain-spotted, ugly yellow carpet. "It was my fault," I said softly. "We were sparring and I was angry." I glanced up.

"Not with her. With Edden. Then she got cocky, and it ticked me off, so I jumped her, catching her off guard . . . landed on her back, pulled her head back by her hair and breathed on her neck."

His lips pressed together, Nick lowered himself to sit on the edge of the chair and put his elbows on his knees. "Let me get this straight. You decided to spar with her while you were angry. You waited until you were both emotionally charged, and then you jumped her?" He exhaled loudly through his nose. "Are you sure you didn't *want* her to bite you?"

I made a sour face at him. "I did say it wasn't her fault." Not wanting to argue with him, I got up and moved his arms to make a spot for me in his lap. He made a surprised grunt, then curved his arms about me as I sat down. I tucked my head against his cheek and shoulder, breathing in his masculine scent. The memory of the vamp-saliva-induced euphoria flickered through me and was gone. I hadn't wanted her to bite me—I hadn't—but a niggling thought wouldn't go away that the baser, pleasure-driven side of me might have. I had known better. It hadn't been her fault. And as soon as I could convince myself of that and get out of Nick's lap, I was going to call and tell her so.

I snuggled and listened to the traffic as Nick ran a hand over my head. He seemed inordinately relieved. "Nick?" I questioned. "What would you have done if I hadn't said no?"

He took a slow breath. "Put your spell pot just inside the door and left," he said, his voice rumbling up through me.

I straightened, and he winced as my body weight shifted against him. "You would have let her tear out my throat?"

He wouldn't meet my eyes. "Ivy wouldn't have drained you and left you for dead," he said reluctantly. "Even in the frenzy you had her whipped up to. I heard what she offered you. That was no one night stand. It was a life commitment."

My demon scar tingled at his words, and frightened, I

pushed the feeling away. "Just how long were you standing there?" I asked, going cold with the thought that the nightmare might have been far more than Ivy simply losing control.

His grip around me tightened as his eyes failed to reach mine. "Long enough to hear her ask to make you her scion. I wasn't going to stand in your way if it was something you wanted."

My mouth dropped open and I pulled my arm from around behind him. "You would have walked away and let her make me into a plaything?"

A flash of anger flickered in his brown eyes. "A scion, Rachel. Not a shadow or plaything, or even a thrall. There's a world of difference."

"You would have walked away?" I exclaimed, not willing to get out of his lap for fear pride might make me leave his apartment. "You would have done nothing?"

His jaw clenched but he made no move to dump me onto the floor. "I am not the one living in a church with a vamp!" he said. "I don't know what you want. I can only go on what you tell me and what I see. You live with her. You date me. What am I supposed to think?"

I said nothing, and he added in a softer voice, "What Ivy wants is not wrong or unusual, it's a cold, scary fact. She's going to need a trustworthy scion in about forty years or so, and she likes you. To tell you the truth, it's a damn fine offer. But you had better make up your mind as to what you want before time and vamp pheromones make it for you." His voice grew halting, reluctant. "You wouldn't be a plaything. Not with Ivy. And you would be safe with her, untouchable by just about every nasty thing Cincinnati has."

Gaze distant, my thoughts lit on small, seemingly unrelated instances of friction between Ivy and Nick, seeing them in a new light. "She's been hunting me all this time," I whispered, feeling the first hints of real fear.

The wrinkles around Nick's eyes creased. "No. It's not just blood she's after, though an exchange is involved. But I have to be honest. You complement each other like no vamp and scion pair I've seen." A flicker of unknown emotion swelled and died within his eyes. "It's a chance at greatness—if you're willing to give up your dreams and bind yourself to hers. You would always be second. But you would be second to a vamp slated to rule Cincinnati."

Nick's hand ceased its motion over my hair. "If I made a mistake," he said carefully, not looking at me, "and you want to be her scion, then fine. I'll drive you and your toothbrush home and walk away, letting you two finish what I interrupted." His hand began moving again. "My only regret will be that I wasn't enough to lure you away from her."

My eyes drifted across Nick's hodgepodge of furniture, hearing the busy traffic outside his apartment. It was so unlike Ivy's church with its wide open spaces and breathing room. All I had wanted was to be her friend. She desperately needed one, unhappy with herself and wanting to be something more, something clean and pure, something untouched and unsullied. She was trying so hard to escape her vampiric existence, and I knew she harbored a belief that someday I might find a spell to help her. I couldn't leave and destroy the one thing that kept her going. God save me if I was a fool, but I admired her indomitable will and belief that someday she'd find what she sought.

Despite the potential threat she posed, her asinine demands for organization, and her strict adherence to structure, she was the first person I'd roomed with who said nothing about my mind-slips, like draining the water heater or neglecting to turn off the heat before opening the windows. I'd lost too many friends over such petty arguments. I didn't want to be alone anymore. The scary thing was that Nick was right. We did do well together.

And now I had a new fear. I hadn't realized the threat of

my vamp scar until she told me. Marked for pleasure and un-claimed. Passed from vampire to vampire until I begged to be bled. Remembering the waves of euphoria and how hard it had been to say no, I saw how easy Ivy's prediction could turn real. Though she hadn't bitten me, I was sure the word on the streets was that I was taken goods and to back off. *Damn. How did I get to this place?*

"Do you want me to take you back?" Nick whispered, pulling me close.

I shifted my shoulder to mold myself into him. If I was smart, I'd ask his help in moving my stuff out of the church tonight, but what came out of my mouth was a small, "Not yet. I'll call to make sure she's all right, though. I'm not go-ing to be her scion, but I can't leave her to be alone. I said no, and I think she'll respect that."

"What if she doesn't?"

I tucked in closer. "I don't know. . . . Maybe I'll put a bell on her."

He chuckled, but I thought I heard a trace of pain in it. I felt his amusement fade. His chest shifted my head as he breathed. What happened had scared me more than I wanted to admit. "You aren't under a death threat anymore," he whispered. "Why don't you leave?"

I didn't move, hearing his heartbeat. "I don't have the money," I protested softly. We'd been over this before.

"I told you that you can move in with me."

I smiled, though he couldn't see it, my cheek scraping against his cotton shirt. His apartment was small, but that wasn't why I had always kept our sleepovers to the week-ends. He had his own life, and I would get in his way if he had to take me in more than small doses. "It would last for a week, and then we would hate each other," I said, knowing from experience it was true. "And I'm the only thing keep-ing her from falling back into being a practicing vamp."

"So let her fall. She's a vampire."

I sighed, not finding the strength to get angry. "She doesn't want to be. I'll be more careful. It'll be all right." I put a confident, persuasive tone in my voice, but was left wondering if I was trying to convince him or me.

"Rachel . . ." Nick breathed, his breath shifting the hair atop my head. I waited, almost able to hear him trying to decide whether he should say anything more. "The longer you stay," he said reluctantly, "the harder it's going to be to resist the vamp-induced euphoria. That demon that attacked you last spring pumped more vamp saliva into you than a master vampire. If witches could be turned, you'd be one by now. As it is, I think Ivy could bespell you simply by saying your name. And she's not even dead yet. You're making unsafe rationalizations for staying in an unsafe situation. If you think you will ever want to leave, you should go now. Believe me, I know how good a vampire scar feels when a vamp's need kicks in. I know how deep the lie goes, and how strong the lure."

I sat up, my hand going to cover my neck. "You know?"

His eyes went sheepish. "I went to high school in the Hollows. You don't think I got through that without being bitten at least once?"

My brow rose at his almost guilty look. "You have a vamp bite? Where?"

He wouldn't meet my eyes. "It was a summer fling. And she wasn't dead so I didn't contract the vamp virus. There wasn't much saliva in it to begin with, so it stays pretty quiet unless I get in a situation where there are a lot of vampire pheromones. It's a trap. You know that, don't you?"

I slumped back into him, nodding. Nick was safe. His scar was old and made by a living vampire barely out of adolescence. Mine was new and laced with so much neurotoxin that Piscary could set it into play with just the weight of his eyes. Nick went still, and I wondered if his scar had flamed to life when he'd walked into the church. It might explain why he had said nothing and simply watched. How good had his scar felt? I wondered, unable to blame him.

"Where is it?" I asked slowly. "Your vamp scar?"

Nick jiggled me farther up onto his lap. "Never mind that—witch," he said playfully.

I suddenly became very aware of him pressing up against me, his arms draped around me to keep me from falling off. I glanced at the clock. I had to go to my mom's and get my old ley line stuff before I could do my homework. If I didn't do it tonight, it wouldn't get done. My gaze tilted to Nick's, and he smiled. He knew why I was looking at the clock.

"Is this it?" I asked. Shifting on his lap, I pulled the collar of his shirt aside to show a faint white scar on his upper shoulder from a deep scratch.

He grinned. "I don't know."

"Mmmm," I said. "Bet I could tell." As he laced his hands to cradle me about the hips, I undid the top button of his shirt. The angle was awkward, and I shifted to straddle his lap, my knees to either side of him. His hands moved to hold me a trifle lower, and arching my eyebrows at our new position, I leaned closer. My fingers went behind his neck and I nuzzled aside his collar to set my lips against the scar, leaving it with an audible pop.

Nick took a noisy breath, shifting under me into more of a slouch so he wouldn't have to hold me from falling. "That's not it," he said. His hand went to my back, tracing a trail down my spine, bumping as he found the waistband of my sweats.

"Okay," I murmured as his fingers tugged the hem of my sweatshirt. He reached up under it, his fingertips making a long tingle across my skin. "I know it isn't this one." Bending over him, I let my hair fall about his chest as I flicked my tongue against first one then the second puncture mark I had given him when I'd been a mink and thought he was a rat trying to kill me. He said nothing, and I carefully worried the three-month-old scar with gentle teeth.

"No," he said, his voice suddenly strained. "You gave me those."

"That's right," I breathed, my lips grazing his neck as I steadily worked my way to his ear with little hop-kisses. "Hmmm . . ." I breathed. "I guess I'll have to do some investigating. You are aware, Mr. Sparagmos, that I am professionally trained in the field of investigation?"

He said nothing, his free hand making a delicious sensation as he traced a path along the small of my back, testing.

I pulled back, and his hands followed the curves of my waist under my sweatshirt with an increasing pressure. I was glad it was near dark. So still and warm. An eager anticipation was in his gaze, and leaning forward to brush the tips of my hair over his face, I whispered, "Close your eyes."

His entire body shifted as he sighed, doing as I asked.

Nick's touch became more insistent, and I settled my forehead into the crook between his neck and shoulder. Eyes closed, I felt for the buttons on his shirt, enjoying the rising feeling of expectation as each one gave way. I struggled with the last, tugging his shirt out from his jeans.

His hands fell from me and he twisted to pull his shirt free. I tilted my head and gently bit his earlobe. "Don't you dare help," I whispered, his lobe still between my teeth. I shivered as he resumed his touch, his hands warm against my back. All the buttons were undone, and I ran my lips across the faint notches rimming his ear.

With a quick motion he reached up, pulling my face to his. His lips were demanding. A soft sound urged me to respond. *Had it been him or me? Don't know. Don't care.* One hand was buried deep in my hair, holding me to him as his lips and tongue explored. His motions grew aggressive, and

I pushed him back into the chair, liking his rough touch. He hit the slats with a thump, pulling me down with him.

His stubble was prickly, and lips still on mine, he reached around, pulling me close. With a grunt of effort, he lurched to his feet, carrying me. My legs wrapped around him as he moved us to the bed. My lips felt cold as he pulled away, setting me down gently. His arms slipped from me as he knelt over me.

I looked up at him, his shirt still on, but open to show lean muscles running down to disappear beneath his waistband. I had tossed one of my arms artfully over my head, and I reached up with the other to draw a line from his chest downward, tugging at his jeans.

Button fly, I thought in a wash of impatience. God help me. I hated button fly. His dusky smile faltered and he almost shuddered as I gave up for a moment and reached behind him, tracing the curve of his back, following it as far as I could reach. It wasn't nearly far enough, and I pulled him down toward me. Slumping forward, Nick supported himself on the flat of a forearm. A sigh escaped me as I got my hands to where I wanted them to be.

Warm, and with the delightful mix of gentle pressure and rough skin, Nick sent his hand searching under my shirt. I ran my hand over his shoulders, feeling his muscles bunch and ease. He scooted lower, and I gasped in surprised as he nuzzled my midriff, his teeth searching for the hem of my sweatshirt.

My breath came faster, and a whispered pant of anticipation slipped from me as he tugged my shirt upward, his hands pushing against my waist. Hasty with a sudden need, I dropped my hands from fumbling at his button fly to help him get my shirt off. It scraped my nose in passing, taking my amulet with it. My held breath slipped out in a sound of relief. Nick's teeth were a teasing hint as he tugged at my tight-fitting exercise bra. I shuddered, arching my upper back in encouragement.

He buried his face at the base of my neck. My demon scar, running from my collarbone to my ear, gave a knife-edged pulse of feeling, and I froze into a frightened wariness. It had never done that before when I'd been with Nick. I didn't know whether to enjoy it or lump the feeling in with the terror of the scar's origin.

Sensing my sudden fear, Nick slowed, his body nudging mine once, twice, then halting. In a slow stillness, he brushed my scar with his lips. I couldn't move as waves of promise raced through me, settling low and insistent in my body. My heart pounded as I compared it to Ivy's vamp-pheromone induced ecstasy and found it identical. It felt too good to dismiss out of hand.

Nick hesitated, his breath harsh in my ear. Slowly the feeling ebbed. "Should I stop?" he whispered, his voice husky with need.

I closed my eyes, reaching downward to work almost frantically at his button fly. "No," I moaned. "It almost hurts. Be—careful."

His breath came in a quick sound, matching mine. More insistent, he ran a hand under my bra and made soft kisses against my scarred neck. An unhelped sound escaped me as I got the last of his buttons undone.

Nick's lips ghosted up the underside of my chin and found my mouth. His touch was gentle, and I lunged my tongue deep into him. He pushed back, his stubble harsh. Our breath came in tandem. His continuing gentle fingers on my neck sent a sudden spasm through me.

I traced my hands down his open shirt to find his jeans. Breath fast, I pushed his clothes down to where I could hook my foot into them and push them all the way off. Hungry for him, I sent my hands searching, stretching to find what I wanted.

Nick's breath caught as I grasped him, feeling the tight, smooth skin between my fingers and thumb. His head dropped from mine, burying it between my breasts, nuzzling, as my bra had somehow disappeared.

He pushed his hips against me, hinting, and I pushed pack. My heart pounded. Strong and insistent, my scar sent waves through me, though Nick's searching lips were nowhere near it.

I abandoned myself to the demon scar, letting the feeling flow through me. I'd figure out later if it was wrong or not. My hands quickened their motion against him, feeling the difference between him and a male witch, finding it roused me further. Leaving one hand to caress him, I grasped the hand not supporting his weight over me and led him to the drawstring on my sweats.

He snatched my wrist, pinning it up over my head on the pillow, refusing to accept my help. A jolt struck through me. He nipped at my neck and darted away, the barest hint of teeth bringing a gasp from me. Nick's hands tugged at my waistband, pulling my sweats and underwear off in a fierce need. I arched my back to help free them from my hips, and a heavy hand pinned my shoulder to the bed.

I opened my eyes, and Nick leaned over me and breathed, "My job, witch." But my sweats were gone.

I reached downward for him, and he shifted his weight, nudging his knee against the inside of my thigh. Again I arched my lower back, reaching, straining to find him. He fell to cover me. His lips on mine, we begin to move against each other.

Slowly, almost tauntingly, he moved inside of me. I clutched at his shoulders, racked with tingling jolts as his lips found my neck.

"My wrist," he panted in my ear. "Oh God, Rachel. She bit my wrist."

The surges of feeling came in time with our bodies'

rhythm as I hungrily found his wrist. He moaned as I fastened on it. I grazed my teeth across it, sucking hungrily as he did the same on my neck. The ache rose in me, and out of my mind in need, I bit Nick's old scar, making it mine, trying to take it away from the one who first marked him.

Pain shot through my neck, and I cried out. Nick hesitated, then again pinched a fold of scarred skin between his teeth. I did the same with his wrist to tell him it was all right. Silent with a desperate need, his mouth lunged hungrily into me. Want crept up from within. I felt it swell. I seduced it closer, willing it to happen. *Now,* I thought, almost crying. *Oh God. Make it now.*

Together Nick and I shuddered, our bodies responding as one as a wave of euphoria washed from me into him. It rebounded, striking me with twofold strength. I gasped, clutching at him. He groaned as if in pain. Again the wave took us, pulling us back. Poised, we hung at the point of climax, trying to hold it forever.

Slowly it ebbed, jolts of dying pleasure sending tremors through us both as the tension eased from us in stages. Nick's weight gradually pressed down atop me. His breath was rough in my ear. Exhausted, I made a conscious effort to unkink my hands from his shoulder. The imprints of my fingers made red lines on his skin.

I lay for a moment, feeling a dying tingle from my neck. Then it was gone. I ran my tongue along the inside of my teeth. No blood. I hadn't broken his skin. *Thank God.*

Still atop me, Nick shifted his weight so I could breathe easier. "Rachel?" he whispered. "I think you almost killed me."

Breath slowing, I said nothing, thinking I could forego my three-mile run today. My heartbeat eased, filling me with a relaxed lassitude. I pulled his wrist close, eyeing the old scar showing a stark white against the red, roughened skin. I felt a twinge of embarrassment to see I had given him a hickey. No guilt, though, for having marked him. He'd probably known what would happen better than I had, and my neck was undoubtedly in a similar state.

Did I care? Not right now. Maybe later when my mom spotted it.

I gave his tender skin a kiss and set his arm down. "Why did it feel like one of us was a vampire?" I asked. "My demon scar was never that sensitive before. And you?" I left my sentence unfinished. I had nibbled a good share of his body over the last two months and never provoked such a response in him. Not that I was complaining.

Looking exhausted, he eased himself off me and fell groaning on the bed. "Must have been from Ivy getting things started," he said, his eyes closed as he faced the ceiling. "I'm going to be sore tomorrow."

I grabbed the afghan and pulled it to cover me, cold now without his body heat. Shifting to my side, I leaned close and whispered, "Sure you want me to move out of the church? I think I'm beginning to see why threesomes are so popular in the vamp circles."

Nick's eyes opened as he grunted. "You are trying to kill me, aren't you?"

Chuckling, I stood, wrapping the afghan around me. My fingers touched my neck to find the skin sore but unbroken. I wouldn't say it had been wrong to take advantage of the sensitivities Ivy set into play, but the vehement need of it had me concerned. Almost too exquisitely intense to control . . . No wonder Ivy had such a hard time.

Thoughts slow and speculative, I dug about in the bottom drawer of Nick's dresser for one of his old shirts and made my way to his shower.

Fourteen

"Hello." Nick's recorded voice came from my answering machine, sounding smooth and polished. "You've reached Morgan, Tamwood, and Jenks of Vampiric Charms, independent runners. They are currently unavailable. Please leave a message and let us know if you would prefer a daylight or evening return call."

I gripped the black plastic of Nick's phone tighter and waited for the beep. Having Nick leave the outgoing message on our machine had been my idea. I liked his voice, and I thought it very posh and professional for us to appear to have a man as a receptionist. 'Course, that all went out the window when they saw the church.

"Ivy?" I said, wincing at the guilt I could hear in my voice. "Pick up if you're there."

Nick walked past me from the kitchen, his hand trailing across my waist as he went into his living room.

The phone remained silent, and I rushed to fill the gap before the machine clicked off. "Hey, I'm at Nick's. Um . . . about earlier. Sorry. It was my fault." I glanced at Nick doing the "bachelor tidy shuffle" as he swooped about, shoving things out of sight under the couch and behind cushions. "Nick says he's sorry for hitting you."

"I do not," he said, and I covered the receiver thinking her vamp hearing might catch it.

"Hey, umm," I continued, "I'm going to my mom's to pick up some stuff, but I'll be back around ten. If you get home before me, why don't you pull the lasagna out and we'll have that tonight. We can eat around midnight? Make it an early dinner so I can get my homework done?" I hesitated, wanting to say more. "Well, I hope you get this," I finished lamely. " 'Bye."

I clicked the phone off and turned to Nick. "What if she's still knocked out?"

His eyes tightened. "I didn't hit her that hard."

I slumped to lean against the wall. It was painted an icky brown and didn't go with anything else. Nothing in Nick's apartment went with anything else, so it kind of fit—in a warped sort of way. It wasn't that Nick didn't care about continuity, but that he looked at things differently. The time I found him wearing a blue sock with a black, he had blinked at me and said they were the same thickness.

His books, too, weren't cataloged alphabetically—his oldest tomes had no title or author—but by some ranking system I had yet to figure out. They lined an entire wall of his living room, giving me the eerie feeling of being watched whenever I was there. He had tried to get me to store them in my closet for him after his mother dumped them on his doorstep early one morning. I'd kissed him soundly and refused. They creeped me out.

Nick leaned into the kitchen and grabbed his keys. The sliding sound of metal pulled me from the wall and to the door. I glanced over my outfit before following him into the hall: blue jeans, tucked-in black cotton T, and the flip-flops I used when we swam in his apartment's pool. I had left them last month and found them washed and hung up in Nick's closet.

"I don't have my bag," I muttered as he gave the door a firm tug to lock it.

"You want to stop at the church on the way?"

His offer didn't sound genuine, and I hesitated. We'd have to cross half of the Hollows to get there. It was after sundown. The streets were getting busy, and it would take forever. There wasn't much in my bag in terms of money, and I wouldn't need my charms—I was only going to my mom's—but the thought of Ivy flat out on the floor was intolerable. "Could we?"

He took a slow breath, and with his long face twisted into a stilted expression, he nodded.

I knew he didn't want to, and the bother of that made me almost miss the step out of the apartment house and onto the dark parking lot. It was cold. There wasn't a cloud in the sky, but the stars were lost behind the city lights. My feet felt drafty in their flip-flops, and when I clutched my arms about myself, Nick handed me his coat. I shrugged into it, my anger at his reluctance to check on Ivy easing at the warmth and lingering smell of him on the thick fabric.

A faint whine came from a street lamp. My dad would have called it a thief light. Just enough illumination to let a thief know what he was doing. The sound of our feet was loud, and Nick reached for my door. "I'll get it," he said gallantly, and I smirked as he fought with the handle, grunting as he gave it a final yank and the latch released.

Nick had been working his new job for only three months but somehow managed to get a beat-up blue Ford truck already. I liked it. It was big and ugly, which was why he had gotten it so cheap. He said it was the only thing they had on the lot that didn't scrunch his legs up to his chin. The clear coat was peeling and the tailgate was rusting out, but it was transportation.

I lurched up and in, putting my feet squarely on the offensive floor mat from the previous owner as Nick slammed the door shut. The truck shook, but it was the only way to be sure the door wouldn't fly open when we went across rail-road tracks.

As I waited for Nick to come around the back, a flickering shadow over the hood caught my eye. I leaned forward, squinting. Something almost smacked the window, and I jumped.

"Jenks!" I exclaimed, recognizing him. The glass between us did nothing to hide his agitation. His wings were a gos-samer blur, shimmering in the street lamp as he frowned. A floppy, wide-brimmed red hat looking gray in the uncertain light was on his head, and his hands were on his hips. My guilty thoughts flashed to Ivy, and I rolled the window down, pushing it along when it got stuck halfway. He darted inside and took off his hat.

"When the hell are you two going to get a speaker phone?" he snarled. "I belong to this crappy firm as much as you, and I can't use the phone!"

He had come from the church? I didn't know he could move that fast.

"What did you do to Ivy?" he continued as Nick silently got in and shut his door. "I spend the afternoon with Glenda the Good trying to calm him down after you yelled at his dad, then I come home to find Ivy having hysterics on the bathroom floor."

"Is she all right?" I asked, then looked at Nick. "Get me home."

Nick started the truck, jerking back as Jenks landed on the gearshift. "She's fine—as much as she ever is," Jenks said, his anger shifting to worry. "Don't go back yet."

"Get off that," I said, flicking a hand under him.

Jenks flitted up, then down, staring at Nick until the man put his hands back on the wheel. "No," the pixy said. "I mean it. Give her some time. She heard your message and is calming down." Jenks flew to sit on the dash before me.

"Man, what did you do to her? She was going on and on about not being able to protect you, and that Piscary was going to be angry with her, and she didn't know what she was going to do if you left." His tiny features grew worried. "Rache? Maybe you should move out. This is too weird, even for you."

I felt cold at the undead vampire's name. Maybe I hadn't pushed her too far; maybe Piscary had put her up to it. We would've been fine had she quit when I first said to. He'd probably figured out that Ivy wasn't the dominant one in our odd relationship and wanted her to rectify the situation, the little prick. It wasn't his business.

Nick put the car in gear, and the tires cracked and popped against the gravel lot. "Church?" he questioned.

I glanced at Jenks, and he shook his head. It was the wisp of fear on him that decided it for me. "No," I said. I'd wait. Give her time to collect herself.

Nick seemed as relieved as Jenks. We pulled out into traffic, headed for the bridge.

"Good," Jenks said. Eyeing my lack of earrings, he vaulted up to sit on the rearview mirror. "What the hell happened, anyway?"

I rolled my window back up, feeling the coldness of the coming night in the damp breeze. "I pushed her too far while we were working out. She tried to make me her—uh—tried to bite me. Nick knocked her out with my spell pot."

"She tried to bite you?"

I looked from the passing night to Jenks, seeing in the light from the car behind us his wings go still, then blur to nothing and go still again. Jenks looked from Nick's embarrassed face to my worried one. "Ohhh," he said, his eyes widening. "Now I get it. She wanted to bind you to her so only *she* could make your vamp scar resonate to vamp pheromones. You turned her down. My God, she must be embarrassed. No wonder she's upset."

"Jenks, shut up," I said, stifling the urge to grab him and toss him out the window. He would only catch up at the first red light.

The pixy flitted to Nick's shoulder, eyeing the lights glowing on the dash. "Nice truck."

"Thanks."

"Stock?"

Nick's gaze slid from the taillights of the car ahead to Jenks. "Modified."

Jenks's wings blurred, then steadied. "What's your top end?"

"One fifty with NOS."

"Damn!" the pixy swore admiringly as he flew back to the rearview mirror. "Check your lines. I smell a leak."

Nick's eyes darted to a grimy, obviously not factory-installed lever under the dash before returning to the road. "Thanks. I wondered." Slowly he rolled his window down a crack.

"No problem."

I opened my mouth to ask, then closed it. Must be a guy thing.

"So-o-o-o-o," Jenks drawled. "We going to your mom's?"

I nodded. "Yeah. Want to come?"

He rose an inch as we hit a pothole, hovering cross-legged. "Sure. Thanks. Her Rose of Sharon is probably still blooming. Think she'd mind if I took some of the pollen home?"

"Why don't you ask her?"

"I will." A grin came over him. "You'd better put some makeup on that love bite."

"Jenks!" I exclaimed, my hand going to cover my neck. I had forgotten. My face warmed as Jenks and Nick exchanged looks in some asinine macho thing. God help me, I felt as if I was back in the cave. *Me mark woman so Glurg keep his furry hands off her.*

"Nick," I pleaded, keenly feeling the lack of my bag. "Can I borrow some money? I have to stop at a charm shop."

But the only thing more embarrassing than buying a complexion spell is buying one with a hickey on your neck. Especially when most of the shop owners knew me. So I opted for autonomy and asked Nick to stop at a gas station. Of course, the spell rack by the register was empty, so I ended up plastering my neck with conventional makeup. Covergirl? Don't you believe it. Nick said it looked all right but Jenks laughed his wings red. He sat on Nick's shoulder and chatted about the attributes of the pixy girls he had known before meeting Matalina, his wife. The randy pixy kept it up all the way to the outskirts of Cincinnati where my mom lived while I tried to touch up my makeup in the visor's mirror.

"Left down that street," I said, wiping my fingers off on each other. "It's the third house on the right."

Nick said nothing as he pulled to the curb in front of my house. The porch light was on for us, and I swear I saw the curtain flutter. I hadn't been there for a few weeks, and the tree I'd planted with my dad's ashes was turning. The spreading maple was almost shading the garage in the twelve years it had been in the ground.

Jenks had already buzzed out Nick's open door, and as Nick leaned to get out, I reached for his arm. "Nick?" I questioned. He paused at the worried tone in my voice, easing back against the age-worn vinyl as I drew my hand away and looked at my knees. "Um, I want to apologize for my mom—before you meet her," I blurted.

He smiled, his long face going soft. He leaned across the front seat and gave me a quick kiss. "Moms are terrible, aren't they?" He got out, and I waited impatiently until he came around and jerked my door open for me.

"Nick?" I said as he took my hand and we started up the walk. "I mean it. She's a little whacked. My dad's death really threw her. She's not a psychopath or anything, but she doesn't think about what she's saying. If it comes into her head, it comes out her mouth."

His pinched expression eased. "Is that why I haven't met her yet? I thought it was me."

"You?" I questioned, then winced inside. "Oh. The human/witch thing?" I said softly, so he wouldn't have to. "No." Actually, I had forgotten about that. Suddenly nervous, I checked my hair and felt for my missing bag. My toes were cold, and the flip-flops were loud and awkward on the cement steps. Jenks was hovering beside the porch light, looking like a huge moth. I rang the bell and stood beside Nick. *Please make it one of her good days.*

"I'm glad it wasn't me," Nick said.

"Yeah," Jenks said as he landed on my shoulder. "Your mom ought to meet him. Seeing as he's bonking her daughter and all."

"Jenks!" I exclaimed, then steeled my face as the door opened.

"Rachel!" my mom cried, swooping forward and giving me a hug. I closed my eyes and returned her embrace. She was shorter than I was, and it felt odd. Hair spray caught in my throat over the faint whiff of redwood. I felt bad about not telling her the full truth about quitting the I.S. and the death threats I'd survived. I hadn't wanted to worry her.

"Hi, Mom," I said, pulling back. "This is Nick Sparagmos. And you remember Jenks?"

"Of course I do. It's good to see you again, Jenks." She stepped back into the threshold, a hand briefly going to her faded, straight red hair and then her calf-length, sweater dress. A knot of worry loosened in me. She looked good. Better than the last time. The mischievous glint was back in her eyes, and she moved quickly as she ushered us inside. "Come in, come in," she said, putting a small hand on Nick's shoulder. "Before the bugs follow you."

The hall light was on, but it did little to illuminate the

shadowy green hallway. Pictures lined the narrow space, and I felt claustrophobic as she gave me another fierce hug, beaming as she pulled away. "I'm so glad you came," she said, then turned to Nick. "So you're Nick," she said, giving him a once-over, her lower lip between her teeth. She nodded sharply as she saw his scuffed dress shoes, then her lips twisted in thought as she saw my flip-flops.

"Mrs. Morgan," he said, smiling and offering his hand.

She took it, and I winced as she pulled him staggering into a hug. She was a great deal shorter than he was, and after his first startled moment, he grinned at me over her head.

"How wonderful to meet you," she said as she let him go and turned to Jenks.

The pixy had put himself at the ceiling. "Hi, Mrs. Morgan. You look nice tonight," he said warily, dipping slightly.

"Thank you." She smiled, her few wrinkles deepening. The house smelled like spaghetti sauce, and I wondered if I should have warned Mom that Nick was human. "Well, come all the way in. Can you stay for lunch? I'm making spaghetti. No problem to make a little more."

I couldn't help my sigh as she led the way to the kitchen. Slowly I started to relax. Mom seemed to be watching her mouth more than usual. We entered the kitchen, bright from the overhead light, and I breathed easier. It looked normal—human normal. My mom didn't do much spelling anymore, and only the dissolution vat of saltwater by the fridge and the copper spell pot on the stove gave anything away. She had been in high school during the Turn, and her generation was very discreet. "We just came to pick up my ley line stuff," I said, knowing my idea to get it and run was a lost cause since the copper pot was full of boiling water for pasta.

"It's no trouble," she said as she added a sheaf of spaghetti, ran her eyes down Nick, then added another. "It's after seven. You're hungry, aren't you, Nick?"

"Yes, Mrs. Morgan," he said, despite my pleading look.

She turned from the stove, content. "And you, Jenks. I don't have much in the yard, but you're welcome to what you can find. Or I can mix up some sugar water if you'd like."

Jenks brightened. "Thank you, ma'am," he said, flitting close enough to send the wisps of her red hair waving. "I'll check the yard. Would you mind if I gathered the pollen from your Rose of Sharon? It will do my youngest a world of good this late in the season."

My mother beamed. "Of course. Help yourself. Those damned fairies have just about killed everything looking for spiders." Her eyebrows arched, and I froze in a moment of panic. She had a thought. No telling what it was.

"Might you happen to have any children who would be interested in a late summer job?" she asked, and my breath escaped me in a relieved sound.

Jenks landed on her offered hand, wings glowing a satisfied pink. "Yes, ma'am. My son, Jax, would be delighted to work your yard. He and my two eldest daughters would be enough to keep the fairies out. I'll send them tomorrow before sunup if you like. By the time you have your first cup of coffee, there won't be a fairy in sight."

"Marvelous!" my mother exclaimed. "Those damn bastards have been in my yard all summer. Drove my wrens away."

Nick started at the foul word coming from such a mild-looking lady, and I shrugged.

Jenks flew an arching path from the back door to me in an unspoken request for me to open it. "If you don't mind," he said, hovering by the knob, "I'll just nip out and take a look. I don't want them running into anything unexpected. He's just a boy, and I want to be sure he knows what to watch out for."

"Excellent idea," my mother said, her heels clacking on

the white linoleum. She flicked on the back light and let him out. "Well!" she said as she turned, eyeing Nick. "Sit down, please. Would you like something to drink? Water? Coffee? I think I have a beer somewhere."

"Coffee would be great, Mrs. Morgan," Nick said as he pulled a chair from under the table and lowered himself into it. I opened the fridge for the coffee, and my mom took the bag of grounds out of my hands, fussing with soft mother sounds until I sat beside Nick. The scraping of my chair was loud, and I wished she wasn't making such a fuss. Nick grinned, clearly enjoying my disquiet.

"Coffee," she said as she puttered about. "I admire a man who likes coffee with lunch. You have no idea how glad I am to meet you, Nick. It's been so long since Rachel brought a boy home. Even in high school she wasn't much for dating. I was starting to wonder if she was going to lean the other way, if you know what I mean."

"Mom!" I exclaimed, feeling my face go as red as my hair.

She blinked at me. "Not that there's anything wrong with that," she amended, scooping out the grounds and filling the filter. I couldn't look at Nick, hearing the amusement in him as he cleared his throat. I put my elbows on the table and dropped my head into my hands.

"But you know me," my mother added, her back to us as she put the coffee away. I cringed, waiting for whatever was going to come out of her mouth. "I'm of the mind that it's better to have no man than the wrong one. Your father, now, he was the right man."

Sighing, I looked up. If she was talking about Dad, she wouldn't be talking about me.

"Such a good man," she said, motions slow as she went to the stove. She stood sideways so she could see us as she took the lid off the sauce and stirred it. "You need the right man to have children with. We were lucky with Rachel," she said. "Even so, we almost lost her."

Nick sat up interested. "How so, Mrs. Morgan?"

Her face went long in an old worry, and I rose to plug the coffeemaker in, since she had forgotten. The coming story was embarrassing, but it was a known embarrassment, much better than what she might come out with, especially after having mentioned children. I sat down beside Nick as my mom started in with the usual opening line.

"Rachel was born with a rare blood disease," she said. "We had no idea it was there, just waiting for an inopportune match to show itself."

Nick turned to me, his eyebrows raised. "You never told me that."

"Well, she doesn't have it anymore," my mother said. "The nice woman at the clinic explained everything, saying that we were fortunate with Rachel's older brother, and that we had a one-out-of-four chance that my next child would be like Rachel."

"That sounds like a genetic disorder," he said. "You usually don't get better from those."

My mother nodded and turned the flame down under the boiling pasta. "Rachel responded to a course of herbal remedies and traditional medications. She's our miracle baby."

Nick didn't look convinced, so I added, "My mitochondria were kicking out this odd enzyme, and my white blood cells thought it was an infection. They were attacking healthy cells as if they were invaders, mostly the bone marrow and anything that had to do with blood production. All I know was, I was tired all the time. The herbal remedies helped, but it was when puberty kicked in that everything seemed to settle down. I'm fine now, except for being sensitive to sulfer, but it did shorten my life span by about ten years. 'Least, that's what they tell me."

Nick touched my knee under the table. "I'm sorry."

I flashed him a smile. "Hey, what's ten years? I wasn't supposed to make it to puberty." I didn't have the heart to tell him that even with ten years sliced off my life expectancy, I was still going to live decades past him. But he probably already knew that.

"Monty and I met at school, Nick," my mother said, bringing the conversation back to its original topic. I knew she didn't like talking about the first twelve years of my life. "It was so romantic. The university had just started their paranormal studies, and there was a lot of confusion about prerequisites. Anyone could take anything. I had no business being in a ley line class, and the only reason I signed up for it was because the gorgeous hunk of witch in front of me at the registrar's office was, and all my alternate classes were full."

Her spoon in the pot slowed, and steam wafted over her. "Funny how fate seems to push people together sometimes," she said softly. "I took that class to sit next to one man, but ended up falling in love with his best friend." She smiled at me. "Your father. All three of us partnered for the lab. I would have flunked if it hadn't been for Monty. I'm not a ley line witch, and since Monty couldn't stir a spell to save his life, he set all my circles for me the next two years in return for me invoking all his charms for him until he graduated."

I had never heard this one before, and as I rose to get three coffee mugs, my gaze fell upon the pot of red sauce. Brow pinching, I wondered if there was a tactful way to spill it down the garbage disposal. She was cooking in her spell pot again, too. I hoped she had remembered to wash it in saltwater, or lunch might be a bit more interesting than usual.

"How did you and Rachel meet?" my mother asked as she nudged me away from the pot and set a loaf of frozen bread to bake in the oven.

Eyes suddenly wide, I shook my head in warning at Nick. His eyes flicked from me to my mother. "Ah, a sporting event."

"The Howlers?" she questioned.

Nick looked to me for help, and I sat beside him. "We met at the rat fights, Mom," I said. "I bet on the mink, and he bet on the rat."

"Rat fights?" she said, making a face. "Nasty business, that. Who won?"

"They got away," Nick said, his eyes soft on mine. "We always imagined they escaped together and fell madly in love and are living in the city's sewers somewhere."

I choked back a laugh, but my mother let hers flow freely. My heart seemed to catch at the sound. I hadn't heard her laugh in delight in a long time.

"Yes," she said as she set her oven mitts aside. "I like that. Minks and rats. Just like Monty and me with no more children."

I blinked, wondering how she had jumped from rats and minks to her and Dad, and how that related to them not having any more children.

Nick leaned close and whispered, "Minks and rats can't procreate, either."

My mouth opened in a silent, Oh, and I thought that perhaps Nick, with his odd way of seeing the world, might understand my mother better than I did.

"Nick, dear," my mom said as she gave the sauce a quick, clockwise turn. "You don't have a cellular disease in your family, do you?"

Oh, no, I thought in panic as Nick answered evenly, "No, Mrs. Morgan."

"Call me Alice," she said. "I like you. Marry Rachel and have lots of kids."

"Mom!" I exclaimed. Nick grinned, enjoying it.

"But not right away," she continued. "Enjoy your freedom together for a while. You don't want children until you're ready. You are practicing safe sex, yes?"

"Mother!" I shouted. "Shut up!" *God, help me get through this night.*

She turned, one hand on her hip, the other holding the dripping spoon. "Rachel, if you didn't want me to bring it up, you should have spelled your hickey."

I stared at her, my mouth agape. Mortified, I rose and pulled her into the hall. "Excuse us," I managed, seeing Nick grinning.

"Mom!" I whispered in the safety of the hall. "You ought to be on medication, you know that?"

Her head drooped. "He seems like a nice man. I don't want you to drive him away like you do all your other boyfriends. I loved your father so. I just want you to be that happy."

Immediately my anger fizzled to nothing, seeing her standing alone and upset. My shoulders shifted in a sigh. *I should come over more often*, I thought. "Mom," I said. "He's human."

"Oh," she said softly. "Guess there isn't much safer sex than that, is there?"

I felt bad as the weight of that simple statement fell on her, and I wondered if that might change her opinion of Nick. There could never be any children between Nick and me. The chromosomes didn't line up right. Finding that out for sure had been the end of a long-running controversy among Inderlanders, proving that witches, unlike vamps and Weres, were a separate species from humans, as much as pixies or trolls. Vamps and Weres, whether bitten or born to their status, were only modified humans. Though witches mimicked humanity almost perfectly, we were as different as bananas from fruit flies at a cellular level. With Nick, I would be barren.

I had told Nick the first time our cuddling turned to something more intent, afraid he would notice if something didn't look quite right. I had been almost sick with the thought he would react in disgust about the different species thing. Then I almost cried when his only wide-eyed question had been, "It all looks and works the same, doesn't it?"

At the time, I honestly hadn't known. We had answered that question together.

Flushing at such thoughts in front of my mother, I gave her a weak smile. She returned it, pulling her slight body up straight. "Well," she said, "I'll go open a jar of alfredo, then."

Tension drained from me, and I gave her a hug. Her grip had a new tightness to it, and I responded in kind. I'd missed her. "Thanks, Mom," I whispered.

She patted my back, and we stepped apart. Not meeting my eyes, she turned to the kitchen. "I've an amulet in the bathroom if you want it, third drawer down." She took a breath, and with a cheerful face headed into the kitchen with quick, short steps. I listened for a moment, deciding nothing had changed as she chattered happily to Nick about the weather while packing the tomato-based sauce away. Relieved, I thumped down the shadowed hall in my flip-flops.

My mom's bathroom looked eerily like Ivy's—minus the fish in the bathtub. I found the amulet, and after washing off the Covergirl, I invoked the spell, pleased at the result. A final primp and sigh at my hair, and I hustled back to the kitchen. No telling what my mom would tell Nick if I left her alone with him too long.

Sure enough, I found them together with their heads almost touching as she pointed at the photo album. He had a cup of coffee in his hands, the steam drifting between them. "Mom," I complained. "This is why I never bring anyone over."

Jenks's wings made a harsh clatter as he rose from my mother's shoulder. "Aw, lighten up, witch. We've already got past the naked baby pictures."

I closed my eyes to gather my strength. Moving with a happy swing in her step, my mother went to stir the alfredo sauce. I took her place by Nick, pointing down. "That's my brother, Robert," I said, wishing he would return my phone calls. "And there's my dad," I said, feeling a soft emotion fill me. I smiled back at the photo, missing him.

"He looks nice," Nick said.

"He was the best." I turned the page, and Jenks landed on it, hands on his hips as he strolled over my life, carefully arranged in neat little rows and columns. "That's my favorite picture of him," I said, tapping an unlikely looking group of eleven- and twelve-year-old girls standing before a yellow bus. We were all sunburned, our hair three shades lighter than usual. Mine was cropped short and stuck out all over. My dad was standing beside me, a hand on my shoulder as he smiled at the camera. I felt a sigh slip from me.

"Those are all my friends at camp," I said, thinking my three years there had been some of my best summers. "Look," I said, pointing. "You can see the lake. It was way up in New York somewhere. I only went swimming once, since it was so cold. Made my toes cramp up."

"I never went to camp," Nick said, looking at the faces intently.

"It was one of those 'Make-a-Wish' camps," I said. "They kicked me out when they figured out I wasn't dying anymore."

"Rachel!" my mother protested. "Not everyone there was dying."

"Most were." My mood went somber as my gaze roved over the faces, and I realized I was probably the only one in the picture still alive. I tried to remember the name of the thin black-haired girl standing beside me, not liking it when I couldn't. She had been my best friend.

"Rachel was asked to not come back after she lost her temper," my mom said, "not because she was getting well.

She got it into her head to punish a little boy for teasing the girls."

"Little boy," I scoffed. "He was older than everyone else there and a bully."

"What did you do?" Nick asked, a glint of amusement in his brown eyes.

I got up to put coffee in my mug. "Threw him into a tree."

Jenks snickered, and my mother rapped the spoon on the side of the sauce pot. "Don't be modest. Rachel tapped the ley line the camp was built on and threw him thirty feet up."

Jenks whistled and Nick's eyes grew wide. I poured out the coffee, embarrassed. It hadn't been a very good day. The brat had been about fifteen, and was tormenting the girl whose shoulder my arm was draped over in the picture. I had told him to leave her alone, and when he pushed me down, I lost it. I hadn't even known how to draw on a ley line; it just kind of happened. The kid landed in a tree, fell, and cut his arm. There had been so much blood, I got scared. The young vamps in the camp all had to take a special overnight trip across the lake until they could dig up the dirt he had bled on and burn it.

My dad had to fly up and sort things out. It was the first time I had used ley lines, and basically the last until I went to college since my dad had tanned my hide but good. I'd been lucky they hadn't made me leave right then and there.

I went back to the table, looking at him smiling at me from the photo. "Mom, can I have this picture? I lost mine this spring when—a misaligned spell took them out." I met Nick's eyes, the shared understanding in them reassuring me he'd say nothing about my death threats.

My mom sidled close. "That's a nice one of your father," she said, pulling the photo out and handing it to me before she went back to the stove.

I sat down in my chair and looked at the faces, searching for a name for any of them. I could recall none. It bothered me.

"Um, Rachel?" Nick said, peering down at the album.

"What?" *Amanda?* I silently asked the dark-haired girl. *Was that your name?*

Jenks's wings flashed into motion, sending my hair to dance about my face. "Holy crap!" he exclaimed.

I looked down to the picture that had been under the one now in my hand and felt my face go white. It was the same day, since the background was of the bus. But this time, instead of being surrounded by preadolescent girls, my dad was next to a man who was a dead ringer for an older Trent Kalamack.

My breath wouldn't come out. The two men were smiling, squinting against the sun. They had an arm companionably about each other's shoulders and were clearly happy.

I exchanged frightened looks with Jenks. "Mom?" I finally managed. "Who is this?"

She came close, making a small sound of surprise. "Oh, I had forgotten I had that one. That's the man who owned the camp. Your father and he were such good friends. It broke your dad's heart when he died. And so tragically, too, not six years after his wife. I think that was part of the reason your dad lost the will to fight. They died only a week apart, you know."

"No, I didn't," I whispered, staring down. It wasn't Trent, but the resemblance was eerie. It had to be his father. My dad had known Trent's father?

I put a hand to my stomach in a sudden thought. I had gone to camp with a rare blood disease and left every year feeling better. Trent dabbled in genetic research. His father might have done the same. My recovery had been called a miracle. Perhaps it had been outlawed, immoral, genetic manipulation. "God help me," I breathed.

Three summers at camp. Months of not waking until almost sundown. The unexplained soreness in my hip. The nightmares I still occasionally woke from, of a cloying vapor.

How much? I wondered. What had Trent's father taken from my dad in payment for the life of his daughter? Had he exchanged it for his own?

"Rachel?" Nick said. "Are you okay?"

"No." I concentrated on breathing, staring at the picture. "Can I have this one, too, Mom?" I asked, hearing my voice as if it weren't my own.

"Oh, I don't want it," she said, and I slipped it out, fingers trembling. "That's why it was underneath. You know I can't throw anything of your father's away."

"Thanks," I whispered.

Fifteen

I wedged one of my fuzzy pink slippers off and dismally scratched the back of my calf with my toe. It was after midnight, but the kitchen was bright, gleams of fluorescent light reflecting off my copper spell pots and hanging utensils. Standing at the stainless steel island, I ground the pestle into the mortar, pulping the wild geranium into a green paste. Jenks had found it in a vacant lot for me, trading one of his precious mushrooms for it. The pixy clan that worked the lot had gotten the better end of the deal, but I think Jenks felt sorry for them.

Nick had made us sandwiches about a half an hour ago, and the lasagna was put away into the fridge still hot. My bologna sandwich had been tasteless. I didn't think I could blame it all on the fact that Nick hadn't put ketchup on it as I asked, saying he couldn't find any in the fridge. Stupid human foible. I'd find it endearing if it didn't tick me off so much.

Ivy had yet to show, and I wouldn't eat the lasagna by myself in front of Nick. I wanted to talk to her but I'd have to wait until she was ready. She was the most private person I knew, not even telling herself what her feelings were until she found a logical reason to justify them.

Bob the fish swam in my next-to-the-largest spell pot beside me on the counter. I was going to use him as my familiar. I needed an animal, and fish were animals, right? Besides, Jenks would flip out if I so much as hinted at a kitten, and Ivy had given her owls to her sister after one narrowly escaped being torn apart when it caught Jenks's youngest daughter. Jezebel was fine. The owl might be able to fly again. Someday.

Depressed, I continued to grind the leaves to a pulp. Earth magic held more power when made between sunset and midnight, but tonight I was having difficulty concentrating, and it was already past one. My thoughts kept circling back to that photo and the Make-a-Wish camp. A heavy sigh escaped me.

Nick looked up from the opposite side of the counter, where he was perched on a bar stool finishing off the last of the bologna sandwiches. "Give it up, Rachel," he said, smiling to soften his words, clearly knowing where my thoughts lay. "I don't think you've been tampered with, and even if you were, how could anyone prove it?"

I let the pestle fall still and pushed the mortar away. "My father died because of me," I said. "If it hadn't been for me and my damned blood disease, he'd still be here. I know it."

His long face went sad. "In his mind, it was probably his fault you were sick."

That made me feel a whole lot better, and I slumped where I stood.

"Maybe they were just friends, like your mom said," Nick offered.

"And maybe Trent's father tried to blackmail my dad into something illegal and died because he wouldn't do it." *At least he had taken Trent's dad with him.*

Nick stretched his long arm out to snag the photo still on the counter where I had dropped it. "I don't know," he said, his voice soft as he gazed at it. "They look like friends to me."

I wiped my hands off on my jeans and leaned to take the

picture. My eyes crinkled as I scanned my dad's face. Sealing my emotions away, I handed it back. "I didn't get well because of herbal remedies and spells. I've been tampered with."

It was the first time I had said it aloud, and my stomach tightened. "But you're alive," he offered.

I turned away and measured six cups of springwater. The tinkling as it ran into my largest copper spell pot sounded loud. "What if it got out?" I asked, unable to look at him. "They'd pack me up and put me away on some frozen island like I was a leper, afraid whatever he did to me might mutate into something and start another plague."

"Oh, Rachel . . ." Nick slipped from his stool. Anxious, I busied myself needlessly drying the measuring cup. He came up behind me, giving me a backward hug before turning me around to face him. "You're not a plague waiting to happen," he cajoled, meeting my eyes. "If Trent's father cured your blood disease, then he did. But it was just that. He fixed it. Nothing's going to happen. See? I'm still here." He smiled. "Alive and everything."

I sniffed, not liking that it bothered me so much. "I don't want to owe him anything."

"You don't. This was between your father and Trent's, and that's assuming it even happened." His hands were warm around my waist. My feet were between his, and I laced my fingers behind his back and balanced my weight against his own. "Just because your dad and Trent's father knew each other, it doesn't mean anything," he said.

Right, I thought sarcastically. We let go of each other at the same time, stepping reluctantly away. While Nick stuck his head in the pantry, I checked over my recipe for the transfer medium. The text I had for binding a familiar was in Latin, but I knew the scientific names of the plants enough to follow it. I was hoping Nick would help with the incantation.

"Thanks for keeping me company," I said, knowing that

he had a half-day shift at the university tomorrow and a night shift at the museum. If he didn't leave soon, he wouldn't get any sleep before he had to go to work.

Nick glanced at the black hallway as he sat down on his stool with a bag of chips. "I was hoping to be here when Ivy came back. Why don't you spend the night at my house?"

My lips curled in a smile. "I'll be fine. She won't come home until she's calmed down. But if you're going stay for a while, how about sketching some pentagrams for me?"

The crackle of plastic stopped. Nick looked at my black paper and silver chalk stacked suspiciously on the counter, then to me. Amusement lit his eyes, and he finished rolling down the edges of the bag. "I'm not going to do your home-work, Ray-ray."

"I know what they look like," I protested, putting the clip-pings of my hair into the spell pot and pushing them down with my ceramic spoon until they sank. "I promise I'll copy them myself later. But if I don't hand them in tomorrow, she'll flunk me and Edden will deduct the cost of tuition from my fee. It's not fair, Nick. The woman has it in for me!"

Nick ate a chip, skepticism pouring from him. "You know them?" I nodded, and he wiped his hand on his jeans before pulling my textbook closer. "All right," he challenged as he tilted the book so I couldn't see. "What does a pentagram of protection look like?"

My breath escaped me in a relieved whoosh, and I added the sanicle decoction I'd prepared earlier. "Standard graph with two braided lines in the outer circle."

"Okay . . . How about divination?"

"New moons sketched at the points, and a mobius strip in the center for balance."

The amused glint in Nick's eye turned to surprise. "Sum-moning?" he prompted.

I smiled and dropped the pulped wild geranium into the brew. The bits of green hung suspended as if the water were a gel. Cool. "Which one? Summoning internal power or a physical entity?"

"Both."

"Internal power has acorns and oak leaves in the mid-points, and summoning an entity uses a Celtic chain binding the points." Smug at his obvious surprise, I adjusted the flame under the pot and dug in my silverware drawer for a finger stick.

"Okay. I'm impressed." The book slipped down and he grabbed a handful of chips.

"You'll copy them for me?" I asked, delighted.

"Promise you'll do them yourself later?"

"Deal," I said cheerfully. I had already finished the short essays. Now all I had to do was make Bob my familiar and I'd be set. Piece of cake. I looked at Bob and cringed. *Yeah. Piece of cake.* "Thanks," I said softly as Nick straightened my black drawing paper by tapping the ends on the counter.

"I'll make them sloppy so she thinks you did them," he said.

I gave him a raised eyebrow look. "Thanks a lot," I amended dryly, and he grinned. Done with the brew, I jabbed my finger and massaged out three drops of blood. The scent of redwood blossomed as they plunked into the pot and the spell quickened. So far, so good.

"Earth witches don't use pentagrams," Nick said as he sharpened the chalk by rubbing it against a piece of scrap paper. "How come you know them?"

Careful to keep my bloodied finger clear, I polished my scrying mirror with a velveteen scarf borrowed from Ivy. A shudder sifted through me at the cold feel of it. I hated scrying. It gave me the willies. "From those pentagram jelly glasses," I said. Nick looked up, the lost look on his face making me feel good for some reason. "You know. Those jelly jars you can use for juice glasses when they're empty? These had pentagrams on the bottom and their uses written on the side. I lived on peanut butter and jelly sandwiches that year." My mood went soft at the memory of my dad quizzing me over toast.

Nick rolled his sleeves up and started sketching. "And I thought I was bad for digging to the bottom of my cereal box for the toy."

I was done with the prep work and ready to do some serious spelling. Time to set my circle. "In or out," I asked, and Nick looked up from my homework, blinking. Seeing his confusion, I added, "I'm ready to set my circle. Do you want to be in or out of it?"

He hesitated. "You want me to move?"

"Only if you want to be out of it."

His look turned incredulous. "You're going to enclose the entire island?"

"Is that a problem?"

"No-o-o-o." Nick scooted his bar stool closer. "Witches must be able to hold more ley line power than humans. I can't make a circle much bigger than three feet across."

I smiled. "I don't know. I'd ask Dr. Anders if she wouldn't make me feel like an idiot. I think it depends. My mom can't hold a circle bigger than three feet, either. So . . . in or out?"

"In?"

My breath slipped from me in relief. "Good. I was hoping you'd say that." Leaning over the counter, I plunked my spell book down beside him. "I need your help translating this."

"You want me to do your homework and help you bind your familiar, too?" he protested.

I winced. "The only spell I could find in my books was in Latin."

Nick looked at me in disbelief. "Rachel. I sleep at night."

I glanced at the clock above the sink. "It's only one-thirty."

Sighing, he slid the book to him. I knew he wouldn't be able to resist once he started, and sure enough, his mild annoyance shifted to hot interest before he had read more than a paragraph. "Hey, this is old Latin."

I leaned across the counter until my shadow covered the print. "I can read the plant names, and I'm sure I made the transfer medium right, as it's standard, but the incantation is iffy."

He wasn't listening anymore, his brow furrowed as he ran a long finger under the text. "Your circle needs to be modified to resolve and gather power."

"Thanks," I said, glad he was going to help. I didn't mind muddling through most things, but spelling was an exact science. And just the idea that I needed a familiar made me uncomfortable. Most witches had them, but ley line witches needed them as a matter of safety. Dividing one's aura helped prevent a demon from pulling you into the ever-after. Poor Bob.

Nick went back to sketching pentagrams for me, glancing up as I pulled my twenty pound bag of salt from under the counter and set it thumping on top. Acutely aware of his eyes on me, I scraped a handful from the clumping mass. At Ivy's insistence, I had blown off the security deposit and etched a shallow circle in the linoleum. Ivy had helped. Actually, Ivy had done all of it, using a string and chalk contraption to be sure the circle was perfect. I'd sat on the counter and let her have at it, knowing it would tick her off if I got in her way. The result was an absolutely perfect circle. She had even taken a compass and marked true north with black nail polish to show me where to start my circle.

Now, peering down to find the black dot, I carefully sifted salt, moving clockwise around the island until I found my starting point. I added the doodads for protection and divination, put the green candles at the appropriate places, then lit them from the flame that I'd used to make the transfer medium.

Nick watched with half his attention. I liked that he accepted me as a witch. When we had met, I'd worried that since he was one of the few humans who practiced the black arts, I would eventually have to smack him up and turn him in, but Nick had taken demonology to improve his Latin and get through a language development class, not to summon demons. And the novelty of a human who accepted magic with such ease was a definite turn-on.

"Last chance to leave," I said as I turned the gas burner off and moved the media to the center island.

Nick made a noise deep in his throat, setting his perfect pentagram aside and starting on the next. Envious of his smooth, straight lines, I pushed my paraphernalia aside to make a clear spot on the counter across from him.

The memory of being punished for having unknowingly tapped into a ley line and flinging the camp bully into a tree flashed through me. I thought it stupid that my dislike of ley lines might stem from the childhood incident, but I knew it was more than that. I didn't trust ley line magic. It was too easy to lose sight of which side one's magic was on.

With earth witchcraft, it was easy. If you have to slaughter goats, it's probably a good bet it's black magic. Ley line magic required a death payment, too, but it is a more nebulous death taken from your soul, much harder to quantify and easier to dismiss—until it's too late.

The cost for white ley line witchcraft was negligible, tantamount to me pulling weeds and using them in my spelling. But the unfiltered power available through ley lines was seductive. It took a strong will to stick to self-imposed limits and remain a white ley line witch. The boundaries that looked so reasonable and prudent when set, often seemed foolish or timid when the strength of a line coursed through you. I'd seen too many friends go from the "pulling weeds" analogy to "slaughtering goats" without even realizing they'd made the jump to the black arts. And they never listened, saying I was jealous or a fool. Eventually I'd find myself hauling their asses down to the I.S. lockup when they put a black charm on the cop who pulled them over for going fifty in a thirty-five zone. Maybe that was why I couldn't keep my friends.

Those were the ones that bothered me, basically good people who had been tempted by a power greater than their will. They were pitiable, their souls slowly eaten away to pay for the black magic they played with. But it was the professional black witches who scared me, those strong enough to foster the soul-death onto someone else to pay for their magic. Eventually, though, the soul-death found its way home, probably dragging a demon along with it. All I knew was, there was screaming, and blood, and great big booms that shook the city.

And then I didn't have to worry about that particular witch anymore.

I wasn't that strong of will. I knew it, accepted it, and avoided the problem by shunning ley lines whenever I could. I hoped that taking a fish as my familiar wasn't the start of a new path but just a speed bump in my current road. Glancing at Bob, I vowed that's all it would be. All witches had familiars. And there was nothing in that binding spell that would hurt anyone.

Taking a slow breath, I closed my eyes to prepare myself for the coming disorientation of connecting to a ley line. Slowly I willed my second sight into focus. The stench of burnt amber tickled my nose. An unseen wind shifted my hair though the kitchen window was closed. It was always windy in the ever-after. I imagined the walls that surrounded me becoming transparent, and in my mind's eye they did.

My second sight strengthened, and the sensation of being outside grew until the mental scenery beyond the walls of the church became as real as the counter, unseen under my fingers. Eyes closed to block my mundane vision, I glanced over the nonexistent kitchen with my mind's eye. Nick didn't show up at all, and the memory of the church's walls had vanished to faint, silvery chalk lines. Through them, I could see the surrounding landscape.

It was parklike, with a glowing red haze reflecting off the bottom of clouds where Cincinnati would be, hiding behind the stunted trees. It was common knowledge that the demons had their own city, built on the same ley lines as Cincinnati. The trees and plants carried a similar reddish glow, and though no wind whispered through the linden tree outside the kitchen, the branches of the stunted ever-after trees tossed in the wind that lifted my hair. There were people who got off on the discrepancies between reality and the ever-after, but I thought it freaking uncomfortable. Someday, I'd go up Carew Tower and look at the broken, glowing demon city with my second sight. My stomach tightened. *Yeah, sure I would.*

My gaze was drawn to the graveyard by the stark, almost glowing white tombstones. They and the moon were the only things that seemed to exist without that red glow, unchanged in both worlds, and I stifled a shudder. The ley line made a solid-looking red smear running due north at head height above the tombstones. It was small—not even twenty yards, I guessed—but so underused that it seemed stronger than the enormous ley line the university straddled.

Conscious that Nick was probably watching with his own second sight, I stretched out my will and touched the ribbon of power. I staggered, forcing my eyes to remain shut as my grip tightened on the counter. My pulse leapt and my breath quickened. "Swell," I whispered, thinking the force surging into me seemed stronger than the last time.

I stood and did nothing as the influx continued, trying to equalize our strengths. My fingertips tingled and my toes ached as it backwashed at my theoretical extremities, which mirrored my real ones. Finally it began to balance, and a trace of energy left me to rejoin the line. It was as if I was part of a circuit, and the line's passage left a growing residue that made me feel slimy.

The link with the ley line was heady, and no longer able to keep my eyelids closed, they flew open. My cluttered kitchen replaced the silver outlines. Queasy with disorientation, I tried to reconcile my mind's eye with my more mundane vision, using them simultaneously. Though I couldn't see Nick with my second sight, it would cast shadows upon him through my usual vision. Sometimes there was no difference, but I was willing to bet Nick wouldn't be one of those people. Our eyes met, and I felt my face go slack.

His aura was rimmed in black. It wasn't necessarily bad, but it pointed to an uncomfortable direction. His narrow build looked gaunt, and where his bookish mien gave him a scholarly air before, now it had undertones of danger. But what shocked me was the black circular shadow upon his left temple. It was where the demon he had saved me from had put its mark, an IOU that Nick would someday have to repay. Immediately I looked at my wrist.

My skin showed only the usual upraised scar tissue in the shape of a circle with a line running through it. That didn't mean that was all Nick could see, though. Holding my arm up, I asked him, "Is it glowing black?"

He nodded solemnly, his usual appearance starting to overshadow his threatening look as my mind's eye began to falter under the strength of my mundane sight.

"It's the demon mark, isn't it?" I said as I ran my fingers over my wrist. I didn't see any hint of black, but I couldn't see my aura, either.

"Yes," he said softly. "Did, uh, anyone tell you that you look really different while channeling a ley line?"

I nodded, my balance wavering as the two realities clashed. "Different" was better than "scary as all hell," which is what Ivy had called me once. "Do you want out of the circle? I haven't closed it yet."

"No."

Immediately I felt better. A properly closed circle couldn't be broken except by its maker. He didn't mind being trapped inside with me, and his show of trust was gratifying.

"All right, then. Here goes." Taking a steadying breath, I mentally moved the narrow rill of salt from this dimension to the ever-after. My circle made the jump with the sharpness of a snapping rubber band against my skin. I started as the salt winked out of existence, replaced with an equal ring of ever-after. The spine-tingling jolt was expected, but it got me every time.

"I hate it when it does that," I said as I glanced at Nick, but he was staring at my circle.

"Whoa," he breathed in awe. "Look at that. Did you know they were going to do that?"

I followed his gaze to the candles, and my jaw dropped. They had gone transparent. The flames still flickered, but the green wax glowed with an utterly unreal look.

Nick slid from his stool, edging carefully around the counter to avoid hitting the circle. He crouched by one of the candles, and I almost panicked when he extended a finger to touch it.

"No!" I shouted, and he jerked his hand back. "Um, I think they shifted to the ever-after with the salt. I don't know what touching them will do. Just . . . don't. Okay?"

He nodded as he stood. Looking properly cowed, he went back to his stool. He didn't pick up the chalk, though. He was going to watch. I smiled weakly at him, not liking that I was at such a disadvantage with ley line magic. But if I followed the recipe, I'd be fine.

All but the barest remnant of power I had drawn from the ley line was now running through my circle. I could feel it pressing against my skin. The molecule-thin slice of the ever-after was a red smear between me and the rest of the world, making a dome arching just over my head.

Nothing could get through the bands of alternating realities. The oblong sphere was mirrored below me as well, and if it had run into any pipes or electrical lines, the circle would not have been perfect, but vulnerable to breakage at that point.

Though most of the ley line force had gone into sealing the circle, there was already a secondary buildup beginning in me. It was slower, almost insidiously so. It would continue until I broke the circle and disconnected from the ley line. Ley line witches knew how to properly store power, but I didn't, and if I remained connected to the line too long, it would drive me insane. The bare hour I'd need would come nowhere near too long.

Satisfied the circle was secure, I let my second sight die completely. The vision of Nick's aura was lost to me. "Ready for step two?" he asked, and I nodded.

Setting his pentagrams completely aside, he pulled the old book closer. His brow furrowed as he ran a finger under the text to leave a chalk mark as he read. "Next, you remove all charms and spells from yourself." He looked up. "Maybe you should have taken a salt bath."

"No. The only charms I have are amulets." I pulled the spell I had gotten from my mom off, the cord tugging at my hair. I felt my neck, giving Nick a lopsided grin at his attention on it. After a moment's hesitation, I worked my pinkie ring off and set it aside.

"I knew it!" Nick exclaimed. "I knew you had freckles. It was the ring, wasn't it?"

He was reaching out, and I handed it to him across the clutter between us. "My dad gave it to me for my thirteenth birthday," I said. "See the wood inlay? I have to renew it every year."

Nick glanced at me from under his bangs. "I like your freckles."

Embarrassed, I took my ring back and set it aside. "What do I do now?"

He glanced down. "Um . . . prepare the transfer medium."

"Done," I said, giving the spell pot a sharp tap to hear it ring. *This wasn't so bad.*

"Okay . . ." He was silent, and the ticking clock seemed to grow loud. Still reading, he said, "Now you have to stand on your scrying mirror and push your aura down into your reflection." His brown eyes pinched in worry as they met mine. "You can do that?"

"In theory. That's why I was so picky about the circle. Until I get my aura back, I'll be vulnerable to all sorts of things." He nodded, his gaze distant in thought. "Will you watch and tell me if it works? I can't see my own aura."

"Sure. It isn't going to hurt, is it?"

I shook my head as I took up the scrying mirror and set it on the floor. Looking down at its black surface, I was reminded of why I had worked so hard to avoid ley line magic. Its perfect blackness seemed to soak up the light, but at the same time was still shiny. I couldn't see myself in it, and it pegged my creepy meter.

"Barefoot," Nick added, and I kicked off my slippers. Taking a deep breath, I stepped onto the mirror. It was as cold as it was black, and I stifled a shiver, feeling I might fall through it as if it were a pothole.

"Euwie," I said, making a face at the pulling sensation from under my feet.

Nick stared, standing up and looking over the counter at my feet. "It's working," he said, his face suddenly pale.

Swallowing, I took my hands and ran them down my head as if pushing off water. An ache set my head to throb.

"Oh, yeah," Nick said, sounding sick. "That pulls it off much faster."

"It feels awful," I muttered as I continued to push my aura

down to my feet. I knew it was going by the soft ache its absence left behind. There was a taste of metal on my tongue, and I glanced at the black surface, my mouth dropping as I saw my reflection in it for the first time. My red hair hung about my face, looking just as I would have expected, but my features were lost behind a smear of amber. "Is my aura brown?" I asked.

"It's bright gold," Nick answered as he dragged his stool around to my side of the counter. "Mostly. I think you got it all. Can we . . . move on?"

Hearing the unease in his voice, I met his eyes. "Please."

"Good." He sat and pulled the book onto his lap. Head bowed, he read the next passage. "Okay, put the scrying mirror into the transfer medium, being careful not to let your fingers touch the media or your aura will reattach and you'll have to start over."

I refused to look in the mirror, worried that I'd see myself trapped in it. Shoulders tense, I scuffed my slippers back on. My feet ached and my head throbbed with the beginnings of a migraine. If I didn't finish this quickly, I was going to be stuck in a dark room with a washcloth all day tomorrow. Taking up the mirror, I gingerly slipped it into the media. The specks of wild geranium flashed to nothing, dissolved by my aura. It was eerie, even by my standards, and I couldn't help an "ooooh" of appreciation. "What's next?" I asked, wanting to be done with it so I could take my aura back.

Nick's head was bent over the book. "Next, you need to anoint your familiar with the transfer medium, but you have to be careful to not touch the media yourself." He looked up. "How do you anoint a fish?"

I felt my face go slack. "I don't know. Maybe I could just slip him into the vat along with the mirror?" I reached for the book on his lap, turning the page. "Isn't there anything about making a fish your familiar?" I questioned. "Everything else is in there."

Nick pushed my hands from the pages as one tore. "No. Go put your fish in the spell pot. If it doesn't work, we'll try something else."

My mood went sour. "I don't want my aura smelling like fish," I said as I dipped a hand into Bob's bowl, and he snickered.

Bob didn't want to go in the spell pot. Trying to catch his darting shape in a round bowl was almost impossible. Getting him out of the bathtub had been easy—I simply drained it until he was beached—but now, after a frustrating moment of near misses, I was ready to dump him onto the floor. Finally I got him and, dripping water over the counter, dropped him in. I peered into the spell pot, watching his gills pump the amber liquid.

"Okay," I said, hoping he was all right. "He's anointed. What's next?"

"Just an incantation. And when the transfer medium goes clear, you can take back the aura your familiar left you."

"Incantation," I said, thinking ley line magic was stupid. Earth magic didn't need incantations. Earth magic was precise and beautiful in its simplicity. My eyes shifted to the not-there candles and I stifled a shudder.

"Here. I'll read it for you." He stood up with the book, and I made a spot for it beside Bob in the bowl. I leaned close to him over the book, thinking he smelled good, manly good. Intentionally bumping into him, I felt a warm current that was probably his aura. Too busy deciphering the text, he didn't notice. Sighing, I put my attention on the book.

Nick cleared his throat. His eyebrows bunched and his lips moved as he whispered the words, sounding dark and dangerous. I caught about one in every three words. He finished, giving me one of his half smiles. "How about that," he said. "It rhymes."

A sigh shifted my shoulder. "Do I need to say it in Latin?"

"I wouldn't think so. The only reason they made these things rhyme is so the witch can remember them. It's the intent behind the words rather than the words themselves that does the trick." He bent back over the book. "Give me a moment and I'll translate it. I think I can even make it rhyme for you. Latin is very loose in its interpretation."

"Okay." Nervous and jittery, I tucked my hair behind an ear and looked into the spell pot. Bob didn't look happy.

" 'Pars tibi, totum mihi. Vinctus vinculis, prece factis.' " Nick looked up. "Ah, 'some to you, but all to me. Bound by ties made so by plea.' "

I dutifully repeated it, feeling silly. Invocations. Could it be any more hokey? Next I'd be standing on one foot and shaking a posy of feathers at the full moon.

Nick's finger ran under the print. " 'Luna servata, lux sanata. Chaos statutum, pejus minutum.' " His brow furrowed. "Let's go with, 'Moon made safe, ancient light made sane. Chaos decreed, taken tripped if bane.' "

I echoed him, thinking ley line witches had a substantial lack of imagination.

" 'Mentem tegens, malum ferens. Semper servus, dum duret mundus.' Ah, I'd say, "Protection recalled, carrier of worth. Bound before the world's rebirth.' "

"Oh, Nick," I complained, "are you sure you're translating that right? That's dreadful."

He sighed. "Try this then." He thought for a moment. "You could also translate it as, 'lee of mind, bearer of pain. Slave until the worlds are slain.' "

That I could live with, and I said it, feeling nothing. We both peered in at Bob, waiting for the amber liquid to go clear. My head pounded, but other than that, nothing happened. "I think I did it wrong," I said, scuffing my slippers.

"Oh—shit," Nick swore, and I looked up to find him staring over my shoulder at the doorway to the kitchen. He swallowed hard, his Adam's apple bobbing.

The hair on the back of my neck pricked. My demon scar gave a pulse. Breath catching, I spun around, thinking Ivy must be home.

But it wasn't Ivy. It was a demon.

Sixteen

"Nick!" I cried, stumbling back. The demon grinned. It looked like an aristocratic Brit, except that I recognized it as the one who put on Ivy's face and tore out my throat that spring.

My back found the counter. I had to run. I had to get out of here! It would kill me! Flailing to put the counter between us, I hit the spell pot.

"Watch the brew!" Nick shouted, reaching out even as the bowl tipped.

I gasped, tearing my gaze from the demon long enough to see Bob's bowl spill. Aura-laced water spilled over the counter in an amber wash. Bob slid out, flopping.

"Rachel!" Nick exclaimed. "Get the fish! He has your aura. He can break the circle!"

I'm in a circle, I thought, strangling my panic. *The demon isn't. It can't hurt me.*

"Rachel!"

Nick's shout tore my eyes from the grinning demon. Nick was desperately trying to catch Bob, flopping on the counter, and keep the spilled water from reaching the edge. My face went cold. I was willing to bet just the aura-laced water would be enough to break the circle.

I lunged for the paper towels. As Nick fumbled for Bob, I

made a mad dash around the counter, laying squares of white to sop up rivulets before they could make puddles on the floor that would run to the circle. My heart pounded and I frantically alternated my attention from the water to the demon standing with a bewildered, amused expression in the archway to the hall.

"Gotcha," Nick whispered, his breath exploding from him in a ragged sound as he finally gained control of the fish.

"Not the saltwater!" I warned as Nick held him over my dissolution pot. "Here." I shoved Bob's original bowl at Nick. Ordinary water sloshed out, and I blotted it up as Nick dropped Bob in. The fish shuddered, sinking to the bottom with his gills pumping.

Silence descended, framed by the heavy rasping of our breathing and the ticking of the clock above the sink. Nick's and my eyes met over the bowl. As one, we turned to the demon.

It looked pleasant enough, having taken the shape of a young man with a mustache, elegant and polished. It was dressed as an eighteenth century businessman in a suit of green velvet with lace trim and long tails. Round glasses were perched atop its thin nose. They were smoked to hide its red eyes. Though able to shift its form and shape at will— becoming everything from my roommate to a punk rocker— its eyes stayed the same unless it made the effort to take on all the abilities of whomever it was mimicking. Hence, my demon bite laced with vamp saliva. A tremor shook me as I recalled that its pupils were slitted like a goat's.

Fear tightened my stomach, and I hated being afraid. I forced my hands to unclench their grip on my elbows, pulled myself straight and tossed my head. "Ever think of updating your wardrobe?" I mocked. *I was safe in a circle. I was safe in a circle.*

My breath caught as a red mist of ever-after hazed it. The demon's clothes molded to a modern-day business suit I'd expect to see on a Fortune-twenty executive. "This is so . . . common," it said, its resonate, British-laden accent perfect for the stage. "But I wouldn't want it said that I wasn't accommodating." It took its glasses off, and my breath hissed in. I stared at the alienness of its eyes, jerking as Nick touched my arm.

Nick looked wary—not nearly scared enough to please me—and I felt a flush of embarrassment at my earlier panic. But damn it, demons scared the crap out of me. No one risked calling up demons since the Turn. Except for whoever called this one up to maul me last spring. And then there had been the one that attacked Trent Kalamack. Maybe demon summoning was more common than I wanted to admit.

I hated that Nick's respect for them stopped short of terror. They fascinated him, and I was afraid his search for knowledge would someday lead him to make a foolish decision, letting the tiger turn and eat him.

The demon smiled to show thick flat teeth as it glanced over its attire. It made a deep-in-thought sound and the wool disappeared, to become a black T-shirt tucked into leather pants with a gold chain belted around narrow hips. A black leather jacket appeared, and the demon stretched in a cloud of sensuality, showing every curve of the new, attractive muscle pulling its T-shirt tight across its chest. Blond hair cut short grew as it shook its head, and its height lengthened.

I felt myself pale. It had become Kist, pulling my old fear of him right out of my head. The demon seemed to take great delight in changing into whatever frightened me the most. I wouldn't let it shake me. I wouldn't.

"Oh, this is nice," the demon said, its accent shifting to a sultry, bad-boy drawl to match its new look. "You're afraid of the prettiest people, Rachel Mariana Morgan. I rather like being this one." Licking its lips suggestively, it sent its gaze across my neck, lingering on the scar it had given me while I was sprawled on the floor of the university library's basement, lost in a haze of vamp-saliva-induced ecstasy as it killed me.

The memory sent my heart pounding. My hand rose to cover my neck. The pressure from its gaze pushed on my skin, making it tingle. "Stop it," I demanded, frightened as it sent the scar into play and tendrils of feeling ran like molten metal from my neck to my groin. My breath hissed in through my nose. "I said stop it!"

The blue of Kist's eyes went wide and flashed to red. Seeing my resolve, the demon's outlines blurred. "You aren't afraid of this one anymore," it said, its voice shifting to become lower and laden with a proper British accent again. "Pity. I do so like to be young and testosterone laden. But I know what frightens you. Let's keep that a secret, hum? No need to let Nick Sparagmos know. Not yet. He may want to buy the information."

Nick's breathing sounded harsh beside me as the demon doffed the biker's hat—which promptly vanished in a haze of ever-after red—and shifted, returning to its previous form of British nobility in lace and green velvet. It smiled at me over its round smoked glasses. "This will do, in the meantime," it said.

I jumped as Nick touched me. "Why are you here?" he asked. "No one called you."

The demon said nothing, glancing over the kitchen with undisguised curiosity. Showing a predatorial grace, it began to circle the bright room, its shiny buckled boots silent on the linoleum. "I know you are new to all of this," it mused aloud as it tapped at Mr. Fish's brandy snifter on the windowsill and the fish quivered, "but generally the summoner is *outside* the circle, and the summoned is on the *inside*." It turned on a heel to send its long coattails furling. "I'll give you that for free, Rachel Mariana Morgan. Because you made me laugh. I haven't laughed since the Turn. We all laughed at that."

My pulse had slowed but my knees felt watery. I wanted to

sit down but didn't dare. "How can you be here?" I asked. "This is holy ground."

The vision of British grace opened my fridge. Making a tsk-tsk sound, it shuffled through the leftovers, coming out with a half-empty container of fudge frosting. "Oh yes, I *do* like this arrangement. Being on the outside is *ever* so much more interesting. I think I'll answer that query for free as well."

Oozing old world charm, it pulled the top of the frosting off. The blue plastic disappeared in a smear of ever-after, and the demon dipped the gold spoon that had taken its place into the container. "This isn't holy ground," it said as it stood in my kitchen in a gentleman's frock and ate frosting. "The kitchen was added after the sanctuary was blessed. You could have the entire grounds sanctified, but then you'd connect your bedroom to the ley line in the graveyard. Ooooh, and wouldn't *that* be delightful."

A sick feeling twisted my stomach at what that might mean. Eyebrows raised, it looked at me over its smoked glasses, its red eyes showing a shocking amount of sudden ire. "You had better have something worth hearing, or I'm going to be royally buggered."

I straightened in understanding. It thought I had summoned it with an offer of information to pay off my IOU. My pulse jackhammered back into full throttle as the container of frosting vanished from the demon's hand and it came close to the circle.

"Don't!" I blurted as it tapped the sheet of ever-after between us. The demon's face lost its amusement and, expression deadly serious, it ran its attention over the seam with the floor. I gripped Nick's arm as it mumbled about tearing summoners limb from limb, interrupted teas, and how inconsiderate it was to pull someone from their dinner or Wednesday night telly. Adrenaline shook me as the demon dissolved to a red mist and sank through the floorboards.

I clutched at Nick, my knees threatening to give way. "He's checking for pipes," I said. "There are no pipes. I looked." Fear made my shoulders hurt as I waited for the demon to rise through the floor at my feet and kill me. "I looked!" I asserted, trying to convince myself.

I knew the circle bisected rocks and roots, and the top of it went into the attic, but as long as there wasn't an open path like a phone or gas line, the circle was secure. Even a laptop could break a circle if it was connected to the net and an e-mail came in.

"Oh good. He's back," Nick breathed as the demon reappeared outside the circle, and I stifled a laugh, knowing it would sound hysterical. What kind of a life did I have when seeing a demon was a good thing?

The demon stood before us, taking a tin of what probably wasn't snuff out of a tiny vest pocket and sniffing a pinch of black powder into both nostrils. "You cast a well-built circle," it said between cultured sneezes. "As good as your father's."

My eyes widened and I stepped to the circle's edge. "What do you know of my dad?"

"Reputation, Rachel Mariana Morgan," it simpered. "Strictly reputation. He was not in my realm of expertise when he was alive. Now that he's dead, I'm interested. I specialize in secrets. As does Nick Sparagmos, it seems." It put the tin away and pulled Ivy's chair out from before her computer. "Now," it said idly as it shook the mouse and brought up the Internet, "as amusing as this is, can we get on with it? Your circle is tight. I won't be killing you now." Its red eyes went sly. "Later, perhaps."

I followed its gaze to the clock over the sink. It was one-forty. I hoped Ivy didn't walk in on this. An undead vamp might survive a demon attack, but a live one would stand as much of a chance as me.

I took a breath to tell it to go away because I didn't call it, but a thought stopped me cold. It knew Nick's last name. It had said it twice.

"It knows your last name," I said, turning to Nick. "Why does it know your name?"

Nick's mouth opened and his eyes slid to the demon. "Ah . . ."

"Why does it know your name?" I demanded, my hands on my hips. I was tired of being afraid, and Nick was a convenient outlet. "You've been calling it up, haven't you!"

"Well . . ." he said, his long face reddening.

"You idiot!" I shouted. "I told you not to call it. You promised you wouldn't!"

"No," he said, his hands taking a grip on my shoulders. "I didn't. You said I wouldn't. And it just sort of happened. I didn't even mean to call him the first time."

"The first?" I exclaimed. "How many times have there been?"

Nick scratched the bristles on his cheek. "See, I was sketching pentagrams—for practice. I wasn't going to do anything. He appeared, thinking I was trying to call him with some information to pay off my debt. Thank God I was in a circle." Nick glanced at the soggy papers with their silver chalk lines. "Just like he showed up tonight."

Together we turned to the demon, and it sent its shoulders to rise and fall in a shrug. It seemed more than willing to wait out our argument, more interested in Ivy's favorites list than us at the moment.

"It's an it, not a him," I said. "And I'm not going to let you blame this on the demon."

"How very kind of you, Rachel Mariana Morgan," the demon said, and I scowled.

Nick was starting to look angry. On sudden impulse I pushed the hair from his left temple. My breath caught as I saw two lines bisecting his demon scar instead of one.

"Nick!" I wailed. "You know what happens when you get too many of those?"

He took a bothered step back, and his brown hair fell to hide it.

"It can pull you into the ever-after!" I shouted, wanting to smack him a good one. I had only one line through my demon scar, and the worry still kept me up at night.

Nick said nothing, watching me with unrepentant eyes. Damn it all to hell, he wasn't even trying to explain himself. "Talk to me!" I exclaimed.

"Rachel," he said. "Nothing is going to happen. I'm being careful."

"But you have two IOUs," I protested. "If you don't make good, you belong to it."

He smiled confidently, and I cursed his belief that the printed word held all the answers and he would be safe if he followed the rules. "It's okay," he said as he took my shoulders again. "I've only entered into a trial contract."

"Trial contract . . ." I stammered, floored. "Nick, this isn't twenty CDs for a penny with only three more to buy. It's trying to take your soul!"

The demon chuckled, and I flicked a glance at it.

"That's not going to happen," Nick soothed. "I can call on him whenever I want, same as if I gave him my soul. And at the end of three years I walk away with no ties or commitments."

"If it sounds like too good a deal, you aren't looking at the fine print."

Still he smiled, his face showing confidence instead of the terror he should have been feeling. "I read the fine print." His finger rose to touch my lips and stop my outburst. "All of it. I get minor questions answered for free, and I can put larger questions to him on credit."

My eyes closed. "Nick. Did you know your aura is rimmed in black? You look like a wraith in my mind's eye."

"So do you, love," Nick whispered, pulling me close.

Shocked, I did nothing as his arms went about me. *My aura was as tainted as his? I hadn't done anything but let it save my life.*

"He has all the answers, Rachel," Nick whispered, and I felt my hair move with his breath. "I can't help it."

The demon cleared its throat, and I pulled away from Nick.

"Nick Sparagmos is my best student since Benjamin Franklin," the demon said, its accent making it sound completely reasonable as it touched Ivy's screen to make it go blue. It didn't fool me, though. The thing couldn't be swayed by pity, guilt, or remorse. If it had found a way past my circle, it would have killed us both for the audacity of calling it from the ever-after—whether it had been intentional or not.

"Though Attila could have gone far if he had been able to look past the military applications," it continued, looking at its nails. "And it is hard to best Leonardo di ser Piero da Vinci for outright cleverness."

"Name dropper," I muttered, and the demon inclined its head graciously. It was more obvious than words that if Nick had the demon at his beck and call for three years, he would agree to anything to keep it there. Which was exactly what the demon was counting on.

"Um, Rachel," Nick said as he took my elbow. "Since he's here, you might want to arrange for a summoning name from him so he doesn't show up every time you close a circle and draw a pentagram. That's how he got my name. I gave it to him for his summoning name."

"I know your names, Rachel Mariana Morgan," the demon said. "I want a secret."

My stomach clenched. "Sure," I said tiredly, scrambling for something. I had a few of those. My eyes fell on the photo of my dad and Trent's father, and I silently held it up to the transparent sheet of ever-after.

"Where's the secret in that?" the demon mocked. "Two

men standing before a bus." Then it blinked. I watched, fascinated, as the horizontal slits went wide until its eyes were almost black. It stood, reaching out for it. A muttered curse slipped past its lips as its fingers smacked into the barrier. I smelled burnt amber.

My pulse leapt at its sudden interest. Maybe it was enough to completely pay off my debt. "Interested?" I taunted. "Clear my debt, and I'll tell you who they both are."

The demon fell back, chuckling. "Oh, you think it's that important?" it mocked. But its eyes tracked the photo as I set it on the counter behind me. Without warning, it shifted forms. The red blur of ever-after melted and flowed. I stared, appalled, as it took on my face. It even had freckles. It was like staring into a mirror, and my skin crawled as my image moved without my volition. Nick went ashen, his long face slack as he stared from me to it.

"I know who both men are," the demon said in my voice. "The one is your father, the other is Trenton Aloysius Kalamack's father. But the camp bus?" Its eyes fastened on me in a devious delight. "Rachel Mariana Morgan, you have indeed given me a secret."

It knew Trent's middle name? Then the same demon attacked us both. Someone had wanted us both dead. For an instant I was tempted to ask the demon who, then dropped my eyes. I could find that out on my own, and it wouldn't cost me my soul.

"Call us even for you having taken me through the ley lines and leave me forever," I said, and the demon laughed. I wondered if my teeth were really that big when I opened my mouth.

"Oh, you are a love," it said in my voice and its accent. "Seeing that picture is enough to buy a summoning name, perhaps, but if you want to absolve your debt, I need something more. Something that could mean your death if it was whispered into the right ear."

The thought that I might be rid of it completely filled me with a reckless daring. "What if I told you why I was there? At that camp?" Nick moved nervously beside me, but if I got rid of the demon forever, it would be worth it.

The demon snickered. "You flatter yourself. That can't be worth your soul."

"Then I'll tell you why I was there if I can summon you safely even without a circle," I blurted, thinking it didn't want to clear my debt simply so it would have a chance at me later.

At that, the demon laughed, turning my stomach as its appearance grotesquely shifted back to the British gentleman even as it roared in mirth. "A promise of safety without a circle?" it said, wiping its eyes when it could speak again. "There's nothing on this God-stinking earth that's worth that."

I swallowed hard. My secret was good—and all I wanted was to be free of it—but it wouldn't believe it was worth it unless I told it first. "I had a rare blood disease," I said before I could change my mind. "I think Trent's father fixed it with his illegal genetic therapy."

The demon chortled. "You and several thousand other brats." Coattails furling, it strode to the edge of the circle. I backpedaled to the counter, heart pounding. "You had better start taking this seriously, or I will lose my good . . ." It jerked as it caught sight of my book, open to the charm for binding a familiar. ". . . temper," it finished, the word trailing to nothing.

"Where did you—" it stammered, then it blinked, sending its goat-slitted eyes over me, then Nick. I couldn't have been more surprised when a small sound of disbelief escaped it. "Oh," it said, sounding shocked. "Damn me thrice."

Nick reached behind me, closing the book and covering it with my sheets of black paper. Suddenly I felt ten times more nervous. My gaze roved over the transparent candles and the pentagram made out of salt. What in hell was I doing?

The demon backed away with a deep-in-thought, toe-to-heel motion. White-gloved hand to its chin, it eyed me with a new intentness, giving me the sensation that it could see through me as easily as I could see through those green candles I had lit, not knowing what they were for. Its quick shift from anger to surprise to an insidious contriving went right to my core, shaking me.

"Well now, let's not be hasty," it amended, its brow furrowed as it glanced at the gadget-strewn watch that appeared on its wrist the instant it looked down. The watch was a twin to Nick's. "What to do, what to do. Kill you or keep you? Hold to tradition or bow to progress? I do believe the only thing that will stand up in court is to let you decide." It smiled, and an unstoppable shiver shook me. "And we do want this to be legal. Very, very legal."

Frightened, I slid down the counter to tuck into Nick. *When did what was legal mean anything to a demon?*

"I will not kill you if you summon me without a circle," the demon said abruptly, its heels making a sharp tap on the linoleum as it backed up, excitement showing in its jerky motions. "If I'm right, I will be giving you this anyway. We'll know soon." It grinned wickedly. "I can hardly wait. Either way, you're mine."

I jumped as Nick took my elbow. "I've never heard of a promise of safety without a circle," he whispered, his gaze pinched. "Ever."

"That's because it's only given to the walking dead, Nick Sparagmos."

The bad feeling in the pit of my stomach started working its way upward, tightening every muscle on the way. There was nothing on this God-stinking earth worth a risk-free summoning, but it gave me that instead of absolving me from my debt? *Oh, that had to be good.*

I had overlooked something. I knew it. Resolute, I pushed the feeling aside. I'd made bad deals before and survived them. "Fine," I said, my voice quavering. "I'm done with you. I want you to go directly back to the ever-after with no deviations along the way."

The demon glanced at its wrist again. "Such a harsh mistress," it said elegantly, in a grand mood as it opened the freezer and took out a frozen box of microwave fries. "But as you're in the circle and I'm out here, I'll leave when I damn well please." Its white-gloved hand was enveloped in a red smear, clearing to show the fries steaming. Opening the fridge, it frowned. "No ketchup?"

Two P.M., I thought, glancing at the clock. *Why was that important?* "Nick," I whispered, going cold. "Take the batteries out of your watch. Now."

"What?"

The clock above the sink said five minutes to two. I wasn't sure how accurate it was. "Just do it!" I shouted. "It's connected to Colorado's atomic clock. It sends out a pulse at midnight their time to reset everything. The pulse will break the circle, just like an active phone line or gas pipe."

"Oh . . . shit," Nick said, his slack face going white.

"Damn you witch!" the demon shouted, furious. "I almost had you both!"

Nick was frantically working at his watch, his long fingers prying at the back. "Do you have a coin? I need a dime to get the back off." His eyes were frightened as they jerked to the clock above the sink. His hand went into a pocket, searching.

"Give it here!" I exclaimed, snatching the watch. I threw it on the counter. Plucking the meat-tenderizing hammer from the rack above me, I swung.

"No!" Nick cried as pieces of watch went everywhere. "We had three minutes yet!"

I shrugged off his grip and beat at it. "You see!" I exclaimed, bringing the hammer down again and again. "You see how clever it is?" Adrenaline made my motions jerky as I brandished the wooden hammer at him. "It knew you had that watch. It was just waiting! That's why it agreed to giving me a safe summoning!" With a cry of frustration, I threw the hammer at the demon. It hit the unseen wall of the circle and bounced back to clatter at my feet. There wasn't much left of Nick's watch but a bent back and shards of quartz.

Nick slumped against the counter, the fingers of one hand pressing into his forehead as he bowed his head. "I thought he *wanted* to teach me," Nick whispered. "All those times, he was just trying to get me to keep him with me until the circle broke."

He jumped as I touched his shoulder, staring at me with frightened eyes. Finally he was frightened. "Do you understand now?" I said bitterly. "It's going to kill you. It's going to kill you and take your soul. Tell me you won't call it again. Please?"

Nick took a quick breath. He met my eyes, shaking his head. "I'll be more careful," he whispered.

Frustrated, I spun to the demon. "Get out of here like I told you to!" I shouted.

With an unearthly grace, the demon stood. The vision of a British gentleman took a moment to adjust the lace about its throat and then its cuffs. Motions slow and deliberate, it pushed the chair back under the table. It inclined its head to me, its red eyes watching from over its glasses. "Congratulations on binding your familiar, Rachel Mariana Morgan," it said. "Summon me with the name Algaliarept. Tell anyone my name, and you're mine by default. And don't think that because you don't have to be in a circle to summon me that you're safe. You are mine. Not even your soul is worth your freedom."

And with that it vanished in a smear of red ever-after, leaving the scent of grease and fried potatoes.

Seventeen

I sat at the lab stool and tapped my ankle against the rungs. "How much longer do you think she can drag this out?" I asked Janine as I tossed my head to Dr. Anders. The woman was at her desk before the blackboard, testing one of the students.

Janine popped her gum and twirled a finger in her enviably straight hair. Her previous fear of my demon mark had turned into a rebellious daring after I told her I got it through my past work with the I.S. Yes, it was ninety percent a lie, but I couldn't bear her distrust of me.

"Familiar evaluations take forever," the young woman agreed. The fingers of her free hand were gentling the fur between her cat's ears. The white Manx had his eyes closed, clearly enjoying the attention. My gaze slid to Bob. I had put him in one of those big peanut butter tubs with a lid to get him there. Janine had "oooohed" over him, but I knew it was a sympathy oooh. Most everyone had cats. One had a ferret. I thought that was cool, and the man to whom it belonged said they made the best familiars.

Bob and I were the only two left to be evaluated, and the room was almost empty, but Janine was waiting for Paula, the student with Dr. Anders. I nervously pulled Bob's bucket closer and glanced out the window to the lights just now flickering on over the parking lot.

I was hoping to see Ivy that night. We still hadn't crossed paths since Nick knocked her out. I knew she'd been around. There was coffee in the pot that afternoon, and the messages were cleared. She had gotten herself up and out before I woke up. That wasn't like her at all, but I knew better than to force a conversation before she was ready.

"Hey," Janine said, jerking my attention back. "Paula and I are going out to Piscary's for some lunch before the sun goes down and the place fills up with undead vamps. Do you want to come? We'll wait for you."

Her offer pleased me more than I wanted to admit, but I shook my head. "Thanks, no. I've already made plans to meet my boyfriend." Nick was working in the next building over, and as he quit today about the time my class was supposed to end, we were going to Micky-d's for his dinner and my lunch.

"Bring him along," Janine urged, her thick blue eyeliner clashing with her otherwise tasteful appearance. "Having one guy at a table of girls always brings the good-looking, single men to the table."

I couldn't help my smile. "No-o-o-o," I hedged, not wanting to tell her Piscary scared the peas out of me, set my demon scar tingling, and was my roommate's uncle, for lack of a better word. "Nick's human," I said. "It'd be kind of awkward."

"You're dating a human!" Janine whispered harshly. "Hey, is it true what they say?"

I gave her a sideways look as Paula finished with Dr. Anders and joined us. "About what?" I asked as Paula shoved her unwilling cat into a collapsible carrier amid yowls and spitting. I stared, appalled, as she zipped the door shut.

"You know . . ." Janine nudged my arm. "Do they have, uh . . . Are they really . . ."

Pulling my eyes from the shaking carrier, I grinned. "Yeah. They do. They really are."

"Yowsers!" Janine exclaimed, reaching to take Paula's arm. "You here that, Paula? I gotta charm me a human before I get too old to appreciate him."

Paula was flushed, looking especially red against her blond hair. "Stop it," she hissed, shooting a glance at Dr. Anders.

"What?" Janine said, not a bit flustered as she opened her carrier and her cat voluntarily went in, curling up and purring. "I wouldn't marry one, but what's wrong with rolling around with a human while you're looking for Mr. Right? My dad's first wife was human."

Our conversation was cut short as Dr. Anders cleared her throat. Janine grabbed her purse and slid off the lab stool. Giving the two women a thin smile, I reluctantly dragged Bob's peanut butter tub off the lab bench and made my way forward. Nick's pentagrams were tucked under my arm, and Dr. Anders didn't look up as I slid the container onto the open space of her desk.

I wanted to wrap this up and get out of here. Nick was going to drive me out to the FIB tonight after lunch so I could talk to Sara Jane. Glenn had asked her to come in so he could get an idea of Dan's daily patterns, and I wanted to ask her about Trent's whereabouts the last few days. Glenn wasn't happy about my angle of investigation, but it was my run, too, damn it.

Nervous, I forced myself to the back of the chair beside Dr. Anders's desk, wondering if Jenks was right and Sara Jane's coming to the FIB was Trent's roundabout way to get his claws into me. One thing was certain. Dr. Anders wasn't the witch hunter. She was nasty, but she wasn't a murderer.

The two women hesitated in the doorway to the hall, their cat carriers pulling them both off balance. "See you Monday, Rachel," Janine said.

I gave her a wave, and Dr. Anders made an annoyed noise deep in her throat. The uptight woman put a blank form on top of the stack of papers and printed my name in large block letters.

"Turtle?" Dr. Anders guessed as she glanced at my container.

"Fish," I said, feeling like an idiot.

"At least you know your limits," she said. "Being an earth witch, it would be difficult for you to hold enough ever-after to bind a rat to you, much less the cat I'm sure you wanted."

Her voice was just shy of patronizing, and I had to unkink my hands from their tight grip.

"You see, Ms. Morgan," Dr. Anders said as she opened the lid and took a peek, "the more power you can channel, the smarter your familiar needs to be. I have an African gray parrot as my familiar." She brought her gaze to mine. "Is that your homework?"

I stifled a surge of annoyance and handed her a pink folder full of short essays. Under it were Nick's water-spotted pentagrams, the black paper curling and warped.

Dr. Anders's lips were so tight, they were bloodless. "Thank you," she said, tossing Nick's sketches aside without even a cursory glance. "You've got a reprieve, Ms. Morgan. But you don't belong in my class, and I will remove you the first chance I get."

I kept my breathing shallow. I knew she wouldn't dare say that if anyone else was in the room.

"Well," she murmured as if tired, "let's see how much aura your fish was able to accept."

"It took a lot." My mood shifted to one of nervousness. Nick had looked over my aura before he left last night, pronouncing it to be rather thin. It would slowly replace itself, but in the interim I felt vulnerable.

Dr. Anders kept her opinion of my obvious fluster to herself. Gaze going distant, she dipped her fingers into Bob's water. The skin on the back of my neck tightened, and it seemed as if my hair drifted in the wind that always seemed to blow in the ever-after. I watched, fascinated, as a blue smear from her hands enveloped Bob. It was ley line power, having turned from red to blue as it reflected the dominant color in the woman's aura.

It was unlikely that Dr. Anders was drawing upon the university's ley line. The power had been taken earlier and stored; it made for faster spell casting. I was willing to bet having a sphere of ever-after in her gut was what made the woman so sour.

The blue haze about Bob vanished as Dr. Anders drew her fingers out of the water. "Take your fish and get out," the woman said brusquely. "Consider yourself flunked."

Floored, I could do nothing but stare. "What?" I finally managed.

Dr. Anders wiped her fingers dry on a tissue and threw it in her trash can under her desk. "This fish isn't bound to you. If it were, the ley line force I cloaked it with would have turned to the color of your aura." Her gaze went indistinct—as if she was looking through me—then her focus sharpened. "Your aura is a sickly gold. What have you been doing, Ms. Morgan, to get it soiled with such a thick haze of red and black?"

"But I followed the instructions!" I cried, not standing up as she began writing on my form. "I'm missing a good chunk of my aura. Where is it?"

"Maybe a bug got into your circle," she said irately. "Go home, call your familiar, and see what comes."

Heart pounding, I licked my lips. *How the hell do you call your familiar?*

She looked up from her writing, putting her crossed arms down upon the page. "You don't know how to call your familiar."

It wasn't a question. I lifted my left shoulder and let it fall in a shrug. What could I say?

"I'll do it," she muttered. "Give me your hand."

I started as she grabbed my wrist. Her bony grip was surprisingly strong. The metallic taste of ash coated my tongue as Dr. Anders muttered an incantation. It was like chewing tinfoil, and I pulled away as soon as her fingers slackened. Rubbing my wrist, I watched Bob, willing him to swim to the surface, or toward me, or something. He just sat on the bottom and swished his tail.

"I don't understand," I whispered, feeling betrayed by my books and the spell-casting abilities I was so confident in. "I followed the instructions to the letter."

Dr. Anders was positively smug. "You will find, Ms. Morgan, that unlike earth magic, ley line manipulation requires more than an unimaginative adherence to rules and to-do lists. It needs talent and a certain amount of freethinking and adaptability. Go home. Make a pet out of whatever shows up on your doorstep. And don't come back to my classroom."

"But I did everything right!" I protested, standing up as she made shooing motions and shuffled her papers in dismissal. "I stood on the scrying mirror and pushed my aura off. I got it into the transfer medium without touching it. I put Bob in with it—"

Dr. Anders jerked, turning her thin face up to me. "Scrying mirror?"

"I said the incantation," I continued. "Nick said it didn't matter if I couldn't say it in Latin." Frustrated, I stood before her desk and fumed. If I left, it would be over. It wasn't the money anymore. It was this woman thinking I was stupid.

"Latin?" Dr. Anders's face was slack.

"I said it," I protested, replaying the night in my head. "And then—" My breath caught and my face went cold. "And then the demon showed up," I whispered, sinking down on the chair before my knees gave way. "Oh God. Did it take my aura? Did the demon take my aura?"

"Demon?" She looked appalled. "You called a demon?"

I panicked, sitting there at the nasty woman's desk. I was scared out of my panties, and I didn't care if she knew it. Algaliarept had my aura. "It got through the circle!" I babbled, forcing myself to not clutch at her arm. "Somehow it got my aura through the circle!"

"Ms. Morgan!" Dr. Anders exclaimed. "If a demon got in your circle, you would not be sitting in front of me. You'd be in the ever-after with it, begging for your death!"

Frightened, I sat where I was with my arms clasped about me. I was a runner, not a demon killer.

The woman looked angry as she tapped her pen on the desktop. "What were you doing summoning a demon? Those things are dangerous."

"I didn't," I gushed. "You gotta believe me. It showed up on its own. See, I owe it a favor for taking me through the ley lines after it was sent to kill me. It was the only way to get back to Ivy before I bled to death. And it thought that I was trying to call it to settle my debt, what with the circle and pentagrams that Nick was copying for—uh—me."

Her eyes flicked to the water-spotted drawings. "Your boyfriend did these, did he?"

Again I nodded, unable to outright lie to her. "I was going to redo them myself later," I said. "I didn't have time to do two weeks of homework and catch a murderer both."

Dr. Anders stiffened. "I did not kill my past students."

My eyes dropped and I felt myself start to calm. "I know."

She took a breath, holding it for a moment before letting it out. I felt some kind of ley line force pass between us, and sat wide-eyed, wondering what she was doing. "You don't think I killed them," she finally said, and the feeling that I was chewing tinfoil stopped. "So why are you in my class?"

"Captain Edden of the FIB sent me to find evidence that

you're the witch hunter," I said. "He won't pay me if I don't follow up on his idea. You're obnoxious, overbearing, and the meanest thing I've seen since my fourth-grade teacher, but you're not a murderer."

The older woman slumped as the tension drained from her. "Thank you," she whispered. "You don't know how good it is to hear someone say that." She pulled her head up, shocking me with a weak smile. "The not-murdering part," she added. "The adjectives I'll ignore."

Seeing a hint of humanity in her, I blurted, "I don't like ley lines, Dr. Anders. Where's the rest of my aura?"

She took a breath to say something, stopping as her gaze went over my shoulder to the door. I spun in my chair at the tentative knock on the frame. Nick peeked round the open door, and I felt my face light up. "I apologize, Dr. Anders," he said, making a show of his university work ID clipped to his shirt. "Can I interrupt for a moment?"

"I'm with a student," she said, the professional tone back in her voice. "I'll be with you in a moment if you'd like to wait in the hall. Could you shut the door, please?"

Nick winced, looking awkward as he stood in his jeans and casual shirt in the doorway. "Ah, it's Rachel I need to see. I'm really sorry for interrupting like this. I'm working in the next building over." He turned to look down the hall and back. "I wanted to see that she was all right. And possibly find out how much longer it was going to be?"

"Who are you?" Dr. Anders asked, her face blank.

"That's Nick," I said sheepishly. "My boyfriend."

Hunched in embarrassment, Nick fidgeted. "I don't know why I'm even bothering you," he said. "I'll go wait in the lounge."

A flash of what looked like horror passed over Dr. Anders. She looked from me to Nick, then surged to her feet. Heels clacking, she pulled him in and shut the door behind him.

"Stay there," she said as she left him bewildered in front

of her desk. Nick's pentagrams sat before us like guilt given substance. Standing before the windows with her back to us, Dr. Anders looked at the dark parking lot. "Where did you get a familiar binding spell that was in Latin?" she asked.

Nick touched my shoulder in sympathy, and I wished I'd never gotten him into this. "Uh, out of one of my old spell books," I admitted, thinking she wanted Nick there for verification. "It was the only charm I could find on such short notice. But I know the pentagrams. I just didn't have the time to do them."

"There's a binding incantation in the appendix of your textbook," she said, sounding tired. "You were supposed to use that one." It wasn't the pentagrams she was worried about, and a cold feeling slid through me as she turned around. The wrinkles in her face looked harsh in the fluorescent light. "Tell me exactly what you did."

At Nick's encouraging nod, I said, "Uh, first I made the transfer medium. Then I closed the circle."

"Modified to summon and protect," Nick interrupted. "And I was inside it with her."

"Wait a moment," Dr. Anders said. "Just how big was your circle?"

I tucked my hair back, glad she wasn't barking at me anymore. "Maybe six feet?"

"Around?"

"Across."

She took a breath and sat down, motioning me to continue.

"Um, then I stood on my scrying mirror and pushed off my aura."

"What was that like?" she whispered, elbows on her desk as she stared out the window.

"Damn—uh—darn uncomfortable. I got the mirror into the transfer medium without touching the surface. My aura precipitated out into the media, and then I put Bob into it."

"Into the transfer medium?"

I nodded, though she wasn't looking at me. "I figured that was the only way to anoint a fish. Then I said the incantation."

"Actually," Nick interrupted. "I said the incantation first in Latin, then translated it for her, giving her an alternate interpretation on the last part."

"That's right," I admitted. "I said it, and then the demon showed up." I glanced at Nick, but it didn't bother him as much as it bothered me. "Then I knocked over Bob's bowl. My aura was all over him. I was afraid he might break the circle if my aura touched it."

"It would have." Dr. Anders was staring at the parking lot again.

"Is that why some of my aura is missing?" I asked. "Did I throw it away with the paper towels?"

Dr. Anders brought her gaze to mine. "No. I think you made Nick your familiar."

My jaw dropped. I spun in my chair and looked up at Nick. His hand had fallen from my shoulder and he took a wide-eyed step back. "What?" I exclaimed.

"You can do that?" Nick asked.

"No. You can't," Dr. Anders said. "Sentient beings with free will can't be bound to another by incantation. But you mixed earth magic with ley line magic. I've never heard of binding a familiar like that. Where did you get that book?"

"My attic," I whispered. I looked up at Nick. "Oh, Nick," I said, embarrassed. "I'm really sorry. You must have picked up my aura when you were trying to catch Bob."

Nick looked confused. "I'm your familiar?" he whispered, his long face quizzical.

Dr. Anders made a bitter-sounding bark of laughter. "It's nothing to be proud of, Ms. Morgan. Taking a human as a familiar is heinous. It's slavery. Demonic."

"Hold up," I stammered, feeling myself go cold. "It was an accident."

The woman's eyes turned hard. "Remember what I said about a practioner's abilities being linked to his or her familiar? Demons use people as familiars. The more powerful the person is, the more power the demon can wield through him or her. That's why they are forever trying to educate the foolish in the dark arts. They teach them, gain control over their souls, then make them their familiars. You used demon magic by mixing earth and ley line witchcraft."

I put a hand to my stomach. "I'm sorry, Nick," I whispered.

He was pale, and he stood unmoving by my shoulder. "It was an accident."

Dr. Anders made a rude noise. "Accident or not, it's the foulest thing I've heard of. You have put Nick in a great deal of danger."

"How?" I fumbled for his hand. It was cold in mine, and he gave my fingers a squeeze.

"Because he's carrying some of your aura. Ley line witches give their familiars a portion of their aura to act as an anchor when they pull on a ley line. If something goes wrong, the familiar is pulled into the ever-after, not the witch. But more important, familiars insulate you from going insane from channeling too much ley line force. Ley line witches don't hold the energy they store from a line in themselves. They keep it in their familiars. Simon, my parrot, holds it for me, and I draw upon it as I need. When we're together, I'm stronger. When he's ill, my abilities decrease. If he's closer to a line than I am, I can reach it through him. If things go wrong, he dies, not me."

I gulped, cold as Dr. Anders eyed me as if I had done it on purpose.

"That's why animals are used as familiars," she said coldly. "Not people."

"Nick," I murmured. "I'm sorry." That was what, three times now I'd said it?

Dr. Anders's face wrinkled up. "Sorry? Until we get him

unbound, you will not store any ley line energy. It's too dangerous."

"I don't know how to bind ley line force," I admitted. *I had made Nick my familiar?*

"Wait a moment." The woman put a thin hand to her forehead. "You don't know how to store ley line force? At all? You made a circle six feet across strong enough to keep out a demon using energy straight from the line? You didn't use any previously stored energy at all?"

I shook my head.

"You don't know how to hold even an ounce of ever-after?"

Again I shook my head.

The woman sighed. "Your father was right."

"You knew my dad?" I questioned. *Why not? Everyone else seemed to.*

"I taught one of his undergrad classes," she said. "Though I didn't know it at the time. I didn't see him again until thirteen years ago when we met to discuss you." She sat back and cocked her eyebrows. "He asked me to flunk you if you ever showed up in my class."

"Wh-Why?" I stammered.

"Apparently he knew how much strength you could pull from a line, as he wanted me to persuade you to turn to earth witchcraft instead of line magic. He said it would be safer. My class was overcrowded that year, and bending to a father's wish to protect his daughter was no skin off my nose. I had assumed he meant safer for you. In hindsight, I think he meant everyone else."

"Safer?" I whispered, feeling ill.

"Making a human your familiar isn't normal, Ms. Morgan," Dr. Anders said.

"Could you do it?" Nick asked, and I flicked a glance at him, glad he had asked, not me.

She looked affronted. "Probably. If I had the binding spell. But I wouldn't. It's demonic. The only reason I'm not calling Inderland Security is because it was an accident which we will soon rectify."

"Thanks," I breathed, numb. *I had made Nick my familiar? I had used demon magic to bind him to me?* Dizzy, I put my head between my knees, figuring it was marginally more dignified then passing out and falling to the floor. I felt Nick's hand on my back and stifled a hysterical laugh. *What had I done?*

Nick's voice came out of the blackness as I closed my eyes and struggled to keep from throwing up. "You can break the spell? I thought familiars were lifelong bonds."

"They generally are—for the familiar." She sounded tired. "But you can unbind one if your skill rises to the point where your familiar is holding you back. And then you have to supplant the old familiar with a better one. But what is better than a person, Nick?"

I pulled my head from between my knees to find Dr. Anders grimacing. "I need to see that book," she said. "There's probably something in it about how to unbind a person. Demons are notorious for taking something better when it comes along. I'd like to know how a book of demon magic ended up in your attic in the first place?"

"I live in a church," I whispered. "It was there when I moved in." I glanced out the window, my sick feeling starting to diminish. Nick had my aura. That was better than a demon having it. And we would be able to undo this—somehow. I had told Glenn I'd meet him at the FIB tonight, but Nick came first.

"I'll go get the book," I said, looking at the closed door. "Can we do this here, or does it have to be somewhere more private? We can go to my kitchen. I've a ley line in the backyard."

Dr. Anders had lost all of her ugliness. Now she looked simply tired. "I can't do anything tonight," she said, glancing apologetically at Nick. "But let me give you my address." She reached for a pen, scribbling across the folded evaluation of me and my familiar. "You can leave the book with the gateman, and I'll get to it this weekend."

"Why not tonight?" I asked as I took the paper.

"I'm busy tonight. I'll be giving a presentation tomorrow, and I have to prepare an updated success/failure statement." She flushed, which turned her years younger.

"Who for?" I asked, the cold feeling returning to the pit of my stomach.

"Mr. Kalamack."

My eyes closed in a strength-gathering blink. "Dr. Anders?" I said, hearing Nick shift from foot to foot beside me. "Trent Kalamack is the one killing the ley line witches."

The woman flashed back to her usual mien of scorn. "Don't be foolish, Ms. Morgan. Mr. Kalamack is no more a murderer than I am."

"Call me Rachel," I said, thinking we ought to be on a first-name basis. "And Kalamack is the witch hunter. I've seen the reports. He talked to every one of the victims within a month before their death."

Dr. Anders opened a lower drawer and pulled out a tasteful black purse. "I talked with him last spring at graduation and I'm still alive. He's interested in discussing my research. If I can capture his attention, he will fund me and I can do what I really want. I've been working six years to put this together, and I'm not going to lose my chance to catch a benefactor because of some fool coincidence."

I shifted to the edge of my chair, wondering how I could go from hating her to being worried so quickly. "Dr. Anders, please," I said, glancing up at Nick. "I know you think I'm a scatterbrained flop. But don't do this. I've seen the reports on the people he's killed. Every one of them died in terror. And Trent talked to all of them."

"Ah, Rachel?" Nick interrupted. "You don't know that for sure."

I spun to him. "You aren't helping!"

Dr. Anders stood with her purse. "Get me the book. I'll look at it this weekend."

"No!" I protested, seeing her tying up the ends of our conversation. "He'll kill you with no more thought than swatting a fly." My jaw gritted as she gestured to the door. "Let me come with you, then," I said as I stood up. "I've done escort service for humans into the Hollows. I know how to stay quiet and watch your back."

The woman's eyes narrowed. "I am a doctor of ley line magic. You think you can protect me better than I can protect myself?"

I took a breath to protest, then let it out. "You're right," I said, thinking it would be easier to follow her without her knowing. "Could you at least tell me when you're meeting with him? I'd feel better if I could give you a call when you're supposed to be home."

She sent one eyebrow up. "Tomorrow night at seven. We're dining at the restaurant atop Carew Tower. Is that a public enough place to please you?"

I would have to borrow some money from Ivy if I was going to follow her up there. A glass of water cost three bucks and a lousy house salad was twelve—or so I'd heard. I didn't think I had a nice enough dress, either. But I wasn't going to let her meet with Trent unwatched.

Nodding, I put the strap of my bag over my shoulder and stood by Nick. "Yes. Thank you."

Eighteen

The early afternoon sun had almost worked its way from the kitchen, a last band making a thin sliver along the sink and counter. I was sitting at Ivy's antique table, leafing through her catalogs and finishing my breakfast of coffee. I'd been up for only an hour or so, nursing my cup and waiting for Ivy. I had made a full carafe, hoping to lure her into talking to me. She still wasn't ready, having evaded me on the excuse of having to research her latest run. I wished she'd talk to me. The Turn take it, I'd be happy if she'd just listen. It didn't seem possible she would put this much weight on the incident. She had slipped before, and we had gotten past it.

Sighing, I stretched my legs out under the table. I turned the page to a collection of closet organizers, my eyes drifting aimlessly. I didn't have much to do today until Glenn, Jenks, and I went to tail Dr. Anders that night. Nick had loaned me some money, and I had a party dress that wouldn't look too cheap and would hide my splat gun.

Edden had been thrilled when I told him I was going to follow the woman—until I stupidly admitted she was meeting with Trent. We had nearly come to blows over it, shocking the officers on the floor. At this point, I didn't care if

Edden threw me in jail. He'd have to wait until I did something, and by then I'd have what I needed.

Glenn wasn't happy with me, either. I'd played the daddy's-boy card to get him to keep his mouth shut and come with me tonight. I didn't care. Trent was killing people.

My eyes, roving over the catalog, fastened on an oak desk, the kind detectives had in pre-Turn movies. A sigh escaped me in an exhalation of desire. It was beautiful, with a deep luster that pressboard lacked. There were all sorts of little cubbies and a hidden compartment behind the bottom left drawer according to the sell line. It would fit nicely in the sanctuary.

A grimace pulled my face down as I thought of my pathetic furniture, some still in storage. Ivy had beautiful furniture, with smooth lines and a heavy weight. The drawers never stuck and the metal latches clicked smartly when they closed. I wanted something like that. Something permanent. Something that arrived on my doorstep fully assembled. Something that could stand a dip in saltwater if I ever got another death threat put on me.

It would never happen, I thought, pushing the catalog away. Getting nice furniture, not the death threat. My eyes slid from the shiny paper to my ley line textbook. I stared at it, thinking. *I could channel more power than most. My dad hadn't wanted me to know. Dr. Anders thought I was an idiot.* There was only one thing I could do.

Taking a breath, I pulled the book closer. I thumbed to the back and the appendices, stopping at the incantation for binding a familiar. It was all ritualistic, with notations referring to techniques I hadn't a clue on. The incantation was in English, and there were no brews or plants involved at all. It was as alien to me as geometry, and I didn't like feeling stupid.

The pages made a pleasant sound as I rifled to the front of the book looking for something I could understand. I slowed, inserting my thumb as I found an incantation for diverting objects in motion. *Cool,* I thought. It was exactly why I had wanted a wand.

Sitting straighter, I crossed my knees and leaned over the book. You were supposed to draw on stored ley line energy to manipulate small things, and connect right to a line for things with a lot of mass or that were moving quickly. The only physical thing I needed was an object to serve as a focal point.

I looked up as Jenks flitted in the open kitchen window. "Hey, Rache," he said cheerily. "Whatcha doing?"

Reaching for the furniture catalog, I slid it smoothly over the textbook. "Not much," I said as I looked down. "You're in a good mood."

"I just got back from your mom's. She's cool, you know." He flew to the center island counter, landing on it to put himself at nearly my eye level. "Jax is doing well. If your mom is cotton to the idea, I'm going to let him have a go at making a garden big enough to support him."

"Cotton?" I questioned, turning a page to some beautiful phone tables. I blanched at the price. How could something that small cost so much?

"Yeah. You know . . . cool, A-okay, keen, kosher."

"I know what it means," I said, recognizing it as one of my mother's favorite phrases and thinking it odd Jenks would have picked it up.

"Have you talked to Ivy yet?" he asked.

"No."

My frustration was obvious in the short word. Jenks hesitated, then, with a clattering of wings, he flew a swooping path to land upon my shoulder. "Sorry."

I forced a pleasant expression as I pulled my head up and tucked a curl behind my ear. "Yeah, me too."

He made an irate noise with his wings. "So-o-o, whatcha

hiding under the catalog? Looking through Ivy's leather outlets?"

My jaw tightened. "It's nothing," I said softly.

"You looking to buy furniture?" he scoffed. "Give me a break."

Peeved, I waved him away. "Yeah. I want furniture, something other than pressboard—excuse me—engineered wood. Ivy's stuff makes mine look like trailer-park plastic."

Jenks laughed, the wind from his wings shifting the hair about my face. "So get yourself something nice the next time you have some money."

"Like that will ever happen," I muttered.

Jenks zipped under the table. Not trusting him, I bent to see what he was doing. "Hey! Stop it!" I cried, moving my foot as I felt a tug on my shoe. He darted away, and when I came up from retying my lace, I found he had pulled the catalog off the textbook. His hands were on his hips as he stood on it, reading. "Jenks!" I complained.

"I thought you didn't like ley lines," he said, flitting up and then right back down where he had been. "Especially now that you can't use them without endangering Nick."

"I don't," I said, wishing I hadn't told him about having accidentally made Nick my familiar. "But look. This stuff is easy."

Jenks was silent, his wings drooping as he looked at the charm. "You gonna try it?"

"No," I said quickly.

"Nick will be okay if you pull your energy right off the line. He'll never know." Jenks turned sideways so he could see me and the print both. "It says right here you don't have to use stored energy but can pull it off the line. See? Right here in black and white."

"Yeah," I said slowly, not convinced.

Jenks grinned. "You learn how to do this, and you could

get back at the Howlers. You still have those tickets for next Sunday's game, don't you?"

"Yeah," I said cautiously.

Jenks strutted down the page, his wings a red blur in excitement. "You could make them pay you, and since you have Edden's paycheck coming for your rent, you could get a nice oak shoe rack or something."

"Ye-e-e-eah," I hedged.

Jenks eyed me slyly from under his blond bangs. "Unless you're afraid."

My eyes narrowed. "Anyone ever tell you you're a real prick?"

He laughed, rising up with a glittering sunbeam of pixy dust. "If I had a quarter . . ." he mused. Flitting close, he landed on my shoulder. "Is it hard?"

Leaning over the book, I swung my hair to one side so he could see, too. "No, and that's what worries me. There's an incantation, and I need a focusing object. I'll have to connect to a ley line. And there's a gesture . . ." My brow furrowed and I tapped the book. *It couldn't be this easy.*

"You gonna try it?"

The thought that Algaliarept might know I was pulling on the line flitted through me. But seeing that it was daylight and we had an agreement, I thought it was safe enough. "Yeah."

Sitting straighter, I settled myself. Reaching out with my second sight, I fumbled for the line. The sun completely overwhelmed any vision of the ever-after, but the ley line was clear enough in my mind's eye, looking like a streak of dried blood hanging above the tombstones. Thinking it was really ugly, I cautiously reached out a thought and touched it.

My breath hissed in through my nose and I stiffened.

"You okay, Rache?" Jenks questioned, launching himself off my shoulder.

Head bowed over the book, I nodded. The energy flowed through me faster than before, equalizing the strengths very quickly. It was almost as if the previous times had cleared the channels. Worried about using too much, I tried to push some of it down through me and out of my feet. It didn't do any good. The incoming force simply filled me back up again.

Resigned to the uncomfortable feeling, I mentally shook my second sight from me and looked up. Jenks was watching me in concern. I gave him an encouraging smile, and he nodded, apparently satisfied. "How about this?" Jenks said, flying to my stash of water paint balls. The red sphere was as big as his head, and clearly heavy, but he managed it all right.

"It's as good as anything," I agreed. "Toss one up, and I'll try to shift it."

Thinking this was easier than grinding plants and boiling water, I said the incantation and made a swooping loop of a figure in the air with my hand, imagining it was like writing your name with a sparkler on the Fourth of July. I said the last word as Jenks tossed the ball up.

"Ow!" I shouted as a surge of ley line force burned my left hand. I looked at Jenks in bewilderment as he laughed. "What did I do wrong?"

He flitted close with the red ball tucked under his arm, caught when it fell back to him. "You forgot your focusing object. Here. Use this."

"Ah." Embarrassed, I took the red ball as he dropped it into my hand. "Let's try it again," I said, and cradled it in my recessive hand as the book had instructed. Feeling the cool smoothness of it, I said the incantation and etched the figure in the air with my right hand.

Jenks tossed a second ball with a sharp whistle of his wings. Startled, I let loose a surge of power. This time it worked. I stifled a yelp as I felt the ley line energy dart through my hand, following my attention right to the ball. It hit it, knocking it into the wall to make a dripping smear. "Yes!" I exclaimed, meeting Jenks's grin with my own. "Look at that! It worked!"

Jenks flew to the counter to get another ball. "Try it again," he prompted, tossing it eagerly to the ceiling.

It came faster this time. I found I could do the incantation and gesture simultaneously, holding the ley line energy with my will until I wanted to release it. With that came a great deal of control, and soon I was no longer hitting them with so much force that they broke when they hit the wall. My aim was getting better, too, and the sink was littered with the balls I'd been bouncing off the screen. Mr. Fish on the sill wasn't happy.

Jenks was a willing partner, zipping about the kitchen, throwing the red balls at the ceiling. My eyes widened as he threw one at me instead. "Hey!" I cried, sending the ball through the pixy hole in the screen. "Not at me!"

"What a good idea," he said, then grinned wickedly as he made a sharp whistle. Three of his kids zipped in from the garden, all talking at once. They brought the smell of dandelions and asters with them. "Toss them at Ms. Morgan," he said, handing his sphere to the girl in pink.

"Hold it," I protested, ducking as the girl pixy threw it with as much skill and power as her father. I looked behind me to the dark splat against the yellow wall, then back to them. My mouth opened. In the instant I had looked away, they all had gotten splat balls.

"Get her!" Jenks cried.

"Jenks!" I said, laughing as I managed to divert one of the four balls. The three I missed rolled harmlessly to the floor. The smallest pixy skimmed over the linoleum, tossing them upward to where his sisters caught them. "Four against one isn't fair!" I shouted as they took aim again.

My eyes darted to the hallway as the phone rang. "Time!"

I called out, lurching to escape into the living room. "Time out!" Still smiling, I reached for the phone. Jenks hovered in the archway, waiting. "Hello. Vampiric Charms. Rachel speaking," I said, ducking the ball he threw at me. I could hear pixy giggles from the kitchen and wondered what they were up to.

"Rachel?" came Nick's voice. "What the blue blazes are you doing?"

"Hi, Nick." I paused to mouth the incantation. I held the energy until Jenks lobbed a ball at me. I was getting better, almost hitting him with the diverted splat ball. "Jenks. Stop it," I protested. "I'm on the phone."

He grinned, then darted out. I flopped into one of Ivy's cushy, matching suede chairs, knowing he wouldn't risk getting water on it and have Ivy come after him.

"Hey, you're up already? You want to do something?" I asked, draping my legs over one arm and lolling my neck on the other. I shifted the red ball I was using as a focusing object between two fingers, daring it to break with the pressure I had it under.

"Um, maybe," he said. "Are you by chance pulling on a ley line?"

I waved Jenks to stop as he swooped in. "Yes!" I said, sitting up and putting my feet on the floor. "I'm sorry. I didn't think you would feel it. I'm not drawing it through you, am I?"

Jenks landed on top of a picture frame. I was sure he could hear Nick, though the pixy was on the other side of the room.

"No," Nick said, a hint of laughter in his voice, tiny through the receiver. "I'm sure I'd be able to tell. But it's odd. I'm sitting here reading, and all of a sudden it feels like you're here with me. The best way to describe it is when you're over here and I'm making dinner, watching you watch TV. You're doing your own thing, not looking for my attention, but being really noisy. It's kind of distracting."

"You watch me watch TV?" I asked, uncomfortable, and he chuckled.

"Yeah. It's a lot of fun. You jump up and down a lot."

My brow furrowed as Jenks snickered. "Sorry," I muttered, but then a faint tickle of warning pulled me straighter. Nick was up reading. He usually spent his Saturday in bed catching up on sleep. "Nick, what book are you reading?"

"Ah, yours," he admitted.

I only had one book that he'd be interested in. "Nick!" I protested as I scooted to the edge of my chair and gripped the phone tighter, "you said you'd take it to Dr. Anders." After blowing off my trip to the FIB because I was frazzled worse than my hair, Nick had taken me home. I'd thought he offered to deliver the book because of my new and healthy phobia of the literally damned tome. Obviously Nick had other plans, and it hadn't made it that far.

"She wasn't going to look at it last night," he said defensively. "And it's safer in my apartment than sitting in a guardhouse getting coffee rings. If you don't mind, I'd like to keep it one more night. There is something in it I want to ask the demon." He paused, clearly waiting for me to protest.

My face warmed. "Idiot," I said, obliging him. "You are an idiot. Dr. Anders told you what that demon is trying to do. It nearly kills both of us, and you're still pumping it for information?"

I heard Nick sigh. "I'm being careful," he said, and I made a frightened bark of laughter. "Rachel, I promise I'll take it over first thing tomorrow. She isn't going to look at it until then anyway." He hesitated, and I could almost hear him gather his resolve. "I'm going to call him. Please don't make me do this behind your back. I'd feel better if someone knew."

"Why? So I can tell your mother what killed you?" I said sharply, then caught myself. Eyes closing, I squeezed the red ball between my fingers. He was silent, waiting. I hated that I had no right to tell him to stop. Not even as his girlfriend. Summoning demons wasn't illegal. It was just really, really, stupid. "Promise you'll call me when you're done?" I asked, feeling my stomach quiver. "I'm up until about five."

"Sure," he breathed. "Thanks. I want to hear how your dinner with Trent goes."

"You bet," I echoed. "Talk to you later." *If you survive.*

I hung up, meeting Jenks's eyes. He was hovering in the middle of the room, a splat ball tucked under his arm. "You two are going to end up as dark smears on ley line circles," he said, and I flicked the splat ball I held at him. He caught it one-handed, moving several feet before stopping its momentum. He flung it back, and I dodged. It hit Ivy's chair without breaking. Thankful for small favors, I picked it up and headed for the kitchen.

"Now!" Jenks shrilled as I entered the bright room.

"Get her!" shrieked a dozen pixies.

Jerked out of my depression, I cowered as a hailstorm of splat balls hit me, breaking against my covered head. Darting to the fridge, I opened the door and hid behind it. Adrenaline made my blood seem to sing. I grinned at the sound of six or more splats against the metallic door. "You little beggars!" I shouted, peeking up to see them flitting over the far end of the kitchen like insane fireflies. My eyes widened; there must have been twenty of them!

Splat balls littered the floor, rolling slowly away from me. Thrilling in it, I said my incantation three times fast and bounced the next three missiles right back at them.

Jenks's kids shrieked in delight, their silk dresses and pants a blur of color. Pixy dust made trails of slowly falling sunshine. Jenks was standing on the ladle hanging from the rack over the center island counter. The sword he used to fight off fairies was in his grip, and he brandished it high as he shouted encouragement.

Under his noisy direction they banded together. Giggled whispers punctuated by excited shouts filled the air as they organized. Grinning, I hid behind the door with my ankles cooling in the draft from the fridge. I said the incantation over and over, feeling the ley line force swell behind my eyes. They were going to attack en masse, knowing I couldn't deflect them all.

"Now!" Jenks shouted. His tiny saber swinging, he launched himself from the ladle.

I cried out at the cheerful ferocity of his kids swarming at me. Laughing in protest, I sent the red balls flying. Little thumps beat at me from the ones I missed. Gasping for air, I rolled under the table. They followed me, bombarding me.

I was out of incantations. "I give up!" I cried, careful not to hit any of Jenks's kids as I put my hands on the underside of the table. I was covered in spots of water, and I pushed back the damp strands of hair stuck to my face. "I give up! You win!"

They cheered, and the phone started ringing again. Proud and exuberant, Jenks bellowed out a stirring song about beating invaders from their land and coming home to seedlings. Sword held high, he made a circuit around the room, gathering his kids up in tow. All singing in glorious harmony, they flowed out the window and into the garden.

I sat in the sudden silence on the kitchen floor under the table. My entire body shifted as I took a deep breath, smiling as I exhaled. "Whew!" I puffed, still chuckling as I wiped a hand under my eye. No wonder the fairy assassins sent to kill me last year hadn't had a chance. Jenks's kids were clever, quick—and aggressive.

Still smiling, I rolled to my feet and padded into the living room to get the phone before the machine picked it up. Poor Nick. I was sure he felt that last one.

"Nick," I blurted before he could say anything. "I'm

sorry. Jenks's kids had me under the kitchen table and were throwing splat balls at me. God help me, but it was funny. They're in the garden right now, making rings around the ash tree and singing about cold steel."

"Rachel?"

It was Glenn, and my mirth died at his worried tone. "What?" I said, looking at the trees through the shoulder-high windows. The spots of water covering me were suddenly cold, and I clasped an arm around myself.

"I'll be there in ten minutes," he said. "Can you be ready?"

I pushed my damp hair back. "Why? What's happened?" I asked.

I heard him cover the receiver and shout something at someone. "You got your warrant to search Kalamack's property," he said when he returned.

"How?" I questioned, not believing Edden had caved. "Not that I'm complaining!"

Glenn hesitated. He took a slow breath, and I heard excited voices in the background. "Dr. Anders called me last night," he said. "She knew you were going to follow her, so she moved her presentation to last night and asked me to go with her instead."

"The witch," I exclaimed softly, wishing I could have seen what Glenn had worn. I bet it had been sharp. But when he remained silent, the cold feeling in my stomach solidified into a sour lump.

"I'm sorry, Rachel," Glenn said softly. "Her car went off Roebling Bridge this morning, pushed over the rail by what appeared to be a huge bubble of ley line force. They just pulled her car from the river. We're still looking for the body."

Nineteen

My foot jiggled as I impatiently stood beside the stack of manuals and empty paper cups that lined the sill of Trent's gatehouse. Jenks was on my earring, muttering darkly as he watched Quen punch a button on the phone. I'd seen Quen only once before—possibly twice. The first time, he was masquerading as a gardener, actually managing to catch Jenks in a glass ball. I had a growing suspicion that Quen had been the third rider who tried to run me down on horseback the night I stole my blackmail disc from Trent. It was a feeling that solidified when Jenks told me Quen smelled just like Trent and Jonathan.

Quen reached in front of me for a pen, and I jerked back, not wanting him to touch me. Still on the phone, he smiled carefully, showing me extremely white, even teeth. *This one,* I thought, *knew what I was capable of.* This one wouldn't underestimate me as Jonathan continually did. And though it was nice being taken seriously for once, I wished Quen was as egotistical and chauvinistic as Jonathan was.

Trent had once said Quen was willing to take me on as a student—after the security officer got over his desire to kill me for infiltrating the Kalamack compound. I wondered if I would have survived having him as a teacher.

Quen looked about the age my father would be if he were

still alive. He had very dark hair that curled about his ears, green eyes that always seemed to be watching me, and a dancer's grace that I knew came from a lifetime of martial arts practice. Dressed in a black security uniform with no insignia, he looked like he belonged to the night. He was a shade taller than I was in heels, and the strength in his lightly wrinkled physique had me on edge. His fingers were quick on a keyboard and his eyes were faster. The only weakness I'd noticed was a slight limp. And unlike everyone else in the room besides me, he had no weapon that I could see.

Captain Edden stood beside me, looking squat but capable in his khaki pants and white shirt. Glenn was in another of his black suits, trying to look collected despite his obvious nervousness. Edden, too, looked worried that he was going to have egg on his face if we didn't find anything.

I adjusted my bag higher onto my shoulder and fidgeted. It was full of charms to find Dr. Anders, dead or alive. I had made Glenn wait while I whipped them up, using the paper she had written her address on as the focal object. If there was a shoe box left of her, the charms would light red. With them was a lie amulet, my wire-framed glasses to see through ley line disguises, and a spell checker. I was going to take the opportunity while talking to Trent to see if he used a charm to disguise his appearance. Nobody looks that good without help.

Outside, parked in the lot beside the gatehouse, were three FIB vans. The doors were open and the officers looked hot as they waited in the heat of an unseasonably warm afternoon. The breeze from Jenks's wings sent a wisp of hair to tickle my neck. "Can you hear him?" I breathed as Quen turned away and began speaking into the phone.

"Oh, yeah," the pixy muttered. "He's talking to Jonathan. Quen is telling him he's standing in the gatehouse with you and Edden with a warrant to search the property and he bloody well just better wake him up."

"Him being Trent?" I guessed, and felt my earring swing as Jenks nodded. I looked at the clock over the door, seeing it was a little after two. Must be nice.

Edden cleared his throat as Quen hung up. Trent's security officer made no bones about letting us know he was unhappy. His light wrinkles deepened as his jaw clenched, and his green eyes were hard. "Captain Edden, Mr. Kalamack is understandably upset, and would like to speak with you while your people carry out your search."

"Of course," Edden said, and a small sound of disbelief escaped me.

"Why are you being so nice?" I muttered as Quen ushered us through the heavy glass and metal doors and back into the strong sun.

"Rachel," Edden breathed, tension carrying through his whisper, "you will be polite and gracious or you will wait in the car."

Gracious, I thought. *Since when were ex–Navy SEALs gracious?* Hard-nosed, aggressive, politically correct to the point of being anal. Ah . . . he was being politically correct.

Edden leaned close as he held the door to one of the vans for me. "And then we're going to nail his ass to a tree," he added, confirming my suspicions. "If Kalamack murdered her, we'll get him," he said, his eyes on Quen as the man swung into an estate vehicle. "But if we bull in here like storm troopers, a jury will let him go even if he confesses. It's all in the procedure. I've stopped traffic in and out. No one leaves without a search."

I squinted at him, putting a hand to my hat to keep it from blowing off. I'd much rather have screamed in with twenty cars and sirens blazing, but I'd have to be satisfied with this.

The drive up the three-mile entry road through the wood Trent maintained about his estate was quiet since Jenks had gone with Glenn in the estate car to try and figure out what kind of Inderlander Quen was. We followed Quen's security vehicle around the last turn and pulled into the empty visitor's parking lot.

I couldn't help but be impressed by Trent's main building. The three-story edifice was settled in among the surrounding vegetation as if it had been here for hundreds of years rather than forty. The white marble sent glints of sunlight to pool against the trees like a sunrise from the west. Large pillars and wide shallow steps made an inviting entry. Surrounded by trees and gardens, the office buildings had a sense of permanence those in the city lacked. Several smaller buildings sprawled from the main one, attached by covered walkways. Trent's renowned walled gardens took up much of the side and back, the acres of well-tended plants surrounded by fields of grass and then his eerie planned-out forest.

I was the first one out of the van, my gaze crossing the road to the distant low-slung buildings where Trent raised his thoroughbreds. A tour bus was just leaving, obnoxiously noisy and emblazoned with advertisements to visit Trent's gardens.

Jenks flitted up to land on my shoulder, since my current earrings were too small for him to perch on, grumbling about his inability to figure out what Quen was. I turned back to the main building and started up the stone steps, heels clicking in a steady cadence. Edden was quick behind me.

My gut tightened when I saw a familiar silhouette waiting for us by the marble pillars. "Jonathan," I whispered, my dislike for the extremely tall man swinging into a slow hatred. Just once I'd like to climb those stairs and not have his haughty eyes on me.

My lips went tight and I suddenly was glad for having worn my best suit-dress despite the unseasonable heat. Jonathan's suit was exquisite. It had to have been tailored to him since he was too tall to be able to buy anything off the rack. His dark hair was graying around the temples, and the wrinkles around his eyes were embedded as if acid had etched them in concrete. He had been a child during the Turn, seemingly marked forever by its fear in his gaunt, almost malnourished stance.

Tidy and overdressed, his manner screamed British Englishman, but his accent was as midwestern as mine. He was clean shaven, his cheeks and thin lips never stirring from a perpetual frown unless it was at someone's expense. He had grinned the entire three days I had been a mink trapped in a cage in Trent's office, his vivid blue eyes alive and eager as he tormented me.

Quen strode quickly up the stairs to pull ahead of me. My eye started to tic as the two men put their heads together. They turned, Jonathan's professional smile laced with professional irritation. Nice.

"Captain Edden," he said, extending his thin hand as Edden and I halted before them. Edden's muscular build looked almost dumpy as he shook hands with him. "I'm Jonathan, Mr. Kalamack's publicity adviser. Mr. Kalamack is waiting for you," he added, the congeniality in his voice never reaching his eyes. "He asked me to relay his desire to help any way he can."

Jenks snickered from my shoulder. "He could tell us where he stashed Dr. Anders."

He whispered it, but both Quen and Jonathan stiffened. I pretended to check the French braid I'd put my hair in—subtly threatening to smack Jenks—then put my hands behind my back to forestall a handshake with Jonathan. I wouldn't touch him. Unless it was my fist in his gut. Damn, I really missed my handcuffs.

"Thank you," Edden said, eyebrows raised at the evil glances Jonathan and I were exchanging. "We'll try to make this as quick and nonintrusive as possible."

As I stood and glowered, Edden pulled Glenn aside. "Keep the search low-key but thorough," he said as Jonathan's eyes flicked over my shoulder to the FIB officers assembling in a loose conglomeration on the wide steps. They had brought several dogs with them, all wearing blue body sleeves with FIB emblazoned on them in yellow. Their tails waved enthusiastically and they were clearly eager to get to work.

Glenn nodded, and I swung my bag around. "Here," I said, pulling out a handful of charms and dumping them into his grip. "I primed them on the way over. They're set to find Dr. Anders whether she is dead or alive. Give them to whoever will take them. They'll turn red if they get within a hundred feet of her."

"I'll make sure every team has one," Glenn said, his brown eyes startled as he tried to keep from dropping them.

"Hey, Rache," Jenks said as he flitted off my shoulder. "Glenn asked me to tag along with him. You mind? I can't do anything sitting pretty on your shoulder."

"Sure, go ahead," I said, thinking he could search the garden better than a pack of dogs.

A worried frown crossed Jonathan's long face, and I beamed sarcastically at him. Pixies and fairies weren't allowed on the grounds as a general rule, and I'd wear my panties on the outside for a week if someone would tell me what Trent was afraid Jenks might find.

Quen and Jonathan exchanged a silent look. The shorter man's lips went tight and his green eyes pinched. Looking as if he'd rather make mud pies out of crap than leave Jonathan alone to accompany us with Trent, Quen hustled after Jenks. My eyes tracked the security officer as he all but flowed down the stairs, his hurried grace mesmerizing.

Jonathan straightened as he returned his attention to us. "Mr. Kalamack is waiting for you in his front office," he said stiffly as he opened a door.

I gave him a nasty smile as I lurched into motion. "Touch me, and I'll hurt you," I threatened as I yanked open the door next to the one Jonathan held.

The main lobby was spacious and eerily empty, the hushed murmur of business silenced with everyone gone for the weekend. Not waiting for Jonathan, I went straight down the wide corridor to Trent's office. Hands fumbling in my purse, I pulled out my ungodly expensive and criminally ugly charmed ley line glasses and put them on my nose. Jonathan gave up on his show of decorum, leaving Edden behind to catch up with me.

I strode down the hallway, my fists clenched and heels thumping. I wanted to see Trent. I wanted to tell him what I thought of him and spit in his face for having tried to break my will by putting me in the city's illegal rat fights.

The frosted doors to either side of me were open, showing empty desks. Farther down was a reception desk tucked into an alcove across from Trent's door. Sara Jane's desk was as neat and organized as the woman herself. Heart pounding, I reached for the handle of Trent's door, jerking back as Jonathan caught up. Giving me a look that could rock an attacking dog back on his haunches, the tall man knocked on Trent's wooden door, waiting until his muffled voice came before opening it.

Edden came even with me, his cross look faltering in shock as he saw my glasses. On edge, I touched my hat and tugged my jacket straight. Maybe I should have asked Ivy for a loan and gotten the pretty ones. The sound of water over rocks filtered out of Trent's office, and I entered hot on Jonathan's heels.

Trent rose from behind his desk as I came in. I took a breath to give him a snide but sincere greeting. I wanted to tell him I knew he had killed Dr. Anders. I wanted to tell him he was scum. I wanted to get in his face and scream that I was better than him, that he would never break me, that he was a manipulative bastard and I was going to *bring him down*. But I did nothing, taken aback by his calm, inner core of strength. He was the most self-possessed man I had ever met, and I stood silent as his thoughts visibly shifted from other matters to focus on me. And no, he didn't use a ley line charm to make him look that good. It was all him.

Every strand of his wispy, almost transparent hair was in place. His gray, silk-lined suit was unwrinkled, accenting the narrow-waisted, wide-shouldered physique I had spent three days ogling as a mink. Standing taller than I was, he gave me his trademark smile: an enviable mix of warmth and professional interest. He adjusted his jacket with a casual slowness, his long fingers drawing my attention as he manipulated the last button. There was only a single ring on his right hand, and like me, he wore no watch at all.

Trent was supposed to be only three years older than I—making him one of the wealthiest bachelors on the freaking planet—but the suit made him look older. Even so, his nicely defined jawline as well as his smooth cheeks and small nose made him look suited more for the beach than the boardroom.

Still smiling that confident, almost pleased smile, he ducked his head, taking his wire-rimmed glasses off and tossing them to the desktop. Embarrassed, I put my own charmed spectacles away in their hard leather case. My eyes went to his right arm as he came around to the front of his desk. It had been in a cast the last time I saw him, which was probably why the gun he'd shot at me missed. There was a faint ring of lighter skin between his hand and the cuff of his jacket that the sun hadn't yet had a chance to darken.

I stiffened as his gaze drifted over me, resting briefly on the pinky ring he had stolen from me and returned to prove he could, finally settling on my neck and the almost invisible scarring from my demon attack. "Ms. Morgan, I wasn't aware you could work for the FIB," he said by way of greeting, making no move to shake my hand.

"I'm a consultant," I said, ignoring how his liquid voice had pulled my breath tight. I had forgotten his voice, all am-

ber and honey—if color and taste could describe a sound—
resonant and deep, each syllable clear and precise yet blend-
ing into the next like liquid. It was mesmerizing in a way
that only ancient vampires could match. And it bothered me
that I liked it.

I met his gaze, trying to show a mirror image of his confidence. Jittery, I extended my arm, forcing him to respond.
His hand came out to meet mine with the barest of hesita-
tions. A stab of satisfaction warmed me in that I had made
him do something he didn't want to, even if it was something this small.

Feeling cocky, I slipped my hand into Trent's. Though his
green eyes were cold with the knowledge that I'd forced him
into touching me, his grip was warm and firm. I wondered
how long he had been practicing it. Satisfied, I loosened my
grip, but instead of doing the same, Trent's hand slipped
from mine with an intimate slowness that wasn't at all professional. I would have said he had just made a pass at me
but for the slight tightening of his eyes, which spoke of a
wary caution.

"Mr. Kalamack," I said, refusing to wipe my hand on my
skirt. "You're looking good."

"As are you." His smile was frozen in place, and his right
hand was almost behind his back. "I understand you're doing reasonably well with your little investigation firm. I
imagine it's difficult when you're just starting out."

Little investigation firm? My unease flashed into irritation. "Thank you," I managed.

A smile quirking the corner of his mouth, Trent turned his
attention to Edden. As the two professional men made polite, politically correct and hypocritical niceties, I glanced
over Trent's office. His fake window still showed a live shot
of one of his yearling pastures, the artificial light shining
through the video screen to make a warm patch of glowing
carpet. There was a new school of black and white fish in the

zoo-size fish tank, and the freestanding aquarium had been moved into a recess built into the wall behind his desk. The spot where my cage had been held a potted orange tree, and the scent-memory of food pellets made my stomach clench. The camera at the ceiling in the corner blinked its little red light at me.

"It's a pleasure to meet you, Captain Edden," Trent was saying, the smooth cadence of his voice luring my attention. "I wish it could be under better circumstances."

"Mr. Kalamack." Edden's sharp staccato sounded harsh against Trent's voice. "I apologize for any inconvenience incurred while we search your grounds."

Jonathan handed Trent the warrant, and he looked at it briefly before handing it back. "Corporal evidence leading to an arrest in the deaths known as the witch hunter murders?" he said, his eyes flicking to mine. "That's a little broad, isn't it?"

"Putting down 'dead body' looked crass," I said tightly, and Edden cleared his throat, the barest hint of worry we might find nothing staining his professional stance. I noticed Edden had fallen into a parade rest, and wondered if the ex–Navy SEAL even knew it. "You were the last person to see Dr. Anders," I added, wanting to see Trent's reaction.

"That's out of line, Ms. Morgan," Edden muttered, but I was more interested in the emotion that passed over Trent. Anger, frustration, but not shock. Trent glanced at Jonathan, who made the slightest shrug I'd ever seen. Slowly, Trent sat back on his desktop, his long, sun-tanned hands clasped in front of him. "I wasn't aware that she had died," he said.

"I never said she was dead," I said. My heart pounded as Edden gripped my arm in warning.

"She's missing?" Trent said, doing a creditable job of showing only relief. "That's good. That she is missing and not—ah—dead. I had dinner with her last night." The barest hint of worry flickered over Trent as he gestured to the two chairs behind us. "Please, sit down," he said as he went behind his desk. "I'm sure you have some questions for me—seeing as you're searching my grounds."

"Thank you, sir. I do." Edden took the seat closest to the hallway. My eyes tracked Jonathan as he closed Trent's door. He remained standing beside it, looking defensive. I eased myself down in the remaining seat in the artificial sun, forcing myself to the back of the chair. Trying for an air of nonchalance, I set my bag on my lap and felt in my jacket pocket for a finger stick. The prick of the blade zinged through me. I eased my bleeding finger into my bag, carefully searching for the charm. *Now let's see Trent lie and get away with it.*

Trent's expression froze at the clatter of my amulet. "Put your truth spell away, Ms. Morgan," he accused. "I said I would be happy to answer Captain Edden's questions, not submit to an interrogation. Your warrant is for search and seizure, not cross-examination."

"Morgan," Edden hissed, his thick hand extended. "Give me that!"

Grimacing, I wiped my fingertip clean and handed the amulet over. Edden stuffed it in a pocket. "My apologies," he said, his round face tight. "Ms. Morgan is tenacious in her desire to find the person or persons responsible for so many deaths. She has a *dangerous*"—this was directed at me—"tendency to forget she has to function within the law's parameters."

Trent's wispy hair rose in the current from the air vents. Seeing my gaze on it, he ran a hand over his head, hinting at irritation. "She means well."

How patronizing was that? Angry, I set my bag on the floor with a thump. "Dr. Anders meant well, too," I said. "Did you kill her after she turned down your offer of employment?"

Jonathan stiffened, and Edden's hands jerked as if he was trying to keep them in his lap and away from around my neck. "I'm not going to warn you again, Rachel. . . ." he growled.

Trent's smile never flickered. He was angry and trying not to show it. I was glad I could paint the walls with my feelings; it was far more satisfying. "No, it's all right," Trent said, clasping his fingers together and leaning forward to set them on his desk. "If it will ease Ms. Morgan's belief that I'm capable of such monstrous crimes, I'll be more than happy to tell you what we discussed last night." Though he was talking to Edden, his gaze didn't shift from mine. "We were discussing the possibility of my funding her research."

"Ley line research?" I questioned.

He picked up a pencil, the motion as he twirled it giving away his discomfort. He really should have broken himself of the habit. "Ley line research," he agreed. "The vein of which has little practical value. I was indulging my curiosity, nothing more."

"I think you offered her a job," I said. "And when she refused to work for you, you had her killed, just like all the other ley line witches in Cincinnati."

"Morgan!" Edden exclaimed, pulling himself upright in his chair. "Go wait in the van." He rose, giving Trent an apologetic look. "Mr. Kalamack, I'm very sorry. Ms. Morgan is entirely out of line, and is not acting under FIB authority in her accusations."

I spun in my chair to face him. "It's what he tried to do to me. Why would Dr. Anders be any different?"

Edden's face went red behind his little round glasses. I clenched my jaw, ready to argue right back. He took an angry breath, letting it out at the knock at the door. Jonathan opened it, stepping back as Glenn came in, ducking his head briefly to Trent in acknowledgment. I could tell by his hunched, furtive expression that the search wasn't going well.

He murmured something to Edden, and the captain

scowled, growling something back. Trent watched the exchange with interest, his brow smoothing and the faint tension in his shoulders easing. The pencil was set aside, and he leaned back in his chair.

Jonathan went to Trent, putting a hand on his desk as he leaned to whisper in Trent's ear. My attention flicked from Jonathan's condescending smile to Edden's worried frown. Trent was going to come out of this looking like an injured citizen brutalized by the FIB. *Damn.*

Jonathan straightened and Trent's green eyes met mine, softly mocking. Edden's voice rasped at my awareness as he told Glenn to have Jenks double-check the gardens. Trent was going to get away with it. He killed those people, and he was going to get away with it!

Frustration gripped me as Glenn gave me a helpless look and left, closing the door behind him. I knew my charms were good, but they might not work if Trent was using ley line magic to hide her. My face went slack. *Ley line magic?* If he was hiding her with ley line magic, I could find her with the same.

I glanced at Trent, seeing his satisfaction falter at the sudden questioning look I knew I must be wearing. Trent held up a finger to Jonathan, keeping the tall man quiet as he focused on me, clearly trying to figure out what I was thinking.

Making a search charm using earth magic was clearly white witchcraft. It followed that one made using ley line magic would be white as well. The cost upon my karma would be negligible, far less than, say, lying about my birthday to get a free drink. And whether stemming from earth or ley line magic, a search charm was covered under the search and seizure warrant.

My heartbeat quickened, and I reached to touched my hair. I didn't know the incantation, but Nick might have it in his books. And if Trent used ley line magic to cover his tracks, there would have to be a line close enough to use. *Interesting.*

"I need to make a call," I said, hearing my voice as if it were from outside my head.

Trent seemed at a loss for words. I liked seeing the emotion on him. "You're welcome to use my secretary's phone," he said.

"I have my own," I said, digging in my bag. "Thank you."

Edden gave me a suspicious glance and went to talk to Trent and Jonathan. By his polite stance and appeaseing look, I thought he might be trying to smooth the political waves his failed FIB visit was going to cause. Tense, I rose, going to the far corner to try and stay out of the camera's view as well as their earshot.

"Be there," I whispered as I scrolled through my short list and hit the send button. "Pick up, Nicky. Please pick up. . . ." He might be getting groceries. He could be doing his laundry or taking a nap or in the shower, but I was willing to bet my nonexistent paycheck that he was still reading that damned book. My shoulders relaxed as someone picked up. He was home. I loved a predictable man.

" 'Ello," he said, sounding preoccupied.

"Nick," I breathed. "Thank God."

"Rachel? What's up?" Concern laced his voice, pulling my shoulders tight again.

"I need your help," I said, glancing at Edden and Trent, trying to keep my voice soft. "I'm at Trent's with Captain Edden. We got a search warrant. Will you look in your books for a ley line charm to find—um—dead people?"

There was a long hesitation. "That's what I like about you, Ray-ray," he said as I heard the sound of a sliding book followed by a thump. "You say the sweetest things."

I waited, my stomach knotting as the sound of turning pages came faintly over the phone.

"Dead people," he murmured, not fazed at all, while the butterflies battered my stomach with jackhammers. "Dead fairies. Dead ghosts. Will an invocation for ghosts do?"

"No." I picked at my nail polish, watching Trent watch me as he talked to Edden.

"Dead kings, dead livestock . . . ah, dead people."

My pulse increased and I fumbled in my bag for a pen.

"Okay . . ." He was silent, reading it over. "It's simple enough, but I don't think you can use it during the daytime."

"Why not?"

"You know how tombstones in our world show up in the ever-after? Well, the charm makes unmarked graves in our world do the same. But you have to be able to see into the ever-after with your second sight, and you can't do that unless the sun is down."

"I can if I'm standing in a ley line," I whispered, feeling cold. I'd never seen that tidbit of information written in a book. My dad had told me when I was eight.

"Rachel," he protested after a moment's hesitation. "You can't. If that demon knows you're in a ley line, he'll try to pull you the rest of the way into the ever-after."

"It can't. It doesn't own my soul," I whispered, turning to hide my moving lips.

He was silent, and my breath sounded loud to me. "I don't like it," he finally said.

"I don't like you calling up demons. And it's an it, not a him."

The phone was silent. I glanced at Trent, then turned my back on him. I wondered how good his hearing was.

"Yes," Nick said, "but he owns two-thirds of my soul, and one-third of yours. What if—"

"Souls don't add up like numbers, Nick," I said, my voice harsh with worry. "It's an all or nothing affair. It doesn't have enough on me. It doesn't have enough on you. I'm not walking out of here without proving Trent killed that woman. What's the incantation?"

I waited, my knees going weak. "Got a pen?" he finally said, and I nodded, forgetting he couldn't see the gesture.

"Yes," I said, jiggling the phone to write on my palm like a test cheat sheet.

"Okay. It's not long. I'll translate everything but the invocation word in English, only because we don't have a word that means the glowing ashes of the dead, and I think it's important you get that part exactly right. Give me a moment, and I can make it rhyme."

"Non-rhyming is fine," I said slowly, thinking this just kept getting better and better. *Glowing ashes of the dead?* What kind of language needed its own word for that?

He cleared his throat and I readied my pen. " 'Dead unto dead, shine as the moon. Silence all but the restless.' " He hesitated. "And then the trigger word is 'favilla.' "

"Favilla," I repeated, writing it phonetically. "Any gesture?"

"No. It doesn't physically act on anything, so you don't need a gesture or focus object. Do you want me to repeat it?"

"No," I said, a little sick as I looked at my palm. *Did I really want to do this?*

"Rachel," he said, his voice sounding worried through the speaker. "Be careful."

"Yeah," I said, my pulse fast in anticipation and worry. "Thanks, Nick." I bit my lower lip in a sudden thought. "Hey, um, keep my book for me until I talk to you, okay?"

"Ray-ray?" he questioned warily.

"Ask me later," I said, flicking a glance at Edden, then Trent. I didn't have to say another word. He was a smart man.

"Wait. Don't hang up," he said, the concern in his voice giving me pause. "Keep me on the line. I can't sit here and feel those tugs on me without knowing if you're in trouble or not."

I licked my lips and forced my hand down from where it had been playing with the end of my braid. Using Nick as my familiar went against every moral fiber I had—and I'd like to think I had a lot of them—but I couldn't walk away. I wouldn't even try it if I wasn't sure Nick would be unaffected. "I'll give you to Captain Edden, okay?"

"Edden?" he said faintly, his worry taking on an edge of self-preservation.

I turned back to the three men. "Captain," I said, drawing their attention. "I'd like to try a different finding spell before we leave."

Edden's round face was pinched with frustration. "We're done here, Morgan," he said gruffly. "We've taken up more than enough of Mr. Kalamack's time."

I swallowed, trying to look like I did this every day. "This one works differently."

His breath went in and out in a rough sound. "Can I have a word with you in the hallway?" he intoned.

Hallway? I would not be pulled into the hallway like an errant child. I turned to Trent. "Mr. Kalamack won't mind. He has nothing to hide, yes?"

Trent's face was a mask of professional politeness. Jonathan stood behind him, his narrow face ugly. "As long as it falls within the parameters of your warrant," Trent said smoothly.

I felt a jolt hearing the concern he was trying to hide. He was worried. I was, too.

I made my steps slow as I crossed the office and handed Edden the phone. "It's a finding spell tuned to find unmarked graves. Nick will tell you all about it, Captain, so you can be sure it's legal. You remember him, don't you?"

Edden took the phone, the slim pink rectangle looking ridiculous in his thick hands. "If it's so simple, why didn't you tell me about it before?"

I gave him a nervous smile. "It uses ley lines."

Trent's face froze. His gaze darted to my demon-marked wrist, and he leaned back into his chair and Jonathan's protection. I arched my eyebrows though my stomach was in knots. If he protested, he would look guilty. His hands moved with a nervous quickness as he reached for his wire-rimmed glasses and tapped them on the desktop. "Please," he said as if he had any say in the matter. "Invoke your charm. I'd be interested to see how much an earth witch such as yourself knows about ley line magic."

"Me, too," Edden said dryly before he put the phone to his ear and began talking to Nick in low, intent tones, making sure what I was going to do fell within the FIB warrant, most likely.

"We'll have to move," I said almost to myself. "I need to find a ley line to stand in."

"Ah, Ms. Morgan," Trent said, clearly agitated as he sat up straight in his chair. The wire-rimmed glasses he had put back on made him look less sophisticated, giving him a softer, almost harmless look. I thought he looked a little pale, too.

Right, I thought snidely as I closed my eyes to make it easier to find a ley line with my second sight. *Like you have a ley line running through your garden.*

I reached out with my thoughts, searching for the red smear of ever-after. My breath hissed in and my eyes flashed open. I stared at Trent.

The man had a freaking ley line running right through his freaking office.

Twenty

Mouth agape, I looked across the office to Trent. His face was tight and drawn as he sat flanked by Jonathan. Neither looked happy. My pulse raced. Trent knew it was there. He could use ley lines. That meant he was either human or witch. Vamps couldn't pull on them, and humans who could and were subsequently infected with the vamp virus lost the ability. I didn't know what frightened me more, that Trent used ley lines or that he knew I knew. God help me. I was halfway to knowing Trent's most precious secret of what the hell he was.

The door to Trent's office smashed into the wall. Adrenaline surged painfully, and I fell into a defensive stance. Quen burst in. "Sa—Sir," he barked, changing his title Sa'hanu, mid-speech. He jerked to a stop, his eyes narrowing as he took in my tense posture in the corner and Edden sitting in his chair with my phone at his ear, carefully not moving one inch.

The man's green eyes fixed upon mine. My heart pounded. Our defensive postures eased, and I tugged my skirt down where it belonged. The door arched closed as Jenks darted in.

"Hey, Rache!" the pixy cried, his wings red in excitement. "Someone's found a ley line and it's got *someone* in an unholy snit." He stopped short, taking in the tense room. "Oh, it's you," he said, grinning. Wings clattering, he lit upon my shoulder, quickly abandoning me for Edden and the chance to overhear what Nick was saying.

Trent leaned forward to put his elbows on the desk. A bead of sweat edged his hairline. I tried to swallow, finding my mouth dry. "Ms. Morgan is demonstrating her ley line skills for us," Trent said. "I'm very interested to see."

I'll bet you are, I thought, wondering how deep in the pile I had stepped. Ley line magic was used heavily in security, and Quen had known the moment I found it.

Uneasy, I took the opportunity to examine everyone's auras with my second sight. Jenks's was all rainbows, as most pixies' were. Edden's was a steady blue tending to yellow about his head. Quen's was a green so dark as to be almost black, shot through with vibrant orange streaks about his middle and his hands—not good. Jonathan's was green as well, much lighter and almost bland in its uniformity and shade. Trent's . . . I hesitated, faltering.

Trent's aura was sunshine yellow, streaked with a sharply defined red. The crimson slashes hinted that he had more than his share of soul-marring tragedy in his past. It was unusually close around him, rimmed in silver sparkles, like Ivy's was. They burst into existence and floated about him when he took a hand and ran it across his head to make his hair lie flat. He was looking for something—the way the sparkles embedded themselves in his main aura indicating that he had dedicated his life to this search. The money, the power, the drive, was all to serve a higher purpose. What was he looking for? I wondered.

I couldn't see my aura. Unless I was standing on a scrying mirror—which I would never do again. But I was sure Trent was looking at it, and I didn't like that he could see the demon mark on my wrist pulsating with a nasty black smear, or than my aura, too, had those same ugly red streaks, or that apart from his sparkles, our auras were almost identical.

Edden looked warily between us, knowing something was going on but not what. Brow pinching, he shifted to the edge of his chair and had a terse, hushed conversation with Nick.

"You have a ley line running through your office?" I said, light-headed.

"You have one in your backyard," Trent answered flatly. Jaw tightening, he glanced at Edden. I could almost see his wish that the FIB captain wasn't there. His expression was laced with a threatening warning. It wasn't publicized that only humans and witches could manipulate ley lines, but anyone could figure it out, and I knew he wanted me to shut up about them. I was more than willing to, knowing that having the information was like holding a cobra by the tail.

My fingers were trembling from adrenaline, and I clenched them into fists as I turned to the three-foot-wide smear of ever-after running through Trent's office. It made an east to west swath before his desk, more accurate than any compass, and I imagined it probably ran through his back office, too. As soon as I stepped into it, I could make an educated guess.

Sweat broke out on the small of my back as I eyed the line. I'd never put myself in one before. Unless you made the effort to tap into a line, you could walk right through it and feel nothing. I took a breath, willing myself to relax. If Algaliarept did show up, all I'd have to do was step out of the line. It couldn't get out of the ever-after as long as the sun was above the horizon.

With a final, wary look at the two men standing protectively behind Trent, I closed my eyes. Stealing myself, I reached out and touched my will to the line.

Power, heady with intent, surged into me. My pulse leapt, and I think I staggered. Breath fast and shallow, I held up a hand to keep Edden from touching me. I had heard him stand. As he shot hushed questions at Nick, I hung my head and did nothing, riding the surges of power rising through me in ever stronger pulses. They backwashed at my extremities, my head throbbing in hurt as they rebounded and crashed into the continuing inflow. I felt a moment of panic as it grew, and grew, and continued to grow. Just how strong was this thing?

I felt like an overinflated balloon and it seemed I was going to burst or go insane. *This,* I thought, almost panting, *was why ley line witches have familiars.* Their animal companions filtered the raw energy, their simpler minds better able to handle the strain. I wouldn't make Nick take my risk. I had to take it all. And I had yet to actually step into the line. How much more potent it would be then was anyone's guess.

Slowly, the demanding influx ebbed, becoming almost bearable. Tingling from the inside, I took a breath that sounded suspiciously like a sob. The balance of energy finally seemed to have equalized. I could feel the wisps of my hair that had escaped my braid tickle my neck as the wind from the ever-after lifted past and through me.

"My God . . ." I heard Edden breathe, and I hoped I hadn't just lost his trust. I don't think he truly understood how different we were until that moment, seeing my hair move in the breeze that only I could feel.

"Not much of a witch," I heard Jonathan say, "staggering in a power drunk at noon."

"It would be if she were tapping it like most people," came Quen's throaty whisper, and I strained to hear him. "She's not using a familiar, Sa'han. She's channeling the entire bloody line by herself."

Jonathan's intake of alarm sent a surge of vindication through me—until he followed it up with an urgent, "Kill her. Tonight. She's not worth the risk anymore."

My eyes almost flew open, but I held them shut so they wouldn't know I had heard. My wildly pounding heart sounded loud in my ears, adding to the slow swelling of ley line force still trickling in. "Jonathan," Trent said, sounding tired. "You don't kill something because it's stronger than you. You find a way to use it."

Use me? I thought bitterly. *Over my dead body.* Hoping it wasn't a premonition, I lifted my head, crossed my fingers for luck, prayed I wasn't making a mistake, and entered the ley line.

My knees buckled as the power swelling in me vanished with a painful suddenness. It was gone. The uncomfortable influx of ever-after was gone. Not believing it, I stood, realizing I had fallen to one knee. I forced my eyes to remain shut lest I lose my second sight, slapping away Edden's hand gripping my shoulder.

The strength of the ley line swirled through me, making my skin prickle and my hair float, but the balance had become perfect. It left me shaken but no longer having to fight the strain of its power. Why had no one ever told me this? Standing in a line was a hell of a lot easier than maintaining a link to one, even if the gritty wind took getting used to.

Eyes still shut, I looked at the ever-after, thinking it was even stranger lit under the demons' sun. The walls of Trent's office were gone, and only Edden's hushed conversation with Nick kept me grounded, telling my frazzled mind that no, I hadn't crossed into the ever-after, I was standing in a trapdoor, seeing a vision of it.

Spreading in all directions was a rolling landscape of scattered groves of trees and wide, open tracts. To the east and west stretched a hazy ribbon of ley line force. I was standing two-thirds down its considerable length, and I would guess it went to Trent's back office. The sky was a washed-out yellow and the sun was intense, beating down as if trying to crush the squat, stubby trees into the ground. I felt as if it was passing right through me, bouncing up and warming the undersides of my feet. Even the coarse grass seemed stunted, barely coming to mid-calf. In the hazy distance to the west were a cluster of sharp lines and angles towering over the landscape. Eerie and strange, the demon city was clearly broken.

"Cool," I breathed, and Edden shushed Nick's demands for information.

Knowing Trent was watching, though I couldn't see him, I turned my back on him so he couldn't read my lips as I whispered the first half of the incantation. Fortunately, I recalled the short translated phrase, since I didn't want to open my eyes to read it off my palm.

As the words fell from me, a slight imbalance of ever-after energy stirred in my feet, swirling up to settle in my belly. My knees grew loose as the grass bent toward me from all sides. Ley line strength flowed into me, carrying a pleasant slurry of tingles with it. I wondered how intense the sensation would grow, not wanting to admit it felt good.

My hair lifted in a sudden swirl of power as I began the second half. With all but the word of invocation said, the energy crested, sending a swirl of prickles to push evenly through me. It hung within me for a moment, then it flashed from me in a flat pulse of yellow, to run like ripples over the contours of the land.

"Holy crap," I said, then covered my mouth, hoping I hadn't just ruined the charm. I hadn't finished it yet. Shocked, I watched with my second sight as the flat sheet of ever-after energy sped away. The pulse was the color of my aura, and I felt uneasy, reminding myself that the spell had taken only the hue of my aura, not my aura itself.

The ring continued to expand until it went faint in the distance. I didn't know whether to be pleased or alarmed that it seemed to have gone all the way to the half-seen city. The outgoing ripple didn't leave the ever-after landscape unchanged, and my awe shifted to alarm as I realized that in its wake was a smattering of glittering green smears.

Bodies. They were everywhere. Beside me I could see the small ones, some no bigger than my pinky nail. Farther out, only the larger ones could be discerned. My first gut-twisting reaction dulled as I realized the charm was picking up everything that was dead: rodents, birds, bugs, everything. A huge number of big ones lay to the west in neat and orderly rows and columns. I had a moment of panic until I realized they were right where Trent's stables lay in the real world and were probably the bodies of his past race winners.

My heart slowed, and I tried to remember the last word, the one that would sensitize the charm to show only human remains. Brow furrowed, I stood in Trent's office, my feet firmly in a gateway to the ever-after, trying to remember what it had been.

"Oh, isn't this a delight," came a richly cultured voice from behind me.

I waited for someone to tell me who had just walked into Trent's office, but no one said a word. The hair pricked on the back of my neck. Anticipating the worst, I kept my eyes closed and my second sight open, and turned. My hand rose to my mouth and I froze. It was a demon dressed in a robe and slippers.

"Rachel Mariana Morgan?" it said, then smiled wickedly. I swallowed hard. Okay—it was my demon. "What are you doing in Trenton Aloysius Kalamack's ley line?" it questioned.

My breath came faster and I waved a hand behind me, trying to find the edge of the line. "I'm working," I said, my hand throbbing as I found it. "What are you doing here?"

It shrugged, its stance lengthening as it molded into the familiar vision of a lanky, leather-clad vamp with blond hair and a torn ear. Slumping into a bad-boy swagger, it licked its pouty lips, the chain running from a back pocket to its belt loop jingling. My breath went shaky. It was getting better at picking Kisten out of my mind; it had him down perfectly.

A pair of smoked glasses with round frames appeared in its hand, and it snapped the earpieces out with a quick flick of the wrist. "I felt you, love," it said, its teeth lengthening to that of a vampire's as it put the glasses on to hide its red goat eyes. "I simply ha-a-a-ad to see if you had come for a visit. You don't mind if I be this one, do you? He's got the balls of a bull."

God, help me. I shuddered, sticking my hand out of the line despite the stabbing hurt of ever-after imbalance. "I wasn't trying to get your attention," I whispered. "Go away."

I felt a touch on my hand and I jerked away. I could smell burnt coffee, and I wished Edden would quit doing that. "Who the devil is she talking to?" the FIB captain asked softly.

"I don't know," Jenks said. "But I'm not going into that line to see."

"Leave?" the demon said, its grin widening. "No, no, no. Don't be silly. I want to see how much ever-after you can manipulate. Go on, love. Finish your little charm," it encouraged.

In the background I could hear Trent and Quen having an intense argument. I wasn't willing to open my eyes and risk losing sight of the demon, but I thought Trent was winning. Nervous, I licked my lips, hating myself when the vision of Kisten did the same with a mocking slowness. "I forgot the last word," I admitted, then stiffened as I remembered. "Favilla," I blurted in relief, and the demon clapped his hands in delight.

I jumped as a second wave of ever-after jolted through me. Clutching my arms about myself as if to keep my aura intact, I watched the flat pulse of yellow dart away, following the path of the first. Algaliarept moaned, staggering as if in pleasure as it passed through it. I watched its reaction in near horror. The demon obviously liked it, but if it could have taken my aura, it would have by now. I think.

"Spun candy," it said, closing its eyes. "Flay me and slay me. Spun candy and nectar."

Swell. I had to get out of there.

While Algaliarept ran its hand over the grass and licked from its fingers the yellow smear of ley line power my charm had left on it, I scanned the surrounding countryside. My shoulders tightened in worry. Every glittering blur marking death was gone. Algaliarept seemed content seining the grass for remnants of my spell, so I snuck a quick look behind me, my fast spin jerking to a stop.

One of the horse graves glowed a bright red. It wasn't a horse, it was a person.

Trent had killed her, I thought, my attention darting to a new shape materializing within the ley line.

It was Trent, having stepped into it to see what I was seeing. His gaze went to the flash of red, widening, but his shock was nothing compared to when the demon shifted into a mirror copy of me, sleek and dangerous in a black silk body stocking.

"Trenton Aloysius Kalamack," it said, making my voice sexier than I ever could. It suggestively licked the last of my spell off its finger, and I wondered if the demon was making me look better than I actually did. "What a dangerous direction your thoughts have taken," the demon said. "You should be more careful whom you invite to play in your ley line." It hesitated, its hip cocked as it squinted over its glasses and compared our auras. "Such a pretty pair you make, like matched horses in my stables."

And it disappeared in a sensation of tingles, leaving me to stare across the ever-after landscape at Trent.

Twenty-One

My heels clacked with more authority than I felt as I walked down the long planked porch of Trent's foaling stable ahead of Trent and Quen. The empty row of box stalls faced the south and the afternoon sun. Atop them were the vet apartments. No one was in them, seeing as it was fall. Though horses could have their foals any time of the year, most stables enforced a strict breeding program so the mares all dropped their foals at once, getting the dangerous period over with at one time.

I thought the temporarily abandoned buildings were a perfect place to hide a body.

God help me, I thought with a sudden wash of ill feeling. How could I be so cavalier? Dr. Anders was dead.

A faint baying of a beagle lifted over the hazy afternoon. My head jerked up and my heart gave a pound. Farther down the dirt road was a kennel the size of a small apartment complex. Dogs were standing against their wire runs, watching.

Trent brushed past me, the breeze of his passage smelling of fallen leaves. "They never forget their quarry," he murmured, and I tensed.

Trent and Quen had accompanied us out here, leaving Jonathan behind to supervise the FIB officers still coming in from the gardens. The two men angled for an alcove tucked dead center between the row of box stalls. The wood-walled room was completely open to the wind and sun on one side. By the rustic furniture, I guessed it was a box stall converted to an outdoor meeting place for the vets to relax during births and such. I didn't like that no one was with them, but I wasn't about to join them. Slowing, I leaned against a support post, deciding I could keep an eye on them from there.

Three FIB officers with their cadaver dogs stood by the dog van parked in the shade of a huge oak tree. The doors were open, and Glenn's authoritative voice drifted to hang over the sun-warmed pastures. Edden was with them, looking out of place on the fringes. It was obvious that Glenn was in charge, by the way Edden kept his hands in his pockets and his mouth shut.

Flitting over them was Jenks, his wings red in excitement as he got in the way and offered a steady stream of unasked for advice that was ignored. The remaining FIB officers stood under the ancient oak that shadowed the parking lot. As I watched, a crime scene van pulled in with an exaggerated slowness. Captain Edden had called it after I found a body.

I snuck a glance at Trent, deciding the businessman looked a bit bothered if anything, as he stood in the informal room with his hands behind his back. Personally, I'd be visibly upset if someone was about to find an unexplained body on my property. I was sure this was where the unmarked grave had been shining.

Cold, I stepped off the covered walkway and into the sun. Hands gripping my elbows, I came to a halt in the sawdust parking lot, surreptitiously watching Trent from around a wisp of hair that had escaped my braid. He had put on a lightweight cream-colored hat against the sun and changed his shoes to boots in deference to our trip out to his stables. Somehow the mix looked right on him. It wasn't fair he should look so calm and relaxed. But then he jerked at the sound of a car door slamming. He was wound as tight as I was; he just hid it better.

Glenn said a few last, loud words and the group broke up. Tails waving, the dogs began a methodical search: two in the nearby pastures, one through the building itself, I couldn't help but notice that the handler assigned to the stables was using his skills, too, instead of relying on the dog's nose alone, looking up into rafters and opening latched panels.

Captain Edden touched his son's shoulder and headed toward me, short arms swinging. "Rachel," he said even before he was close, and I looked up, surprised he had used my first name. "We've been over this building already."

"If it isn't this building, then it's near here. Your men may not have been using my charms properly." *Or not at all,* I finished silently, knowing the prejudice humans felt was often covered up in smiles, lies, and hypocrisy. I knew I shouldn't jump to conclusions, though. I was fairly sure Trent had used a ley line charm to cover up her whereabouts, and so my spells would have been less than useful. My attention went from the dogs to Trent as Quen leaned to speak into his ear. "Shouldn't he be under arrest, or detained, or something?" I asked.

Edden squinted from the low sun. "Keep your panties on. Murder cases are won and lost in the collection of evidence, Morgan. You ought to know that."

"I'm a runner, not a detective," I said sourly. "Most of the people I tagged were charged before I brought them in."

He grunted at that. I thought that Captain Edden's adherence to "the rules" might lead to Trent vanishing in a puff of smoke to never be seen again. Seeing me fidget, he pointed at me and then at the ground, to tell me to stay where I was before he moseyed down to Quen and Trent. The squat human's hands were in his pockets but not far from his weapon. Quen hadn't a weapon, but looking at him shifting lightly on his feet, I didn't think he needed one.

I felt better when Edden subtly moved the two men apart, snagging a passing officer and telling him to ask Quen to detail their security procedures while he talked to Trent about the upcoming FIB fund-raiser dinner. Nice.

I turned away, watching the sun shine on the dog's yellow coat. The heat soaked into me, and the smell of the stables was warm with memory. I had enjoyed my three summers at camp. The scent of sweaty horse and hay mixing with the hint of aged manure was like a balm.

My riding lessons had been to help increase my balance, improve my muscle tone, and up my red blood cell count, but I think its largest benefit had been the confidence I gained from being in control of a big beautiful animal that would do anything I asked of it. To an eleven-year-old, that feeling of power was addictive.

A smile curved over me and I closed my eyes, feeling the autumn sun soak deeper. My friend and I had snuck out of our camp house one morning to sleep in the stables with the horses. The soft sounds of their breathing had been indescribably comforting. Our cabin mother had been furious, but it was the best I had slept the entire time.

My eyes opened. It had probably been the only night I'd slept uninterrupted. Jasmin, too, had slept well at the stables. And the pale girl had desperately needed sleep. *Jasmin!* I thought, clutching at the name. That's what the dark-haired girl's name had been. Jasmin.

The sound of radio chatter pulled my gaze from the field, leaving me feeling more melancholy than I would've expected. She had possessed an inoperable brain tumor. I didn't think even Trent's father's illegal activities could have fixed that.

My attention went to Trent. His green eyes were intent on me even as he talked to Edden, and I tugged my hat straight and tucked a wisp of hair behind an ear. Refusing to let him rattle me, I stared back. His gaze flicked behind me, and I turned as Sara Jane's red car pulled up with a scattering of sawdust beside the FIB vehicles.

The small woman bolted from her car, looking like a different person in her jeans and casual blouse. Slamming the door, she stalked forward. "You!" she accused, coming to a flustered halt before me, and I took a surprised step back. "This is your doing, isn't it!" she shouted up at me.

My face went blank. "Uh."

She put herself in my face, and I took another step back. "I asked for your help in finding my boyfriend," she said shrilly, eyes flashing. "Not accuse my employer of murder! You are an *evil* witch, so evil, you could—*could fire God*!"

"Um," I stammered, glancing at Edden for help. He and Trent were on their way over, and I backed up another step, holding my bag tight against me. I hadn't thought of this.

"Sara Jane," Trent soothed even before he was close. "It's all right."

She spun to him, her blond hair catching the highlights of the sun. "Mr. Kalamack," she said, her face shifting abruptly to fear and worry. Eyes pinched, she wrung her hands. "I'm sorry. I came as soon as I heard. I didn't ask her to come here. I—I . . ." Her eyes welled, and making a small noise, she dropped her head into her hands and started crying.

My lips parted in surprise. Was she worried about her job, her boyfriend, or Trent?

Trent gave me a dark look, as if it were my fault she was upset. It melted into genuine sympathy as he put a hand upon the small woman's shaking shoulders. "Sara Jane," he soothed, ducking his head to try and meet her eyes. "Don't even think that I blame you for this. Ms. Morgan's accusations have nothing to do with you going to the FIB about Dan." His wonderful voice rose and fell like puddles of silk.

"B-But she thinks you murdered those people," she stammered, sniffing as she pulled her hands from her face and smeared her mascara into a brown blur under her eye.

Edden shifted uneasily from foot to foot. The radio chatter from the FIB vehicles rose over the crickets. I refused to feel sorry that I had made Sara Jane cry. Her boss was dirt, and the sooner she realized that, the better off she would be. Trent hadn't killed those people with his hands, but he had arranged it, making him as guilty as if he had carved them up himself. My thoughts went to the picture of the woman on the gunnery, and I steeled myself.

Trent pulled Sara Jane's gaze up with a gentle encouragement. I wondered at his compassion. I wondered how it would feel to have his beautiful voice soothing me, telling me that everything was all right. Then I wondered if there was a chance in hell of Sara Jane getting away from him with her life intact.

"Don't jump to conclusions," Trent said, handing her a linen handkerchief embroidered with his initials. "No one has been accused of anything. And there's no need for you to stay here. Why don't you go back home? This ugly business will be done as soon as we find the stray dog that Ms. Morgan's charm has fixed on."

Sara Jane shot me a poisonous look. "Yes sir," she said, her voice harsh.

Stray dog? I thought, torn between my desire to take her out to lunch for a heart-to-heart and my need to slap some sense into the woman.

Edden cleared his throat. "I'd ask Ms. Gradenko and yourself to stay here until we know more, sir."

Trent's professional smile faltered. "Are we being detained?"

"No sir," he said respectfully. "Merely a request."

"Captain!" a dog handler shouted from the second floor landing. My heart pounded at the excitement in the man's voice. "Socks didn't point, but we have a locked door."

Adrenaline zinged through me. I looked at Trent. His face showed nothing.

Quen and a small man started forward, accompanied by an FIB officer. The short man was obviously a past jockey now turned manager. His face was leathered and wrinkled, and he had a wad of keys with him. They jingled as he pulled one off and handed it to Quen. Body tense with that unnerving liquid menace, Quen handed it in turn to Edden.

"Thank you," the FIB captain said. "Now go stand with the officers." He hesitated, smiling. "If you would, please." He crooked his finger at a pair of FIB officers who had just arrived, pointing at Quen. They jogged over.

Glenn left the crime scene van with its radio and headed in our direction. Jenks was with him, and the pixy circled him three times before zipping ahead. "Give me the key," Jenks said as he came to a pixy-dust-laced halt between Edden and me. "I'll take it up."

Glenn looked at the pixy in bother as he joined us. "You're not FIB. Key, please."

An unheard sigh lifted through Edden. I could tell he wanted to see what was in that room and was making a conscious effort to let his son handle it. By rights, he had no business being out here. I imagine accusing a city council member of murder gave him more justification than he might have otherwise.

Jenks's wings clattered harshly as Captain Edden handed the key to Glenn. I could smell Glenn's sweat over his cologne, his eagerness. A cluster of people had joined the dog and her handler about the door, and gripping my bag tightly, I started to the stairs right along with him.

"Rachel," Glenn said, coming to a stop and catching my elbow. "You're staying here."

"I am not!" I exclaimed, jerking out of his grip. I glanced at Captain Edden for support, and the squat man shrugged, looking put out that he hadn't been invited, either.

Glenn's face hardened as he saw the direction of my gaze.

Letting go of me, he said, "Stay here. I want you to watch Kalamack. Read his emotions for me."

"That's a load of crap," I said, thinking, crap or not, it was probably a good idea. "Your d—" I bit my tongue. "Your captain can do that," I amended.

Bother pinched his brow. "All right. It's crap. But you're going to stay here. If we find Dr. Anders, I want this crime scene tighter than—"

"A straight man's butt cheeks in prison?" Jenks offered, his tiny shape starting to glow.

He landed on my shoulder, and I let him stay. "Come on, Glenn," I wheedled. "I won't touch anything. And you'll need me to tell you if there are any lethal spells."

"Jenks can do that," he said. "And he doesn't have to step on the floor to do it."

Frustrated, I cocked my hip and fumed. I could tell that under his official veneer, Glenn was worried and excited all at the same time. He had only made detective recently, and I imagined this was the biggest case he'd worked. Cops spent their entire professional lives on the job and were never assigned a case with this many potential political ramifications. All the more reason I should be there. "But I'm your Inderland consultant," I said, grasping at straws.

He put a dark hand on my shoulder, and I pushed it off. "Look," he said, the rims of his ears going red. "There are procedures to follow. I lost my first court case because of a contaminated crime scene, and I'm not going to risk losing Kalamack because you were too impatient to wait your turn. It needs to be vacuumed, photographed, dusted, analyzed, and anything else I can think of. You come in right after the psychic. Got it?"

"Psychic?" I questioned, and he frowned.

"Okay, I'm kidding about the psychic, but if you put one

manicured nail over that threshold before I say, I'll throw you out of here faster than stink on snake."

Faster than stink on snake? He must have been serious if he was mixing his metaphors.

"You want an ACG suit?" he asked, his eyes shifting from mine to the dog van.

I took a slow breath at the subtle threat. Anticharm gear. The last time I tried to take Trent down, he had killed the witness right out from under me. "No," I said.

My subdued tone seemed to satisfy him. "Good," he said, turning and striding away.

Jenks hovered before me, waiting. His dragonfly wings were red in excitement and the sun caught the glitter of pixy dust. "Let me know what you find, Jenks," I said, glad at least one representative from our sorry little firm would be there.

"You bet, Rache," he said, then zipped after Glenn.

Edden silently joined me, and I felt as if we were the only two people in high school who hadn't been invited to the big pool party, standing across the road and watching. We waited with an edgy Trent, an indignant Sara Jane, and a tight-lipped Quen as Glenn knocked at the door to announce his FIB presence—as if it wasn't obvious—and unlocked it.

Jenks was the first one in. He darted out almost immediately, his flight somewhat ragged as he landed on the railing. Glenn leaned in, then out of the black rectangular opening. "Get me a mask," I heard him mutter, clear through the hush.

My breath came fast. He had found something. And it wasn't a dog.

Hand over her mouth, an FIB officer extended a surgical mask to Glenn. A foul stench came faintly over the comforting aroma of hay and manure. My nose wrinkled, and I glanced at Trent to see his face empty. The parking lot went silent. An insect shrilled and another answered it. By the upstairs door, Socks whined and pawed at her handler's legs as she looked for reassurance. I felt ill. How had they missed the smell before? I'd been right. It had to have been spelled to keep it contained in the room.

Glenn took a step into the room. For a moment his back was bright with sun, then he took another to disappear, leaving an empty black door frame. A uniformed FIB officer handed him a flashlight from the threshold, a hand over her mouth. Jenks wouldn't look at me. His back was to the door as he stood on the railing, his wings bowed and unmoving.

My heart hammered and I held my breath as the woman in the doorway backed up and Glenn came out. "It's a body," he said to a second young officer, his soft voice carrying clear down to us. "Detain Mr. Kalamack for questioning." He took a breath. "Ms. Gradenko, too."

The officer's response was subdued, and she headed down the stairs to find Trent. I triumphantly looked to Trent, then sobered as I imagined Dr. Anders dead on the floor. I superimposed the memory of watching Trent kill his leading researcher, so quick and clean with a ready alibi waiting to be implemented. I had caught him this time, having moved too fast for him to cover his butt.

Sara Jane clutched at Trent. Fear, real and full, made her eyes wide and colored her pale cheeks. Trent didn't seem to notice her grip, his face seriously blank as he looked at Quen. Knees weak, I watched Trent take a slow breath as if steadying himself.

"Mr. Kalamack?" the young officer said, gesturing for Trent to accompany him.

A flicker of emotion flickered over Trent as the FIB officer said his name. I would have said it was fear if I thought anything could shake the man. "Ms. Morgan," Trent said in parting to me as he helped Sara Jane into motion. Edden and Quen went with them, the captain's round face slack with relief. He must have put his reputation further on the line than I had thought.

Sara Jane pulled from Trent and turned to me. "You bitch," she said, fear and hatred in her high, childlike voice. "You have no idea what you've done."

Shocked, I said nothing as Trent took her elbow with what I thought might be a warning strength. My hands started shaking and my stomach clenched.

Glenn was on the stairway. There was a disposable wipe in his hands and he was running it over his fingers as he made his way to me. He pointed to the crime scene van and then the black rectangle the door made. Two men lurched into motion. With a calm tension, they wheeled a black hard-walled suitcase forward.

I was going to get Trent Kalamack arrested, I thought. *Can I survive that?*

"It's a body," Glenn said as he came to a squinting halt before me, wiping his hands with yet another wipe. "You were right." He saw my face, and I knew I must have looked anxious as he followed my gaze to Trent standing with Quen and Edden. "He's just a man."

Trent was confident and unruffled, the picture of cooperation, a sharp contrast to Sara Jane's anger and hysterics. "Is he?" I breathed.

"It's going to be a while before you can go in," he said, taking a third towel and swabbing the back of his neck. He looked a little gray. "Maybe tomorrow, even. You want a ride home?"

"I'll stay." My stomach felt light. It occurred to me that I should probably call Ivy and let her know what was going on. If she'd talk to me. "Is it bad?" I asked. By the door, the two men chatted to a third as they unpacked a vacuum from the battered suitcase and put paper sleeves on over their shoes.

Glenn didn't answer, his eyes going everywhere but to me and that black doorway. "If you're staying, you'll need this," he said as he handed me an FIB badge with the word TEM-

PORARY on it. People were stringing yellow crime scene tape, and it looked like they were settling in. The radio was thick with short, terse requests, and everyone but the dogs and I seemed happy. I had to get upstairs. I had to see what Trent had done to Dr. Anders.

"Thanks," I whispered, looping the badge's necklace over my head.

"Get yourself a coffee," he said, looking toward one of the vans that had come in with us. FIB officers with nothing to do were already clustered around it. I nodded, and Glenn headed back to the stairway, his long legs taking them two at a time.

I glanced only once at Trent, in the open room between the box stalls. He was talking to an officer, apparently having waived his right to counsel. To foster a perception of innocence? I wondered. Or did he think he was too smart to need one?

Numb, I joined the FIB personnel around the van. Someone handed me a soda, and after I avoided everyone's eyes, they obligingly ignored me. I didn't particularly want to make friends, and I wasn't comfortable with the lightness of the conversations. Jenks, though, proceeded to charm sips of sugar and caffeine from everyone, doing impersonations of Captain Edden that got everyone laughing.

Eventually I found myself on the outskirts listening to three conversations as the sun moved and a new chill came into the air. The vacuum cleaner was faint, the on-again, off-again sound making me jittery. Finally it quit and didn't start up. No one seemed to have noticed. My eyes rose to the upper apartments, and I pulled my jacket closer about me. Glenn had come down just moments before to vanish inside the crime scene van. My breath slid in and out of me, as easy as the day I was born. Giving myself a push, I found myself moving to the stairway.

Immediately Jenks was on my shoulder, making me wonder if he had been keeping an eye on me. "Rache," he warned. "Don't go in there."

"I have to see." I felt unreal, the rough banister under my hand still warm from the sun.

"Don't," he protested, his wings clattering. "Glenn is right. Wait your turn."

I shook my head, the swinging of my braid forcing him off my shoulder. I needed to see before the atrocity was lessened with little bags, white cards with neatly printed words, and the careful collection of data designed to give madness structure so it could be understood. "Get out of my way," I said flatly, waving at him as he hovered belligerently in front of my face. He darted back, and I jerked to a stop as I felt a fingertip flick one of his wings. *I'd hit him?*

"Hey!" he shouted. Surprise, alarm, and finally anger washed over him. "Fine!" he snapped. "Go see. I'm not your daddy." Still swearing, he flew away at head height. Heads turned in his path as a torrent of foul words spilled nonstop from him.

My legs felt heavy as I forced myself to rise up the stairs. A sharp clattering of feet drew my attention up, and I stood sideways as the first of the vacuum guys hustled past me. A rank smell of decayed flesh trailed after him, and my gore rose. Forcing it down, I continued, smiling sickly at the FIB officer standing beside the door.

The smell was worse up there. My thoughts flashed to the pictures I had seen in Glenn's office, and I almost lost it. Dr. Anders could have only been dead a few hours. How could it have gotten so bad so quickly?

"Name?" the man said, his face stiff as he tried to look unaffected by the cloying stench.

I stared for a moment, then saw the notebook in his hand. There were several names on it, the last followed by the word "photographer." The remaining man on the outside walkway snapped his suitcase shut and dragged it thumping down the stairs. By the doorway was a video camera, its sophistication somewhere between that of a news crew and the one my dad used before he died to record my and my brother's birthdays. "Oh, um, Rachel Morgan," I said faintly. "Special Inderland consultant."

"You're the witch, right?" he said, writing my name down with the time and my temporary badge number. "You want a mask with your boots and gloves?"

"Yes, thank you."

My fingers felt weak as I put the mask on first. It reeked of wintergreen, blocking the stink of decayed flesh. Thankful, I looked in at the wooden floor, shining polished and yellow under the last of the sunlight. From around the corner and out of sight came the *snick snick snick* of a camera shutter. "I'm not going to bother him, am I?" I asked, my words muffled.

The man shook his head. "Her," he said. "And no, you won't bother Gwen. Watch it, or she'll have you holding tape measures."

"Thanks," I said, resolving to not do anything of the kind. My gaze flicked to the parking lot below me as I snapped the paper covers over my shoes. The longer I stayed there, the more likely it was that Glenn would realize I wasn't where he had left me. Stealing myself, I pinched the clip of the mask tighter, jerking as the pungent fragrance hit my nose. My eyes started to water, but I wasn't going to take it off for anything. I put my gloved hands in my pockets as if I were in a black-charm shop and entered.

"Who are you?" a strong, feminine voice challenged as my shadow eclipsed the sun.

My attention jerked to a willowy woman with dark hair tied in a no-nonsense ponytail. She had a camera in hand and was dropping a roll of film into a black bag tied to her hip.

"Rachel Morgan," I said. "Edden brought me in as a—" My words cut off as my eyes fell onto the torso tied to a hard-backed chair partially hidden behind her. My hand rose to my mouth and I forced my throat closed.

It's a mannequin, I thought. It had to be a mannequin. It couldn't be Dr. Anders. But I knew it was. Yellow nylon ropes bound her to the chair, and her top-heavy upper torso sagged, sending her head forward to hide her face. Stringy hair caked with black hung to further hide her expression, and I thanked God for that. Her legs were missing below both knees, the stumps sticking out like a small child's feet at the end of a chair. The ends were raw and ugly, swollen with decay. Her arms were gone at the elbows. Old black blood covered her clothes in a fantastic rivulet pattern so thick the original color couldn't be guessed.

My eyes flicked to Gwen, shocked at her blasé expression. "Don't touch anything. I'm not done yet, okay?" she muttered as she went back to her photographing. "God bless it. Can't I have even five minutes before everyone comes traipsing in here?"

"Sorry," I breathed, surprised I could still talk. Dr. Anders's slumped body was covered in blood, but there was surprisingly little of it under the chair. I felt light-headed, but I couldn't look away. Her lower cavity had been opened at her belly button, a perfectly round patch of skin the size of my fist propped open with a silver knife to show a careful dissection of her insides. There were suspicious gaps, and the incision was entirely bloodless, as if washed—or licked—clean. Where the flesh wasn't covered in blood, it was white, like wax. My gaze went to the pristine walls and floors. The body didn't match. It had been mutilated elsewhere and moved.

"This one is a real sicko," Gwen said, camera chattering away. "Look at the window."

She pointed with her chin, and I turned. It looked like a little cityscape was arranged on the wide shadowed sill. Squatty buildings were set out in straight lines in no apparent order of size. Small lumps of gray putty held them upright like glue. They were arranged around a thick class ring, placed like a monument among the city's streets. I looked closer, horror tightening my gut. I spun to the limbless corpse and back again.

"Yup," Gwen was saying as she clicked away. "He put them there on display. The larger parts he tossed into the closet."

My gaze shot to the tiny closet, then back to the shady windowsill. They weren't buildings, they were fingers and toes. He had cut her fingers off knuckle by knuckle, arranging them like Tinkertoys. The putty was bits of her insides, the viscera keeping it all together.

I felt hot, then cold. My stomach went light and I thought I might pass out. I held my breath as I realized I was hyperventilating. I was willing to bet she'd been alive during it.

"Get out," Gwen said, casually framing another shot. "If you spew in here, Edden will have a hissy."

"Morgan!" came a faint irate shout from the parking lot. "Is that witch in there?"

The outside officer's answer was muffled. I couldn't take my eyes off the wreck of a body on the chair. The flies crawled among the city streets the mutilated digits made, climbing the buildings like monsters in a B-movie. Gwen's clicks were like my heartbeat, fast and furious. Someone grabbed my arm and I gasped.

"Rachel," Glenn said, spinning me around to him. "Get your witch ass out of here."

"Detective Glenn," the officer by the door stammered. "She signed in."

"Sign her out," he growled. "And don't let her in again."

"You're hurting me," I whispered, feeling light and unreal.

He dragged me to the door. "I told you to stay out," he muttered fiercely.

"You're hurting me," I repeated, pushing at his fingers encircling my arm as he pulled me out. I hit the setting sun. It struck me like a goad, and I took a huge breath, snapping out of my stupor. That wasn't Dr. Anders. The body was too old, and it had been a man's ring. It looked like it had the university's logo on it. I thought I'd just found Sara Jane's boyfriend.

Glenn dragged me to the stairs. "Glenn," I said as I stumbled on the first step. I would have fallen but for his hold on me. Another FIB vehicle was easing into the lot. A mobile morgue this time. Glenn, not taking any chances, was bringing everything there.

Slowly my legs lost their watery feeling as I put distance between me and what I had seen upstairs. I watched the FIB officers joking among themselves, not understanding. I was clearly not cut out for crime scene work. I was a runner, not an investigator. My father had worked in the arcane division where most of the bodies showed up. Now I knew why he never said much about his day at the dinner table.

"Glenn," I tried again as he pulled me into the open room between the stalls. Trent stood in a corner with Sara Jane and Quen, quietly answering questions. Glenn jerked to a stop as he saw them. He looked at his father, who shrugged. The FIB captain sat before a laptop resting on a bail of straw propped up on its end. Someone had run a line from the crime van, and Edden's stubby fingers skated over the keyboard as he played subordinate so he could stay.

Irritation pinched Glenn's face and he gestured to the young FIB officer with Trent.

"Glenn," I said as the officer edged his way to us. "That isn't Dr. Anders up there."

Edden's round face went questioning behind his glasses. Glenn flicked a glance at me. "I know," he said. "The body is too old. Sit down and shut up."

The FIB officer came to a halt beside us, and my eyes widened as Glenn put an aggressive arm across his shoulders. "I told you to detain them," he said softly. "What are they still doing here?"

The man went white. "You meant in one of the cruisers? I

thought Mr. Kalamack would be more comfortable here."

Glenn's lips pressed together and his neck muscles tensed. "Detained for questioning means move them to the FIB offices. You don't question people at the crime scene when it's this important. Get them out of here."

"But you didn't say . . ." The man swallowed. "Yes sir." Glancing once at Edden, he headed toward Trent and Sara Jane, looking apologetic, frightened, and very young. I didn't have time to spare him any pity.

Still angry, Glenn went to stand over his father's shoulder, typing in his own password with a stiff finger. My stomach gave a lurch and settled. I pushed the top of the computer down on his hands. Glenn clenched his jaw as they both looked up at me. I turned to Trent and Sara Jane on their way out, waiting until Edden and Glenn followed my gaze to them before saying, "I can't say for sure, but I think that's Dan."

Sara Jane's face remained blank for a telling moment. Eyes widening, she clutched at Trent. Her mouth opened and closed. Burying her face in his shoulder, she began sobbing. Trent patted her shoulder gently, but his eyes on me were narrowed in anger.

Edden pursed his lips in thought, which made his graying mustache stick out as we exchanged shrewd looks. Sara Jane didn't know Dan as well as she wanted everyone to think. Why would Trent make Sara Jane come to the FIB with a phony complaint of a missing boyfriend when he knew I'd find the body on his grounds? Unless he hadn't known about it? How could he not know?

Glenn, apparently, missed everything as he grabbed my upper arm and yanked me past a hysterical Sara Jane and out into the shadows of the oak tree. "Damn it, Rachel," he hissed as Sara Jane was led sobbing to a cruiser. "I told you to shut up! You're leaving. Now. That little stunt of yours might be enough to let Kalamack walk."

Even in my heels, Glenn was taller than me, and it ticked

me off. "Yeah?" I shot back. "You asked me to read Trent's emotions. Well I did. Sara Jane doesn't know Dan Smather from her mailman. Trent had him killed. And that body has been moved."

Glenn reached for me, and I stepped out of his reach. His face tightened and he took a step back, exhaling slowly. "I know. Go home," he said, extending his hand for the temporary FIB badge. "I appreciate your assistance in finding the body, but as you said, you aren't a detective. Every time you open your mouth, you're making it easier for Trent's attorney to sway a jury. Just . . . go home. I'll call you tomorrow."

Anger warmed me, the last dregs of adrenaline making me feel weak, not strong. "I found his body. You can't make me leave."

"I just did. Give me the badge."

"Glenn," I said as I ducked out of the necklace before he snapped it off my neck, "Trent murdered that witch as sure as if he had twisted the knife."

He held my badge in a tight grip, his anger slowing enough to show his frustration. "I can talk to him, even hold him for questioning, but I can't arrest him."

"But he did it!" I protested. "You've got a body. You've got a weapon. You've got probable cause."

"I have a body that's been moved," he said, his voice flat from his repressed emotions. "My probable cause is conjecture. I've got a weapon six hundred employees could have planted. There is nothing to link Trent to the murder yet. If I arrest him now, he could walk even if he confesses later. I've seen it happen. Mr. Kalamack may have done this on purpose, planted the body and made sure there was nothing to link him to it. If this one doesn't stick, it will be twice as hard to pin another corpse to him, even if he makes a mistake later."

"You're afraid to take him down," I accused, trying to goad him into arresting Trent.

"Listen to me real good, Rachel," he said, jolting me into taking a step back. "I don't give a dingo's ass if you *think* Kalamack did it. I have to *prove* it. And this is the only chance I'm going to get." Turning halfway around, he scanned the parking lot. "Someone take Ms. Morgan home!" he said loudly. Without a backward glance, he stomped to the stables, his heavy steps silent on the sawdust.

I stared, not knowing what to do. My attention went to Trent getting into a FIB cruiser, his expensive suit making it look wrong. He gave me an unfathomable look before the door shut with a metallic thump. Lights off and slow, the two cars pulled out.

My blood hummed and my head was pounding. Trent wasn't going to get away with this unscathed. Eventually I would tie each and every murder back to him. Having found Dan's body on his grounds would give Captain Edden the clout to get whatever warrant I wanted. Trent was going to fry. I could play it slow. I was a runner. I knew how to stalk prey.

I turned away, disgusted. I hated the law even as I relied on it. I'd much rather fight a coven of black witches than a courtroom any day. I understood witches' mores better than lawyers'. At least witches used theirs.

"Jenks!" I shouted as Captain Edden emerged from the stables, keys jingling in his hands. Great. Now I was going to have to listen to a lecture of wise-old-man crap all the way home. It felt good to shout, and I took another breath to yell for Jenks again when the pixy came to a short stop in front of me. He was literally glowing in excitement, the dust that had sifted from him drifting into me from his momentum.

"Yeah, Rache? Hey, I heard Glenn kicked you out. I told you not to go up there. But did you listen to me? No-o-o-o-o-o. No one listens to me. I've got thirty some kids, and the only one who listens to me is my dragonfly."

My anger hesitated for an instant as I wondered if he really had a pet dragonfly. Then I shook myself, sending my thoughts onto how to salvage something from this. "Jenks," I said, "can you get home from here all right?"

"Sure. I'll hitch with Glenn or the dogs. No problem."

"Good." I glanced at Captain Edden as he approached. "Tell me what happens, okay?"

"Gotcha. Hey, for what's it's worth, I'm sorry. You gotta learn to keep your mouth shut and your fingers to yourself. See you later."

This coming from a pixy? "I didn't touch anything," I said, peeved, but he had already flitted back to Glenn's temporary office, leaving a head-high trail of dust to slowly dissipate.

Edden spared me a single glance as he passed me. Frowning, I followed him, yanking my door open. The car started, and I got in and slammed the door shut. Belt latched, I draped my arm on the open window and stared at the empty pasture.

"What's the matter?" I said nastily. "Glenn kick you out, too?"

"No." Edden shifted the car into reverse. "I need to talk to you."

"Sure," I said, for lack of anything better. A frustrated sigh slipped from me, catching as my gaze fell upon Quen. He stood unmoving in the shade of the old oak. There was no expression on his face. He must had heard my entire conversation with Glenn concerning Trent. A chill went through me, and I wondered if I had just put myself on Quen's "special people" list.

Green eyes fixed to me with a shocking intensity, Quen reached up to a low branch and swung himself up with the ease of picking a flower, disappearing into the old oak as if he had never existed.

Twenty-Two

Edden swung the car into the church's tiny weed-choked parking lot. He hadn't said much on the way back, his white knuckles and red neck telling me what he thought of the free-flow stream of consciousness that I had been spewing forth ever since he confessed the reason why he was playing chauffeur for me.

Shortly after finding the body, word had come over the radio that I was to be "removed from the FIB payroll." Seems it got out that a witch was helping them and the I.S. called foul. I might have been able to swing it if Glenn had cared to explain that I was merely a consultant, but he hadn't said a word, apparently still sulking over me contaminating his precious crime scene. That there wouldn't even *be* a crime scene if it hadn't been for me didn't seem to mean anything.

Slamming the car into park, Edden stared out the front window and waited for me to get out. I had to give him credit. It's not easy to sit and listen while someone compares your son to squid suckers and bat guano in the same breath.

Shoulders slumping, I didn't move. If I got out, it would mean it was over, and I didn't want it to be. Besides, keeping up a tirade for twenty minutes is tiring, and I probably owed him an apology if nothing else. My arm hung out the car's open window, and I could hear a piano playing some elaborate complicated thing that composers made up to show off their dexterity rather than any artistic expression. I took a breath. "If I could just talk to Trent—"

"No."

"Can I at least listen to the tape of his interview?"

"No."

I rubbed my temples, an escaped curl tickling my cheek. "How does anyone expect me to do my job if they won't let me do it?"

"It's not your job anymore," Edden said. The hint of anger pulled my head up. I followed his gaze to the pixy children sliding down the steeple on the tiny squares of wax paper I had cut for them yesterday. Neck stiff, Edden shifted in his seat to take his wallet from a back pocket. Flipping it open, he handed me some bills. "I was told to pay you in cash. Don't claim it on your taxes," he said flatly.

My lips pressed together and I snatched it, counting the money. *Pay me in cash? Out of the captain's pocket?* Someone had fallen deep into "cover your ass" mode. My stomach tightened as I realized it was far less than what we had agreed upon. I'd been almost a week on this. "And you'll get me the rest later, right?" I asked as I shoved it into my bag.

"Management won't pay for Dr. Anders's canceled class," he said, not looking at me.

Stiffed again. Not looking forward to telling Ivy I was short with my rent, I opened the door and got out. If I didn't know better, I'd say the piano was coming from the church. "Tell you what, Edden." I slammed the door shut. "Don't call me again."

"Grow up, Rachel," he said, jerking me back around. His round face was tight as he leaned across the seat to talk to me through the window. "If it had been me, I would have arrested you and given you to the I.S. to play with. He told you to wait, and you stepped all over his authority."

Fingers pulling the strap of my bag higher up my shoulder, my scowl faltered. I hadn't thought about it like that.

"Look," he said, seeing my sudden understanding. "I don't want to break our working relationship. Maybe when things cool off, we can try this again. I'll get the rest of the money to you somehow."

"Yeah. Sure." I straightened, my beliefs in the asinine, knee-jerk reactions of upper management reinforced, but maybe I owed Glenn an apology.

"Rachel?"

Yup. I owed Glenn an apology. I turned to Edden, a depressed, frustrated sigh shifting through me. "Tell Glenn I'm sorry," I muttered. Before he could respond, I sent my heels clacking on the cracked sidewalk and up the wide stone steps. For a moment there was silence. Then the car's fan belt whined as Edden backed up and drove away. The music was coming from inside. Still upset about my missing rent, I yanked open the heavy door and went in.

Ivy must be home. My frustration with Edden died with the chance to finally talk to her. I wanted to tell her that nothing had changed and she was still my friend—if she'd have me for one. Turning down the offer to be her scion might be an insurmountable insult in the vamp world. I didn't think so, though. What little I had seen of her showed guilt, not anger.

Ivy?" I called cautiously.

The piano cut off in mid-chord. "Rachel?" Ivy responded from the sanctuary. There was a worrisome hint of alarm in her voice. Damn, she was going to run. Then my eyebrows rose. That wasn't a recording. We had a piano?

Shrugging out of my coat, I hung it up and went into the sanctuary, blinking at the sudden light. We had a piano. We had a beautiful, black, baby grand piano sitting in an amber and green sunbeam coming in through the stain-glassed windows. Its top was propped up to show its insides, the wires gleaming and the stops all velvety smooth.

"When did you get the piano?" I asked, seeing her poised and ready to run. *Double damn. If she would just slow down enough to listen.*

My shoulders eased as she took up a chamois cloth and started rubbing the gleaming wood. She was wearing jeans and a casual top, and I felt terribly overdressed in my dress suit. "Today," she said as she dusted wood that needed no dusting. Maybe if I didn't say anything about what had happened, we could get back to the way things were. Ignoring a problem was a perfectly acceptable way to deal with it, as long as both people agree to never bring it up again.

"You didn't have to stop because of me," I said, scrambling to say something before she found a reason to leave.

She edged around to polish the back as I went to hit middle C.

Ivy straightened, her eyes slipping shut and her dust cloth stopping. "Middle C," she said as peace slackened her pale oval face.

I chose another, holding the key down to listen to it echo among the rafters. It sounded wonderful in the open, hard-walled space. Especially since the exercise mats were gone.

"F-sharp," she whispered, and I hit two at a time. "C and D-sharp," she said, opening her eyes. "That's an awful combination."

I smiled, relieved when she met my gaze. "I didn't know you could play," I said, hitching my bag up higher on my shoulder.

"My mother made me take lessons."

Nodding absently, I dug the money out of my bag. My thoughts went to the discrepancy between us as I leaned through the piano and handed it to her. Ivy was buying a baby grand piano and my dresser was made of pressboard.

Head bent over the money, she counted it. "You're missing two hundred," she said.

Taking a breath, I went into the kitchen. Guilt tugged at me as I dropped my bag on Ivy's antique kitchen table and went to the fridge for the juice. "Edden shorted me," I shouted to the sanctuary, thinking she probably wouldn't leave if we were talking about money. "I'll get the rest. I'm going to talk to the baseball team again."

"Rachel . . ." Ivy said from the hall, and I spun, my heart pounding. I hadn't heard her footsteps. She took in my surprise, and a wash of inner pain flickered over her. Edden's freakin' attempt at compensation was in her hand, and I hated everything. Just everything.

"Forget it," she said, making me feel even better. "I can cover for you this month."

Again, I finished silently for her. Damn it to hell. I ought to be able to pay my own bills.

Depressed, I took off my hat and hung it on my chair. My heels were next, and I kicked them off, sending them flying out the archway to land thumping somewhere in the living room. In my stocking feet, I sat slumped at the table and nursed my juice as if it was a beer at closing time. There was an open bag of cookies on the table, and I pulled them closer. Chocolate cream would make everything better if I could get enough into me.

Ivy stretched to drop the money into the jar atop the fridge. It wasn't the safest place to keep the money we pooled to pay our bills, but who was going to steal from a Tamwood vampire? Saying nothing, she slipped into her chair across from me, the length of the table between us. The fan of her computer whirled up to speed as she jiggled the mouse. My bad mood eased. She hadn't left. She was working at her computer. I was in the same room with her. Maybe she felt safe enough that she could at least listen.

"Ivy—" I started.

"No," she said, flicking me a frightened look.

"I just want to say I'm sorry," I rushed. "Don't go. I'll drop it." How could someone so strong and powerful be so afraid of herself? The woman was a conflicting mass of strength and vulnerability that I didn't understand.

Her eyes went everywhere but to mine. Slowly her wire-tight posture relaxed. "But it wasn't your fault," she whispered. *Then why do I feel like crap?* "I'm sorry, Ivy," I said, pulling her eyes to mine for a brief moment. They were as brown as chocolate, with no hint of black rimming them. "It's just—"

"Stop," she said, her gaze going to her hand clutching the table, the nails still shiny from the clear polish she had put on to go to Piscary's. She visibly forced her grip to relax. "I . . . won't ask you to be my scion again if you don't say anything more." The last was hesitant, disquieting in her vulnerability.

It was almost as if she knew what I was going to say and couldn't bear to hear it. I would not be her scion—I couldn't. The tie that would bind us would be too tight and take from me my independence. While I knew in the vampire existence that the giving and receiving of blood was not necessarily equated with sex, to me they were the same. And I didn't want to say, "Can we just be friends?" It was trite and degrading, even if to be her friend was all I wanted. She'd take the words as the brush-off most people used them for. I liked her too much to hurt her that way. And I could tell it wasn't a lingering bitterness that prompted her promise. She wouldn't ask me to be her scion because she didn't want the pain of being rejected again.

I didn't understand vampires. But that's where Ivy and I were.

She met my eyes with a faltering sureness that strengthened as she saw my silent agreement to ignore what had happened. Her shoulders eased and she regained a wisp of her usual confidence. But as I sat in our kitchen with my feet in the sun, I went cold with the knowledge of how badly I was using her. She was freely giving me protection against the many vampires that would take advantage of my scar—in essence, she was ensuring my free will—and she was willing to overlook that I wasn't paying for it in the usual vampiric fashion. God help me, it was enough to make me hate myself. She wanted something I couldn't give her, and she was content to take my friendship in the hopes that someday I could give more.

I took a slow breath, watching her pretend not to notice my eyes on her as I let the pieces fall into place. I couldn't leave. It was more than not wanting to lose the only real friend I had had in eight years or my desire to help her win the war she fought against herself. It was the fear of being turned into a plaything by the first vampire I ran into in a moment of weakness. I was trapped by convenience, and the tiger with me was willing to lap cream and purr, betting she'd find a way to change my mind. *Great. I'd have no problem sleeping tonight.*

Ivy's eyes met mine, her breathing hesitating a bare second as she realized that I'd finally figured it out. "Where's Jenks?" she asked, turning to her screen as if nothing had happened.

I exhaled slowly, coming to grips with my new outlook. I could leave and fight off every lustful vamp I ran into, or I could stay under Ivy's mantle, trusting I'd never have to fight her off instead. As my dad was fond of saying, a known danger was far better than an unknown one.

"At Trent's helping Glenn," I said, my fingers trembling as I reached for another cookie. I'd stay. We had an understanding. Or was Nick right, in that I really did want her to bite me but couldn't accept that my "preferences" had slid a little? Surely the former. "I'm off the case. I found a body and word got out a witch was helping the FIB."

Her eyes met mine over the screen between us, her thin eyebrows high. "You found a body? At Trent's compound? You're kidding."

I nodded, slumping with my elbows on the table, unwilling to delve any deeper into my psyche right now. I was too tired. "I'm pretty sure it's Dan Smather's, but it doesn't matter. Glenn is more uptight than a pixy in a room full of frogs, but Trent's going to walk." My thoughts shifted from what I was going to do about Ivy to the memory of Dan's mutilated body strapped to the chair. "Trent is too smart to leave anything to connect him to the body," I said. "I don't understand why it was on his property to begin with."

She nodded, her attention going back to her screen. "Maybe he put it there."

A wry grimace crossed me. "That's what Glenn thinks. That Trent is the murderer but wanted us to find it, knowing we couldn't link it to him, and therefore making it twice as hard to catch him if he makes a mistake later on. It fits with Sara Jane's reaction. She doesn't know Dan Smather better than her UPS man, but something . . ." I hesitated, trying to put my feeling into words. "Something isn't right." I thought back to the picture she'd given me. It had been the same photo as the one on his TV. I should've known then that their courtship was contrived.

I was starting to doubt my own, grudge-laced belief that Trent was responsible for the murders, and that was disturbing. He was capable of murder—I'd seen that firsthand—but the mutilated, bloodless body tied to that chair and tortured was far and away from the clean, fast death he had inflicted upon his head geneticist last spring. Thinking, I reached for a cookie. Biting the head off, I got up to hunt through the fridge to decide what I was going to fix for dinner and let my subconscious work on it. Maybe I'd make something special. It had been a while since I had done more than open boxes and stir things on the stove.

I glanced at Ivy, feeling guilty and relieved all at the same time. No wonder she thought I wanted more than to be her roommate. Some of this was my fault. Most maybe.

"So what did Trent do when you found the body?" Ivy asked, mouse clicking as she checked out her chat rooms. "Any guilt?"

"Ah, no," I said, pushing my uncomfortable feelings aside even as I took a half pound of lean hamburger out of the freezer and set it clunking into the sink. "And the surprise he let slip wasn't that I found a body but that it was Dan's body. That's why I don't like the idea that he put it there to cover himself. He knows more than he's saying, though." I gazed out the window at the sunlit garden and the glimmers of pixy wings as Jenks's kids fought off a migrating hummingbird from the last of the lobelias. It had to be migrating. Jenks would have killed it before letting competition get a foothold in his garden.

As the children shouted and called, working together to drive the hapless bird away, my thoughts returned to the worry Trent had let show when I found that ley line running through his office. He had been more upset about me finding that line than finding Dan's body.

The ley line. That's where the real question lurked. My fingers tingled as I turned, wiping the frost from the hamburger off on a towel instead of my suit dress. I glanced at the window, wondering if I would draw more attention by shutting it or if I should press my luck and hope Jenks's kids were too busy to eavesdrop. Ivy pulled back from her computer screen as she saw my sudden secrecy. Jenks had a big mouth, and I didn't want him knowing of my suspicions of Trent's possible ancestry. He would blab it around, and Trent would hire a plane to "accidentally" drop Agent Orange on the entire block to stop the rumors.

Splitting the difference, I shut the curtains and stood by the window where I could see the shadow of pixy wings should any flit close enough to hear. "Trent has a ley line in his office," I said, my voice hushed.

Ivy stared at me in the blue-tinted sun. "No kidding? What are the chances of that?"

She didn't get it. "So that means he must use them," I prompted.

"And . . ." Her eyebrows rose in question.

"So who can use ley lines?" I shot back.

Her jaw dropped in sudden understanding. "He's human or a witch," she breathed. She got to her feet in a movement so quick, it set me on edge. Coming to the sink, she pushed the curtain aside and shut the window with a thump. "Does Trent know you saw it?" she asked, her eyes black in the dimmer light.

"Oh, I'd say he does." I went to get another cookie to subtly put some space between us. "Seeing as I had to use the line to find the body."

Her lips pressed together and her lanky stance went tight. "You put your head on the block again. You, me, Jenks, and his entire family. Trent will do anything to keep this quiet."

"If he was that worried about it, he wouldn't have risked putting his office on the line," I protested, hoping I was right. "Anyone looking would find it. He could still be Inderlander or human. We're safe, especially if I don't say anything about the ley line."

"Jenks might figure it out," she insisted. "You know how he'll blab it. He'd love the prestige of finding out what Trent is."

I snatched a cookie. "What am I supposed to do? If I tell him to keep his mouth shut about the line, he'll only try to figure out why."

Her fingers drummed on the counter as I ate the shortbread and cream. In an unnerving display of strength, she used one hand to lever herself up to sit atop the cabinets. Her face had come alive, her thin eyebrows creased with the chance to solve the long-running mystery. "So what do you think he is? Human or witch?"

Returning to the sink, I ran hot water over the frozen meat. "Neither." It was a flat admission. Ivy remained silent, and I turned the water off. "He's neither, Ivy. I would stake my life that he isn't a witch, and Jenks swears he's more than human."

Is this why I stayed? I wondered, seeing her eyes alight and her mind working with mine. Her logic, and my intuition. In spite of the problems, we worked well together. We always had.

Ivy shook her head, her features blurred in the blue-curtained dusk, but I could feel her tension rising. "It's the only choices we have. You eliminate everything, and whatever remains, no matter how improbable, is the answer."

It didn't surprise me she was quoting Sherlock Holmes. The anal logic and brusque nature of the fictional detective fit right in with Ivy's personality. "Well, if you want to entertain the improbable," I muttered, "you can lump demons in with the possibilities."

"Demons?" Ivy's tapping fingers stilled.

I shook my head in bother. "Trent's not a demon. I only mentioned it because demons are from the ever-after and so can manipulate ley lines, too."

"I'd forgotten that," she breathed, the soft sound sending a shiver down my spine, but she was intent on her thoughts and had no idea how creepy she was getting. "That you're related, I mean. Witches and demons." An affronted snort slipped past me, and she shrugged apologetically. "Sorry. Didn't know it was a sore spot."

"It isn't," I said tightly, though it was. There had been a flurry of controversy about a decade ago when a nosy human in the field of Inderland genealogy got hold of the few genetic maps that had survived the Turn, theorizing that because witches could manipulate ley lines, we had originated in the ever-after along with demons. Witches aren't related to demons. But much to our embarrassment, science forced us to admit aloud that we had evolved right along next to them in the ever-after.

Finding funding with that unsavory tidbit, the woman then went beyond her original theory, using the rates of RNA mutation to properly place the time of our en masse migration to this side of the ley lines about five thousand years ago. Witch mythology claimed that a demon uprising had prompted the move, leaving the elves to foolishly wage a losing battle, since they wouldn't leave their beloved fields and woods to be raped of their natural resources and polluted. It sounded like a viable theory, and the elves had lost all their history by the time they gave up and followed suit a measly two thousand years ago.

That humans had developed skill in ley line magic about that time was blamed on the elves' practice of using their magic to hybridize with humanity to stave off the extinction the demons started and the Turn finished. My thoughts turned to Nick, and I slumped. It was just as well witches were so far from humanity that even magic couldn't bridge the gap. Who knew what an uninformed witch/human hybrid skilled in ley lines might do? That the elves had brought humanity into the ley-line-using family was bad enough. The elves' dexterity with line magic had slipped into the human genome as if it belonged. It was enough to make you wonder.

Elves? I thought, going cold. It had been staring me right in the face. "Oh—my—God," I whispered.

Ivy looked up, her swinging legs stilling as she took in my expression.

"He's an elf," I whispered, the thrill of discovery bubbling up making my pulse race. "They didn't die out in the Turn. He's an elf. Trent is a freaking elf!"

"Whoa, wait a minute," Ivy warned. "They're gone. If any were alive, Jenks would know. He'd be able to smell it."

I shook my head, pacing to the hallway to look for winged eavesdroppers. "Not if the elves went underground for a pixy/fairy generation. The Turn pretty much did them in, and it wouldn't be hard to hide what survived until the last pixy who knew what they smelled like died. They only live about twenty years or so, pixies I mean." My words tumbled over themselves as I rushed to get it out. "And you saw how Trent doesn't like them or fairies. It's almost a phobia. It fits! I can't believe it! We figured it out!"

"Rachel," Ivy cajoled as she shifted atop the counter. "Don't be stupid. He's not an elf."

Arms crossed, I pressed my lips together in frustration. "He sleeps at noon and midnight," I said, "and he's most active at dawn and dusk, just like elves were. He possesses nearly vamplike reflexes. He likes his solitude but is damn good at manipulating people. My God, Ivy, the man tried to ride me down on horseback like prey under the full moon!" I tossed my arms as I gestured. "You've seen his gardens and that artificial forest of his. He's an elf! And so are Quen and Jonathan."

She shook her head. "They died. All of them. And what would they have to gain by letting even Inderland think they were gone if they weren't? You know how we throw money at endangered species. Especially intelligent ones."

"I don't know," I said, exasperated with her disbelief. "Humanity was never keen on their history of stealing human babies and substituting their own failing infants. That would be enough for me to keep my mouth shut and my head down until everyone thought we were dead."

Ivy made a noise of doubt deep in her throat, but I could see her belief shifting. "He works ley lines," I insisted. "You said it yourself. Eliminate the impossible, and what's left, no matter how improbable, is the truth. The man isn't human or witch." My eyes closed as I remembered biting both Jonathan and Trent when I had been a mink, struggling to escape. "He can't be. His blood tastes like cinnamon and wine."

"He's an elf," Ivy said, her voice shockingly flat. I opened my eyes. Her face was alive and alight. "Why didn't you tell me he tasted like cinnamon?" she said as she slipped from the counter, her black ankle boots hitting the linoleum without a sound.

Self-preservation pulled me a step from her before I knew I had moved. "I thought it might have been from the drugs he had knocked me out with," I said, not liking that the mention of blood had jerked her into motion. The brown of her irises was shrinking behind her widening pupils. I was sure it was from discovering Trent's ancestry and not me standing in her kitchen with my blood pounding and my palms sweating. But still . . . I didn't like it.

Mind whirling, I gave her a warning look and put the island counter between us. *Okay, so I knew Trent's history.* Telling him would certainly get me an audience with him, but how do you tell a serial killer you know his secret without ending up dead?

"You aren't going to tell him you know," Ivy said, giving me an apologetic look before putting her back against the counter in a blatant show of keeping her distance.

"I have to talk to Trent. He'll talk to me if I drop this on his plate and serve it up with gravy. I'll be okay. I have that blackmail on him."

"Edden will slap you with a harassment suit if you so much as call him," Ivy warned.

My eyes lit upon the bag of sandwich cookies with their little oak tree and clapboard sign. Moving slowly, I slid the bag closer, picking out a figure with all his limbs intact. Ivy's eyes dropped to the cellophane, then rose to me. I could almost see her thoughts aligning themselves to mine. She gave me one of her few honest smiles, letting slip only the barest glimmer of teeth as a wicked yet almost shy look brought her alive.

A shiver laced through me, pulling my insides tight. "I think I know how to get his attention," I said, biting the head clean off the chocolate-covered cookie and wiping the crumbs from my lips. But in the back of my head, a new question niggled, incited by Nick's constant worry. Was the thrill of anticipation I felt rising through me from my coming conversation with Trent . . . or that tiny whisper of white teeth?

Twenty-Three

The clamor of the bus's diesel engine was obnoxious as it jolted into motion and struggled to find momentum while going uphill. I stood on the weed-edged sidewalk and waited for it to pass before crossing the street. The soft whooshes of cars made a comforting background to the birds, insects, and the occasional quacking of a duck. I turned, feeling someone's eyes on me.

It was a Were, with black hair to his shoulders and a trim body that said he ran on two legs as much as he did four. His attention went from me to the park, and he sank back into the tree he was leaning against, adjusting his worn leather coat. My pace faltered as I recognized him from the university, but he looked away and pulled his hat down over his eyes, dismissing me. He wanted something, but it was obvious he knew I was busy and was willing to wait.

Loners were like that, and from his confident, set-apart look, I imagined that's what he was. He probably had a run for me and wasn't willing to knock on my door, more comfortable with waiting to catch me when I wasn't busy. It had happened before. Weres had a tendency to view anyone who lived on hollowed ground as mysterious and esoteric.

Appreciating his professionalism, I started down the sidewalk in the opposite direction of the bus, the noon sun warm on my shoulders. I liked Eden Park, especially this little used end of it. Nick worked at the art museum cleaning artifacts just down the road, and we occasionally had my lunch and his dinner alfresco at the small overlook above Cincinnati. But my favorite place was the end that looked the other way, over the river and to the Hollows.

My father had brought me here Saturday mornings, where we would eat doughnuts and feed crumbs to the ducks. My mood went somber as I recalled the one occasion when he brought me after one of his few arguments with my mother. It had been night, and we'd watched the lights of the Hollows flicker across the river, the world seeming to continue around us as we were caught in a drop of time hanging on the lip of the present, reluctant to fall and make room for the next. Sighing, I tugged my short leather jacket closer and watched my step.

Yesterday I had sent a bag of cookies to Trent by special messenger with a card that simply said "I know." The cellophane bag and sandwich cookies had been just rife with an insulting mix of elf and magic propaganda that even the enlightened times after the Turn hadn't been able to quell. Sure enough, I was awoken that morning by the phone ringing. Then ringing again when the machine clicked off. And ringing again. And again. And again.

Eight o'clock in the morning is an ungodly time for witches—I had only been asleep four hours—but Jenks couldn't answer the phone, and waking Ivy up wasn't a good idea. The long and short of it was that Trent invited me to his garden for tea. No freaking way. I told Jonathan I'd meet Trent in Eden Park at four at Twin Lakes Bridge, right after his boss's nappies.

Twin Lakes Bridge was a rather grand name for the concrete footbridge, but I knew the troll that lived under it and felt I could rely on him in a pinch. The water chattering over the artificial rapids would distort any listening spell. Better yet, on football Sunday, the park would be almost deserted, giving us enough privacy to talk, yet retain enough people to deter any stupid choices Trent might be tempted to make, like outright killing me.

I forced my gaze up from the sidewalk as I passed Glenn's unmarked FIB car parked illegally at the curb. He had probably been assigned to keep an eye on Trent. Good. That meant I wouldn't have to truss up whatever FIB officer Edden had tailing the man so Trent and I could talk uninterrupted.

I had made a point to bring no spells with me, other than my usual pinky ring. No cumbersome bag, either. Just my little used driver's license and my bus pass. The reason for the lack of personal effects was twofold. Not only could I run faster if Trent tried something, but I wouldn't give Trent the opportunity to claim I'd slipped him a charm.

The strain from my quick pace made my calves ache, and I scanned the large park, finding it as sparsely populated as I'd hoped. I had ridden past the first stop since I wanted a good look-see before getting off. Not to mention it was impossible to make a graceful entrance from a bus. Even the leather pants, matching leather jacket, and red halter top wouldn't help.

I slowed, taking in the pond water, green with copper sulfate, and the lush grass. The trees were tipped with color, not yet hurried on by frost. Trent's red blanket made a vivid splash upon the ground. He was alone, pretending to read. I wondered where Glenn was, thinking that unless he was in the few large trees or the skinny apartments across the street, he was likely lurking in the bathrooms.

Arms swinging, I waved across the park to Jonathan, standing sullen by the Gray Ghost Limo in the sun. Clearly unhappy, he raised his wrist and spoke into his watch. My stomach tightened as I imagined Quen watching me from the trees. I forced my pace to a sedate saunter as I went to the public rest rooms, my vamp-made boots silent on the walkway.

For bathrooms, they were elegant, speaking of a more gracious time, with the ivy covered stone and cedar shingles. The metal shutters and doors lent themselves to the permanence of the structure as much as the fading perennials smothering it. Sure enough, I found Glenn inside the men's room, his back to me as he stood on the toilet with a pair of binoculars, watching Trent through the broken window. The bridge was within his view, and I felt better knowing he would be watching me.

"Glenn," I said, and he spun, almost slipping off the toilet.

"God bless it!" he swore, giving me a dark look before returning his attention out the window. "What are you doing here?"

"And good morning to you, too," I said politely, wanting to smack him a good one and ask why he hadn't stuck up for me yesterday and kept me working. The room reeked of chlorine and had no partitions at all. The ladies' bathroom at least had stalls.

His neck tensed, and I gave him credit for not looking from Trent for even a moment. "Rachel," he warned. "Go home. I don't know how you found out Mr. Kalamack was here, but if you go near him, I'll give you to the I.S. myself."

"Look, I'm sorry," I said. "I made a mistake. I should have stayed put until you said I could enter that crime scene, but Trent asked me to meet him here, so you can go Turn yourself."

Glenn lowered his binoculars, his face slack as he looked at me.

"Scouts honor," I said, giving him a sarcastic salute.

His eyes went distant in thought. "This isn't your run anymore. Get out of here before I have you arrested."

"You could have at least gotten me in to Trent's FIB interview yesterday," I said, taking an aggressive step forward. "Why did you let them shut me out? This was *my run*!"

His hand rested on the two-way on his hip, right next to

his weapon. His brown eyes were angry with a past incident that didn't include me. "You were ruining the case I was building against him. I told you to stay out, and you didn't."

"I said I was sorry. And there wouldn't even be a case if it wasn't for me," I exclaimed. Frustrated, I put my hand on my hip and raised my other in an angry gesture, jerking to a halt as someone came in. It was a frumpy looking man in a frumpy looking coat. He stood in shock for three heartbeats, running his eyes over Glenn in his expensive black suit standing on the can to me in my leather pants and jacket.

"Uh, I'll come back," he said, then hastened out.

I turned back to Glenn, having to tilt my head at an awkward angle to look up at him. "I can't work for the FIB anymore, thanks to you. I'm informing you of my meeting with Trent as a courtesy from one professional to another. So back off and don't interfere."

"Rachel . . ."

My eyes narrowed. "Don't mess with me, Glenn. Trent asked for this meeting."

The faint worry lines around Glenn's eyes deepened. I could see his thoughts warring among themselves. I wouldn't have bothered telling him at all except he probably would have called in everyone from his dad to the bomb squad when he saw me with Trent.

"Are we clear on this?" I asked belligerently, and he stepped off the toilet.

"If I find out you lied to me—"

"Yeah, yeah, yeah." I turned to go.

He reached for me. I felt his hand coming and jerked away, spinning. I shook my head in warning, but his eyes were wide at how fast I had moved. "You just don't get it, do you?" I said. "I am not human, this is Inderland business, and you are in way over your head." And with that thought to keep him awake at night, I strode back out into the sunlight, trusting he would keep an eye on me and not get in my way.

My arms swung as I attempted to dispel the last of the adrenaline, and my skin seemed to prickle as Jonathan's eyes fell on me. Ignoring him, I tried to spot where Quen had hidden himself as I made my way to the concrete bridge. On the other side of the twin ponds was Trent upon his blanket. He still had that book in his hand, but he knew I was here. He was going to make me wait, which was fine by me. I wasn't ready for him yet.

Deep in the shadows of the bridge ran a wide ribbon of fast water connecting the two ponds. My foot hit the bridge, and the puddle of purple amidst the current shuddered.

"Heyde-hey," I said, stopping just shy of the bridge's apex. Yeah, it was kind of stupid, but it was the traditional greeting between trolls. If I was in luck, Sharps would still have possession of this bridge.

"Heyde-ho," said the dark puddle of water, pulling itself up in a series of ripples until a dripping, craggy face showed. Algae grew on his otherwise bluish skin and his fingernails were white with the mortar he scraped from the bottom of the bridge to supplement his diet.

"Sharps," I said, truly pleased as I recognized him by his one white eye, blinded by a past fight. "How's the water flowing?"

"Officer Morgan," he said, sounding tired. "Can you wait until sundown? I promise I'll leave tonight. The sun is too bright right now."

I smiled. "It's just Rachel now. I quit the I.S. And don't move on account of me."

"You did?" The puddle of water sank back down until only a mouth and good eye showed. "That's fine. You're a nice girl. Not like the warlock they have now, coming at noon with electric prods and clangy bells."

I winced in sympathy. Trolls had extremely sensitive skin that kept them out of direct light most of the time. They tended to destroy whatever bridge they were under, which was why the I.S. continually chased them out. But it was a losing battle. As soon as one left, another took his place, and then there was a fight when the original troll wanted his home back.

"Hey, Sharps," I said. "Maybe you could help me."

"Anything I can manage." A purple-hued, skinny arm reached up to pick a grain of mortar from the underside of the bridge.

I glanced at Trent, seeing he was making motions to head my way. "Has anyone been around your bridge this morning? Maybe leaving a spell or charm behind?"

The puddle of oily water drifted to the opposite side of the bridge and into a patch of dappled shade where I lost sight of him. "Six kids kicked rocks off the bridge, one dog took a leak at the footing, three adult humans, two strollers, a Were, and five witches. Before dawn, there were two vamps. Someone got bit. I smelled the blood that hit the southwest corner."

I looked over, seeing nothing. "No one left anything, though?"

"Just the blood," he whispered, sounding like bubbles against rocks.

Trent had stood and was brushing his pants off. My pulse quickened and I pulled the strap to my shirt straight under my jacket. "Thanks, Sharps. I'll watch your bridge if you want to take a swim."

"Really?" His voice took on a hopeful, incredulous sound. "You'd do that for me, Officer Morgan? You're a damn fine woman." The smear of purple water hesitated. "You won't let anyone take my bridge?"

"No. I may have to leave quick, but I'll stay as long as I can."

"Damn fine woman," he said again. I leaned to watch a surprisingly long ribbon of purple slip out from under the bridge and flow around the rocks to the deeper pool of water in the lower basin. Trent and I would have a good measure of privacy, but a troll's territorial drive was so strong, I knew Sharps would keep an eye on me. I felt unjustifiably secure with Glenn on one side in the men's bathroom and Sharps in the water on the other.

Putting my back to the sun and Glenn's eyes, I leaned against the railing of the bridge to watch Trent stride over the grass to me. Behind him on the blanket he left an artfully arranged set of two wineglasses, a bottle packed in ice, and a bowl of out-of-season strawberries looking as if it were June, not September. His pace was measured and sure on the surface, but I could see it was fraught with nervousness beneath, giving away how young he really was.

He had covered his fair hair with a lightweight sun hat to shadow his face. It was the first time I had seen him in anything other than a business suit, and it would be easy to forget he was a murderer and a drug lord. The confidence of the boardroom was still there, but his trim waist, wide shoulders, and smooth face made him look more like an especially fit soccer dad.

His casual attire accentuated his youth instead of hiding it, as his Armani suits did. A wisp of blond hair peeked from behind the cuffs of his tasteful, button-down shirt, and I spared a thought that it was probably as soft and light as the pale hair drifting about his ears. His green eyes were pinched as he approached, squinting from the reflected sun or from worry. I was betting the latter since his hands were behind his back so I wouldn't shake with him.

Trent slowed as he stepped upon the bridge. His expressive eyebrows were slanted, and I remembered his fear when Algaliarept had turned into me. There was only one reason the demon would have done that. Trent was afraid of me, either for still falsely thinking I had set Algaliarept on him, or for having snuck into his office three times in as many weeks, or for me knowing what he was.

"None of the above," he said, his casual shoes scuffing as he came to a halt.

A wash of cold shocked through me. "I beg your pardon?" I stammered, pulling myself up and away from the railing.

"I'm not afraid of you."

I stared, his liquid voice melting itself into the chatter of water surrounding us.

"And I can't read your mind, either, just your face."

My breath came in a soft sound and I shut my mouth. *How had I lost control so fast?*

"You took care of the troll, I see," he said.

"Detective Glenn, too," I said as I touched my hair to be sure my curls hadn't escaped my braid. "He won't bother us unless you do something stupid."

His eyes tightened at the insult. He didn't move, keeping that same five feet between us. "Where's your pixy?" he asked.

Irritation pulled me straight. "His name is Jenks, and he's somewhere else. He doesn't know, and I'd just as soon keep it that way as he has a big mouth."

Trent visibly relaxed. He went to stand opposite me, the narrow width of the bridge between us. It had been hard to slip Jenks this afternoon, and Ivy finally stepped in, taking him out on a nonexistent run. I think she was actually going for doughnuts.

Sharps was playing with the ducks, pulling them under to bob to the surface and fly away quacking. Turning from the sight, Trent leaned his back against the railing and crossed one ankle against another, his position mirroring mine exactly. We were two people meeting by chance, sharing a few words and the sun. Ri-i-i-ight.

"If it gets out," he said, his eyes on the distant bathroom behind me, "I'll make the records concerning my father's little camp public. You and every one of those sorry little snots will be tracked down and treated like lepers. That is if they don't simply cremate you out of fear something will mutate and start another Turn."

My knees went loose and watery. I had been right. Trent's father had done something to me, fixed whatever had been wrong. And Trent's threat wasn't idle. The best-case scenario would involve a one-way ticket to the Antarctic. I moved my tongue around on the inside of my mouth, trying to find enough spit to swallow. "How did you know?" I asked, thinking my secret was more deadly than his.

Eyes fixed to mine, he pushed the sleeve of his shirt up to show a nicely muscled arm. The hair was bleached from the sun and his skin was well-tanned. A ragged scar marred its even smoothness. My eyes rose to his, reading an old anger.

"That was you?" I stammered. "That was you I threw into the tree?"

With motions short and abrupt, he tugged his sleeve back down, hiding the scar. "I've never forgiven you for making me cry in front of my father."

A childhood anger flared from coals I had thought long extinct. "It's your own fault. I told you to stop teasing her!" I said, not caring that my voice was louder than the surrounding water. "Jasmin was sick. She cried herself to sleep for three weeks because of you."

Trent jerked upright. "You know her name?" he exclaimed. "Write it down. Quick!"

I stared at him in disbelief. "Why do you care what her name was? She had a hard enough time without you picking on her."

"Her name!" Trent said, patting his pockets until he found a pen. "What's her name?"

Scowling, I tucked a curl behind an ear. "I'm not going to tell you," I said, embarrassed that I had forgotten it again.

Trent pressed his lips together and put the pen away. "You forgot already, didn't you?"

"Why do you care anyway? All you did was pester her."

He looked cross as he tugged his hat lower over his eyes. "I was fourteen. A very awkward fourteen, Ms. Morgan. I teased her because I liked her. Next time you recall her name, I would appreciate it if you would write it down and send it to me. There were long-term memory blockers in the camp's drinking water, and I would like to know if—"

His voice cut off, and I watched the emotion flicker behind his eyes. I was becoming good at reading them. "You want to know if she survived," I finished for him, knowing I had guessed right when his gaze went elsewhere. "Why were you there?" I asked, almost afraid he'd tell me.

"My father owned the camp. Where else would I spend my summers?"

The cadence of his voice and the slight tightening of his brow told me it had been more than that. A thrill of satisfaction warmed me; I'd found his tell for when he lied. Now all I needed was the same for when he was speaking the truth, and he'd never be able to successfully lie to me again.

"You are as filthy as your father," I said, disgusted, "blackmailing people by dangling a cure within their reach and making them your puppets. Your parents' fortune was built on the misery of hundreds, maybe thousands, Mr. Kalamack. And you're no different."

Trent's chin trembled almost imperceptibly, and I thought I saw a shimmer of sparkles about him, the memory of his aura playing tricks on me. Must be an elf thing. "I will not justify my actions to you," he said. "And you have become very adept in the art of blackmail yourself. I'm not going to waste my time bickering like children over who hurt whose feelings over a decade ago. I want to hire your services."

"Hire me?" I said, unable to keep my voice lowered as I put my hands on my hips in disbelief. "You tried to kill me in the rat fights, and you think I'm going to work for you? To help clear your name? You murdered those witches. I'm going to prove it."

He laughed, his hat shadowing his face as he bowed his head and chuckled.

"What's so funny?" I demanded, feeling foolish.

"You." His eyes were bright. "You were never in any danger in that rat pit. I was only using it to knock home your current sordid state. But I did make a few astounding contacts while I was there."

"You son of—" Lips pressed tight, I clenched my hand into a fist.

Trent's mirth vanished and his head tilted in warning as he took a step away. "I wouldn't," he threatened, raising a finger. "I really wouldn't."

I slowly rocked back, my knees shaking in the memory of the pit. The gut-twisting feeling of helplessness, of being trapped and forced to kill or be killed, washed through me. I had been Trent's toy. Him running me down on horseback was nothing compared to that. After all, I had been thieving from him at the time.

"Listen to me really good, Trent," I whispered, the thought of Quen forcing me to retreat until the concrete pressed cold into the small of my back. "I'm not working for you. I'm going to take you down. I'm going to figure out how to tie you to every one of those murders."

"Oh please," he said, and I wondered how we went so quickly from a Fortune-twenty businessman and a slick independent runner to two people squabbling over past injustices. "Are you still on that? Even Captain Edden realizes Dan Smather's body was dumped in my stables, which is why he sent his son to watch me instead of filing charges. And as for having contact with the victims, yes, I talked to them all, trying to employ them, not kill them. You have a very strong skill set, Ms. Morgan, but detective is not among them. You are far too impatient, driven by your intuitive skills, which seem to only work forward, not backward."

Affronted, I put my hands on my hips and made a sound of disbelief. *Who did he think he was, lecturing me?*

Trent reached into a shirt pocket, pulling out a white envelope and handing it to me. Leaning forward and back, I snatched it, flipping it open. My breath caught as I realized it held twenty crisp hundred-dollar bills.

"That's ten percent up front, the rest on completion," he said, and I froze, trying to look cavalier. *Twenty thousand dollars?* "I want you to identify who is responsible for the murders. I've been trying to hire a ley line witch for the last three months, and every one of them ends up dead. It's growing tiresome. All I want is a name."

"You can go to hell, Kalamack," I said, dropping the envelope when he didn't take it back. I was angry and frustrated. I had come here with information so fine, I was sure I was going to get a confession. What I got was threatened, insulted, and then bribed.

Looking unperturbed, he stooped to pick up the envelope, smacking it against his palm several times to get the grit off before tucking it away. "You do realize that with that little stunt you pulled yesterday, you are next on the killer's list? You fit the profile nicely, having shown yourself as proficient in ley line magic, and then adding our little tryst today."

Damn. I'd forgotten about that. If Trent really wasn't the murderer, than I had nothing to stop the real one from coming after me. Suddenly the sun wasn't warm enough. I felt breathless, sick that I was going to have to find the real killer before he found me.

"Now," Trent said, his voice smoother than the water. "Take the money so I can tell you what I've managed to learn."

Stomach twisting, I met his mocking gaze. I was going to

do just what he wanted. He had manipulated me into helping him. Damn, damn, and double damn. Crossing to his side of the bridge, I put my elbows atop the thick railing with my back to Glenn. Sharps was deep underwater, only the lack of ducks to say he was here. Beside me stood Trent.

"Did you send Sara Jane to the FIB with the sole intention that Edden would involve me?" I asked bitterly.

Trent shifted, putting himself so near I could smell the clean scent of his aftershave. I didn't like how close he was, but if I moved, he'd know it bothered me. "Yes," he said softly.

In his voice was the sound of truth I had been waiting for, and a trickle of excitement pulled my breath tight. There it was. Now I had it. He'd never be able to lie to me again. Looking back over our past conversations in a new light, I realized that apart from the reason he'd given me for being at his father's camp, he never had. Ever.

"She doesn't know him, does she?" I asked.

"A few dates to get the picture, but no. It was a calculated certainty that he would be murdered after he agreed to work for me, though I tried to protect him. Quen is very upset," he said lightly, his gaze on Sharps's ripples. "That Mr. Smather turned up in my stables means the killer is getting cocky."

My eyes closed briefly in frustration as I scrambled to realign my thinking. Trent hadn't killed those witches. Someone else had. I could either take the money and help Trent solve his little employment problem or not take the money and he'd get it for free. I'd take the money. "You're a bastard, you know that?"

Seeing my new understanding, Trent smiled. It was all I could do to not spit in his face. His long hands hung out over the edge of the railing. The sun turned his tan a warm golden color that almost glowed against his white shirt, and his face was shadowed. Wisps of his hair moved in the breeze, almost touching my own wayward strands.

With a casual movement, he reached into his shirt pocket, and with our bodies hiding the action from Glenn, he extended the envelope. Feeling dirty, I took it, shoving it out of sight behind my jacket and into my waistband.

"Excellent," he said, warm and sincere. "I'm glad we can work together."

"Go Turn yourself, Kalamack."

"I'm reasonably confident that it's a master vampire," he said, easing away from me.

"Which one?" I asked, disgusted with myself. *Why was I doing this?*

"I don't know," he admitted, flicking a bit of mortar off the railing to land in the water. "If I did, I'd have taken care of it already."

"I just bet you would," I said sourly. "Why not take them all out? Get it over with?"

"I can't go about staking vampires at random, Ms. Morgan," he said, worrying me because he'd taken my question seriously instead of the sarcasm it was. "That's illegal, not to mention it would start a vamp war. Cincinnati might not survive it. And I know my business interests would suffer in the interim."

I snickered. "Oh, we can't let that happen, now. Can we?"

Trent sighed. "Using sarcasm to cover your fear makes you look very young."

"And twirling your pencil in your fingers makes you look nervous," I shot back. It felt good to argue with someone who wouldn't bite me if things got out of control.

His eye twitched. Lips bloodless, he turned back to the large pond before us. "I'd appreciate it if you would keep the FIB out of this. It's an Inderland matter, not human, and I'm not sure the I.S. can be trusted, either."

I found it interesting how fast he had fallen into the "them" and "us" verbiage. Apparently I wasn't the only one who knew Trent's background, and I didn't like the higher degree of intimacy it put between us.

"I'm thinking it might be a rising vamp coven trying to gain a foothold by removing me," he said. "It would be a lot less risky than taking out one of the lesser houses."

It wasn't a boast—just a tasteless fact—and my lips curled at the thought I was taking money from a man who played the underworld like a chessboard. For the first time in my life I was glad my dad was dead and couldn't ask me "Why?" The picture of our fathers standing before the camp bus intruded, and I reminded myself I couldn't trust Trent. My father had, and it killed him.

Trent sighed, the sound both regretful and tired. "Cincinnati's underground is very fluid. All of my usual contacts have gone quiet or dead. I'm losing touch with what's happening." He flicked a glance at me. "Someone is trying to keep me from increasing my reach. And without a ley line witch at my disposal, I've reached an impasse."

"Poor baby," I mocked. "Why not do the magic yourself? Bloodline too polluted with nasty human genes to manage the heavy magic anymore?"

The knuckles of his fingers whitened as he gripped the rail, then relaxed. "I will have a ley line witch. I would much rather hire someone willing than abduct them, but if every witch I talk to ends up dead, I will steal someone."

"Yes," I drawled caustically. "You elves are known for that, aren't you?"

His jaw clenched. "Be careful."

"I'm always careful," I said, knowing I wasn't a good enough witch to have to worry about him "stealing" me. I watched the rims of his ears slowly lose their red tint. I squinted, wondering if they were a little pointed or if it was my imagination. It was hard to tell with the hat he had on. "Can you narrow it down for me?" I said. *Twenty thousand dollars to sift through Cincinnati's underworld to find out who wanted to put a crimp in Mr. Kalamack's day by killing his potential employees. Yeah. That sounded like an easy run.*

"I have lots of ideas, Ms. Morgan. Lots of enemies, lots of employees."

"And no friends," I added snidely, watching Sharps make serpentlike humps like a miniature Loch Ness. My breath slipped from me in a slow sound as I imagined what Ivy was going to say when I came home and told her I was working for Trent. "If I find out you're lying, I'll come after you myself, Kalamack. And this time, the demon won't miss."

He made a scoffing bark of laughter and I turned to him. "You can drop the bluff. You didn't send that demon after me last spring."

The slight breeze was cold, and I pulled my jacket closed as I turned. "How did you . . ."

Trent gazed distantly over the lower basin. "After overhearing your conversation with your boyfriend in my office and seeing your reaction to that demon, I knew it had to have been someone else, though I'll admit seeing you beaten and blue after I freed that demon to go back to kill its summoner nearly had me convinced."

I didn't like that he had overheard me talking to Nick. Or that he had responded the exact same way as I had after gaining control over Algaliarept. Trent's shoes scuffed, and a cautious inquiry came into his eyes. "Your demon scar . . ." He hesitated, and the flicker of haunted emotion strengthened. "It was an accident?" he finished.

I watched the ripples from Sharps's disappearing humps. "It bled me so badly that—" I stopped, my lips pressing together. Why was I telling him this? "Yeah. It was."

"Good," he said, his gaze still upon the pond. "I'm glad to hear that."

Ass, I thought, thinking whoever had sent Algaliarept after us had gotten a double whammy of pain that night. "Someone sure didn't like us talking, did they," I said, then froze. My face went cold and I held my breath. What if the attacks on our lives and the recent violence were connected?

Perhaps I was supposed to have been the witch hunter's first victim?

Heart pounding, I held myself still, thinking. Every single one of the victims had died in their own personal hell: the swimmer drowned, the rat caretaker ripped apart and eaten alive, two women raped, a man working with horses pressed to death. Algaliarept had been told to kill me in terror, taking the time to find out what my strongest fear was. *Damn. It was the same person.*

Trent tilted his head at my silence. "What is it?" he asked.

"Nothing." I leaned heavily into the railing. Dropping my head into my cupped hands, I willed myself to not pass out. Glenn would call someone, and that would be that.

Trent pushed away from the railing. "No," he said, and I pulled my head up. "I've seen that look on you twice before. What is it?"

I swallowed. "We were supposed to be the first victims of the witch hunter. He tried to kill both of us, giving up after we showed him we could best a demon and I made it clear I wasn't going to work for you. Only the witches who agreed to work for you were killed, yes?"

"They all agreed to work for me," he breathed, and I stifled a shudder at how the words seemed to flow over my spine. "I never thought to connect the two."

You can't accuse a demon of murder. Because there was no way to contain it if sentenced, the courts had long ago determined to treat demons as weapons, even if the comparison wasn't quite right. Free choice was involved, but as long as the payment was commensurate with the task, a demon wouldn't turn down murder. Someone, though, had summoned it. "Did the demon ever tell you who sent it to kill you?" I asked. Easiest twenty thousand I'd ever made. *God help me.*

Anger tinted in fear crossed Trent. "I was trying to stay alive, not have a conversation. You seem to have a working relationship with it, though. Why don't you ask it?"

My breath come in a jerky sound of disbelief. "Me? I already owe it one favor. You can't pay me enough to dig myself in deeper. I'll tell you what, though. I'll call it up for you, and you can ask it. I'm sure the two of you can come to some agreement about payment."

His sun-tanned face went pale. "No."

Satisfied, I looked over the small pond. "Don't call me a coward unless it's something you would do yourself. I'm reckless. Not stupid." But then I hesitated. *Nick would do it.*

A faint smile, surprising and genuine, came over Trent. "You're doing it again."

"What," I said flatly.

"You had another thought. You are such fun, Ms. Morgan. Watching you is like watching a five-year-old."

Insulted, I looked out over the water. I wondered if Nick asking who had sent it to kill me would be considered a small question or a large one, necessitating further payment. Pushing myself away from the railing, I decided I'd walk over to the museum and find out.

"So?" Trent prompted.

I shook my head. "I'll have your information after sundown," I said, and he blinked.

"You're going to call it?" His sudden, unguarded surprise caught at me, and I kept my face impassive, thinking that managing to startle him was an ego boost I badly needed. How quickly he hid it made the feeling twice as satisfying. "You just said—"

"You're paying for results, not a play-by-play. I'll let you know when I find something."

His expression shifted to what might be respect. "I've misjudged you, Ms. Morgan."

"Yeah, I'm just full of surprises," I muttered, reaching up to keep the hair out of my eyes as the wind gusted. Trent's hat threatened to blow off into the water, and I stretched to catch it before it left his head. My fingers brushed his hat, then nothing.

Trent leapt backward. I stared, blinking at where he had been. He was gone.

I found him a good four feet away, entirely off the bridge. I'd seen cats move like that. He looked frightened as he straightened, then angry that I'd seen the emotion on him. The sun glinted on his wispy hair; his hat was in the water, turning a sickly green.

I stiffened as Quen dropped out of the nearby tree to land softly before him. The man stood with his arms hanging loose, looking like a modern-day samurai in his black jeans and shirt. I didn't move as a whoosh of water came from behind me. I could smell copper sulfate and scum. I felt, more than saw, Sharps loom behind me, cold, wet, and almost as big as the bridge he lived under, having sucked in a huge amount of water to give himself more mass. A faint clatter from the nearby bathroom told me Glenn was on his way.

My heart pounded as no one moved. *I shouldn't have touched him. I should not have touched him.* Licking my lips, I tugged my jacket straight, glad Quen had the sense to know I hadn't been trying to hurt Trent. "I'll call you when I have a name," I said, my voice sounding thin. Giving Quen an apologetic look, I turned on a heel and strode quickly to the street, my heels thumping soundlessly up through my spine.

And you are afraid of me, I thought silently. *Why?*

Twenty-Four

"**F**or the third time, Rachel. Would you like another piece of bread?"

I looked from the light glinting on the surface of my wine, finding Nick waiting with a curious, amused expression. He was holding out the plate with the bread. By his wondering expression, I guessed he'd held it there for a while. "Um, no. No, thank you," I said, glancing down to find the supper Nick had made for me almost untouched. Giving him an apologetic smile, I sent my fork under another bite of pasta and white sauce. It was his supper, my lunch, and both delicious, and even more so since I hadn't done anything but make the salad. It would likely be the last thing I ate today because Ivy had a date with Kist. That meant I'd be having dinner with Ben and Jerry in front of the TV. I thought it unusual she would go out with the living vamp, seeing as he was worse than a monkey when it came to sex and blood, but it was resolutely *not* my business.

Nick's plate was empty, and after setting the bread down, he sat back and played with the end of his knife, making it lay just so atop his napkin. "I know it's not my food," he said. "What's the matter? You've hardly said a word since you—ah—came over to the museum."

I covered my smirk with a napkin and wiped the corner of

my mouth. I had caught him napping, sitting with his lanky legs up, his feet propped on his cleaning table, the eighteenth century tea towel he was supposed to be restoring draped over his eyes. If it wasn't a book, he really didn't care about it. "Is it that obvious?" I said, taking a bite.

A familiar, lopsided smile came over him. "It's not like you to be this quiet. Is it about Mr. Kalamack not being arrested after finding, er, that—body?"

I pushed the plate away in a flush of guilt. I hadn't yet told Nick I'd switched sides in the "Let's get Trent" issue. I hadn't, really, and that's what bothered me. The man was slime.

"You found a body," he said as he leaned across the table and took my hand. "The rest will follow."

I cringed, worried Nick might tell me I'd sold out. My distress must have shown because he squeezed my hand until I looked up. "What is it, Ray-ray?"

His eyes were soft with encouragement, their brown depths catching the glint from the ugly light hanging over Nick's tiny kitchen/dining room. My attention went over the short, chest-high mantel dividing it from the living room as I tried to decide how to broach the subject. I had been harping on him for months about letting sleeping demons lie, and here I was, wanting to ask him to call Algaliarept up for me. I was sure the answer was going to cost more than what Nick's "trial contract" would cover, and I didn't want to risk him paying it for me anyway. Nick had a chivalrous streak as wide as the Ohio River.

"Tell me?" he asked, ducking his head to try and see my eyes.

I licked my lips and met his gaze. "It's about Big Al." I didn't like chancing that Algaliarept would conveniently assume I was calling it every time I said its name, so I had begun referring to the demon by the somewhat insulting moniker. Nick thought it was funny; that I was worried about it showing up unsummoned, not that I called it Al.

Nick's fingers slipped from mine and he pulled away to take up his wineglass. "Don't start," he said, his eyebrows furrowed in the first signs of anger. "I know what I'm doing, and I'm going to do it whether you like it or not."

"Actually," I hedged, "I wanted to see if you might ask it something for me."

Nick's long face went slack. "Beg pardon?"

I winced. "If it won't cost you anything. If it does, forget it. I'll find another way."

He set the glass down and leaned forward. "You want me to call him?"

"See, I talked to Trent today," I said quickly, so he couldn't interrupt, "and we figure that the demon that attacked us last spring is the same one that's doing the murders—that I was supposed to be the first witch hunter victim, but because I turned Trent's job offer down, it let me go. If I can find out who sent it to kill us, then we have the murderer."

Lips parted, Nick stared at me. I could almost see his thoughts fall in place: Trent was innocent and I was working for him to find the real murderer and clear his name of suspicion. Uncomfortable, I pushed the fork around on the plate. "How much is he giving you?" Nick finally asked, his voice giving me no clue to his thoughts.

"Two thousand up front," I said, feeling it light in my pocket, since I had yet to go home. "Eighteen more when I tell him who the witch hunter is." *Hey. I'd made my rent. Whoop-de-do.*

"Twenty thousand dollars?" he said, his brown eyes large in the fluorescent light. "He's giving you twenty thousand dollars for a name? You don't have to bring him in or anything?"

I nodded, wondering if Nick thought I was selling out. I felt like I was.

Nick held himself still for three heartbeats, then rose, his chair scraping the worn linoleum. "Let's find out how much that costs," he said, halfway out of the room.

I was left blinking at his wire and plastic chair. My heart thumped. "Nick?" I stood, taking a moment to move our plates to the sink. "Doesn't it bother you I'm working for Trent? It bothers me."

"Did he kill those witches?" came his voice from the hallway to his room, and I followed it through the living room to find him moving everything out of his linen closet and stacking it on his bed with a methodical quickness.

"No. I don't think so." *God help me if I misread his tells.*

He handed me a stack of brand new, lusciously green towels. "So what's the problem?"

"The man is a biodrug lord and runs Brimstone," I said, juggling the towels to take the oversize gardener boots he handed me. I recognized them as the ones from my belfry, and I wondered why he was keeping them. "Trent is trying to take over Cincinnati's underworld, and I'm working for him. That's what's the matter."

Nick grabbed his spare sheets and edged past me to drop them on his bed. "You wouldn't be helping him unless you believed he didn't do it," he said as he returned. "And for twenty thousand dollars? Twenty thousand dollars buys a lot of therapy if you're wrong."

I grimaced, not liking Nick's "money makes everything right" philosophy. I suppose growing up watching your mother struggle for every dollar might have a lot to do with it, but I sometimes questioned Nick's priorities. But I had to find out just to save my own skin, and I'd be damned if I cleared Trent of suspicion for free.

I stood sideways in the hallway as Nick went into his room with a pile of sweaters. The closet was empty—there hadn't been much in it to start with—and after dumping everything, he took the towels and boots from my arms, adding them to the mound on the bed before returning to the closet. My eyebrows rose as he pulled a square of carpet up to reveal a circle and pentagram etched in the floor. "You summon Al into a closet?" I said in disbelief.

Nick looked up from where he was kneeling, his long face devious. "I found the circle when I moved in," he said. "Isn't it a nice one? It's lined in silver. I checked it out, and it's almost the only spot in the apartment where there are no electric or gas lines. There's another in the kitchen that you can see with a black light, but it's bigger and I can't make a circle that large that's strong enough to hold him."

I watched as he wedged the shelves off their brackets with a stiff, underhand thunk, stacking them against the wall in the hallway. Finished, he stepped into the closet and held out a hand for me to join him. I stared, surprised.

"Al said the demon was supposed to be in the circle, not the summoner," I said.

His hand dropped. "It's part of the trial membership thing. I'm not so much summoning him as asking for an audience. He can say no and not show up at all, though that hasn't happened since you gave me the idea to put myself in the circle instead of him. He shows up just to laugh now." Nick held out his hand again. "Come on. I want to make sure we both fit."

I looked to the slice of living room I could see, not wanting to get in a closet with Nick. Well, not under these circumstances, anyway. "Let's use the circle in the kitchen," I suggested. "I don't mind closing it."

"You want to risk him thinking you called him?" Nick asked, eyebrows high.

"It's an it, not a him," I said, but at his exasperated expression, I took his hand and stepped into the closet. Immediately, Nick dropped my grip and ran his gaze over where our elbows went. The closet was good-sized and deep. Right now it was okay, but add a demon trying to get in, and it would be claustrophobic. "Maybe this isn't such a good idea," I said.

"It'll be fine." Nick's motions were quick and jerky as he stepped out of the closet and reached up to the last shelf, still in place above our heads. Taking down a rattling shoe box, he opened it to show a zippy bag of gray ash and about a dozen milky green tapers already burnt. My mouth opened as I recognized them as the candles he had lit one night when we were, ah, utilizing Ivy's tub to its fullest potential. What were they doing in a box with ashes?

"Those are my candles," I said, only now realizing where they had gone.

Setting the box on his bed, he took the zippy bag and the longest candle and went into the living room. I heard a thump, and he soon reappeared, dragging the stool that I had put his obligatory housewarming plant on. Still silent, he set the candle where the peace lily had once been.

"Buy your own candles for summoning demons," I said, affronted.

He frowned as he opened the drawer under the footstool to pull out a box of matches. "They have to be lit the first time on hallowed ground or they don't work."

"Well, you've got everything figured out, don't you." I sourly wondered if the entire night had been an excuse to get those candles. How long had he been calling this demon anyway? Lips pursed, I watched him light the candle and shake the match out. But it wasn't until he took a handful of gray dust from the zippy bag that I started getting nervous. "What is that?" I asked, worried.

"You don't want to know." His voice carried a surprising amount of warning.

My face warmed as I recalled that I use to bring his kind in for grave robbing. "Yes, I do."

He looked up, his brow pinched in irritation. "It's a focus object so Algaliarept materializes outside the circle instead of in it with us. And the candle is to make sure he doesn't focus on anything but the ash on the table. I bought it, okay?"

Muttering a quick, "Sorry," I backed off. Somehow I seemed to have found the only nerve Nick had and stomped on it. I wasn't up on my demon summoning; obviously he was. "I thought all you had to do was make a circle and call them," I said, feeling nauseated. Someone had sold their grandmother's ashes so Nick could call a demon with her remains.

Nick dusted his hands together and resealed the bag. "You might be able to get away with that, but I can't. The guy at the store kept trying to sell me this outrageously expensive amulet to make a proper binding circle, not believing a human could close one of his own. He gave me ten percent off everything after I put him in a circle he couldn't break. I guess he thought I knew enough to survive to come back and buy something more."

His irritation had vanished the moment I quit barking at him. I realized that this was the first time—well, the second— he had the chance to show me his skills, something he was obviously very proud of. Humans had to work hard to manipulate ley lines as well as witches, which is why humans were known to align themselves with demons so they could keep up. Of course, they didn't last long after that, eventually making a mistake and being pulled into the ever-after. *This was so unsafe. And here I was encouraging him.*

Seeing my face, he came to me and put his hands atop my shoulders. I could feel the ash, gritty between his hands and my skin. "It's okay," he soothed, his narrow face smiling. "I've done this before."

"That's what I'm afraid of," I said, stepping back to make room for him.

As Nick tossed the zippy bag of ash to land next to the shoe box, I tried to wipe the ash off my shoulders. Nick got in the closet with me, and then, with a grunt of remembrance, wedged a piece of wood into the crack of the hinges. "He shut the door on me once," he said, shrugging.

This is not good, I thought again as the small of my back started to sweat.

"Ready?"

I glanced at the lit candle and its little mound of ash. "No."

My fingertips tingled as Nick closed his eyes and opened his second sight. An eerie feeling of my insides being rearranged started in my belly, swirling up into my throat. My eyes widened. "Whoa, whoa, whoa!" I cried as the sensation wrenched into an uncomfortable pull. "What is that?"

Nick opened his eyes. They were glazed, and I could tell he was seeing everything in that confusing mix of reality and ever-after sight. "That's what I've been telling you about," he said, his voice hollow. "It's from the binding spell. Nice, isn't it?"

I shifted from foot to foot, making sure I stayed in the circle. "It's awful," I admitted. "I'm sorry. Why didn't you tell me it was that bad?"

He shrugged, closing his eyes.

The pull through me strengthened, and I struggled to find a way to deal with it. I could feel the ever-after energy slowly building in him, paralleling what I experienced when I tapped into a ley line. The power swelled, and though it was a fraction of what I had channeled in Trent's office, it urged me to react.

With an excruciating slowness, the levels built to a usable level. My palms started to sweat and my stomach clenched. I wished he'd hurry up and close the circle. The eddies of power went deep through me, the need to do something growing.

"Can I help?" I finally asked, gripping my hands together so they wouldn't spasm.

"No."

The tingling in my palms rose to become an itch. "I'm sorry," I said. "I didn't know you could feel all this. Is this why you haven't been sleeping? Have I been waking you up?"

"No. Don't worry about it."

My heel started tapping, the jolts going up my calves feeling like fire. "We have to break the charm," I said, jittery. "How can you stand this?"

"Shut up, Rachel. I'm trying to concentrate."

"Sorry."

His breath slipped from him in a slow sound, and I wasn't surprised when he jumped, mirroring the sudden cutoff of ever-after energy I could feel running through him. Through us.

"Circle's up," he said breathlessly, and I resisted the urge to look at it. I didn't want to insult him, and having felt its construction, I knew it was good. "I'm not sure, but I think because I'm carrying some of your aura, you can break the circle, too."

"I'll be careful," I said, suddenly a lot more nervous. "So what happens now?" I questioned, looking at the candle on the footstool.

"Now I invite him over."

I stifled a shudder as Latin flowed from Nick. My lips curved down at the alienness of it. As he spoke, Nick seemed to take on a different cast, shadows under his eyes growing, to make him look ill. Even his voice changed, more resonant and somehow echoing in my head. Again there was a slow buildup of ever-after energy, rising until it was almost intolerable. I was antsy and nervous, almost relieved when Nick said Algaliarept's name with a drawn-out, careful precision.

Nick sagged, taking a clean breath. I could smell his sweat over his deodorant in the close confines. His fingers slipped into my hand, giving me a quick squeeze before dropping it.

The clock ticked from the living room, and the sound of the traffic past the window was hushed. Nothing happened.

"Is something supposed to happen?" I asked, starting to feel silly, standing in Nick's closet.

"It might take a while. Like I said, it's a trial membership, not the real thing."

I took three slow breaths, listening. "How long?"

"Since I've been putting myself in the circle instead of him? Five, ten minutes."

Nick's mood was easing, and I could feel the heat from our shoulders almost touching. An ambulance sounded faint in the distance, disappearing.

I eyed the burning candle. "What if it doesn't show?" I asked. "How long do we have to wait before we can get out of the closet?"

Nick gave me a noncommittal, stranger-in-the-elevator smile. "Uh, I wouldn't step out of the circle until sunup. Until he appears and we can banish him properly back to the ever-after, he can show up anytime between now and then."

"You mean if it doesn't show, we're stuck in this closet until morning?"

He nodded, his eyes jerking away as the smell of burnt amber came to me. "Oh, good. He's here," Nick whispered, standing straighter.

Oh, good. He's here, I repeated sarcastically in my head. God help me. My life was so screwed up.

The pile of ash at the end of the hallway was hazed with a smear of ever-after. It grew with the speed of flowing water, up and out to take a rough, animal shape. I forced myself to breathe as eyes appeared, red and orange and slit sideways like a goat's. My stomach clenched as a savage muzzle formed, saliva dripping to the rug even before it finished coalescing into the pony-size dog I remembered from the basement vault of the university library: Nick's personal fear of dogs brought to life.

Harsh panting rasped, the sound pulling an instinctive fear from the depths of my soul that I hadn't even known I had. Paws tipped with nails and powerful hindquarters appeared as it shook itself, the last of the mist forming a thick mane of yellow hair. Beside me, Nick shuddered. "You okay?" I asked, and he nodded, his face pale.

"Nicholas Gregory Sparagmos," the dog drawled, sitting on its haunches and giving us a savage doggy smile. "Already, little wizard? I was just here."

Gregory? I thought as Nick shot an unrepentant grimace at me. Nick's middle name was Gregory? And what had Nick gotten in return for telling it that?

"Or did you call me to impress Rachel Mariana Morgan?" it finished, a long red tongue lolling out as it turned its doggy smile to me.

"I've a few questions," Nick said, his voice bolder than his body language.

Nick's breath caught as the dog rose and padded into the hallway, its shoulders almost brushing the walls. I stared, horrified, as it licked the floor beside the circle, testing it. The film of ever-after reality hissed as it sent its tongue over the unseen barrier. Smoke smelling like burnt amber rose, and I watched as if through a pane of glass as Algaliarept's tongue began to char and burn. Nick stiffened, and I thought I heard a whispered oath or prayer. Making an annoyed growl, the demon's outline went hazy.

My heart hammered as the dog lengthened and rose into its usual vision of a British gentleman. "Rachel Mariana Morgan," it said, hitting every accent with an elegant precession. "I must congratulate you, love, on finding that corpse. It was the sharpest bit of ley line magic I've seen in twelve years." It leaned close, and I smelled lavender. "You made quite a stir, you know," it whispered. "I was invited to all the parties. My witch's spell went to the city's square to chime the bells. Everyone got a taste, though not as much as I did."

Eyes closing, the demon shuddered, its outlines wavering as its concentration lapsed.

I swallowed hard. "I'm not your witch," I said.

Nick's fingers on my elbow tightened. "Stay in that form," Nick said, his voice firm. "And stop bothering Rachel. I have questions, and I want to know the cost before I ask them."

"Your mistrust will kill you if your cheek doesn't." Algaliarept spun in a quick motion of furling coattails to return to the living room. From where I stood, I could see it open the glass-door cabinet to Nick's books. Its white-gloved fingers stretched and reached, pulling one out. "Oh, I wondered where this one had gotten to," it said, its back to us. "How splendid that you have it. We will read from this next time."

Nick glanced at me. "That's what we do, usually," he whispered. "He deciphers the Latin for me, letting all sorts of things slip."

"And you trust him?" I frowned, nervous. "Ask it."

Algaliarept had replaced the tome and taken out another, its mood lightening as it cooed and fussed as if having found an old friend.

"Algaliarept," Nick said, mouthing the word slowly, and the demon turned, the new book in its hand. "I'd like to know if you were the demon that attacked Trent Kalamack last spring."

It didn't look up from the open book cradled in his hands. I felt queasy as I realized it had lengthened its fingers to better support it. "That comes under our arrangement," it said, its voice preoccupied. "Seeing as Rachel Mariana Morgan has already guessed the answer." It looked up, its eyes over the smoked glasses orange and red. "Oh, yes, I tasted Trenton Aloysius Kalamack that night as well as you. I ought to have killed him directly, but the novelty of him was so fine, I tarried until he managed to circle me."

"Is that why I survived?" I asked. "You made a mistake?"

"Is that a question coming from you?"

I licked my lips. "No."

Algaliarept closed the book. "Your blood is common, Rachel Mariana Morgan. Tasty with subtle flavors I don't understand, but common. I didn't play with you; I tried to kill you. Had I known you could ring the tower bells, I might have handled things differently." A smile came over it, and I felt its gaze spill over me like oil. "Maybe not. I should have known you would be as your father. He rang the bells, too. Once. Before he died. Do hope it's not a premonition for you."

My stomach clenched, and Nick grabbed my arm before I could touch his circle. "You said you didn't know him," I said, anger making my voice harsh.

It simpered at me. "Another question?"

Heart pounding, I shook my head, hoping it would tell me more.

It put a finger to its nose. "Then Nicholas Gregory Sparagmos better ask another question before I'm called away by someone who is willing to pay for my services."

"You're nothing but a squealing informant, you know that?" I said, shaking.

Algaliarept's gaze resting on my neck pulled a memory of me on the basement floor with my life spilling from me. "Only on my bad days."

Nick straightened. "I want to know who summoned you to kill Rachel, and if he or she is now summoning you to kill ley line witches."

Moving almost out of my line of sight, Algaliarept murmured, "That is a very expensive set of questions, the two together far more than our agreement." It dropped its attention back to the book in its hands and turned a page.

Worry crashed over me as Nick took a breath. "No," I said. "It isn't worth it."

"What do you want for the answers?" Nick asked, ignoring me.

"Your soul?" it said lightly.

Nick shook his head. "Come up with something reasonable, or I'll send you back right now, and you won't be able to talk to Rachel anymore."

It beamed. "You're getting cocky, little wizard. You're halfway mine." It closed the book in its hand with a sharp snap. "Give me leave to take my book back across the line, and I'll tell you who sent me to kill Rachel Mariana Morgan. If they are the same person who is summoning me to kill Trenton Aloysius Kalamack's witches? That stays with me. Your soul isn't enough for that. Rachel Mariana Morgan's, perhaps. Pity when a young man's tastes are too expensive for his means, isn't it?"

I frowned, even as I realized it had admitted it was killing the witches. It must have been luck that kept Trent and me alive when every other witch had died under it. No, not luck. It had been Quen and Nick. "And why do you even want that book?" I asked it.

"I wrote it," it said, its hard voice seeming to wedge the words into the folds of my mind.

Not good. Not good, not good, not good. "Don't give it to him, Nick."

He turned in the tight confines, bumping me. "It's just a book."

"It's your book," I agreed, "and my question. I'll find out some other way."

Algaliarept laughed, a gloved finger shifting the curtain so he could see the street. "Before I'm sent again to kill you? You're quite the topic of conversation, both sides of the ley lines. You'd best ask quick. If I'm called away suddenly, you may want to settle your affairs."

Nick's eyes went round. "Rachel! You're next?"

"No," I protested, wanting to smack Algaliarept. "It's just saying that so you'll give him the book."

"You used ley lines to find Dan's body," Nick said shortly.

"And now you're working for Trent? You're on the list, Rachel. Take your book, Al. Who sent you to kill Rachel?"

"Al?" The demon brightened. "Oh, I like that. Al. Yes, you can call me Al."

"Who sent you to kill Rachel?" Nick demanded.

Algaliarept beamed. "Ptah Ammon Fineas Horton Madison Parker Piscary."

My knees threatened to give way, and I gripped Nick's arm. "Piscary?" I whispered. *Ivy's uncle was the witch hunter? And the man had seven names? Just how old was he?*

"Algaliarept, leave to not bother us again this night," Nick said suddenly.

The demon's smile sent shivers through me. "No promises," it leered, then vanished. The book in its hand hit the carpet, followed by an unseen sliding thump from the bookshelves. I listened to my heart beat, shaken. What was I going to tell Ivy? How could I protect myself from Piscary? I'd hid in a church before. I didn't like it.

"Wait," Nick said, pulling me back before I could touch the circle. I followed his gaze to the pile of ash. "He's not gone yet."

I heard Algaliarept swear, then the ash vanished.

Nick sighed, then edged his toe past the circle to break it. "Now you can leave."

Maybe Nick was better at this than I thought.

Hunched and worried looking, he went to blow the candle out and sit on the edge of his couch with his elbows on his knees and his head in his hands. "Piscary," he said to the flat carpet. "Why can't I have a normal girlfriend who only has to hide from her old prom date?"

"You're the one calling up demons," I said, my knees shaking. The night was suddenly a lot more threatening. The closet seemed bigger now that Nick wasn't in it, and I didn't want to get out. "I should go back to my church," I said, thinking I was going to set my old cot up in the sanctuary and sleep on the abandoned altar tonight. Right after I called Trent. He said he'd take care of it. *Take care of it.* I hoped that meant staking Piscary. Piscary didn't care about the law; why should I? I searched my conscience, not finding even a twinge.

I reached for my jacket and went to the door. I wanted to be in my church. I wanted to wrap myself in the ACG blanket I'd stolen from Edden and sit in the middle of my God-blessed church. "I need to make a call," I said numbly, stopping short in the middle of his living room.

"Trent?" he asked needlessly, handing me his cordless phone.

I made a fist to hid my shaking fingers after I punched in the number. I got Jonathan, sounding irate and nasty. I gave him a hard time until he agreed to let me talk to Trent directly. Finally I heard the click of an extension, and Trent's river-smooth voice came on to give me a professional "Good evening, Ms. Morgan."

"It's Piscary," I said by way of greeting. There was silence for five heartbeats, and I wondered if he had hung up.

"It told you Piscary is sending it to kill my witches?" Trent asked, the sound of his fingers snapping intruding. There followed the distinctive scratch of him writing something, and I wondered if Quen was with him. The weariness Trent had put in his voice to cover his worry didn't work.

"I asked it if it was sent to kill you last spring, and who summoned it for the task," I said, my stomach roiling as I paced. "I suggest you stay on hallowed ground after sunset. You can walk on hallowed ground, can't you?" I asked, not sure how elves handled that sort of thing.

"Don't be crass," he said. "I have a soul as much as you do. And thank you. As soon as you confirm the information, I'll send a courier with the rest of your compensation."

I jerked, my eyes meeting Nick's. "Confirmed?" I said. "What do you mean, confirmed?" I couldn't stop my hands from shaking.

"What you gave me was advice," Trent was saying. "I only pay my stockbroker for that. Get me proof, and Jonathan will cut you a check."

"I just gave you proof!" I stood up, heart pounding. "I just talked to that damned demon and it said it's killing your witches. How much more proof do you need?"

"More than one person can summon a demon, Ms. Morgan. If you didn't ask it if Piscary summoned it to murder those witches, you have only speculation."

My breath caught, and I turned my back to Nick. "That was too expensive," I said, lowering my voice and running a hand over my braid. "But it attacked us both under Piscary's binding, and it admitted to killing the witches."

"Not good enough. I need proof before I go about staking a master vampire. I suggest you get it quickly."

"You're going to stiff me!" I shouted, spinning to the curtained window as my fear shifted to frustration. "Why not?" I cried sarcastically. "The Howlers are. The FIB is. Why should you be any different?"

"I'm not stiffing you," he said, anger making the gray of his voice turn from silk to cold iron. "But I won't pay for shoddy work. As you said, I'm paying you for results, not a play-by-play—or speculation."

"Sounds to me you aren't paying me anything! I'm telling you it was Piscary, and a lousy twenty thousand isn't enough to get me to waltz into a four-hundred-year-old-plus vampire's lair and ask him if he has been sending his demon to kill citizens of Cincinnati."

"If you don't want the job, then I expect you to return my retaining fee."

I hung up on him.

The phone was hot in my grip, and I set it gently on the

mantel between Nick's kitchen and living room before I threw it at something. "Get me home, please?" I asked tightly.

Nick was staring at his bookshelf, running his fingers over the titles.

"Nick," I said louder, angry and frustrated. "I really want to get home."

"Just a minute," he mumbled, intent on his books.

"Nick!" I exclaimed, gripping my elbows. "You can pick out your bedtime story later. I really want to get home!"

He turned, a sick look on his long face. "He took it."

"Took what?"

"I thought he was talking about the book in his hand. But he took the one that you used to make me your familiar."

My lip curled. "Al wrote the book on how to make humans into familiars? He can have it."

"No," he said, his expression drawn and pale. "If he's got it, how are we going to break the spell?"

My face went slack. "Oh." *I hadn't thought of that.*

Twenty-Five

The low *lub-lub-lub-lub* of a bike pulled my eyes up from my book. Recognizing the cadence of Kist's motorbike, I pulled my knees to my chin, tugged my covers farther up, and clicked off my bedside lamp. The sliver of black beyond my propped-open stained-glass window showed a lighter gray. Ivy was home. If Kist came in, I was going to pretend to be asleep until he left. But his bike hardly paused before it idled back up the street. My eyes went to the glowing green numbers of my clock. Four in the morning. She was early.

Closing the book upon my finger to mark the page, I listened for her footsteps on the walk. The cold, predawn September air had pooled in my room. If I were smart, I'd get up and close my window; Ivy would probably turn the heat on when she came in.

I thanked all that was holy that my bedroom was part of the original church and fell under the sacred-ground clause: guaranteed to keep out undead vamps, demons, and mothers-in-law. I was safe in my bed until the sun came up. I still had to worry about Kist. But he wouldn't touch me while Ivy breathed. He wouldn't touch me if she were dead, either.

A stirring of unease pulled my finger out of the book, and

I set it on the cloth-covered box I was using as a table. Ivy hadn't come in yet. It *had* been Kist's bike I heard driving away.

I listened to my heartbeat, waiting for Ivy's soft steps or the closing of the church's door. But what met me was the sound of someone retching, faint through the cold-silenced night.

"Ivy," I whispered, throwing off my covers. Chilled, I lurched from my bed, snatched my robe, jammed my feet into my fuzzy pink slippers, and went into the hall. Skittering to a halt, I retraced my steps. Standing before my pressboard chest of drawers, I sent my fingers over the shadowed bumps of my perfumes.

Choosing the new one I had found among the rest just yesterday, I impatiently dumped a splash on me. Citrus blossomed, clean and sharp, and I set the bottle down, knocking over half of what remained with a harsh clatter. Feeling unreal and disoriented, I almost ran through the empty church, tugging my robe on as I went. I hoped this one worked better than the last.

A sharp clattering of wings was my only warning as Jenks dropped from the ceiling. I jerked to a stop as he hovered before me. He was glowing black. I blinked in shock. He was freaking glowing black.

"Don't go out there," he said, fear thick in his high voice. "Go out the back. Get on a bus. Go to Nick's."

My gaze shot past him to the door as I heard Ivy vomiting again, the ugly sounding gags mixing with heavy sobs. "What happened?" I asked, frightened.

"Ivy fell off the wagon."

I stood there, not understanding. "What?"

"She fell off the wagon," he repeated. "She's sipping the B-juice. She's sampling the wine. She's practicing again, Rachel. And she's off her rocker. Go. My family is waiting for you by the far wall. Get them to Nick's for me. I'll stay here and keep an eye on her. To make sure she—" He glanced at the door. "I'll make sure she isn't going to come after you."

The sound of Ivy vomiting stopped. I stood in my nightgown and robe in the middle of the sanctuary, listening. Fear soaked in with the stillness, settling in my gut. I heard a small noise that grew into a steady, soft crying.

"Excuse me," I whispered, moving around Jenks. My heart was pounding and my knees were weak as I pushed open one side of the heavy door.

The glow from the streetlight was enough to see. Deep in the shadows cast by the oaks, Ivy was sprawled in her biker leather, half laying across the church's two lowest steps, dumped and left to fend for herself. A gelatinous dark vomit spread over the steps, dripping to the sidewalk in ugly syrupy clumps. The cloying smell of blood was thick, overpowering my citrus scent.

Gathering the hem of my robe, I went down the steps with a calm born in fear.

"Rachel!" Jenks shouted, his wings a harsh clatter. "You can't help her. Leave!"

I faltered as I stood over Ivy, her long legs askew and her hair sticking to the black vomit. Her sobs had turned silent, shaking her shoulders. *God, help me through this.*

Breath held, I reached from behind, gripping under her arms to try to get her to her feet. She flinched at my touch. Coherency flickered over her. Focus wavering, she angled her feet under her to help. "I told him no," she said, her voice cracking. "I said no."

My stomach clenched at the sound of her voice, bewildered and confused. The acidic smell of vomit caught in my throat. Under it was a rich scent of well-turned earth, mixing with her burnt ash smell.

Jenks flitted around us as I got her to her feet. Pixy dust

sifted from him to make a glowing cloud. "Careful," he whispered, first on my left side, then my right. "Be careful. I can't stop her if she attacks you."

"She's not going to attack me," I said, anger joining my fear to make a nauseating mix. "She didn't fall off the wagon. Listen to her. Someone pushed her."

Ivy shuddered as we reached the top step. Her hand touched the door for support, and she jerked as if burned. Like an animal, she clawed her way from me. Gasping, I fell back, wide-eyed. Her crucifix was gone.

She stood before me on the church's landing, tension pulling her tall. Her gaze took me in, and I went cold. There was nothing in Ivy's black eyes. Then they flashed into a ravenous hunger, and she lunged.

I had not a chance.

Ivy grabbed me by my neck, pinning me to the door of the church. Adrenaline surged, flashed through me in a pained assault. Her hand was like warm stone under my chin. My last breath made an ugly sound. Toes brushing the stone landing, I hung. Terrified, I tried to kick out, but she pressed into me, heat going through my robe. Eyes bulging, I pried at her fingers about my throat.

Struggling to breathe, I watched her eyes. They were utterly black in the streetlight. Fear, despair, hunger all mixed. Nothing there was her. Nothing at all.

"He told me to do it," she said, her feather-light voice a shocking contrast to her twisted face, terrifying in its absolute hunger. "I told him I wouldn't."

"Ivy," I rasped, managing a breath. "Put me down." Again I made that ugly noise as her grip tightened.

"Not this way!" Jenks shrilled. "Ivy! It's not what you want!"

The fingers on my neck clenched. My lungs struggled, a fire burning as they tried to fill. The black of Ivy's eyes grew as my body started to shut down. Panicking, I stretched for my ley line. The disorientation of connection flashed through the chaos almost unnoticed. Reeling from the lack of oxygen, I let the surge of power explode from me, uncontrolled.

Ivy was flung back. I fell to my knees, drawn forward even as her grip around my neck pulled away. My breath came in a ragged gasp. Pain went all the way to my skull as my knees hit the stone landing. I coughed, feeling my throat. I took a breath, then another. Jenks was a blur of green and black. The black spots dancing before me shrank and vanished.

I looked up to find Ivy curled in a fetal position against the closed doors, her arms over her head as if she had been beaten, rocking herself. "I said no. I said no. I said no."

"Jenks," I rasped, watching her around the strands of my hair. "Go get Nick."

The pixy hovered before me as I staggered to my feet. "I'm not leaving."

I felt my neck as I swallowed. "Go get him, if he's not already on his way here. He must have felt me pull on that line."

Jenks's face was set. "You should run. Run while you can."

Shaking my head, I watched Ivy, her confident self-assurance shattered into nothing as she rocked herself and cried. I couldn't go. I couldn't walk away because it would be safer. She needed help, and I was the only one who stood a chance of surviving her.

"Damn it all to hell!" Jenks shouted. "She's going to kill you!"

"We'll be okay," I said as I lurched to her. "Go get Nick. Please. I need him to get through this."

The pitch of his wings rose and fell in tandem with his visible indecision. Finally he nodded and left. The silence his absence made reminded me of the quiet left in a cruddy little hospital room when two faltered to one. Swallowing, I tightened my robe tie. "Ivy," I whispered. "Come on, Ivy.

I'm going to get you inside." Stealing myself, I reached out and put a shaking hand on her shoulder, jerking away as she shuddered.

"Run away," she whispered as she stopped rocking, falling into a wire-tight stillness.

My heart pounded as she looked up at me, her eyes empty and her hair wild.

"Run away," she repeated. "If you run, I'll know what to do."

Trembling, I forced myself to remain still, not wanting to trigger her instincts.

Her face went slack, and with a sudden creasing of her brow, a ring of brown showed in her eyes. "Oh God. Help me, Rachel," she whimpered.

It scared the crap of me.

My legs trembled. I wanted to run. I wanted to leave her on the steps of the church and go. No one would say anything if I did. But instead I reached out and put my hands under her shoulders and lifted. "Come on," I whispered as I pulled her to her feet. All my instincts screamed to drop her as her hot skin touched mine. "Let's get you inside."

She hung slack in my grip. "I said no," she said, her words starting to slur. "I said no."

Ivy was taller than I, but my shoulder fit nicely under hers, and supporting most of her weight, I wedged the door open.

"He didn't listen," Ivy said, all but incoherent as I dragged her inside and shut the door behind us, shutting out the vomit and blood on the steps outside.

The black of the foyer was smothering. I staggered into motion, the light brightening as we entered the sanctuary. Ivy doubled over, panting around a moan. There was a dark smear of new blood on my robe, and I looked closer. "Ivy," I said. "You're bleeding."

I went cold as her new mantra of "He said it was all right"

turned into a giggle. It was a deep, skin crawling giggle, and my mouth went dry.

"Yes," she said, the word sliding from her with a sultry heat. "I'm bleeding. Want a taste?" Horror settled into me as her giggle slipped into a sobbing moan. "Everyone should have a taste," she whimpered. "It doesn't matter anymore."

My jaw clenched and I tightened my grip on her shoulders. Anger mixed with my fear. Someone had used her. Someone had forced her to take blood against her will. She was out of her mind, an addict coming off a high.

"Rachel?" she quavered, her steps slowing. "I think I'm going to be sick. . . ."

"We're almost there," I said grimly. "Hold on. Just hold on."

We barely made it, and I held Ivy's vomit-strewn hair out of the way as she gagged and retched into her black porcelain toilet. I looked once in the glow of the seashell night-light, then closed my eyes as she vomited thick, black blood over and over. Sobs shook her shoulders, and when she finished, I flushed the toilet, wanting to get rid of what ugliness I could.

I stretched to flick the light on, and a rosy glow filled her bathroom. Ivy sat on the floor with her forehead on the toilet, crying. Her leather pants were shiny with blood down to her knees. Under her jacket, her silk blouse was torn. It clung to her, sticky with blood coming from her neck. Ignoring the warning coursing through me, I carefully gathered her hair to see.

My stomach knotted. Ivy's perfect neck had been ravaged, one long low tear marking the austere whiteness of her skin. It was still bleeding, and I tried not to breathe on it lest the lingering vamp saliva might set it into play.

Frightened, I let her hair fall and backed away. In vampire terms, she had been raped.

"I told him no," she said, her sobs slowing as she realized I wasn't standing over her anymore. "I told him no."

The image of me in the mirror looked white and scared. I

took a breath to steady myself. I wanted it to go away. I wanted it all to just go away. But I had to get the blood off her. I had to get her in bed with a pillow to cry on. I had to get her a cup of cocoa and a really good shrink. Did they have shrinks for abused vampires? I wondered as I put a hand on her shoulder.

"Ivy," I coaxed. "It's time to get cleaned up." I looked at her bathtub where that stupid fish still swam. She needed a shower, not a bath where she would be sitting in the filth she had to get off her. "Let's go, Ivy," I encouraged. "A quick shower in my bathroom. I'll get your nightgown. Come on . . ."

"No," she protested, eyes not focused and unable to help as I lugged her upright. "I couldn't stop. I told him no. Why didn't he stop?"

"I don't know," I murmured, my anger growing. I supported her across the hall and into my bathroom. Hitting the light switch with my elbow, I left her slumped upright against the washer and dryer and went to start the shower.

The sound of the water seemed to revive her. "I smell," she whispered vacantly, looking down at herself.

She wouldn't look at me. "Can you take your shower by yourself?" I asked, hoping to spark some motion.

Face empty and slack, she looked down at herself, seeing she was covered in coagulated, vomited blood. My stomach clenched as she touched the shiny blood with a careful finger and licked it. Tension tightened my shoulders until they hurt.

Ivy started to cry. "Three years," she said in a soft exhalation, tears running down her oval face until she ran the back of her hand under her chin to leave a smear of blood. "Three years . . ."

Head bowed, she reached for the side zipper on her pants, and I lurched to the door. "I'll make you a cup of cocoa," I said, feeling entirely inadequate. I hesitated. "Will you be all right for a few minutes?"

"Yeah," she breathed, and I shut the door softly behind me.

Feeling weightless and unreal, I went into the kitchen. I flicked on the light, gripping my arms around myself, hearing the emptiness of the room. Her makeshift desk with its silver technology smelling faintly of ozone looked oddly right beside my shiny copper pots, ceramic spoons, and herbs hanging from a sweater rack. The kitchen was full of us, carefully separated by space but contained by the same walls. I wanted to call someone, to rage, to rant, to ask for help. But everyone would tell me to leave her and get out.

My fingers shook as I methodically got the milk and cocoa out and started to make Ivy a drink. *Hot cocoa,* I thought bitterly. Someone had raped Ivy, and all I could do was make her a damned cup of cocoa.

It had to be Piscary. Only Piscary was strong or bold enough to rape her. And it had been rape. She told him to stop. He took her against her will. It had been rape.

The timer on the microwave dinged, and I tightened the tie on my robe. My face went cold as I saw the blood on it and my slippers, some of it black and coagulated, some fresh and red from her neck. The former was smoldering. It was undead vampire blood. No wonder Ivy was retching. It must be burning inside her.

Ignoring the rank smell of cauterized blood, I resolutely finished making Ivy's cocoa, taking it to her room as the shower was still running.

The light from her bedside table filled the pink and white room with a soft glow. Ivy's bedroom was as far from a vampire's lair as her bathroom was. The leather curtains to keep out the morning light were hidden behind white curtains. Gunmetal-framed pictures of her, her mother, father, sister, and their lives took up an entire wall, looking like a shrine.

There were grainy photos taken before Christmas trees with robes, smiles, and uncombed hair. Vacations in front of roller coasters, with sunburned noses and wide-brimmed hats. A sunrise on the beach, her father's arms about Ivy and her sister, protecting them from the cold. The newer pictures were in focus and in vibrant color, but I thought them less beautiful. The smiles had become mechanical. Her father looked tired. A new distance existed between Ivy and her mother. The most recent photos didn't have her mother in them at all.

Turning away, I pulled Ivy's soft coverlet down to expose the black satin smelling of wood ash. The book on the nightstand concerned deep meditation and the practice of reaching altered states of consciousness. My anger swelled. She had been trying so hard, and now she was back to square one. Why? What had it all been for?

Leaving the cocoa beside the book, I went across the hall to get rid of my bloodied robe. Motions quick with spent adrenaline, I brushed through my hair and threw on a pair of jeans and my black halter top, the warmest clean thing I had since I hadn't gotten my winter stuff out of storage yet. Leaving my robe and smoldering slippers in an ugly pile on the floor, I padded barefoot through the church, getting her nightgown from the back of her bathroom door.

"Ivy?" I called, knocking hesitantly on my bathroom door, hearing only the water running. There was no answer, and so knocking again, I pushed the door open. A heavy mist blurred everything, filling my lungs and making them seem heavy. "Ivy?" I called again, worry striking through me. "Ivy, are you all right?"

I found her on the floor of the shower stall, crumpled in a huddle of long legs and arms. The water flowed over her bowed head, blood making a thin rivulet to the drain from her neck. A shimmer of lighter red colored the bottom of the stall, coming from her legs. I stared, unable to look away. Her inner thighs were marred with deep scratches. Maybe it had been rape in the traditional sense as well.

I thought I was going to be sick. Ivy's hair was plastered to her. Her skin was white and her arms and legs were askew. The black of the twin ankle bracelets showed dark against the white of her skin, looking like shackles. She was shivering though the water was scalding, her eyes closed and her face twisted in a memory that would haunt her the rest of her life and into her death. Who said vampirism was glamorous? It was a lie, an illusion to cover the ugly reality.

I took a breath. "Ivy?"

Her eyes flashed open, and I jerked back.

"I don't want to think anymore," she said softly, unblinking though the water flowed over her face. "If I kill you, I won't have to."

I tried to swallow. "Should I leave?" I whispered, but I knew she could hear me.

Her eyes closed and her face scrunched up. Drawing her knees to her chin to cover herself, she wrapped her arms around her legs and started to cry again. "Yes."

Shaking inside, I stretched over her and turned off the water. The cotton towel was rough on my fingertips as I grabbed it and hesitated. "Ivy?" I said, frightened. "I don't want to touch you. Please get up."

Tears silently mixing with the water, she rose and took the towel. After she promised she would get herself dried off and dressed, I took her blood-soaked clothes along with my slippers and robe through the church to drop them on the back porch. The smell of burning blood turned my stomach like bad incense. I'd bury them in the cemetery later.

I found her huddled in her bed when I came back, her damp hair soaking her pillow and her untouched cocoa on the nightstand. Her face was to the wall and she wasn't moving. I pulled the afghan from the foot of the bed over her, and she trembled. "Ivy?" I said, then hesitated, not knowing what to do.

"I told him no," she said, her voice a whisper, torn gray silk drifting to rest atop snow.

I sat down on the cloth-draped trunk against the wall. *Piscary.* But I wouldn't say his name for fear of triggering something.

"Kist took me to him," she said, her words having the cadence of repeated memory. She had crossed her arms over her chest, only her fingers showing as they clutched her shoulders. I blanched as I saw what must be flesh under her nails, and I tugged the afghan up to hide it.

"Kisten took me to see him," she repeated, her words slow and deliberate. "He was angry. He said you were causing trouble. I told him you weren't going to hurt him, but he was angry. He was so angry with me."

I leaned closer, not liking this.

"He said," Ivy whispered, her voice almost unheard, "that if I couldn't curb you, that he would. I told him I'd make you my scion, that you would behave and he wouldn't have to kill you, but I couldn't do it." Her voice got higher, almost frantic. "You didn't want it, and it's supposed to be a gift. I'm sorry. I'm so sorry. I tried to tell you," she said to the wall. "I tried to keep you alive, but he wants to see you now. He wants to talk to you. Unless . . ." Her trembling ceased. "Rachel? Yesterday . . . when you said you were sorry, was it because you thought you'd pushed me too far, or that you said no?"

I took a breath to answer, shocked when my words got stuck in my throat.

"Do you want to be my scion?" she breathed, softer than a guilty prayer.

"No," I whispered, frightened out of my mind.

She started shaking, and I realized she was crying again. "I said no, too," she said around her gulps for air. "I said no, but he did anyway. I think I'm dead, Rachel. Am I dead?" she questioned, her tears cutting off in her sudden fear.

My mouth was dry and I clutched my arms around myself. "What happened?"

Her breath came in a quick sound, and she held it for a moment. "He was angry. He said I had failed him. But he said it was all right. That I was the child of his heart, and that he loved me, that he forgave me. He told me he understood about pets. That he once kept them himself but that they always turned on him and he had to kill them. It hurt him, when they betrayed him time and again. He said if I couldn't bring myself to make you safe, that he'd do it for me. I said I'd do it, but he knew I was lying." A frightening moan came from her. "He knew I was lying."

I was a pet. I was a dangerous pet to be tamed. That's what Piscary thought I was.

"He said he understood my want for a friend instead of a pet, but that it wasn't safe to let you stay as you were. He said I had lost control and people were talking. I started to cry then, because he was so kind and I had disappointed him." Her words came in short bursts as she struggled to get the words out. "And he made me sit beside him, holding me as he whispered how proud he was of me and that he loved my great-grandmother almost as much as he loved me. That was all I ever wanted," she said. "Him to be proud of me."

She made a short gasp of pained laugher. "He said he understood about wanting a friend," she said to the wall, her face hidden behind her hair. "He told me he had been looking for centuries for someone strong enough to survive with him, that my mother, grandmother, and great-grandmother were all too weak but that I had the will to survive. I told him I didn't want to live forever, and he shushed me, telling me I was his chosen, that I would stay with him forever."

Her shoulders shook under the coverlet. "He held me, soothing my fears of the future. He said he loved me and was proud of me. And then he took my finger and drew blood from himself."

Stomach acid bubbled up, and I swallowed it down.

Her voice had gone wispy, her hunger and need a hidden ribbon of steel. "Oh God, Rachel. He's so old. It was like liquid electricity, welling up from him. I tried to leave. I wanted it, and I tried to leave, but he wouldn't let me. I said no, and then I ran. But he caught me. I tried to fight, but it didn't matter. Then I begged him no, but he held me and forced me to taste him."

Her voice was husky and her body shook. I moved to sit on the edge of the bed, horrified. Ivy went still, and I waited, unable to see her face, afraid to.

"And then I didn't have to think anymore," she said, the flat sound of her voice shocking. "I think I passed out for a moment. I wanted it. The power, the passion. He's so old. I pulled him to the floor and straddled him. I took everything he had as he clutched me to him, urging me to go deeper, to draw more. And I took it, Rachel. I took more than I should have. He should have stopped me, but he let me take it all."

I couldn't move, riveted by the terror of it.

"Kist tried to stop us. He tried to get between us, to stop Piscary from letting me take too much, but with every swallow, I lost more of myself. I think I—hurt Kist. I think I broke him. All I know is he went away, and Piscary . . ." A soft, pleasure-filled sound escaped her as she said his name again. ". . . Piscary drew me back." She moved languorously beneath the black sheets, suggestively. "He gentled my head against him and pressed me closer until I was sure he wanted me and I found he had more to give."

A harsh breath shook her, and she clenched into a huddled knot, the sated lover flashing into a beaten child. "I took everything. He let me take everything. I knew why he let me, and I did it anyway."

She was silent, but I knew she wasn't done yet. I didn't want to hear anymore, but she had to say it or she would drive herself slowly insane.

"With every pull, I could feel his hunger growing," she said, whispering. "With my every swallow his need swelled. I knew what would happen if I didn't stop, but he said it was all right, and it had been so long," she almost moaned. "I didn't want to stop. I knew what would happen, and I didn't want to stop. It was my fault. My fault."

I recognized the phrase from rape victims. "It wasn't your fault," I said, resting my hand upon her covered shoulder.

"It was," she said, and I pulled away as her voice became low and sultry. "I knew what would happen. And when I had everything he was, he asked for his blood back—like I knew he would. And I gave it to him. I wanted to, and I did. And it was fantastic."

I forced myself to breathe.

"God help me," she whispered. "I was alive. I hadn't been alive for three years. I was a goddess. I could give life. I could take it away. I saw him for what he was, and I wanted to be like him. And with his blood burning in me as if it was mine, his strength wholly mine, and his power wholly mine, burning into me the ugly, beautiful truth of his existence, he asked me to be his scion. He asked me to take Kisten's place, that he had been waiting for me to understand what it meant before he offered it to me. And that when I died, I would be his equal."

I kept my hand moving over her head in a soothing motion as her eyes closed and her shaking stopped. She was getting drowsy, her face going slack as her mind unwound her nightmare, finding a way to deal with it. I wondered if it had anything to do with the sky past her curtains brightening with the coming dawn.

"I went to him, Rachel," she whispered, color starting to come back into her lips. "I went to him, and he tore into me like a beast. I welcomed the pain. His teeth were God's truth, cutting clean into my soul. He savaged me, out of control from the joy of getting his power back after giving it to me so freely. And I gloried in it even as he bruised my arms and tore my neck open."

I forced my hand to keep moving.

"It hurt," she whispered, sounding like a child as her eyelids fluttered. "No one has enough vamp saliva in them to transmute that much pain, and he lapped up my misery and anguish along with my blood. I wanted to give him more, prove my loyalty to him, prove that though I failed by not taming you, that I would be his scion. Blood tastes better during sex," she said faintly. "The hormones make it sweet, so I opened myself to him. He said no, even as he moaned for it, that he might kill me by mistake. But I worked him until he couldn't stop himself. I wanted it. I wanted it even as he hurt me. He took it all, bringing us to climax even as he killed me." She shuddered, her eyes closed. "Oh God, Rachel. I think he killed me."

"You aren't dead," I whispered, frightened because I wasn't sure. She couldn't be in a church if she was dead, yes? Unless she was still in transition. The space of time when the chemistry shifted over had no hard and fast rules. What the hell was I doing?

"I think he killed me," she said again, her voice starting to slur as she fell asleep. "I think I killed myself." Her voice grew childlike. Her eyelids fluttered. "Am I dead, Rachel? Will you watch over me? Make sure the sun doesn't burn me while I sleep? Will you keep me safe?"

"Shhhh," I whispered, scared. "Go to sleep, Ivy."

"I don't want to be dead," she mumbled. "I made a mistake. I don't want to be Piscary's scion. I want to stay here with you. Can I stay here with you? Will you watch over me?"

"Hush," I murmured, running a hand over her hair. "Go to sleep."

"You smell good . . . like oranges," she whispered, setting my pulse pounding, but at least I didn't smell like her. I kept my hand moving until her breathing slowed and grew deep. I wondered if, when she fell asleep, it would stop. I wasn't sure Ivy was alive anymore.

My gaze went to the stained-glass window, the hint of dawn leaking around the edges. The sun would be up soon, and I didn't know anything about vampires crossing over except they had to be six feet under or in a light-tight room. That, and that they woke hungry the next sunset. *Oh God. What if Ivy was dead?*

I looked at the jewelry box on her mahogany dresser that held her "in case of death" bracelet that she refused to wear. Ivy had good insurance. If I called the number engraved on the silver band, an ambulance would be there in a guaranteed five minutes, whisking her away to a nice dark hole in the ground to emerge when darkness fell as a beautiful reborn undead.

My stomach churned and I rose to go to my room for my tiny cross. If she was dead, there would be some reaction, even if she was in transition. Passing out in a church is one thing; having a consecrated cross touch your skin is another.

Nauseated, I returned. Charms jingling, I held my breath and dangled my bracelet over Ivy. There was no response. I brought the cross close to her neck behind her ear, breathing easier when again there was no reaction. Silently asking for her forgiveness if I was wrong, I touched the cross to her skin. She didn't move, her pulse at her neck staying slow and sedate. Her skin, when I pulled the cross away, was white and unblemished.

I straightened, saying a silent prayer. I didn't think she was dead.

Slowly I crept from Ivy's room, shutting the door behind me. Piscary had raped Ivy for one reason. He knew I had figured it out. Ivy said he wanted to talk to me. If I stayed in my church, he would go for my mother next, then Nick, and then probably track down my brother.

My thoughts returned to Ivy, huddled under her covers in

a shock-induced sleep. My mother would be next. And she would die not even knowing why she was being tortured.

Shaking inside, I went into the living room for the phone. My fingers were trembling so badly, I had to dial it twice. It took a precious three minutes of arguing to get to Rose.

"I'm sorry, Ms. Morgan," the woman said, her voice so politically correct I could freeze an egg on it. "Captain Edden is not available, and Detective Glenn left word that he is not to be disturbed."

"Not to be—" I stammered. "Listen. I know who murdered them. We have to go out there now. Before he sends someone after my mother!"

"I'm sorry, Ms. Morgan," the woman said politely. "You are no longer a consultant. If you have a complaint or death threat, please hold and I'll transfer you back to the front desk."

"No! Wait!" I pleaded. "You don't understand. Just let me talk to Glenn!"

"No, Morgan." Rose's calm, reasonable voice was suddenly thick with an unexpected anger. "You don't understand. No one here wants to talk to you."

"But I know who the witch hunter is!" I exclaimed, and the connection clicked off.

"You sorry-assed *idiots!*" I shouted, throwing the phone across the room. It hit the wall, the back coming off and the batteries rolling over the floor. Frustrated, I stomped into the kitchen, spilling Ivy's pens over the table as I reached for one. Heart pounding, I scratched a note to thumbtack to the door of the church.

Nick was coming. Glenn would talk to Nick. He could convince them I was right, tell them where I'd gone. They'd have to come out, if only to arrest me for interfering. I would have told him to call the I.S., but Piscary probably owned them. And though humans had as much chance of besting a master vampire as I did, perhaps just the interruption might be enough to save my butt.

Spinning, I reached for the cupboard, pulling amulets from hooks and jamming them into my bag. I yanked open a bottom drawer and grabbed three wooden stakes. I added the big butcher cleaver from the knife block. My splat gun was next, loaded with the strongest spell a white witch would have: sleepy-time charms. From the island counter I took a bottle of holy water. Thinking for a moment, I pulled up the valve top, took a swallow, recapped it, then shoved it in with the rest. Holy water wasn't much good unless it was all you'd been drinking for the last three days, but I'd take all the deterrent I could scrape together.

Not slowing, I strode into the hall for my boots. I slipped them on and headed for the front door, laces flapping. Jerking to a halt in the hallway, I spun, returning to the kitchen. Grabbing a handful of change for the bus, I left.

Piscary wanted to talk to me? Good. I wanted to talk to him.

Twenty-Six

The bus was crowded at five in the morning. Living vamps, mostly, and vamp wannabes on their way home to take stock of their sorry existence. They gave me a wide birth. It could have been that I stank of holy water. It could have been that I looked like hell warmed over in my ugly, heavy winter coat with the fake fur around the collar that I had worn so the driver wouldn't recognize me and pick me up. But I was betting it was the stakes.

Face tight, I got off the bus at Piscary's restaurant. I stood where my feet hit the pavement and waited while the door shut and the bus drove away. Slowly the noise faltered until it melted into the background hum of swelling morning traffic. My eyes pinched as I looked straight up at the brightening sky. The mist from my breath obscured the fragile-looking, pale blue. I wondered if it was going to be the last sky I'd ever see. It would be dawn soon. If I were smart, I would wait until the sun was up before I went in.

I pushed myself into motion. Piscary's was two stories tall, and all the windows were dark. The yacht was still tied to the quay, and the water lapped softly. There were only a few cars in the lot at the outskirts. Employees, probably. As I walked, I swung my bag around. Pulling out the stakes, I flung them away. Their harsh clatters on the asphalt shocked my ears. Bringing them had been stupid. Like I could stake an undead vampire. The splat gun at the small of my back was probably a futile gesture, too, since I was sure I would be searched before they took me to Piscary. The master vampire said he wanted to talk, but I'd be a fool to think it would stop there. If I wanted to meet him with all my spells and charms, I'd have to fight my way to him. If I let them take away everything I had, I'd get to him unscathed but pretty much helpless.

I opened the bottle of holy water and chugged it, spilling the last drops into my hands and patting my neck. The empty bottle clattered after the stakes. I strode forward in my soundless boots, my fear for my mother and my anger at what he had done to Ivy keeping my feet moving. If there were too many of them, I'd go in charmless. Nick and the FIB were my ace in the hole.

My stomach knotted as I pushed open the heavy door. The faint hope that there might be no one died as half a dozen people looked up from their scattered work, all of them living vamps. The human staff was gone. I'd be willing to bet that the pretty, scarred, adoring humans had gone home with favorite customers.

The lights were up high while the wait staff cleaned, and where the large room with it log-cabin walls had looked mysterious and exciting, now it looked dirty and tired. Kind of like me. The shoulder-high wall of stained glass that divided the room was broken. A petite woman with hair to her waist was sweeping the shards of green and gold toward the wall. She stopped to lean on the broom as I came in. There was an odd smell at the back of my throat, rich and cloying. My feet faltered as I realized the vamp pheromones were so thick I could taste them.

At least Ivy had put up a fight, I thought, realizing most of the vamps were sporting a bandage or bruise, and all of them, with the exception of the vamp sitting at the bar, were in a bad mood. One had been bit, his neck torn and his uniform ripped at the collar. In the bright light of morning, their glamour and sexual tension had been wiped away, to leave only a tired ugliness. My lip curled in distaste. Seeing them like this, they were repellant. And yet my scar on my neck started to tingle.

"Well, look who showed," the vamp sitting at the bar drawled. His uniform was more elaborate than the rest, and he took his name tag off as he saw my eyes on it. It read SAMUEL, the vampire that had let Tarra upstairs the night we were there. Samuel got up, leaning to flick a switch behind the counter. The open sign behind me in the window went out. "You're Rachel Morgan?" he asked, his vamp-confident voice slow and patronizing.

Clutching my bag, I boldly walked past the WAIT HERE FOR HOST sign. Yeah, I was a bad girl. "That's me," I said, wishing there were fewer tables. My feet slowed as caution finally worked its way past my anger. I had broken rule number one: going in mad. I would have been okay if I hadn't also broken the more important rule number two: confronting an undead vamp on his own turf.

The wait staff was watching, and my pulse quickened as Samuel went to the door and locked it. Turning, he casually threw the wad of keys clear across the room. A figure by the unused fireplace raised his arm, and I recognized Kisten, unseen in the shadows until he moved. The keys hit Kist's palm with a jingle and disappeared. I didn't know if I should be angry with him or not. He had dumped Ivy and driven off, but he had tried to stop them, too.

"This is what Piscary is worried about?" Samuel said, his beautiful face sneering. "Skinny little thing. Not much on top." He leered. "Or bottom. I thought you'd be taller."

He reached for me. Jerking into motion, I stiff-armed him, feeling my fist pop into his open palm. I twisted my wrist, grabbing his. I yanked him forward into my upraised foot.

His breath whooshed out as it hit his stomach, knocking him backward. I followed him down, giving him a jab at his crotch before I got to my feet. "And I thought you'd be smarter," I said, backing away as he writhed on the floor, gasping.

It probably hadn't been the smartest thing to do.

Dropping their rags and broom, the wait staff converged on me with an unnerving, unhurried pace. My breath came fast, and I shimmied out of my coat, shoving one of the tables away with my foot to make room to move. Seven spells in my gun. Nine vamps. I'd never get them all. My face went cold and I shivered in the draft on my bare shoulders.

"No," Kist said from his corner, and they hesitated. "I said no!" he shouted as he got to his feet and started over, his fast pace jerking into a slower one to hide a new limp.

Their faces twisting to an ugly promise, they stopped, making a ring about me a good eight feet back. *Eight feet,* I thought, feeling ill as I remembered my and Ivy's workouts. That was a living vamp's reach.

Crotch-boy got to his feet, his shoulders hunched and his face pained. Kist pushed through the circle to stand opposite him, hands on his hips and feet spread wide. His dark silk shirt and dress pants gave him more sophistication than his usual leather. A bruise spread upward across his lightly stubbled cheek to just miss his eye. By the way he held himself, I guessed his ribs were hurting, but I thought the real damage was to his pride. He had lost his scion status to Ivy.

"He said bring her down, not rough her up," Kist said, his lips going bloodless as my gaze lingered on the fingernail gouge behind his bangs.

Though Samuel was bigger, Kist's demand for obedience was unmistakable. A hard, bad temper had replaced his usual mien of casual flirtation, giving him a rough edge that I'd always found attractive in men. Like every manager, Kist had problems with his employees, and somehow the fact that he had to deal with crap just like everyone else made him more appealing. My gaze roved over him, my thoughts following my eyes. *Damn vamp pheromones.*

Still panting, the larger vamp darted his eyes to me and back to Kist. "She needs to be searched." He licked his lips, looking at me to make my pulse race. "I'll do it."

I stiffened, my thoughts going to my splat gun. There were too many of them.

"I'm doing it," Kist said, his blue eyes starting to vanish behind a swelling circle of black.

Swell.

Samuel sullenly backed off, and Kist held out his hand for my bag. I hesitated, then seeing him arch his eyebrow as if to say, "Just give me a reason," I extended it. He took it, roughly setting it on a nearby table. "Give me what you have on you," he said softly.

Eyes on his, I slowly reached behind me and handed him my splat gun. There wasn't a sound from the surrounding vampires. Perhaps some respect for my little red paint-ball gun? They didn't know what it was loaded with. I had known the moment I tucked it behind my waistband I'd never get to use it, and I frowned at lost chances that never really existed.

"The cross?" he asked, and I worked the clasp of my charm bracelet, dropping it into his waiting hand. Saying nothing, he set it and my gun on the table behind him. Stepping forward, he put his arms out wide. I obediently mimicked him, and he came close to pat me down.

Jaw gritted, I felt his hands run over me. Where he touched, a warm tingling started, working its way to my middle. *Not the scar, not the scar,* I thought desperately, knowing what would happen if he touched it. The vamp pheromones were almost thick enough to see, and just the breeze from the fan was making a pleasant sensation run from my neck to my groin.

I shook in relief when his hands fell away. "The charm on

your pinky," he demanded, and I took it off, slapping it in his palm. He dropped it beside my gun. A tight look came into his eye as he stood before me. "If you move, you die," he said.

I stared at him, not understanding.

Kist eased close, and my breath hissed. I could smell his tension, his wire-tight reactions balancing on the possibility of my next move. He sent his breath against my collarbone, and my thoughts jerked back to his lips brushing my ear four days ago. Head tilted, he looked down at me, hesitating, an empty look in his blue eyes, his hunger well-hidden.

Reaching up, he ran a finger from my ear, across my neck and the bumps of my scar.

My knees buckled. Sucking in air, I pulled myself upright, and with waves of need demanding to be met, I backhanded him. He caught my wrist before it landed, yanking me into him. Twisting, I swung my foot up. He caught it.

Kist jerked me off my feet and let go.

I fell on my can, the wooden floor bruising. I stared up at him as the vamps laughed. Kist's face, though, was empty. No anger, no speculation. Nothing.

"You smell like Ivy," he said as I got to my feet, my heart hammering. "You aren't bound to her, though." A sliver of satisfaction marred his stoic expression. "She couldn't do it."

"What are you talking about?" I snarled, embarrassed and angry as I brushed myself off.

His eyes narrowed. "It felt good, didn't it? Me touching your scar? Once a vamp binds you by blood, only they can elicit that kind of a response. Who bit you and didn't bother to claim you?" His face went thoughtful, and I thought I saw a glimmer of lust. "Or did you kill your attacker afterward to prevent being bound? You're a bad little girl."

I said nothing, letting him believe what he wanted, and he shrugged. "Since you aren't tied to anyone, any vamp can entice that kind of reaction." His eyebrows rose. "Any vamp," he repeated, and a chill went through me at the thought of Piscary waiting for me. "You should have an interesting morning," he added.

Vision clearing, he reached behind him and dragged my bag from the table. The vamps had begun to talk among themselves, making casual, unnerving speculations as to how long I would last. Kist pulled out the butcher knife first, and hooting laughter rippled over them. My gaze went over the destruction of Piscary's as Kist set a handful of charms clattering on the table.

"Did Ivy do this?" I asked, trying to find a sliver of my confidence. The longer I kept them talking, the better the chance that Nick would get the FIB out there in time.

The vamp I had crotch-punched sneered. "In a manner of speaking." He looked at Kist, and I thought I saw the blond vamp's jaw clench. "Your roommate's a good lay," Samuel said, going smug as Kist's breath quickened and his fingers digging through my bag became rough.

"Yeah," Samuel continued in a good-old-boy's drawl. "She and Piscary got the entire restaurant hopped-up on vamp pheromones. Ended up with three fights, a couple of bites." He leaned against a table, crossed his arms and smirked. "Someone died and got carted off to the city's temporary vaults. See? He got his picture on the wall and a coupon for a free dinner. We were damned lucky we figured out what was going on and got everyone not a vamp outta here before all hell broke loose. God help us if Piscary lost his MPL and had to reapply. Took him almost a year last time." Samuel took a peanut from a bowl and threw it into the air, catching it with his mouth and grinning as he chewed.

Kist's face was red with anger. "Shut up," he said, pulling the ties to my bag closed.

"Whatsa matter?" Samuel mocked. "Just 'cause you never got Piscary that worked up doesn't mean he's gonna make her his scion."

Kist stiffened. He hadn't told anyone that Piscary already did. My eyes darted to him, his anger keeping my mouth shut.

"I said shut up," Kist warned, the heat from him almost visible.

The surrounding vamps were casually shifting back. Samuel laughed, clearly wanting to push Kist as far as he could. "Kist is jealous," he said to me with the sole intent to irritate him. "The most that ever happened when he and Piscary were going at it was a bar fight." His full lips split into a nasty grin, and he glanced cockily at the surrounding vamps. "Don't worry, old man," he directed to Kist. "Piscary will get tired of her as soon as she dies, and you'll be back on top—or bottom—or somewhere in between if you're lucky. Maybe they'll let you sit in and Ivy can teach you a thing or two."

Kist's fingers trembled. In the space between one heartbeat and the next, he moved. Too fast to follow, he crossed the circle, grabbed Samuel by the shirtfront, and shoved him up against a thick support post. The timber groaned, and I heard something snap in Samuel's chest. The bigger man's face showed a surprised shock, his eyes wide and his mouth open in pain he hadn't had time to feel.

"Shut up," Kist said softly. His jaw clenched and his eye twitched. Dropping him, Kist gave Samuel a shove, twisting his arm at an unnatural angle as the larger man fell to his knees. My breath caught at the audible pop of his shoulder dislocating.

Samuel's eyes bulged. Mouth open in a silent scream, he knelt, his arm still bent behind him, since Kist had never let go of his wrist. Kist dropped it, and Samuel gasped for air.

I stood—unable to move—frightened at how fast it had been.

Kist was suddenly before to me, and I jerked. "Here's your bag," he said, handing it to me. I snatched it, and Kist gestured that I should go before him. An opening parted in the circle. The surrounding vamps looked properly cowed. No one had gone to help Samuel, and his ragged pants for air as he lay unmoving struck me to my core.

"Don't touch me," I said as I passed Kist. "And none of you had better mess with my things while I'm gone," I added, shaking inside. My pace faltered as I took a last look at my charms and realized only about half of what I had brought was on the table.

Kist took my elbow and pulled me into motion. "Let me go," I said, the memory of him dislocating Samuel's arm keeping me from pulling away.

"Shut up," he said, the tension in his voice giving me pause.

Mind whirling, I followed his not-so-subtle direction, weaving through the tables to pass through a set of swinging doors and into the kitchen. Behind us the wait staff went back to their work, the speculations flying as they ignored Samuel.

I couldn't help notice that though smaller, my kitchen was nicer than Piscary's. Kist led me to a metal institutional-looking fire door. He opened it and flicked on a light to show a small white room floored in oak. The silver doors of an elevator were tucked out of the way. A wide-mouthed, spiral stairway leading downward took up much of one wall. The stairway was elegant, the modest chandelier above it clinking faintly in the upwelling draft. A wooden clock the size of a table hung on the wall opposite the stairway, ticking loudly.

"Down?" I said, trying to keep from looking scared. If Nick didn't find my note, there was no chance I'd be coming back up those stairs.

The fire door snicked shut behind him, and I felt the air pressure change. The draft smelled like nothing, almost a void in itself. "Let's take the elevator," Kist said, his voice unexpectedly soft. His entire posture changed as he focused on an unknown thought. *He had left me some of my charms. . . .*

The elevator doors opened immediately when he pushed the button, and I got in. Kist was tight behind me, and we faced the doors as they closed. With a soft pull at my stomach, the elevator started down. Immediately I swung my bag around and opened it.

"Idiot!" Kist hissed.

A tiny shriek escaped me as he slid, pinning me into a corner. The room shifted under me and I froze, poised to act. His teeth were inches from me. My demon scar pulsed and I held my breath. The pheromones were less in here, but it didn't seem to matter. If there was elevator music, I was going to scream.

"Don't be stupid. You don't think he's got cameras in here?"

My breath came in a soft pant. "Get away from me."

"Don't think so, love," he whispered, his breath sending tingling jolts from my neck and making my blood pound. "I'm going to see just how far that scar on your neck can take you . . . and when I'm done, you're going to find a vial in your purse."

I stiffened as he pressed closer. The scent of leather and silk was a pleasing assault. I couldn't breathe as he nuzzled my hair out of the way. "It's Egyptian embalming fluid," he said, and I tensed as his lips shifted against my neck with his words. I didn't dare move, and if I was honest, I'd admit that I didn't want to as tingling ribbons of promise flowed from my scar. "Get it in his eyes, and it will knock him unconscious."

I couldn't help it. My body demanded I do something. Shoulders easing, I closed my eyes and ran my hands up the smooth expanse of his back. He paused in surprise, then his hands slid down my sides to grasp my waist. The muscles under his silk shirt bunched beneath my fingers. Reaching upward, my nails played with the hair at the nape of his neck. The soft strands had a uniform color that you can only find in a box, and I realized he dyed his hair.

"Why are you helping me?" I breathed, fingering the

black chain about his neck. The body-warm links were the same pattern as the bracelets about Ivy's ankle.

I felt his muscles shift, tightening with pain instead of desire. "He said I was his scion," he said as he hid his face in my hair to hide his moving lips from the unseen camera—at least, that's what I told myself. "He said I would be with him forever, and he betrayed me for Ivy. She doesn't deserve him." Hurt stained his voice. "She doesn't even love him."

My eyes closed. I would never understand vampires. Not knowing why I did, I sent my fingers gently through his hair, soothing him as his breath caressed my demon scar into mounting surges demanding to be met. Common sense told me to stop, but he was hurt, and I'd been betrayed like that, too.

Kist's breath faltered as I sent the hint of my fingernails under his ear. Making a low guttural sound, he pressed closer, his heat obvious through the thin material of my shirt. His tension became deeper, more dangerous. "My God," he whispered, his voice a husky thread. "Ivy was right. Leaving you unbound and free of compulsion would be like fucking a tiger."

"Watch your mouth," I said breathily, his hair tickling my face. "I don't like that kind of language." *I was already dead. Why not enjoy my last few moments?*

"Yes, ma'am," he said obediently, his voice shocking in its submissiveness even as he forced his lips to mine. My head hit the back of the elevator with the force of his kiss. I pushed back, unafraid.

"Don't call me that," I mumbled around his mouth, remembering what Ivy had said about him playing the subordinate. Maybe I could survive a submissive vampire.

His weight pressing harder into me, he pulled his lips from mine. I met his eyes—his faultless blue eyes—studying them with the breathless understanding that I didn't know what was going to happen next, but praying that whatever it was, it would happen.

"Let me do this," he said, his rumbling voice just shy of a growl. His hands were free, and he took my chin and held my head unmoving. I caught a glint of tooth, then he was too close to see anything. Not a shimmer of fear struck me as he kissed me again, pushed out by a sudden realization.

He wasn't after blood. Ivy wanted blood; Kist wanted sex. And the risk that his desire might turn to blood catapulted me past my sensibilities and into a reckless daring.

His lips were soft with a moist warmth. His blond stubble was a striking contrast, adding to my fervor. Heart pounding, I hooked a foot behind his leg and pulled him closer. Feeling it, his breath came and went in a pant. A soft sound of real bliss escaped me. My tongue found the smoothness of his teeth, and his muscles under my hands tensed. I pulled my tongue away, teasing.

Our mouths parted. Heat was in his eyes, black and full of a fervent, unashamed desire. And still there was no fear. "Give this to me. . . ." he breathed. "I won't break your skin if . . ." He took a breath. ". . . you give this to me."

"Shut up, Kisten," I whispered, closing my eyes to block what I could of the confusing swirl of rising tensions.

"Yes, Ms. Morgan."

It was the softest whisper. I wasn't even sure I had heard it. The need in me swelled, compelling beyond sanity. I knew I shouldn't, but heart quickening, I ran my nails down his neck to leave red pressure trails. Kisten shuddered, his hands falling to find the small of my back, firm and questing. Liquid fire raced from my neck as he angled his head and found my scar. His breath came in strong surges, sending wave after delicious wave through me from his lips alone.

"I will not—I will not," he panted, and I realized he was balanced on the brink of something more. A tremor passed through me as he traced a path across my neck with his gentle teeth. A whisper of words unrecognized pattered through my thoughts, pinging my sensibilities. "Say yes . . ." he urged, a wisp of urgent promise in his low, coaxing voice. "Say it, love. Please . . . give me this, too."

My knees trembled as the coolness of his teeth grazed over my skin again, testing, luring. His hands on my shoulders held me firm. *Did I want this?* Eyes warming with unshed tears, I admitted I didn't know anymore. Where Ivy couldn't move me, Kisten did. I prayed Kisten didn't feel it in my fingers gripping his arms as if he was the only thing keeping me sane at this brink of time.

"You need to hear me say yes?" I breathed, recognizing the passion in my voice. I would rather die here with Kisten then in fear with Piscary.

The ding of the elevator intruded and the doors opened.

A flush of cool air drifted about my ankles. Reality flashed back in a painful rush. It was too late. I had tarried too long. "Do I have the vial?" I questioned, breathless as my fingers twined among the short hair at the nape of his neck. His weight was heavy against me, and the scent of leather and silk would forever mean Kisten to me. I didn't want to move. I didn't want to get out of this elevator.

I felt Kist's heartbeat and heard him swallow. "It's in your purse," he breathed.

"Good." My jaw clenched and my grip in his hair tightened. Yanking his head back, I brought my knee up.

Kist flung himself away from me. The elevator shook as he hit the opposite wall. I'd missed him. Damn.

Breathless and disheveled, he pulled himself straight and felt his ribs. "You have to move faster than that, witch." Flipping the hair from his eyes, he gestured for me to go out before him.

Knees watery and loose, I gathered myself and walked out of the elevator.

Twenty-Seven

Piscary's daytime quarters were not what I had expected. I walked out of the elevator, my head swinging from side to side, taking it all in. The ceilings were high—I guessed ten feet—and were painted white where they weren't covered with warm, primary-colored sheets of fabric draped into soothing folds. Large archways hinted at equally spacious rooms farther in. It had the soft comfort of a playboy mansion mixed with the air of a museum. I spared a moment to try to find a ley line, not surprised to find I was too deep underground.

My boots trod upon a plush off-white carpet. The furniture was tasteful, and there was occasional artwork under spotlights. Floor-to-ceiling curtains at regular intervals gave the illusion of windows behind them. Bookshelves behind glass were between them, every tome looking older than the Turn. Nick would have loved it, and I spared a thought, desperately hoping he had found my note. The first hints of possible success made me walk with more confidence than I deserved. Between Kisten's vial and Nick's note, maybe I could escape with my life.

The doors to the elevator shut. I turned, noticing there was no button to push to make them open up again. The stairway, too, was missing. It must come out somewhere else. My heart gave a pound and settled. Escape with my life? *Maybe*.

"Take off your boots," Kist said.

I cocked my head in disbelief. "Excuse me?"

"They're dirty." His attention was on my feet. He was still flushed. "Take them off."

I looked at the expanse of white carpet. *He wanted me to kill Piscary, and he was worried about my boots on the carpet?* Grimacing, I slipped them off and left them askew by the elevator. I did not believe this. I was going to die in my bare feet.

But the carpet felt nice on my arches as I followed Kisten, forcing myself to not feel the outside of my bag for the vial he had promised was there. He was tense again, his jaw tight and his manner sullen, far from the domineering vampire that had driven me to the brink of capitulation. He looked jealous and wronged. Just what I would expect from a betrayed lover.

Give me this. . . . echoed in my memory, pulling an unstoppable shudder through me. I wondered if he begged Piscary like that, knowing that he had been asking for blood. And I wondered if, to Kisten, the taking of blood was a casual commitment or something more.

The sound of muted traffic drew my attention from the picture of what looked like Piscary and Lindburgh sharing a pint in a British pub. Steps slow to hid his limp, Kisten led me into a sunken living room. At the end of it was a tiled breakfast nook before what looked like, for all the world, a window overlooking the river from the second story. Piscary was lounging at a small metal-weave table dead center of the circular tiled space, surrounded by carpet. I knew I was underground and that it was only a live video feed, but it sure looked like a window to me.

The sky was brightening with the coming dawn, giving the gray river a soft sheen. Cincinnati's taller buildings were dark silhouettes against the lighter sky. Smoke came from the paddleboats as they stoked their boilers, readying them-

selves for the first wave of tourists. Sunday traffic was light,
and the individual whooshes of cars were lost behind the
thousands of clatters, clanks, and unseen calls that make up
the background of a city. I watched the water ripple under
the breeze, and my hair lifted in a gust in time with a soft
hush of wind. Taken aback at the detail, I searched the ceiling and floor until I found a vent. A horn blew in the distance.

"Enjoy yourself, Kist?" Piscary said, pulling my attention
away from the jogger and his dog running the footpath beside the river.

Kist's neck went red and he ducked his head. "I wanted to
know what Ivy was talking about," he mumbled, looking like
a child caught kissing the neighbor girl.

Piscary smiled. "Exciting, isn't it? Leaving her unbound
like that is loads of fun until she tries to kill you. But then,
that's where the thrill comes from, yes?"

My tension flowed back. Piscary looked relaxed, sitting at
one of the table's two wireweave chairs in a lightweight,
midnight-blue silk robe. The morning paper sat folded by his
hand. The deep color of his robe went nicely with his amber
skin. His bare feet were visible through the table. They were
long and skinny, the same honey hue as his bare scalp. My
anxiety strengthened at his bedroom-casual appearance.
Great. This is just what I needed.

"Nice window," I said, thinking it was better than Trent's,
the toad. He could have taken care of all of this had he acted
when I told him Piscary was the murderer. Men were all
alike: take what they can get without paying for it, lie about
the rest.

Piscary shifted in his chair, and his robe parted to show
his knee. I quickly looked away. "Thank you," he said. "I
hated sunrises when I was alive. Now it's my favorite part of
the day." I sneered, and he gestured to the table. "Would you
like a cup of coffee?"

"Coffee?" I said. "I would have thought it was against the gangster code to have coffee with someone before killing them."

His thin black eyebrows rose. I realized he must want something from me, otherwise he would have just sent Algaliarept to kill me on the bus.

"Black," I said. "No sugar."

Piscary gave Kisten a directive nod, and he slipped soundlessly away. I pulled out the second chair across from Piscary, flopping down with my bag on my lap. I glanced out the fake window in the silence. "I like your lair," I said sarcastically.

Piscary raised one eyebrow. I wished I could do that. Too late to learn how now. "It was originally part of the underground railroad," he said. "A foul hole in the ground under someone's shipping dock. Ironic, isn't it?" I said nothing, and he added, "This used to be the gateway to the free world. It still is, occasionally. There's nothing like death to free a person."

A small sigh slipped from me, and I turned to the window, wondering how much wise-old-man-crap he was going to make me listen to before killing me. Piscary cleared his throat, and I looked back. A wisp of black hair showed behind the V of his robe, and his calves visible through the wire mesh of the table were hard with muscle. I recalled my lust rising hot and fast in the elevator with Kisten, knowing it had mostly been vamp pheromones. *Liar.* That Piscary could to that to me and more with nothing more than a sound turned my stomach.

Unable to stop myself, I sent my hand over my neck as if to brush my hair from my eyes. I wanted to hide my scar, though Piscary was probably more aware of it than the nose on my face. "You didn't have to rape her to get me to come see you," I said, deciding to be angry instead of afraid. "A dead horse head in my bed would have done it."

"I wanted to," he said, his low voice carrying the strength of the wind. "Much as you'd like to think otherwise, this isn't all about you, Rachel. Some of it, but not all."

"My name is Ms. Morgan."

He acknowledged this with a three-second, mocking silence. "I have been spoiling Ivy. People are beginning to talk. It was time to bring her back into the fold. And it was a pleasure—for both of us." A smile of remembrance came over him, a glint of fang and a soft, almost subliminal, guttural sigh. "She surprised me, going far past my intended purpose. I haven't lost control like that for at least three hundred years."

My stomach quivered as a surge of his vamp-induced desire flashed through me and was gone. Its potency took my breath away, and I found myself reaching out to catch it. "Bastard," I said, wide-eyed as my blood pounded in me.

"Flatterer," he said back, his eyebrows high.

"She changed her mind," I said, as the last of his need died in me. "She doesn't want to be your scion. Leave her alone."

"It's too late. And she does want it. I put no compulsion on her when she made her decision. I didn't need to. She had been bred and raised for the position, and when she dies, she will have the complexity to be a suitable companion, varied and sophisticated enough in her thoughts so that I don't become bored with her and she with me. You see, Rachel, it's not honest to say that the lack of blood is what causes a vampire to go insane and walk out into the sun. It's the boredom that brings upon a lack of appetite that leads to insanity. Working to bring Ivy about has helped me stave that off. Now that she is poised upon her potential, she's going to keep me from going insane." He inclined his head graciously. "And I'll do the same for her."

His attention went over my shoulder, and the hair on the back of my neck pricked. It was Kisten. The whisper of his passage brushed against me, and I stifled a shudder. The bruised and beaten vamp silently set a cup of coffee on a saucer before me and left. He never met my eyes, his manner holding a subdued pain. The steam from the porcelain rose three inches before the artificial wind caught it and blew it away. I didn't reach for the cup. Fatigue pulled at me and adrenaline made me feel ill. I thought of the charms in my bag. Why was Piscary waiting?

"Kist?" the undead vampire said softly, and Kisten turned. "Give it to me."

Piscary held out his hand, and Kisten dropped a crumpled paper in his palm. My face went slack in panic. It was my note to Nick.

"Did she call anyone?" Piscary asked Kist, and the young vampire ducked his head.

"She called the FIB. They hung up on her."

Shocked, I looked at Kisten. He had watched the entire thing. He had hidden in the shadows while I held Ivy's hair as she vomited, watched as I made her cocoa, and listened as I sat beside Ivy while she relived her nightmare. While I had been taking forever on the bus, Kisten had ripped my salvation from the door. No one was coming. No one at all.

Not meeting my eyes, he walked away. There was the distant sound of a door closing. My gaze flicked to Piscary's and my breath froze. His eyes were entirely black. *Shit.*

The unblinking obsidian orbs made my palms sweat. With the coiled tension of a predator, he reclined before me in his midnight-blue robe with that fake wind moving the wisps of hair on his bare arms, tan and healthy looking. The hem of his robe shifted with his subtle movements. His chest moved as he breathed in an effort to ease my subconscious. And as I sat before him, the enormity of what was going to happen fell on me.

My breath came and went, and I held it. Seeing me recognize my death, he blinked slowly and smiled with a knowing glint. *Not yet, but soon. When he could wait no longer.*

"It's amusing you care for her so deeply," he said, the power seeping from his voice to clench about my heart. "She betrayed you so utterly. My beautiful, dangerous *filiola custos*. I sent her to watch you four years ago, and she joined the I.S. I bought a church and told her to move into it; she did. I asked her to put in a witch's kitchen and stock it with appropriate books; she went beyond to arrange for a garden that would be irresistible."

My face was cold and my legs trembled. *Her friendship had been a lie? A sham to keep tabs on me?* I couldn't believe it. Remembering the lost sound of her voice as she asked me to keep the sun from killing her, I couldn't believe her friendship had been a lie.

"I told her to follow you when you quit," Piscary said, the blackness in his eyes taking on the tension of a remembered passion. "It was our first argument, and I thought that I had found the point where I could make her my scion, where she would show her strength and prove she could hold her own against me. But she capitulated. For a time I thought I might have made a mistake and she lacked the strength of will to survive infinity with me and I'd have to wait yet another generation and try with a daughter born of her and Kisten. I was so disappointed. Imagine my delight when I realized she had her own agenda and was using me."

He smiled, the slip of teeth a little bigger, showing a little longer. "She had fastened upon you as her way out of the future I saw for her. She thought you could find a way to keep her from losing her soul when she dies." He shook his head in a controlled motion, the light glinting across his smooth scalp. "Can't be done, but she won't believe."

I swallowed, making fists as my feelings of betrayal faltered. She had been using him, not following his direction. "Does she know you murdered those witches?" I whispered, sick at heart that she might have known and never told me.

"No," Piscary said. "I'm sure she suspects, but my interest

in you stems from an older reason, having nothing to do with Kalamack's current holy grail of a ley line witch."

I kept my eyes from my hands gripped tightly in my lap above the opening of my bag. I couldn't reach for the vial. *If it wasn't for that, why did Piscary want me dead?*

"It must have cost her pride dearly to come to me, begging for clemency when you survived your demon attack. She was so upset. It's hard to be young. I understood more than she knows what it is to want an equal. And I was inclined to spoil her more once I realized she had used me without my knowing. So I let you live, provided she break her fast and take you completely. You being her shadow had an ironic twist I liked. She promised she would, but I knew she was lying. Even so, I didn't mind as long as she kept you and Kalamack apart."

"But I'm not a ley line witch," I said, keeping my voice soft so it wouldn't shake. I could have breathed the words and he would have heard. "Why?"

He hadn't taken a breath since he stopped talking. The balls of his feet were pressed to the floor. His calves were tense. *Almost,* I thought, moving my fingers to the opening of my bag. *He was almost ready. What was he waiting for?*

"You are your father's daughter," he said, the skin around his eyes tightening. "Trent is his father's son. Apart you are annoying. Together . . . you have the potential to be a problem."

My gaze went distant then sharpened as I met his eyes, knowing my face had taken on a horrified expression. The picture of my father and Trent's outside a yellow camp bus. Piscary had killed them. It had been Piscary.

Hard and strong, my blood pounded in my temples. My body demanded I do something, but I sat, knowing if I moved, he would move.

He shrugged, a calculated motion that pulled my eyes to a flash of amber skin beneath his robe. "They were getting too close to solving the elven riddle," he said, watching my reaction.

I kept my face impassive as he said Trent's most precious secret, telling him I, too, knew. Apparently it was the right thing to do.

"I'm not going to let you two pick up where they left off," he added, prodding.

I said nothing, stomach roiling. Piscary had killed them. Trent's father and my dad had been friends. They had been working together. They had been working together against Piscary.

Piscary went very still. "Has he sent you into the everafter yet?"

My gaze shot to his, fear in my gut. There it was. The question he wanted answered, the one he hid among others so I wouldn't know. As soon as I answered it, I'd be dead.

"I'm not in the habit of breaking my client confidentiality," I said, my mouth dry.

His cool dispassion cracked as he took a breath. It was subtle, but there it was. "He has. Did you find one?" he asked, catching himself before he could lean forward over the table. "Was it sound enough to read?"

One? Read what? I said nothing, desperately wanting to hide my pulse pounding in my neck, but though his eyes were black, he wasn't interested in my blood. That was almost too frightening to believe. I didn't know how to answer. Would yes save my life or damn it?

Frowning, he studied me a long moment while I listened to my heart pound and sweat broke out on my arms. "I can't interpret your silence," he said, seeming irritated.

I took a breath.

Piscary moved.

The adrenaline hurt. I pushed myself from the table in a blind panic. My chair tipped over backward, with me still in it.

Piscary flung the table out of the way. It crashed aside, my untouched coffee making a fantastic pattern on the white carpet.

I scrabbled backward, my bare feet squeaking against the circle of tile. My fingers found the carpet and I clutched at it, rolling over and pulling myself forward.

A shriek escaped me as he yanked me up by my wrist. I clawed at him in panic. He took it all. Face dispassionate, he drew a fingernail across my right arm, follow the blue of a vein. Fire traced his nail as he opened my skin, then bliss. Silently, savagely, I fought to get free as he held me by my wrist, unmoving as a tree. My blood welled and I felt the bubble of insanity swell in me. *Not again. I couldn't be ravaged by a vampire again!*

He looked at my blood, then my eyes. Taking his free hand, he swiped it across my arm.

"No!" I screamed.

He let go of my wrist, and I fell to the carpet. Breath a harsh pant, I scrabbled backward. I found my feet, adrenaline pounding through me as I headed for the elevator.

Piscary jerked me back.

"You son of a bitch!" I screamed. "Leave me alone!"

He gave my head a smack to make me see stars.

I crumpled. Panting, I lay at his feet as he stood above me, an amulet in his hand. He smeared my blood across it, and it glowed red. His hand was enveloped in a red haze as he nudged my fallen chair farther onto the surrounding carpet. I pulled my head up, seeing past my hair that the pattern on the tiled floor before us made a perfect circle. The circle of blue tile around the white stone was one piece of marble. It was a summoning circle.

"God help me," I whispered, knowing what was going to happen when Piscary tossed the amulet to land dead center of the circle. I watched the ball of ever-after energy expand to form a protective bubble. My skin hummed with the power from another witch, kindled to life with my blood as Piscary prepared to call his demon.

Twenty-Eight

Piscary brought his hand to his mouth to lick away my remaining blood, recoiling. "Holy water?" he said, his dispassionate face showing a glimmer of distaste. Taking his robe hem, he wiped my blood from him, leaving his palm showing only a mild redness. "You need more than that to do more than annoy me. And don't flatter yourself. I wasn't going to bite you. I don't even like you, but you'd enjoy it. Instead, you will be dying slowly and in pain."

"Bring it on . . ." I panted, slumped at his feet as my eyes remembered how to focus.

He moved that hated eight feet away, staying between the elevator and me. Carefully pronounced Latin came from him. I recognized some of the words from Nick's summoning. My pulse quickened and I looked frantically over the plush, spacious white room for anything. I was too far underground to tap into a ley line. Algaliarept was coming. Piscary was going to give me to it.

I froze as Piscary said its name. The taste of burnt amber coated my tongue, and a haze of ever-after red melted into existence within the summoning circle. "Oh, look. A demon," I whispered, dragging myself to the fallen table and pulling myself up. "This just keeps getting better and better."

Swaying, I watched as it swelled to grow into a six-foot-high figure. The ever-after red soaked inward, coalescing as an athletic, amber-skinned body dressed in a loincloth decorated with stones and colored ribbons. Algaliarept had bare muscular legs, an impossibly thin waist, and a magnificently sculptured chest that would make Schwarzenegger weep. And atop it was a jackal head, alive with pointing ears and a long savage muzzle.

My mouth dropped open and I looked from the vision of the Egyptian god of death to Piscary, seeing the vampire's features with new meaning. Piscary was Egyptian?

Piscary stiffened. "I told you not to appear before me like that," he said tightly.

The death mask grinned, fascinating in that it was alive and part of him. "I forgot," it drawled in an incredibly deep voice that seemed to set my insides resonating. A thin red tongue slipped past the jackal teeth to caress its muzzle. There was the clopping sound of teeth and lips.

My heart pounded, and as if hearing it, Algaliarept slowly turned to me. "Rachel Mariana Morgan," it said, its ears pricked. "You are the little gadabout."

"Shut up," Piscary said, and Algaliarept's eyes narrowed to slits. "What do you want for making her tell me what she knows about Kalamack's progress?"

"Six seconds with you outside your circle." The sheer desire to kill Piscary in its voice was like ice down my back.

Piscary shook his head, his cool compassion unshaken. "I'll give you her. I don't care what you do with her as long as she doesn't walk this side of the ley lines ever again. In return, you will make her tell me how far Trent Kalamack is in his research. Before you take her. Agreed?"

Not the ever-after. Not with Algaliarept.

Algaliarept's canine grin was pleased. "Rachel Mariana Morgan as payment? Mmmm, I agree." The Egyptian god clenched its hands and took a step forward, halting at the edge of the circle. Its jackal ears pricked and its doggy eyebrows rose.

"You can't do that!" I protested, heart pounding. I looked at Piscary. "You can't do that. I don't agree." I turned to Algaliarept. "He doesn't own my soul. He can't give it to you!"

The demon spared me a glance. "He has your body. Control the body, control the soul."

"That's not fair!" I shouted, ignored.

Piscary came close to the circle. He put his hands upon his hips, taking an aggressive stance. "You will," he intoned, "not attempt to kill or touch me in any fashion. And when I say, you will leave and return directly to the ever-after."

"Agreed," the jackal head said. A drop of saliva fell from a fang, hissing as it flowed down the ever-after between them.

Never dropping the demon's gaze, Piscary rubbed his big toe over the circle to break it.

Algaliarept lunged out of the circle.

Gasping, I backpedaled. A powerful hand reached out and grasped my throat.

"Stop!" Piscary shouted.

My breath choked and I pried at the golden fingers. It had three rings with blue stones, all pinching my skin. I swung to kick it, and Algaliarept shifted me higher to avoid my strike. A wet sound escaped me.

"Drop her!" Piscary demanded. "You can't have her until I get what I want!"

"I'll get your information some other way," the jackal said, the rumble of its words joining the rushing sound of my blood. My head felt as if it was going to explode.

"I called you to get information from *her*," Piscary said. "If you kill her now, you violate your summoning. I want it now, not next week or next year."

The fingers around my throat dissolved. I dropped to the

carpet, gasping. Its sandals were made of leather and thick ribbons. Slowly I pulled my head up, feeling my throat.

"A reprieve only, Rachel Mariana Morgan," the jackal head said, its tongue moving in fantastic patterns as it spoke. "You will be warming my bed tonight."

I knelt before it, sucking in air as I tried not to figure out how I could be warming its bed if I was dead. "You know," I wheezed, "I'm really getting tired of this." Heart pounding, I got to my feet. It had agreed to a task. It was susceptible to being summoned again. "Algaliarept," I said clearly. "I call you, you dog-faced, murdering son of a bitch."

Piscary's face went slack in surprise, and I swear Algaliarept winked at me. "Oh, let me be the one in leather?" the jackal head said. "Be afraid of him. I like being him."

"Sure, whatever," I said, knees shaking.

Black leather driving gloves slit into existence over the amber-skinned hands, and the jackal-headed Egyptian god's stance melted from a ramrod stiffness into a confidant slouch. Kisten took shape, wearing head-to-toe leather and thick-heeled black boots. There was a jingle of chain and a whiff of gasoline. "This is good," the demon said, showing a glint of fang as it slicked its blond hair back, its passing hand leaving it shower-wet and smelling of shampoo.

I thought it looked good, too. Unfortunately.

Exhaling slowly, the image of Kist bit its lower lip to make it redden, a tongue slipping out to leave it with a wet shine. A shudder went through me as I recalled how soft Kist's lips were. As if reading my mind, the demon sighed, strong fingers reaching down its leather pants to draw my eyes to it. A scratch melted into existence over its eye, mirroring Kist's new wound.

"Damn vamp pheromones," I whispered, pushing the memory of the elevator away.

"Not this time," Algaliarept said, smirking.

Piscary was staring in confusion. "I summoned you. You do what I say!"

The image of Kisten turned to Piscary, belligerently flipping him off. "And Rachel Mariana Morgan summoned me, too. The witch and I have a preexisting debt to settle. And if she has enough guile to win a circleless summoning from me, then I will hold to it."

Piscary's teeth ground together. He lunged at us.

I gasped, lurching back. There was a wrenching sensation, and I stared as Piscary slammed into a wall of ever-after, falling in a shocked tangle of arms and legs. I went cold as I realized Algaliarept had put us in a circle of its own construction.

The thick haze of red pulsed and hummed, pressing down against my skin though I was two feet away. As Piscary got to his feet and adjusted his robe, I extended a finger and touched the barrier. A sliver of ice shivered through me as the surface rippled. It was the strongest, thickest sheet of ever-after I'd ever witnessed. Feeling Algaliarept's eyes on me, I pulled my hand back and wiped it on my jeans.

"I didn't know you could do that," I said, and it chuckled. In hindsight it made sense. It was a demon. It existed in the ever-after. Of course it would know how.

"And I'm willing to teach you how to survive manipulating as much ever-after, too, Rachel Mariana Morgan," it said as if reading my mind. "For a price."

I shook my head.

"Later, perhaps?"

With a cry of frustrated rage, Piscary took a wire-weave chair and slammed it against the barrier. I jumped, my mouth going dry.

Algaliarept gave the incensed vampire a sideways glance as Piscary ripped the leg off the chair and tried to pierce the barrier like a sword. The demon took a belligerent stance at the edge of the circle, showing me its tight butt in leather pants. "Bugger off, old man," it mocked in Kist's fake accent, infuriating Piscary all the more. "The sun will be up soon. You'll have another chance at her in about three minutes."

My head came up. *Three minutes? Was the sun that close to rising?*

Furious, Piscary threw the bar, which skittered and rolled across the carpet. His eyes black pits, he began to make slow, sedate circles about us in anticipation.

But for the moment I was safe in Algaliarept's circle. *What's wrong with this picture?*

Forcing my arms down from the tight grip around myself, I glanced at Piscary's fake window, seeing the glint of sun on the highest buildings. Three minutes. I pushed my fingertips into my forehead. "If I ask you to kill Piscary, will you call us even?" I asked as I looked up.

It struck a sideways pose. "No. Even though killing Ptah Ammon Fineas Horton Madison Parker Piscary is on my to-do list, it is still a request and would cost you, not absolve your debt. Besides, if you send me after him, he will likely summon me again as you did and you'd be right back where you started. The only reason he can't summon me now is because we haven't agreed on anything and we're in summoning limbo, so to speak."

It grinned, and I looked away. Piscary stood and listened, clearly thinking.

"Can you get me out of here?" I asked, thinking of escape.

"Through a ley line, yes. But this time, it will cost you your soul." It licked its lips. "And then, you're mine."

Happy, happy choices. "Can you give me something to protect myself from him?" I pleaded, getting desperate.

"Just as expensive . . ." It tugged its gloves tighter to its fingers. "And you already have what you need. Tick-tock, Rachel Mariana Morgan. Anything that will save your life will require your soul."

Piscary was grinning, and my stomach turned as he came

to a standstill eight feet away. My eyes darted to my bag with the vial Kist had given me. It was out of reach on the wrong side of the barrier. "What should I ask for?" I cried desperately.

"If I answer that, you won't have enough left to pay for it, love," it breathed, bending close and sending my curls drifting. I jerked back as I smelled Brimstone. "And you're a resourceful witch," it added. "Anyone who can ring the city's bells can survive a vampire. Even one as old as Ptah Ammon Fineas Horton Madison Parker Piscary."

"But I'm three stories down!" I protested. "I can't reach a ley line through that."

Leather creaked as it circled me, hands laced behind its back. "What *will* you do?"

I swore under my breath. Past our circle, Piscary waited. Even if I managed to escape, Piscary would walk. It wasn't as if I could ask Algaliarept to testify.

Eyes widening, I looked up. "Time?" I asked.

The vision of Kist looked at its wrist, and a watch twin to the one I had smashed with my meat tenderizer appeared about it. "One minute, thirty."

My face went cold. "What do you want for you to testify in an I.S. or FIB courtroom that Piscary is the witch serial killer?"

Algaliarept grinned. "I like the way you think, Rachel Mariana Morgan."

"How much?" I shouted, looking at the sun creeping down the side of the buildings.

"My price hasn't changed. I need a new familiar, and it's taking too long to get Nicholas Gregory Sparagmos's soul."

My soul. I couldn't do it, even if it would satisfy Algaliarept and ultimately save Nick from losing his soul and being pulled into the ever-after to be the demon's familiar. My face went slack and I stared at Algaliarept so intently that it blinked in surprise. I had an idea. It was foolish and risky, but maybe it was crazy enough to work.

"I'll voluntarily be your familiar," I whispered, not knowing if I could survive the energy it might pull through me or force me to hold for it. "I'll freely be your familiar, but I get to keep my soul." Maybe if I retained my soul, it couldn't pull me into the ever-after. I could stay on this side of the ley lines. It could use me only when the sun was down. Maybe. The question was, would Algaliarept take the time to think it through? "And I want you to testify before my end of the agreement becomes enforceable," I added in case I managed to survive.

"Voluntarily?" it said, its form blurring at the edges. Even Piscary looked shocked. "That's not how it works. No one has ever willingly been a familiar before. I don't know what that means."

"It means I'm your damn familiar!" I shouted, knowing that if it thought about it, it would realize it was only getting half of me. "You say yes now, or in thirty seconds either I or Piscary is going to be dead, and you will have nothing. Nothing! Do we have a deal or not?"

The vision of Kist leaned forward and I shirked away. It looked at its watch. "Voluntarily?" Its eyes were wide in wonder and avarice.

In a wash of panic, I nodded. I'd worry about it later. If I had a later.

"Done," it said, so quickly I thought for sure I'd made a mistake. Relief filled me, then reality hit with a soul-shaking slap. *God help me. I was going to be a demon's familiar.*

I jerked back as it reached for my wrist.

"We agreed," it said, snatching my arm with a vamp quickness.

I kicked it square in the stomach. It did nothing, rocking back with the transfer of momentum but otherwise unmoved. A gasp slipped from me as it scratched a line across my demon mark. Blood flowed. I jerked back, and making shushing noises, the demon bent its head over my wrist and blew on it.

I tried to pull away, but it was stronger than me. I was sick of the blood, of everything. It let me go and I fell back, sliding down the arch of its barrier, feeling my back tingle. Immediately I looked at my wrist. There were two lines where one had once been. The new one looked as old as the first. "It didn't hurt this time," I said, too strung-out to be shocked.

"It wouldn't have hurt the first time had you not tried to stitch it up. What you felt was the fiber burning away. I'm a demon, not a sadist."

"Algaliarept!" Piscary shouted as our agreement was sealed.

"Too late," the grinning demon said, and disappeared.

I fell backward as its barrier vanished from behind me, shrieking as Piscary lunged. Bracing myself against the floor, I brought my legs up into him, flipping him over me. I scrambled for my bag and the vial. My hand dove into my bag, and Piscary jerked me back.

"Witch," he hissed, gripping my shoulder. "I'll have what I want. And then you'll die."

"Go to hell, Piscary," I snarled, thumbing the vial open with a soft pop and throwing it into his face.

Crying out, Piscary violently pushed away from me. From the floor, I watched him lurch away, wiping at his face with frantic motions.

Heart in my throat, I waited for him to fall, waited for him to pass out. He did neither.

My gut tightened in fear as Piscary wiped his face, bringing his fingers to his nose. "Kisten," he said, his disgust melting into a weary disappointment. "Oh, Kisten. Not you?"

I swallowed hard. "It's harmless, isn't it."

He met my eyes. "You don't think I survived this long by telling my children what can really kill me, do you?"

I had nothing left. For three heartbeats I stared. His lips curved into an eager smile.

I jerked into motion. Piscary casually reached out and grabbed my ankle as I tried to rise. I fell, kicking out, managing to hit his face twice before he pulled me to him and immobilized me under his weight.

The scar on my neck gave a pulse, and fear surged through it, making a nauseating mix.

"No," Piscary said softly, pinning me to the carpet. "You will be in pain for this."

His fangs were bared. Saliva dripped from them.

I struggled for air, trying to get out from under him. He shifted, holding my left arm over my head. My right arm was free. Teeth gritted, I went for his eyes.

Piscary jerked back. With a vamp strength, he grasped my right arm and snapped it.

My scream echoed against the high ceilings. My back arched and I gasped for air.

Piscary's eyes flashed black. "Tell me if Kalamack has a viable sample," he demanded.

Lungs heaving, I tried to breathe. The wave of misery thrummed from my arm and echoed in my head. "Go to hell . . ." I rasped.

Still pinning me to the carpet, he squeezed my broken arm.

I writhed as agony sang through me. Every nerve ending pulsed into a burn. A guttural sound escaped me, pain and determination. I wouldn't tell him. I didn't even know the answer.

He leaned his weight onto my arm, and I screamed again so I wouldn't go insane. Fear made my skull hurt as Piscary's eyes flashed into hunger. His instinctive need had risen high, triggered by my struggles. The black of his eyes swelled. I heard my sounds of pain as if outside my head. Silver sparkles from shock started between me and Piscary's eyes, and my cries turned to relief. I was going to pass out. *Thank you, God.*

Piscary saw it, too. "No," he whispered, his tongue making a quick pass over his teeth to catch the saliva before it fell. "I'm better than that." He took his weight from my arm. A groan came from me as the agony dulled to a throb.

He leaned to put his face inches from mine, watching my pupils with a cool detachment as the sparkles disappeared and my focus returned. Under his impassivity was a growing excitement. If he hadn't already sated his hunger with Ivy, he wouldn't have been able to keep from draining me. He knew the instant my will returned, smiling in anticipation.

Taking a breath, I spit in his face, tears mixing with my saliva.

Piscary closed his eyes, his expression showing a tired irritation. He let go of my left wrist to wipe his face.

I swung the heel of my hand up to smash it into his nose.

He caught my wrist before it hit. Fangs glinting, he held my arm. My eyes traveled down the scratch he had cut in me to invoke the amulet. My heart gave a hard pound. A ribbon of blood trailed slowly to my elbow. A drop of red swelled, quivered, and fell to land upon my chest, warm and soft.

My breath was shaking. I stared, waiting. His tension rose, his muscles tightening as he lay atop me. His gaze was fixed to my wrist. Another drop fell, feeling heavy against me.

"No!" I shrieked as a carnal groan slipped from him.

"I see now," he said, his voice terrifyingly soft, harnessed need pulsing under it. "No wonder Algaliarept took so long finding out what frightens you." Pinning my arm to the floor, he leaned closer until our noses lay side by side. I couldn't move. I couldn't breathe. "You're afraid of desire," he whispered. "Tell me, little witch, what I want to know or I will slice you open, filling your veins with me, making you my plaything. But I will let you remember your freedom—mine forever."

"Go to hell. . . ." I said, terrified.

He eased back to see my face. It was hot where his robe had shifted and his skin touched mine. "I will start here," he said, pulling my dripping arm to where I could see it.

"No . . ." I protested. My voice was soft and frightened. I couldn't help it. I tried to bring my arm closer, but Piscary had it tight. He pulled my arm in a slow controlled motion as I fought to keep it unmoving. My broken arm sent surges of nausea through me as I tried to use it, pushing at him with the strength of a kitten.

"God no, God no!" I screamed, redoubling my struggles as he tilted his head and sent his tongue across my elbow, moaning as he cleaned it, his tongue moving slowly to where the blood flowed freely. If his saliva reached my veins, I would be his. Forever.

I wiggled. I thrashed. The warm wetness of his tongue was replaced with the cool sharpness of teeth, grazing but not piercing.

"Tell me," he whispered, tilting his head so he could see my eyes, "and I'll kill you now instead of in a hundred years."

Nausea bubbled up, mixing with the darkness of insanity. I bucked under him. The fingers of my broken arm found his ear. I tore at them, reaching for his eyes. I fought like an animal, instinct a hazy mist between me and madness.

Piscary's breath came in a harsh pant as my struggles and pain whipped him into a frenzy of restraint I'd seen in Ivy far too often. "Oh, the hell with it," he said, his flowing voice cutting through me. "I'm going to drain you. I can find out some other way. I may be dead, but I'm still a man."

"No!" I shrieked. But it was too late.

Piscary's lips pulled back. Forcing my bleeding arm to the

floor, his head tilted to reach my neck. The haze of pain swelled into ecstasy as he ground his fingers into my broken arm. I screamed into his moan of anticipation.

A distant boom of sound struck through me, and the floor trembled. I spasmed, the warm rapture of my arm shocking into a breathless feeling of pain. The sound of men shouting filtered in through the haze of nausea.

"They won't reach us in time," Piscary murmured. "They're too late for you."

Not like this, I thought, out of my mind in fear and cursing the stupidity of it all. I didn't want to die like this. He bent to me, his face savage with hunger. I took a last breath.

It exploded from me as a green ball of ever-after smashed into Piscary.

I wiggled in the minuscule shifting of weight. Still on me, Piscary snarled and looked up.

My arm was free, and I wedged my knees between us. Tears blurred my vision as I fought with renewed desperation. Someone was there. Someone was there to help me.

Another blast of green smashed into Piscary. He rocked back. I got a leg under me and levered us up, flipping Piscary off me.

Scrabbling to my feet, I grabbed a chair and swung. It hit him, the shock echoing up my arm.

Piscary turned, his face savage. He tensed, gathering himself to leap at me.

I backpedaled, my broken arm clutched tight to me.

A third blast of green ever-after hissed past me, hitting Piscary and sending him flying backward into a wall.

I spun to the distant elevator.

Quen.

The man stood beside a huge hole in the wall beside the elevator in a cloud of dust, a growing ball of ever-after in his hand, still red but taking on the tinges of his aura. He must have had the energy stored in his chi, since we were too deep underground to reach a line. A black satchel sat beside his feet, several wooden swordlike stakes extending out from the open zipper. Beyond the hole was the stairway. "It's about time you got here," I panted, staggering.

"I got caught behind a train," he said, his hands moving in ley line magic. "Bringing the FIB into this was a mistake."

"I wouldn't have had to if your boss wasn't such a prick!" I shouted, then took a shallow breath, trying not to cough at the dust. Kisten had taken my note. How did the FIB get there if Quen didn't bring them?

Piscary had regained his feet. He took us in, showing his fangs in a wide smile. "And now elf blood? I haven't fed this well since the Turn."

With a vamp's speed, he raced across the large room to Quen, backhanding me in passing. I was flung backward. My back hit the wall and I slumped to the floor. Dazed and hovering on the edge of unconsciousness, I watched Quen evade Piscary, looking like a shadow in his black bodysuit. He had a wooden stake the length of my arm in one hand, a growing ball of ever-after in the other. The Latin spilled from him, the words of the black charm burning themselves into my mind.

The back of my head throbbed. Nausea flooded me as I touched a spot of agony, but I found no blood. The black spots before me cleared as I got to my feet. Dazed, I looked for my bag of charms through the haze of wall-dust.

A masculine cry of agony jerked my attention to Quen. My heart seemed to stop.

Piscary had caught him. Holding him like a lover, Piscary was fastened to his neck, supporting both their weights. Quen went slack and the wooden sword fell to the floor. His shriek of pain swelled into a moan of ecstasy.

Using the wall for support, I got to my feet. "Piscary!" I shouted, and he turned, his mouth red with Quen's blood.

"Wait your turn," he snarled, showing me his red-smeared teeth.

"I *was* here first," I said.

Angry, he dropped Quen. If he had been hungry, nothing would have moved him from downed prey. Quen's arm lifted weakly. He didn't get up. I knew why. It felt too good.

"You don't know when to leave well enough alone," Piscary said, coming at me.

Latin fell from me, burned into my mind from Quen's attack. My hands moved, etching black magic. My tongue swelled at the taste of tinfoil. I stretched for a ley line, not finding it.

Piscary slammed into me. I gasped, unable to breathe. He was on me again, reaching.

In the fear, something broke. A flood of ever-after flowed into me. I heard my scream at the shock of the unexpected influx of power. Gold laced with black and red burst from my hands. Piscary lifted from me. He crashed into a wall, shaking the lights.

I pulled myself up as he slumped on the floor, realizing where the energy had come from. "Nick!" I cried in fear. "Oh God. Nick! I'm sorry!"

I had pulled on a line through him. I had pulled the energy through him as if he had been a familiar. It had raced through him as it had me. I had pulled more than he could handle. *What had I done?*

Piscary was slumped where the wall met the floor. His foot shifted and he swung his head up. His eyes weren't focused, but they were black with hatred. I couldn't let him get up.

Racked in pain, I grabbed the leg of the chair Piscary had torn free and staggered across the room.

He lurched to his feet, supporting himself with a hand against the wall. His robe was almost undone. His eyes suddenly focused.

I gripped the metal rod in one hand like a bat, pulling it back even as I ran. "This is for trying to kill me," I said, swinging.

The bar of metal hit him behind the ear with a sodden smack. Piscary staggered, but didn't go down.

My breath came in an angry sound. "This is for raping Ivy!" I shouted, my anger at him for hurting something so strong and vulnerable giving me strength. I swung, grunting in effort.

The metal rod met the back of his skull with the sound of a melon.

I stumbled, catching my balance. Piscary fell to his knees. Blood seeped from his scalp.

"And this," I said, feeling my eyes grow hot and my vision blur from tears, "is for killing my dad," I whispered.

With a cry of anguish, I swung a third time. It smacked into Piscary's head. Spinning from the momentum, I fell to my knees. My hands stung and the rod slipped from my senseless grip. Piscary's eyes rolled up and he dropped.

Breath sounding like sobs, I looked at him and wiped the back of my hand across my cheek. He wasn't moving. I looked past my hair at the fake window. The sun was up, shining on the buildings. He would probably stay down until nightfall. Probably.

"Kill him," Quen croaked.

I pulled my head up, I'd forgotten he was there.

Quen had risen, a hand against his neck. The blood seeping through his fingers made an ugly pattern on the white carpet. He threw a second wooden sword at me. "Kill him now."

I caught it as if I had been catching swords my entire life. Trembling, I turned its point into the carpet and used it to get up. Shouts and calls were coming from the hole in the wall. The FIB had arrived. Late as usual. "I'm a runner," I said, my throat sore and my words rough. "I don't kill my marks. I bring them in alive."

"Then you're a fool."

I lurched to an overstuffed chair before I fell down. Dropping the sword, I put my head between my knees and stared at the carpet. "You kill him, then," I whispered, knowing he could hear me.

Quen moved unsteadily to his satchel by the ragged hole in the wall. "I can't. I'm not here."

The puff of air that escaped me hurt. I looked up as he crossed the room to me, his steps slow and careful. He took the sword from the floor, jamming it into in his duffle bag with a bloody hand. I thought I saw a gray square of explosive in there, too, telling me how he had blown a hole in the wall.

He looked tired, his lanky stature hunched in pain. His neck didn't look bad, but I'd rather be in traction for six months than have one saliva-laced bite from Piscary. Quen was an Inderlander and so couldn't be turned vampire, but by the look of fear edging his veneer of confidence, he knew he might be tied to Piscary. With a vampire that old, the bond might last a lifetime. Time would tell how much binding saliva, if any, Piscary had laced the bite with.

"Sa'han is wrong about you," he said wearily. "If you can't survive a vampire without help, your value is questionable. And your unpredictability makes you unreliable and therefore unsafe." Quen gave me a nod before he turned and headed for the stairway. I watched him go, my mouth hanging open.

Sa'han is wrong about me, I thought sarcastically. *Well goodie for Trent.*

My hands hurt, the palms red with what looked like first-degree burns. Edden's voice in the stairway was loud. The FIB could take care of Piscary. I could go home. . . .

Home to Ivy, I thought, closing my eyes briefly. *How did my life get this ugly?*

Tired beyond belief, I got to my feet as Edden and a string of FIB officers exploded out of the hole Quen had made.

"It's me!" I croaked, putting my good hand in the air since there was a frightening clatter of safeties going off. "Don't shoot me!"

"Morgan!" Edden peered through the sifting dust and lowered his weapon. Only half the FIB officers did the same. It was a better than average number. "You're alive?"

He sounded surprised. Bent in pain, I looked down at myself, my broken arm clutched close. "Yeah. I think so." I started shivering, cold.

Someone snickered, and the remaining weapons were lowered. Edden made a motion, and the officers fanned out. "Piscary is over there," I said, looking that way. "He's down until sunset. I think."

Coming closer, Edden eyed Piscary, his robe fallen open to show a good portion of muscular thigh. "What was he trying to do, seduce you?"

"No," I whispered, so my throat wouldn't hurt so much. "He was trying to kill me." I met his eyes and added, "There is a living vamp named Kisten around somewhere. He's blond and angry. Please don't shoot him. Other than him and Quen, I haven't seen anyone but the eight living vamps upstairs. You can shoot them if you want."

"Mr. Kalamack's security officer?" Edden's gaze roved over me, cataloging my hurts. "He came with you?" He put a hand on my shoulder to steady me. "It looks like your arm is broken."

"It is," I said, jerking back as he reached for it. *Why do people do that?* "And yeah, he came out here. Why didn't you?" Suddenly angry, I poked him in the chest. "You ever refuse to take my call again, and I swear I'll have Jenks pix you every night for a month."

Arrogance crossed Edden's face and he flicked a glance at the FIB officers warily circling Piscary. Someone called for an I.S. ambulance. "I didn't refuse your call. I was asleep.

Being woken up by a frantic pixy and a panicking boyfriend telling me you went out to stake one of Cincinnati's master vampires is not my favorite way to wake up. And who gave you my unlisted number?"

Oh God, Nick. The remembered burst of ley line energy I'd pulled through him made my face go cold. "Nick," I stammered. "I have to call Nick." But as I looked over the room for my bag and the phone in it, I hesitated. Quen's blood was gone. All of it. I guess Quen was serious about not wanting any evidence that he was here. How had he done that? *A little elven magic, perhaps?*

"Mr. Sparagmos is in the parking lot," Edden said. Peering at me and my cold face, he snagged a passing officer. "Get me a blanket. She's going shocky."

Numb, I let him help me across the room and the hole in the wall. "Poor guy passed out, he was so worried about you. I wouldn't let him or Jenks out of the car." Eyes alight in a sudden thought, he reached for the radio on his belt. "Tell Mr. Sparagmos and Jenks that we found her and she's all right," he said into it, getting a garbled answer back. Taking my elbow, he muttered, "Please tell me you didn't really leave a note on your door saying you were going to stake Piscary?"

My eyes were fixed upon my bag with its pain amulet clear across the room, but my head snapped up at his words. "No!" I protested as my vision swam at the quick movement. "I said I was going to talk to him and that he was the witch hunter. Kisten must have done that, because my note is here somewhere. I saw it!" *Kisten had replaced my note?*

I stumbled in confusion as Edden pulled me forward. Kisten had replaced my note, giving Nick the only number that would bring the FIB out here. Why? Had it been to help me, or simply to cover his betrayal of Piscary?

"Kisten?" Edden questioned. "That's the living vamp you don't want me to shoot, right?" He took the blue FIB blanket someone held out and draped it over my shoulders. "Come on. I want to get you upstairs. We can figure this out later."

Leaning heavily on him, I tugged the blanket closer, wincing as the rough wool hurt my hands. I wouldn't look at them, thinking they were nothing compared to the smut on my soul for having invoked that black charm Quen had taught me. I took a slow breath. *What did it matter if I knew black charms? I was going to be a demon's familiar.*

"My God, Morgan," Edden said as he put the two-way back on his belt. "Did you have to blow a hole in his wall?"

"I didn't," I said, focusing on the carpet three feet in front of me. "It was Quen."

More officers clattered down the stairs and into the room, a hoard of official presences suddenly making me feel like an alien. "Rachel, Quen isn't here."

"Yeah," I said, shivering violently as I looked over my shoulder at the pristine carpet. "I probably imagined it all." The adrenaline was gone, and fatigue and nausea pulled at me. People were moving quickly around us, making me dizzy. My arm was a solid ache. I wanted my bag and the pain amulet in it, but we were moving in the wrong direction, and it looked as if someone had dropped an evidence card by it. Swell.

My mood darkened even further when a woman in an FIB uniform stopped us short by dangling my gun in front of Edden. It was in an evidence bag, and I couldn't stop my hand from reaching out. "Hey, my splat gun," I said, and Edden sighed, not sounding at all happy.

"Tag it," he said, his voice laced with guilt. "Put Ms. Morgan as a positive ID."

The woman looked almost frightened as she nodded and turned away.

"Hey," I protested again, and Edden kept me from following her.

"Sorry, Rachel. It's evidence." He ran a quick look over the surrounding officers before whispering, "But thanks for leaving it where we could find it. Glenn couldn't have downed those living vamps without it."

"But . . ." I stammered, seeing the woman disappear upstairs with my splat gun. The dust was worse here, and I swallowed hard so I wouldn't cough and make myself pass out.

"Let's go," Edden said, sounding tired as he tried to pull me forward. "I hate to do this, but I should get a statement from you before Piscary wakes up and presses charges."

"Presses charges? For what?" I jerked out of his grip, refusing to move. What in hell was going on? I had just tagged the witch hunter, and I was the one being arrested?

The nearby officers were carefully listening, and Edden's round face went even more guilty. "For assault and battery, slander, trespassing, illegal entry, malicious destruction of private property, and whatever else his pre-Turn lawyer can come up with. What did you think you were doing, coming down here and trying to kill him?"

I struggled to speak, affronted. "I didn't kill him, though he by God deserves it. He raped Ivy to get me to come here so he could kill me because I found out he was the witch hunter!" I reached up with my good hand as if it could sooth the raw ache of my throat from the outside. "And I have a witness willing to testify that Piscary contracted it to kill the victims. Is that enough for you?"

Edden's brow rose. "It?" He turned to look at Piscary, surrounded by nervous FIB officers until the I.S. ambulance got there. "Which *it* would that be?"

"You don't want to know." I closed my eyes. I was going to be a demon's familiar. But I was alive. I hadn't lost my soul. Focus on the positive.

"Can I go?" I asked as I saw the first of the stairs past the hole in the wall. I had no idea how I was going to make it up all of them. Maybe if I let Edden arrest me, they would carry me up. Not waiting for his permission, I pulled away and held my arm close as I limped to the ragged hole in the wall. I had just tagged Cincinnati's most powerful vampire as a serial murderer, and all I wanted to do was throw up.

Edden took a step to catch up, still not having answered me. "Can I at least have my boots?" I asked as I saw Gwen taking pictures of them, carefully making her way through the room, her video camera recording everything.

The FIB captain started, looking down at my feet. "You always tag master vampires in your bare feet?"

"Only when they're in their pj's." I clutched the blanket around myself miserably. "Want to keep it sporting, you know."

Edden's round face broke into a grin. "Hey, Gwen! Knock it off," he said loudly as he took my elbow and helped me wobble to the stairs. "This isn't a crime scene. It's an arrest."

Twenty-Nine

"Hey! Here!" I shouted, sitting straighter on the hard ballpark seat and waving to get the attention of the wandering vendor. It was almost a good forty minutes before the game was scheduled to start, and though the stands were starting to fill, the vendors weren't very attentive.

I squinted and held up four fingers as he turned, and he held up eight in return. I winced. *Eight bucks for four hot dogs?* I thought, passing my money down. Oh well. It wasn't as if I had bought the tickets.

"Thanks, Rachel," Glenn said from beside me as the paper-wrapped package hit his hand, thrown by the vendor. He set it on his lap and caught the rest since my arm was in a sling and obviously not working. He handed one to his dad and Jenks on his left. The next he gave to me, and I passed it to Nick on my other side. Nick flashed me a thin smile, immediately looking down to where the Howlers were warming up.

My shoulders slumped, and Glenn leaned closer under the excuse of unwrapping my hot dog and handing it to me. "Give him some time."

I said nothing, my gaze riveted to the highly manicured ballpark. Though Nick wouldn't admit it, a new ribbon of fear had slid between us. We'd had a painful discussion last week where I had apologized profusely for having pulled such a massive amount of ley line energy through him and told him it had been an accident. He insisted that it was all right, that he understood, that he was glad I had done it since it saved my life. His words were earnest and heartfelt, and I knew to the depths of my soul he believed them. But he would only rarely meet my eyes anymore, and he worked hard to keep from touching me.

As if to prove nothing had changed, he had insisted on our usual weekend sleepover last night. It had been a mistake. The dinner conversation was stilted at best: *How was your day, dear? Fine, thank you; how was yours?* We followed that with several hours of TV where I sat on the couch and he sat on the chair across the room. I had hoped for some improvement after retiring at an ungodly early one o'clock in the morning, but he pretended to fall asleep right away, setting me almost to tears when he moved away from the touch of my foot.

The night was brilliantly capped off at four in the morning when he woke from a sound sleep in a nightmare. He all but panicked when he found me in bed with him.

I had quietly excused myself and took the bus home, saying that as long as I was up, I should make sure Ivy got home all right and that I'd see him later. He hadn't stopped me. He sat on the edge of his bed with his head in his hands and hadn't stopped me.

I squinted into the bright afternoon sun, sniffing back any hint of tears. It was the sun. That's all. I took a bite of hot dog. It seemed to take a lot of effort to chew, and it sat heavy in my middle when I finally swallowed. Below, the Howlers called and threw the ball about.

Setting the hot dog down on the paper wrapping across my lap, I took up a baseball in my injured hand. My lips moved in unvoiced Latin as I quietly sketched a complex figure with my good left hand. The fingers about the ball tingled as I said the last word of the charm. A melancholy satisfaction stirred me as the pitcher's throw went wild. The catcher stood to reach it, hesitating in question before he returned to his crouch.

Jenks rubbed his wings together to get my attention, giving me a merry thumbs-up for the bit of ley line magic. I returned his grin with a weak smile. The pixy was sitting on Captain Edden's shoulder so he could see better. The two had mended their fences over a conversation about country western singers and a night out at a karaoke bar. I didn't want to know. Really.

Edden followed Jenks's attention to me, his eyes behind his round-framed glasses suddenly suspicious. Jenks distracted him by loudly extolling the features of a trio of women headed up the concrete steps. The squat man's face reddened but the smile remained.

Grateful, I turned to Glenn, finding he had already finished his hot dog. I should have gotten him two. "How's Piscary's court case shaping up?" I asked.

The tall man shifted in his seat with a bound excitement as he wiped his fingers off on his jeans. Out of his suit and tie, he looked like another person, the sweatshirt emblazoned with the Howlers' logo making him appear comfortable and safe. "With your demon's testimony, I think it's reasonably secure," he said. "I've been waiting for a surge in violent crimes, but they've dropped." He glanced at his dad. "I'm thinking the lesser houses are waiting until Piscary is officially incarcerated before they start vying for his territory."

"They won't." My fingers and words sent another ball clean out of the park with a boost of ever-after energy. It was harder to gather the power from the nearby line. The park's safeguards were kicking in. "Kisten is handling Piscary's affairs," I said sourly. "It's business as usual."

"Kisten?" He leaned closer. "He's not a master vamp. Won't that cause problems?"

Nodding, I sent a pop fly to bounce wrong. The players became slow with tension as it hit the wall and rolled in an odd direction. Glenn had no idea how much trouble it was going to be. Ivy was Piscary's scion. By unwritten vamp law, she was in charge whether she wanted to be or not. It put the retired I.S. runner in a huge moral dilemma, caught between her vampire responsibilities and her need to be true to herself. She was ignoring Piscary's summons to his jail cell, along with a lot of other things that were quietly building.

Hiding behind the excuse that everyone thought Kist was still Piscary's scion, she did nothing, claiming that Kisten had the clout, if not the physical presence, to hold everything together. It didn't look good, but I wasn't about to advise her to start handling Piscary's affairs. Not only had she devoted her life to bringing in those who broke the law, but she'd snap while trying to best the pull of blood and domination such a position would magnify.

Seeing no more comments forthcoming, Glenn crumbled his paper and dropped it into a coat pocket. "So, Rachel," he said, glancing at the empty seat beside Nick. "How is your roommate? Better?"

I took another bite. "She's handling it," I said around my full mouth. "She would have come today but the sun really bothers her—lately."

Lots of things bothered her since having glutted herself on Piscary's blood: the sun, too much noise, not enough noise, the lack of speed of her computer, the pulp in her orange juice, the fish in her bathtub until Jenks took it out back and had a fish fry to boost his kids' protein levels before fall hibernation. She had been violently ill after returning from midnight church services this morning, but she wouldn't stop going. She told me it would help keep space between her and Piscary. Mental space, apparently. Time and distance were enough to break the bond a lesser vamp could put on another with a bite, but Piscary was a master vampire. The bond would last until Piscary wanted it ended.

Slowly Ivy and I were finding a new balance. When the sun was high and bright, she was Ivy, my friend and partner, cheerful with her dry, sarcastic humor as we thought up practical jokes to play on Jenks or discussed possible improvements to the church to make it more livable. After sunset, she left so I wouldn't see what the night did to her now. She was strong in the sunlight, a cruel goddess after sunset, balanced on the edge of helplessness in the battle she fought against herself.

Uncomfortable with my thoughts, I pulled on the ley line and sent a pitched ball wild, to smack into the wall behind the catcher.

"Rachel?" Captain Edden said, his eyes behind his glasses taking on a hard look as he leaned past his son to see me. "Let me know if she wants to talk to Piscary. I'd be glad to look the other way if she wants to smack him around."

He eased back as I gave him a wan smile. Piscary had been extradited to I.S. custody, safe and sound in a vamp jail cell. The preliminary hearing had gone well, the sensationalism of the situation prompting an unexpected opening in the court docket. Algaliarept showed up to prove he was a reliable witness. The demon made all the papers, morphing into all sorts of figures to scare the pants off everyone in the courtroom. What disturbed me most was that the judge was afraid of a little towheaded girl with a lisp and a limp. I think the demon enjoyed it.

I adjusted my red Howlers' hat against the sun as a batter came to the mound to pop a few into the infield. Hot dog in my lap, I shifted my fingers and mouthed the incantation. The park's safeguards had risen higher, and I had to punch a hole through them to reach the line. A sudden influx of ever-after coursed through me, and Nick stiffened. Excusing himself, he slid past me, muttering about the bathroom. His lanky form hastened down the steps and vanished.

Unhappy, I sent the ever-after energy into the pitcher's throw. There was a sharp crack as the bat broke. The batter dropped the shattered ash, swearing loud enough that I could hear him. He turned to look at the stands in accusation. The pitcher put his mitt on his hip. The catcher stood. My eyes narrowed in satisfaction as the coach whistled, pulling everyone in.

"Nice one, Rache," Jenks said, and Captain Edden started, giving me a questioning look.

"That you?" he asked, and I shrugged. "You're going to get yourself banned."

"Maybe they should have paid me." I was being careful. No one was getting hurt. I could make their runners twist their ankles and the wild throws hit players if I wanted. I wasn't. I was just messing with their warm-up. I poked about in the napkin the hot dog had been wrapped in. *Where was my ketchup packet? This hot dog was utterly tasteless.*

The FIB captain moved uneasily. "Ah, about your compensation, Morgan . . ."

"Forget it," I offered quickly. "I figure I still owe you for paying off my I.S. contract."

"No," he said. "We had an agreement. It's not your fault the class was canceled—"

"Glenn, can I have your ketchup?" I said brusquely, cutting Edden off. "I don't know how you people can eat hot dogs without it. Why the Turn didn't that guy give me any ketchup?"

Edden leaned back, a heavy sigh slipping from him. Glenn obediently shuffled about his wad of paper until he came up with a white plastic packet. Face drawn, he looked at my broken arm and hesitated. "I'll—uh—open it for you," he offered.

"Thanks," I muttered, not liking being helpless. Trying not to scowl, I watched the detective carefully tear open the packet. He handed it to me, and with the hot dog balanced on my lap, I awkwardly squeezed the ketchup out. So intent was I on getting it on the right spot, I almost missed Glenn raising his hand and surreptitiously licking a red smear off his fingers.

Glenn? I thought. My face went slack as I remembered

our missing ketchup and the pieces fell into place. "You . . ." I sputtered. *Glenn had stolen our ketchup?*

The man's face went panicked, and he reached out, almost covering my mouth before he drew back. "No," he pleaded, leaning close. "Don't say anything."

"You took our ketchup!" I breathed, shocked. Beyond Glenn I could see Jenks rocking in mirth on Edden's shoulder, able to hear our whispers and keep up a running conversation to distract the FIB captain at the same time.

Glenn shot a guilty look at his dad. "I'll pay you for it," he begged. "Anything you want. Just don't tell my dad. Oh God, Rachel. It would kill him."

For a moment I could only stare. *He had taken our ketchup. Right off our table.* "I want your handcuffs," I said suddenly. "I can't find anything real without fake purple fur glued to it."

His panicked look eased and he shifted back. "Monday."

"Soon enough for me." My words were calm, but inside I was singing. *I was going to get my cuffs back!* It was going to be a good day.

He darted a guilty look toward his dad. "Will you—get me a bottle of spicy?"

My eyes jerked to his.

"Maybe some barbecue sauce?"

I closed my mouth before a bug flew into it. "Sure." I did not believe this. I was pimping ketchup to the son of the FIB's captain.

I looked up to see a park official wearing a red polyester vest loping up the stairs toward us, scanning the faces. A smile curved over me as he met my eyes. He worked his way down the relatively empty aisle in front of us as I wrapped up what was left of my hot dog and set it on Nick's seat, then dropped the baseball into my bag out of sight. It had been fun while it lasted. I wasn't going to interfere with the game, but they didn't know that.

Jenks flitted from Captain Edden to me. He was wearing

all red and white in honor of the team, the brightness hurting my eyes. "Oooooh," he mocked. "You're in trouble now." Edden gave me one last warning look before putting his attention on the field, clearly trying to divorce himself from me lest they kick him out, too.

"Ms. Rachel Morgan?" the young man in the red vest questioned as he reached us.

I stood with my bag. "Yes."

"I'm Matt Ingle. Park ley line security? Could you come with me, please?"

Glenn got to his feet, standing with his feet spread wide and his hands on his hips. "Is there a problem?" he asked, turning the angry-young-black-man mien on high. I was too thrown by him liking ketchup to get angry at him wanting to protect me.

Matt shook his head, not cowed at all. "No sir. The Howlers' owner heard about Ms. Morgan's efforts to retrieve their mascot and would like to speak with her."

"I'd be happy to talk to her," I said as Jenks chortled, his wings turning a bright red. Despite Captain Edden keeping my name out of the paper, the entirety of Cincinnati and the Hollows knew who had solved the witch hunter murders, made the tag, and summoned the demon into the courtroom. My phone was ringing off the hook with requests for help. Overnight, I had gone from struggling entrepreneur to bad-ass runner. What did I have to fear from the owner of the Howlers?

"I'm coming with you," Glenn said.

"I can handle this," I said, mildly affronted.

"I know, but I want to talk to you, and I think they're going to kick you out of the park."

Edden chuckled, shifting his squat bulk deeper into the hard seat. Taking a key chain from his front pocket, he handed it to Glenn.

"You think?" I said, waving 'bye to Jenks and telling him with a finger motion and a nod that I'd see him back at the church. The pixy nodded, settling himself back on Captain Edden's shoulder, hooting and hollering, having too much fun to leave.

Glenn and I followed the ley line security guy to a waiting golf cart, and he drove us deeper into the stadium. It grew cool and quiet, the thrum of the unseen thousands around us a low, almost subliminal thunder. Far into the authorized personnel areas and amid black suits and champagne, Matt stopped the cart. Glenn helped me out, and I took my cap off, handing it to him as I fluffed my hair. I was dressed nice in jeans and white sweater, but everyone I'd seen in the last two minutes was wearing a tie or diamond earrings. Some had both.

Matt looked nervous as he took us up an elevator and left us in a long plush room that overlooked the field. It was comfortably full of talk and nicely dressed people. The faint smell of musk tickled my nose. Glenn tried to give me my hat back, and I motioned for him to keep it.

"Ms. Morgan," a small woman said, excusing herself from a group of men. "I am so glad to meet you. I'm Mrs. Sarong," she said as she approached, her hands extended.

She was shorter than me, and clearly a Were. Her dark hair was graying in wispy streaks that looked good on her, and her hands were small and powerful. She moved with a predatory grace that drew attention, her eyes seeing everything. Were men had to work hard to hide their rough edges. Were women got more dangerous-looking.

"I'm pleased to meet you," I said as she briefly touched my shoulder in greeting since my right arm was in a sling. "This is Detective Glenn, of the FIB."

"Ma'am," he said shortly, and the small woman smiled to show flat, even teeth.

"Delighted," she said pleasantly. "If you would excuse us, Detective? Ms. Morgan and I have a need to chat before the game begins."

Glenn bobbed his head. "Yes ma'am. I'll get you both a drink if I might."

"That would be lovely."

I rolled my eyes at the political niceties, relieved when Mrs. Sarong put a light hand on my shoulder and led me away. She smelled like ferns and moss. Every man watched us as we moved together to stand by a window with an excellent view of the field. It was a long way down, making me slightly queasy.

"Ms. Morgan," she said, her eyes not at all apologetic, "it has just come to my attention that you were contracted to retrieve our mascot. A mascot that was never missing."

"Yes ma'am," I said, surprised how the title of respect just seemed to flow out of me. "When I was told, my time and energies were given no consideration."

She exhaled slowly. "I detest digging out prey. Have you been magicking the field?"

Pleased at her frankness, I decided to be the same. "I spent three days planning how to break into Mr. Ray's office when I could have been working on other cases," I said. "And while I admit that isn't your fault, someone should have called me."

"Perhaps, but it remains that the fish was not missing. I am not in the habit of paying out blackmail. You will stop."

"And I'm not in the habit of offering it," I said, having no trouble keeping my temper as her pack surrounded me. "But I'd be remiss if I didn't make you aware of my feelings in the matter. I give my word I won't interfere with the game. I don't need to. Until I get paid, every time a ball goes foul or a bat cracks, your players will wonder if it's me." I smiled without showing my teeth. "Five hundred dollars is a small price for your players' peace of mind." *Lousy five hundred dollars. It should have been ten-times that. Why Ray's henchmen wasted bullets on me for a lousy stinking fish was still beyond me.*

Her lips parted and I swear I heard a small growl in her sigh. Athletes were notorious for being superstitious. She'd pay.

"It's not the money, Mrs. Sarong," I said, though at first it had been. "But if I let one pack treat me like a cur, then that's what I'll be. And I'm not a cur."

She brought her gaze up from the field. "Not a cur," she agreed. "You are a lone wolf." With a graceful motion, she motioned to a nearby Were, one that looked oddly familiar, in fact. He hastened forward with a leather-bound check-book the size of a Bible, which took two hands to handle. "It's the lone wolf that is the most dangerous," she said as she wrote. "They also have extremely short life spans. Get yourself a pack, Ms. Morgan."

The rip of the check was loud. I wasn't sure if she was giving me advice or a threat. "Thank you, I have one," I said, not looking at the amount as I tucked it in my bag. The smooth shape of the baseball touched my knuckles and I pulled it out. I set it into her waiting hand. "I'll leave before the game starts," I said, knowing there was no way they would let me back in the stands. "How long am I banned for?"

"Life," she said, smiling like the devil herself. "I, too, am not a cur."

I smiled back, genuinely liking the older woman. Glenn drifted closer. I took the champagne he handed me and set it on the windowsill. "Good-bye, Mrs. Sarong."

She inclined her head as way of dismissal, the second flute of champagne Glenn had brought resting easy in her grip. Three young men lurked behind her, sulky and well-groomed. I was glad I didn't have her job, though it looked as if the perks were great.

Glenn's shoes sounded loud on the concrete as we made our way back to the front gate without the help of Matt and his golf cart.

"You'll tell everyone good-bye for me?" I asked, meaning Nick.

"Sure." His eyes were on the huge signs with their letters and arrows pointing to the exits. The sun was warm when we found it, and I relaxed as I went to stand at the bus stop. Glenn came to a halt beside me and handed me my hat. "About your fee—" he started.

"Glenn," I said as I put it on, "like I told your dad, don't worry about it. I'm grateful for them paying off my I.S. contract, and with the two thousand Trent gave me, I've enough to see me through until my arm heals."

"Would you shut up?" he said, digging in his pocket. "We worked something out."

I turned, my gaze dropping to the key in his hands and then rising to his eyes.

"We couldn't get approval to reimburse you for the canceled class, but there was this car in impound. The insurance agency salvaged the title, so we couldn't put it up for auction."

A car? Edden was going to give me a car?

Glenn's brown eyes were bright. "We got the clutch and the transmission repaired. There was something wrong with the electrical system, too, but the FIB garage guys fixed it, no charge. We would have gotten it to you sooner," he said, "but the DMV office didn't understand what I was trying to do so it took three trips down there to get it transferred to your name."

"You guys bought me a car?" I said, excitement bubbling up into my voice.

Glenn grinned and handed me a zebra-striped key on a purple rabbit's foot key chain. "The money the FIB put into it just about equals what we owed you. I'll drive you home. It's a stick, and I don't think you can handle shifting gears yet with your arm."

Heart suddenly pounding, I fell into step beside him, scanning the lot. "Which one?"

Glenn pointed, and the sound of my heels on the pavement faltered as I saw the red convertible, recognizing it. "That's Francis's car," I said, not sure what I was feeling.

"That's okay, isn't it?" Glenn asked, suddenly concerned. "It was going to be scrapped. You aren't superstitious, are you?"

"Um . . ." I stammered, drawn forward by the shiny red paint. I touched it, feeling the clean smoothness. The top was down, and I turned, smiling. Glenn's worried frown eased into relief. "Thank you," I whispered, not believing it was really mine. *It was mine?*

Steps light, I walked to the front, then the back. It had a new vanity plate: RUNNIN'. It was perfect. "It's mine?" I said, heart racing.

"Go on, get in," Glenn said, his face transformed by his pleased enthusiasm.

"It's wonderful," I said, refusing to cry. *No more expired bus passes. No more standing in the cold. No more disguise charms just so they would pick me up.*

I opened the door. The leather seat was warm from the afternoon sun and as smooth as chocolate milk. The cheerful dinging of the door being opened was heaven. I put in the key, checked that it was in neutral, pushed in the clutch, and started it up. The thrum of the engine was freedom itself. I shut the door and beamed at Glenn. "Really?" I asked, voice cracking.

He nodded, beaming.

I was delighted. With my broken arm, I couldn't safely manage the gearshift, but I could try all the buttons. I turned on the radio, thinking it must be an omen when Madonna thundered out. I turned "Material Girl" down and opened the glove box just to see my name on the registration. A thick yellow business-size envelope slid out, and I picked it up off the floor.

"I didn't put that there," Glenn said, his voice carrying a new concern.

I brought it to my nose, my face going slack as I recognized the clean scent of pine. "It's from Trent."

Glenn straightened. "Get out of the car," he said in a hard staccato, every syllable laced with authority.

"Don't be stupid," I said. "If he wanted me dead, he wouldn't have had Quen bail me out."

Jaw tight, Glenn opened the door. My car started chiming. "Get out. I'll have it looked at and bring it over tomorrow."

"Glenn . . ." I cajoled as I opened the envelope and my protests wavered. "Um," I stammered. "He's not trying to kill me, he's paying me."

Glenn leaned to see, and I tilted the envelope to him. A muttered oath came from him. "How much is that, you think?" he asked as I closed it and shoved it in my bag.

"I'm guessing eighteen thousand." I tried to be cavalier, ruining it with my trembling fingers. "It was what he offered me to clear his name." Brushing the hair from my eyes, I looked up. My breath caught. Visible in the rearview mirror was Trent's Gray Ghost limo sitting in the fire lane. It hadn't been there a moment ago. At least, I hadn't seen it. Trent and Jonathan were standing beside it. Glenn saw where my attention was and turned.

"Oh," he said, then a concerned wariness tightened the corners of his eyes. "Rachel, I'm going to go over to the ticket booth right over there . . ." He pointed. ". . . and talk to the lady about possibly buying a block of seats for the FIB's company picnic next year." He hesitated, shutting my door with a solid thump. His dark fingers stood out against the bright red paint. "You going to be all right?"

"Yeah." I pulled my eyes from Trent. "Thanks, Glenn. If he kills me, tell your dad I loved the car."

A trace of a smile crossed him, and he turned away.

My eyes were fixed to my rearview mirror as his steps grew faint. Behind me came a roar of fans as the game began. I watched Trent have an intent conversation with

Jonathan. He left the angry tall man and ambled slowly to me. His hands were in his pockets and he looked good. Better than good, really, dressed in casual slacks, comfortable shoes, and a cable-knit sweater against the slight chill in the air. The collar of a silk shirt the color of midnight showed behind it, contrasting wonderfully with his tan. A tweed cap shaded his green eyes and kept his fine hair under control.

He came to a slow halt beside me, his eyes never leaving mine to touch upon the car even once. Feet scuffing, he half turned to look at Jonathan. It stuck in my craw that I had helped clear his name. He had murdered at least two people in less than six months—one of them Francis. And here I was, sitting in the dead witch's car.

I said nothing, gripping the wheel with my one good hand, my broken arm sitting in my lap, reminding myself that Trent was afraid of me. From the radio, a fast-talking announcer took over, and I turned the radio almost off. "I found the money," I said as way of greeting.

He squinted at me, then shifted to stand by the side mirror to put his face in shadow. "You're welcome."

I peered up at him. "I never said thank you."

"You're welcome anyway."

My lips pressed together. *Ass.*

Trent's eyes dropped to my arm. "How long until it heals?"

Surprised, I blinked. "Not long. It was a clean break." I touched the pain amulet about my neck. "There was some muscle damage, though, which is why I can't use it well yet, but they say I don't need any therapy. I'll be back on the streets in six weeks."

"Good. That's good."

It had been a quick comment—and it was followed by a long silence. I sat in my car, wondering what he wanted. There was a jittery cast to him, his eyebrows a shade too high. He wasn't afraid, and he wasn't worried. I couldn't tell what he wanted. "Piscary said our fathers worked together," I said. "Was he lying?"

The sun glinted on Trent's white hair as he shook his head. "No."

A sliver of ice dropped down my spine. I licked my lips and brushed a spot of dust from the steering wheel. "Doing what?" I asked casually.

"Come work for me, and I'll tell you."

My eyes went to his. "You are a thief, a cheat, a murderer, and a not-nice-man," I said calmly. "I don't like you."

He shrugged, the motion making him look utterly harmless. "I'm not a thief," he said. "And I don't mind manipulating you into working for me when I need it." He smiled, showing me perfect teeth. "I enjoy it, actually."

I felt my face warm. "You are so full of yourself, Trent," I said, wishing I could shift the car into reverse and drive over his foot.

His smile widened.

"What?" I demanded.

"You called me by my first name. I like that."

I opened my mouth, then closed it. "So throw a party and invite the Pope. My dad may have worked for your dad, but you are scum, and the only reason I'm not throwing your money back in your face is a, I earned it, and b, I need something to live on while I recover from injuries gained from keeping your ass out of prison!"

His eyes were glinting in amusement, and it made me furious. "Thank you for clearing my name," he said. He went to touch my car, stopping as I made an ugly noise in warning. He turned the motion into seeing if Jonathan had moved. He hadn't. Glenn, too, was watching us.

"Just forget it, okay?" I said. "I went after Piscary to save my mom's life, not yours."

"Thank you anyway. If it means anything, I'm sorry now for putting you in that rat pit."

I tilted my head to see him, holding the hair out of my face as the wind gusted. "And you think that means anything to me?" I said tightly. Then I squinted. He was almost jiggling where he stood. What was up with him?

"Scoot over," he finally said, looking at the empty seat beside me.

I stared at him. "What?"

He looked past me to Jonathan and back. "I want to drive your car. Scoot over. Jon never lets me drive. He says it's beneath me." He looked over at Glenn skulking beside a pillar. "Unless you would rather have an FIB detective drive you home at the posted speed limit?"

Surprise kept the anger out of my voice. "You can drive a stick?"

"Better than you."

I looked at Glenn, then back to Trent. I slowly sank back into the seat. "Tell you what," I said, my eyebrows rising. "You can drive me home if we keep to one topic on the way."

"Your father?" he guessed, and I nodded. I was getting used to this deal-with-a-demon business.

Trent put his hands back in his pockets and rocked back and forth once on his heels in thought. Bringing his attention from the blue sky, he nodded.

"I do not believe I'm doing this," I muttered as I threw my bag in the back and awkwardly shifted over the gear stick to the other seat. Taking my red Howlers cap off, I wound my hair up into a bun and jammed the hat back on against the coming wind.

Glenn had started forward, slowing as I waved good-bye to him. Shaking his head as if in disbelief, he turned and went back inside the ballpark.

I buckled my belt as Trent opened the door and slid into the front. He adjusted the mirrors, then revved the engine twice before pushing in the clutch and shifting it into first. I